Everything's Better With You

An MM Sports Romance

R.L. Merrill

Published By: Celie Bay Publications, LLC
Edited and Proofread By: Reina - Rickrack Books
Cover Design By: Reese Dante

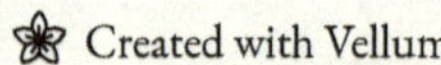 Created with Vellum

To Mom…Thank you for teaching me to soar and giving me the wings to do so. I promise I won't roller skate in the house, nor will I do cartwheels in the living room.

FOREWORD

Pain sucks. Living with chronic pain is exhausting. Knowing you did most of it to yourself while chasing a dream? Just desserts or paying the piper or karma. Whatever you want to call it.

I spent the first seventeen years of my life in constant motion. Dancing, gymnastics, cheerleading, bicycling, roller skating, and swimming all filled my formative years with joy...and injuries. It was worth it, even if it meant a broken collarbone, sprained ankle and wrist, countless knee injuries, back pain, and multiple scars and concussions. At 50 years old, I feel all of them, but I wouldn't change a thing about how I earned them.

I am grateful for the sacrifices my mom made to give me the opportunity to attend J&J's Academy of Dance. Driving the "bus" (an orange and white VW bus and then a bright orange van) to pick up other dancers, making costumes, etc, all of those things meant I could continue to do this activity that helped me focus, gave me an outlet for my endless energy (what happened to all that energy?) and gave me confidence. I gained a lot of my identity from my dancing talent as a young person. For the longest time, though, I thought it was all I was good for, the only way to get attention and respect from my peers and family. I never felt like I completely fit in, but I made friends that helped me get through those tough years.

I started cheerleading in sixth grade and continued through tenth, then I switched to swim. Being a cheerleader meant having people form opinions about who you were, and were not. You were a party girl and easy, not smart. This was 1985-1988 so things were a lot different then. We had little supervision, we worked hard, and we fought for every opportunity. If you look at pics of my squads back then, you'll see nine or so girls, most with dark, curly hair, and one tow-headed blond with long straight hair. I didn't fit, but it was better than not being able to do what I loved. Dancing.

I slowed down in college for a few years, but then I joined my college coed cheer squad my senior year at Graceland University (Go Jackets!) in an attempt to reclaim that joy. It was probably the most fun I ever had cheerleading, since high school cheerleading was fraught with drama. For once I wasn't the biggest one on the squad and therefore I wasn't at the bottom of precarious pyramids. I once had a male cheerleader from UMKC pick up my 5'10" 135 pound self and throw me around like I was one of the tiny flyers. It was a humbling experience and did a lot to make me feel like less of a giantess for a few seconds. I also slid across the basketball court on my ass once in front of several hundred spectators, but I digress.

Post college, I was focused on my career as a teacher, but I kept my fingers in dance by coaching cheerleading squads, and choreographing various musicals and show choir teams. I took dance classes from a friend and auditioned for the Golden State Warriors Dance Team. What an exciting day, to be dancing on the floor of the Oakland Coliseum and still able to keep up. I didn't have the look and was too tall, but I loved being out there. I also took Polynesian classes, danced in a local college's summer musical... and then I got married. And had kids. And that was that.

I miss dancing. Of course I still dance around my house and embarrass my kids. I'll get out on the floor any time we gather at bookish events. But it hurts. Everything hurts. All the time. All of this is to say I channeled my hope, fears, and pain into creating Joe Judd. After watching my football player students and then my daughter go through Traumatic Brain Injuries, I thought up Leslie Payton. I wrote this book in the fall of 2021 when the pandemic had hold of us and I needed something positive to focus on. I was beginning to work out in earnest after my diabetes diagnosis and it was *hard*, but it was the first time that moving brought me joy in a long time. In addition to my treadmill, I take barre classes and dance cardio through Peloton, and I've managed to continue my streak since January 2021. Sure, I've got to do physical therapy for my neck to avoid dizzy spells and migraines, and I work on strengthening my knee daily, but that's what I have to do. I'll be having knee surgery this summer, and then I'll keep moving. Maybe it will be enough to get me back to dance classes. In the meantime, have this book, my love letter to dance, and take care of your bodies. Hopefully I'll see you out on the dance floor soon...

One

J oe

Joe Judd pulled his cigarette-smoke-infested rental minivan into a spot in front of the imposing brick building that represented an important slice of his formative years. His ties to the place ran deep; his liberal arts education, his adult education, his physical education, all happened in this very place, and the building before him was a symbol of the chapter in his life that paved the way for where he was now.

Where am I?

Right. Spring Fling weekend. Greenvale College. Go Jackets!

This was the first year he'd returned to his alma mater for this momentous occasion since graduating in 2008. Joe left Ayre Valley, Iowa in his rearview mirror fifteen years ago and his life had been all glitz and glamour ever since.

Okay, the minivan he was currently sitting in wasn't glamorous. He couldn't even pretend to be an old Hollywood starlet whose leading man lit his cigarettes for him. He'd quit smoking a long time ago, and the way this car reeked, it was a damn good thing he had. Everything else in Joe's life was glitz and glamour, though.

And pain.

Ugh, the pain.

He turned off the ignition of the Chrysler and listened for the *clunk clunk* of the engine shutting down. The airport car rental place had given him their last available vehicle and charged him a premium since he'd wrongly assumed Kansas City, Missouri wouldn't be so packed that he couldn't land a nice Mustang for the two-hour drive up to Ayre Valley. The woman working the register let him know in no uncertain terms that his thinking was wrong.

The engine clunked once more and a grinding sound emanated from the other side of the dash as if the thing had given up the ghost.

He could relate. His body felt like that when he stopped moving these days.

At thirty-six years old, Joe had the appearance of a fit man in his twenties. He liked to think he resembled his beloved Porsche at home in West Hollywood rather than this current hunk of junk. Gleaming chrome and a flashy paint job on the outside gave people the impression that he was all power and sleek lines, when in reality, his engine needed an overhaul under the hood, and his shocks and struts had seen better days. He pushed his Porsche to the same limits he pushed his body and both protested loudly. Just like the minivan.

"Time to move before you freeze up like this piece of shit."

He gritted his teeth and opened the door, feeling his lower back protest. He had to get his feet planted under him just right and push himself to standing, putting the least amount of pressure on his knees. Once he was upright, he arched his back and felt the L5 bulging disc, the torn tendon in his hip, and the stubborn rib that would not stay in place no matter how hard his chiropractor back in Hollywood pounded on it.

He let out a harsh exhale as everything settled into place and then he swung the door closed. It was a chilly April morning and he was glad he'd brought his wool coat and worn his fleece-lined jeans. He'd kept them around past their expiration date because when his arthritis acted up, they kept him toasty. His fur-lined Palladium boots kept his aching feet supported and warm. The frigid temps here in the Midwest were hell on his joints, but he knew once he started moving, he'd feel better. He was just about to head up the walkway when he heard the rumble of tailpipes and the screeching of...heavy metal?

A ginormous four-by-four truck complete with a rack of lights and a winch mounted on the front grill kicked up gravel as it pulled into the spot next to Joe's rental. The windows were tinted but he had a feeling he knew exactly who the monstrosity belonged to.

"Well, if it isn't fancy-pants, twinkle-toes, *Dance Machine*'s own Joe Judd! I'll be damned."

The six-foot-five, Northern European ruddy complexioned, long and not-quite-as-lean these days, blond-mulleted, monster-truck madman currently lowering himself gingerly out of the gas-guzzling giant was none other than Leslie Payton. Three-time Super Bowl-winning—now retired—NFL quarterback, championship university football coach, and fellow alum of Greenvale College.

The tremors running through Joe's body had nothing to do with the temperature. No, this was a reunion long in the making, and now that he was here, he struggled to keep his snarky demeanor front and center.

"You always did know how to make an entrance," Joe said, shaking his head. He strolled toward the back of his car to greet Les, who already had his hand out, seemingly just as eager.

"And you're a sight for sore eyes," Les said, taking Joe's hand and pulling him in for a back-pounding bro-hug that made Joe's teeth smack together. "I can't believe you're really here."

Joe couldn't either, honestly. He'd told himself he'd never come back here after graduation. The fact that he'd returned to the site of the best and most difficult years of his life was due entirely to the sheer amount of respect he held for Barry Payton—Leslie's older brother and the new president of Greenvale College—and the complicated feelings he had for the man standing before him.

"I'm glad you could make it out. Barry was thrilled when you agreed to arrive early and meet with him."

Joe raised an eyebrow. "I agreed to come for Spring Fling and the recognition of the cheer squad...Am I missing something? Was there another part to the invitation?"

Les stepped back but didn't let go of Joe's hand, nor did he remove his other hand from Joe's shoulder.

"I'll let him explain it all to you. I'm just glad you're here. Man, you look good."

Joe did not miss the fact that Les's gaze traveled hungrily over Joe's body. Joe stood a little taller under the appraisal, glad he wasn't the only one struggling with propriety.

"You just off a show?"

Les's hands were rough, his knuckles thick on long fingers. His hands were huge, as they needed to be for a storied career as a professional football player. They were strong, too. Sturdy, like Les's shoulders—

"Uh, yeah. Just finished choreography for the next season of *Dance Machine* and I'm headed from here to New York for a limited run of *West Side Story*."

"*When you're a jet...doo doo doo doo doo,*" Les sang, snapping his fingers. He laughed and pounded on Joe's shoulder again, hard enough to make him stagger. "Oh, sorry, man. That's great. I loved watching you on that live broadcast. You've still got those moves."

Les's smile held more wattage than all the lights in Levi Stadium, and Joe felt a blast of heat being the recipient of one of those smiles.

He had a flash of the first time he'd been the recipient of a Leslie Payton smile and how that night changed his life.

He watched my show. Joe fought to hide a triumphant smile.

"How 'bout you? How's your mom?"

Joe skimmed the alumni newsletter from time to time, only stopping if there was mention of Greenvale's Golden Boy alum. He knew, for example, that Les had built a sprawling estate on his grandparents' farmland outside of Ayre Valley for his family to live in while he was still playing for the 49ers, and that his mother Agnes lived there.

"She's good, thank you for asking. I'm actually here for the same reason you are," Les said as he gestured to the administration building. "Brother Barry calls and I come running."

"Right. That's great he was promoted to president this year. How exciting for him."

Les laughed. "It suits him. He's been an old man my whole life. Figures he'd end up all respectable and shit."

Les's eyes crinkled as he talked about his brother. They were close, the whole Payton clan. Joe wouldn't know about that. It was just Joe. No siblings and he'd lost his mom a long time ago.

"I'm not sure why he asked me to be here early. I don't think the big game is until later, right? It's been a while, but I figured they still played at night."

The Yellowjacket's Spring Fling tradition was for the cheerleaders to play flag football against half of the football team. The rest of the players learned a cheer routine to be performed at halftime. It was all in fun and the ticket sales went to the athletic department scholarships.

"Yeah, well..." Les trailed off. He rubbed his hands together. "Why don't we go inside, huh?"

He'd started moving toward the building before he finished talking.

Joe realized that there was something more to this invitation than he'd been led to believe. He wasn't sure whether he was more intrigued or concerned, honestly, but he wasn't going to miss out on finally being in the same place at the same time with Leslie Payton.

"Right," Joe said, following Les up the walkway. He clicked the remote lock on his rental car once more, not that anyone in Ayre Valley would break in or steal it. It was just a habit after living in LA for so long.

A big crowd of kids dressed in green and gold matching T-shirts and shorts came bursting out of the student center. The women all had their hair pulled up in space buns with green and gold ribbons to match and they carried poms.

"Omg is that...JOE JUDD!"

Under normal circumstances, Joe didn't care for fan mobs, but this was different.

These kids were literally here because of him.

"That's right!" Les used his best TV commentator voice. "Please welcome the Godfather of Jackets Cheer, Mr. Joe Judd." He clapped and whistled while the kids gathered around giggling in that starstruck way Joe had experienced many times since making his TV debut on *Dance Machine.*

"Hey," Joe said, and he cleared his throat. *Allergies this time of year were brutal.* Of course that was why he felt the sudden urge to rub his eyes. "Looking forward to seeing you play tonight."

"You'll watch our demo too, won't you?" one of the young men asked. "We're doing our competition routine for the school this afternoon. Then there's the barbecue and—"

"Sure. Can't wait to see what you guys came up with this year."

The kids squealed and one by one they all reached in to shake his hand. After twenty handshakes, Joe was a little out of breath.

"You're their goddamned hero, you know that?" Les shook his head and chuckled. "They didn't even recognize me."

"Well, you have to admit the long hair and the Motörhead shirt don't scream NFL star. I bet you wouldn't be recognized in most bars around here."

"Yeah, I would." He laughed that big belly laugh of his. "Cheerleaders just don't watch football typically unless they're cheering for it."

"Not true," Joe said, and then he backpedaled. "I'm sure I watched one of your games at some point."

Bullshit, Joe. You watched every single one you could. Hell, you even recorded the games he commentated on after he retired.

Joe had thirsted after Les Payton since they spent a magical Spring Fling night together fifteen years ago. Talking. Laughing. Dreaming of the future, but nothing beyond that. No, they'd been on two very different paths and therefore it hadn't made sense to let anything start. Graduation for Joe was weeks away and Les had already been playing in the NFL for eight years. They'd met at Spring Fling but hadn't, uh, flung anything together. Over the years, they'd kept in occasional contact, which became more regular—and intimate—and Joe had never stopped wondering.

Two

L eslie

What if?

Many times over the years, Les had asked that question regarding the incomparable Joe Judd. Even though Les had been the visiting hero that Spring Fling weekend fifteen years ago, Joe had been the star, and Les hadn't been able to take his eyes off him. The dancer played a mean game of flag football, leaping over potential tackles as he ran at top speed down to the opposing team's end zone, doing back flips in celebration. But later at the bar while folks danced and had too much to drink, he'd taken a seat next to the cocky kid white kid with the dark, brooding good looks, and then spent hours standing in the parking lot. Les had cornered him for conversation, but had refused to take advantage of the tipsy coed.

Joe hadn't been intimidated by him at all.

No, what Joe *had* been intimidated by was the thought of getting involved with someone. No way, no how was he going to stop moving long enough to fall for a guy, not as long as he had breath in his lungs and feeling in his feet. He'd made that very clear. So for Leslie, it was a no-brainer. He wasn't interested in a one-time thing, especially not with someone as incredible as Joe Judd.

But that was fifteen years ago. A lot had changed for both of them since then.

"I would have gotten you tickets, you know. If you ever wanted them."

"Little old cheerleader Joey?" Joe raised his eyebrows at him and batted his eyes. "I didn't think you'd even remember me...at first."

"Yeah right. You know better. I saw every show of yours I could."

Joe smirked. "You never asked me to get tickets for you."

Les grinned. "I bought out a whole section at Madison Square Garden. I had to see you dance with JLo. When the team heard about the show, they all wanted in." Les shrugged and smiled innocently. "What could I do?"

Joe raised an eyebrow. "You could have let me know you were going to be there. You'd only ever tell me after."

Their eyes met for a long moment and then they broke off, laughing nervously. Leslie was pumped like he'd just scored a touchdown and he couldn't wait to make the next play. His muscles twitched with their desire to do...something. Anything. Especially if it involved getting closer to Joe.

"It really is damn good to see you."

"You too."

Les held the door for Joe at the top of the stairs and he didn't miss his wince when he climbed the last step.

"Stairs, man, am I right?" He chuckled, but Joe just scowled and brushed past him. The playfulness momentarily gone.

"Hey Caroline," Les said, giving the secretary a big hug. "You remember Joe Judd."

She blushed as Les set her back on her feet. "Of course. It's good to have you back, Mr. Judd. Mr. Payton will see you both now."

"Darn right he'll see me," Les said as he strutted into the President's office like he was on set at the NFL Postgame Show on network TV but dressed more like a drunken spectator tailgating before the big game.

"Brother Barry," Les said. He trotted over to the president's desk with his arms spread.

"Jesus, Leslie, you've got a wider wingspan than a pterodactyl." Barry stood and accepted his brother's bear hug. Barry was three years older than Les's forty-five years with buzz-cut blond and white hair, and was about six inches shorter. He looked the part of the responsible older brother, always had.

Les put an arm around him and gestured to Joe. "Joe and I met up in the parking lot. Joe, you remember my brother Barry?"

Barry reached out to shake Joe's hand. "I was teaching Economics, I believe, when you were a student here. Thank you for coming."

Joe nodded. "Yes, sir. I had you for Macro."

Barry grinned. "And of course we are in debt to you for pushing us to make the cheerleading program coed. We've won several national championships, and the squads have traveled to Europe and Japan to perform. All thanks to you."

Joe took the praise with only the slightest hint of a blush.

"It helped me as well," Joe said. "*Dance Machine* never would have been possible without my experience here."

Barry nodded. "Which is why we've asked you to come." He shot a glance in Les's direction, which made Joe frown.

"We?"

"We-e-e," Les said, trying to hide his excitement, "asked you to come because we have a proposition for you."

Joe crossed an ankle over his knee and looked between Les and Barry.

"A proposition? I thought I was coming for Spring Fling."

Les glanced at Barry and he leaned forward, lacing his fingers in front of him on the desk.

"You know I was recently made president here at Greenvale, Mr. Judd—"

"Joe, please."

Barry nodded and continued. "I have a mandate from the board. They want to see some significant changes. Our enrollment has been declining the past five years, we're losing qualified students and staff to the larger schools, but we firmly believe that the education we provide is top rate and a special experience for our students. We want to continue to offer unique programs as well as quality extracurricular activities. Which is where you come in."

Joe's eyebrows rose as he glanced between Les and Barry, but he didn't speak.

Les had been standing next to Barry's desk, but he took a seat in the chair next to Joe and turned it to face him. He didn't want to seem like they were on the attack. What they were about to propose could send Joe running for the hills. No one knew that possibility more than Les. It was a huge departure from Joe's current lifestyle, and Les knew from their brief encounter fifteen years ago that Joe was destined for greatness and a big life. But he had exactly what Greenvale needed, and wasn't that advantageous for Les?

"What my brother is so eloquently trying to say is that we need your special skill set. We want to revamp the athletic program at Greenvale, make it possible to recruit the top athletes in our various sports programs, and put Greenvale College back on the winning track, financially as well as with our alumni. Participation and donations have been dwindling, attendance at our events have petered out. We need to make this an exciting place to be again."

Joe chuckled. "I don't mean to offend, but exciting is not exactly a word I would have ever used to describe Greenvale. Safe? Yes. Nurturing? Absolutely. Fun? Sometimes. But not exciting."

This was going to be a hard sell. Les had known that, but he was determined. There was no better option for Greenvale, and no better way to make his plan work.

"All right, maybe I could have chosen a different word. But I'm going to whip this football program into shape and get the team into the playoffs year one. Year two and beyond, I plan to clinch the conference title at the very least. But it's not just about football. In the past, Greenvale had champion soccer, volleyball, and softball teams...and of course, the Yellowjackets Cheer program. We want to bring that winning spirit back. And how could we even possibly consider rebuilding our championship sports programs without talking to you?"

Joe shrugged. "Sounds great. I'm glad you are including the cheerleaders in your plans."

Barry cleared his throat. "Leslie has agreed to end his run at the network as an NFL talking head to coach the Jackets Football program and to help me recruit the best of the best coaches for the rest of the teams."

Joe shifted in his chair, swapping one long leg for the other. "I'm happy to hear it."

Les leaned closer to Joe. "Actually, Joe, we asked you here because we want you to join our coaching staff as well."

Joe blinked. "I'm sorry, what? Want me for what? I'm not a coach."

"You've been an instructor and a choreographer. You've coached contestants on your show. You're a motivator." Les wasn't sure how much to divulge of his borderline unhealthy fixation on the man, which included having all twelve seasons of *Dance Machine* saved on his DVR. "You're exactly what we need."

No, that definitely didn't sound like you were hitting on him.

"To be completely transparent," Barry said, cutting in before Les made a total fool out of himself. He was always so damn awkward when it came to discussing, well, anything other than football. "Your accomplishments and reputation will give the program the credibility it's been lacking in recent years. Recruitment is going to be key to the success of this endeavor and I'll be honest and say that having Joe Judd join the faculty at Greenvale will go a long way in easing the board's concerns about this gamble."

Joe sat for a long time without speaking. An uncomfortably long time. Then he folded his arms over his chest and licked his lips. "I'm... flattered?" He let out a burst of nervous laughter. "Never in a million years would I have ever imagined my name would ease anyone's concerns about anything. I mean, what exactly are we talking about?"

Barry held out his hands. "Carte blanche. Oversee the cheer program, foster its growth and improvement. There is significant interest in offering a dance program as part of our Fine Arts department, which we could see you spearheading. You certainly have the experience. Year one would be a building year, and classes would have to be approved by the board, of course."

From what Les knew about Joe's past—what he'd gleaned from watching countless interviews and reading anything in print he could get his hands on—Joe had been a ballet dancer as a child, had switched over to more contemporary disciplines when he was a teenager, and by the time he hit college he was primarily a hip-hop dancer. Then, after two years of attending workshops and auditions, he was chosen for *Dance Machine*'s debut season. The reality show put dancers through a grueling competition where they were challenged to develop their skills in multiple disciplines. Joe soared, coming in second behind a bubbly young woman who was a social media darling. Joe's darker disposition turned some of the audience off...and then there were those in the show's demographics who would never vote for an openly queer dancer no matter how much he danced circles around the competition. He took it all in stride and used the attention to launch his career. Nabbing Joe Judd to coach the cheer program and potentially found a dance program at Greenvale would be a huge win for Barry...and it would please Les to no end. He just didn't know if it was possible to tie Joe Judd to one place for any length of time.

Leslie certainly hadn't been able to tempt him with previous attempts.

"I don't know what to say. Thank you, obviously. I'm flattered you would even think of me for such an opportunity," Joe said.

Les was impressed at the lengths Joe was going to come across professionally. Les knew from experience that Joe had a sharp temper and snarky sense of humor.

"But I'm not exactly collegiate leadership material."

"And *I* am?" Les said, gesturing to himself. He knew it would make Joe laugh, and he succeeded.

"But you're a proven commodity. I'm an unknown quantity."

"Not true," Barry said. "You're an important part of the athletic history of this school and it makes perfect sense to offer you the position."

Again with the blinking.

"I don't know what to say," Joe said, his voice not quite as strong. "I...wow."

Barry held up a hand. "Think about it. Spend the weekend thinking about it. Les will tell you more about what the position entails, and then we can talk more about salary and benefits. Leslie will introduce you around and take you to your accommodations as well." He stood from his desk and held out his hand, prompting Joe to pop up from his seat. Les moved a little slower as he got up and moved around next to his brother. "I've got a meeting with alumni donors and then I'm going to introduce the cheer squad for their exhibition. Thanks for coming this weekend, Joe. I hope you enjoy Spring Fling."

Joe shook his hand. "Thanks for the invite. I always meant to come back."

Les squeezed Barry's shoulder and then turned to Joe. "You're here now, that's what counts. We'll see if we can't persuade you to join us over the weekend." He was laying it on thick, but he couldn't help himself. Joe Judd was here, in person, and Les was determined to convince him to stay. Well, to take the job.

"We'll see you two in a bit." Barry left them alone in the office.

Les's cheeks hurt from smiling.

"What do you think?" he asked. "I know you'd be great."

Joe planted his hands on his hips and the confused look on his face made Les crack up.

"Do you honestly see me as an educator? An upstanding citizen and a fucking role model? Oh my god, listen to my mouth, are you serious right now? How could anyone see me as an academic? I graduated from here with mediocre marks, and that's being generous."

He put a hand to his forehead and Les wanted nothing more than to say the right thing, but he knew better.

"Joe, you're great at everything you do and you know it."

He looked at Les funny and his shoulders dropped from up and around his ears. "Maybe *you* should be the cheer coach," he finally said. "You're good at this."

A memory from the night they'd met hit Les like a left tackle, catching him just as he was about to pass and surprising the hell out of him.

The two of them sitting at a bar, Joe with a frou-frou drink, Les with a nonalcoholic beer as he was coming off his latest concussion. Knees touching under the bar, not giving a shit who was watching, high off the vibe you get when you connect with someone on that level, where the attraction is obvious to both parties, the conversation is flowing, and neither party can take their eyes off the other. Les tried to memorize every word that came out of Joe's mouth that night, but he was more focused on Joe's mouth than his words.

Like now.

"Les?"

"Hmmm?"

Joe laughed, the tension gone from his frame. "I asked 'what now?' Are you gonna show me a good time?"

Les's face must have showed his shock because Joe gave a devilish chuckle.

"All right, Leslie Payton. Show me a good time while I try to comprehend why on *Earth* you and your brother think this is a good idea."

THREE

J oe

Joe smiled and nodded as he followed Les out of the office and down the walkway, but he was fixated on the Payton brothers' proposition.

Me? Joe Judd living in Ayre Valley? Educating America's youth?

In what reality was *that* a good idea?

"You'd have housing, a great salary, and the eternal gratitude of the Greenvale community."

"Housing?"

"Yeah, you remember the cottages on the road coming onto campus?"

Joe snorted. "I remember getting drunk with the former dean after graduation in one of those cottages." He laughed at Les's expression. "What? You're not surprised by that, are you?"

Les shook his head. "At least he waited until you graduated. That old queen had a hard time keeping his hands to himself. Thank goodness there were no scandals."

"That you knew of," Joe muttered and Les chuckled.

"You're trouble."

"That's what I'm trying to tell you!"

Les smiled. "You can't convince me you're not perfect for the job, so don't even try. Besides, I need a partner in crime, right?"

Joe cocked his head. The idea of him and Les being partners in crime had been fodder for his fantasies over the years. He'd occasionally stop moving long enough to contemplate what life would be like if he and Les were in the same place at the same time and trying to make a go of a life together. Had Les really thought as much about him?

They walked around the campus and Joe was shocked at how small everything seemed. He'd been a reluctant student there as a freshman, angry that his mother had blackmailed him into going to the Midwest for school. Okay, she'd given him the choice of staying home or going to Greenvale. It was her alma mater and the only place she felt safe sending him. He'd outgrown his hometown and wanted a fresh start, but his mom wanted him to be safe and was sure if he went to a big city, he'd be murdered in the first month.

"And the plan is to expand the training center, add a staff of full-time trainers and interns from the sports medicine program."

Joe snapped into the present as Les pointed to a board with the drawings for the new center.

"They're really serious about this."

Thoughts climbed all over each other in Joe's mind. He had rehearsals for the next two weeks for a show that was going to run from June through early August. Then there was the new season of *Dance Machine*...

"Come on. I can see that crease on your forehead trying to dig in. It's not Broadway or Madison Square Gardens but you'd have a big impact."

The sound system on the field crackled and they heard applause and shouts.

"It's time for the expo. Let's go."

Joe and Les trotted over to the field and Joe ignored the pain in his knees.

"If this didn't hurt so damned much, I'd race you."

Joe laughed. "And you'd win because my running days are over." That was a lie, but he knew Les wouldn't call him on it. He'd run out on the quarterback fifteen years ago, setting a precedent. Maybe it was time to stop running, but then Joe wasn't sure he was ready to accept the implications of what it would mean to slow down.

Maybe he could consider a year? That thought made him shudder. A year in Smalltown, America with its potentially small-minded ways? In the Midwest with its freezing cold winters and sweaty summers?

They came through the gates and climbed the steps to the bleachers as the music blared through the speakers. Les waved to several groups of folks before gesturing for Joe to take a seat on the bleachers, but he shook his head and took a seat on the left behind a large group of folks. Les sat down next to him, obviously confused.

"It will throw them off if I'm seated right in front," he said by way of explanation.

"Ah," Les responded. "I could see that. You are quite imposing." He made a point to look down his nose at Joe and then cracked up. Their size difference was quite comical. "No, I get it. You're a big deal around here."

Joe was about to argue but the team trotted out onto the field and got into formation. He clenched his fists to keep from biting his nails, a terrible habit he had whenever watching something he created. And he had created this program, if not this particular team. When he'd shown up on campus in the fall of 2004 a cocky badass in his own mind, he'd thought some time off dancing would do him good. Then he went to a football game and saw the tiny cheer squad. They were good dancers, great crowd leaders, but their choreography was dated. He'd thought, "I could do something with this." And why not? His classes had been a breeze to that point, he didn't know anyone, and he'd been itching to get into some trouble, all signs he needed to find something productive to do with his time. All it took was crashing their practice, showing them some of his ideas, and they'd been elated. So many of the area schools had coed teams, but Greenvale didn't put much stock in their cheerleaders. No one had made noise about it, not until Joe Judd showed up.

The team kicked off their routine with coordinated jumps, level changes, and drops and then they moved into their first stunt. So far so good. But the minute they started climbing, Joe's hand flew to his mouth.

Their technique was terrible.

They didn't have enough spotters.

"Shit," Joe exclaimed when one of the flyers fell. "He didn't have a good grip. They need another set of hands." He rubbed his hands on his thighs and exhaled through pursed lips.

They got through the rest of the routine with some rudimentary stunts, definitely not the latest skills out there. Joe was already thinking of little things they could do immediately to improve this routine, even though they'd already taken it to Nationals. They apparently took fourth in their division, which was pretty good for Greenvale, at least from what Joe had seen over the past few years. He still kept tabs on college cheer, especially his Jackets. Since his team won nationals twice, the team had qualified to go eight more times, won twice, and placed four times.

"They're good," Les said, clapping when they finished. They both stood up with the crowd as they cheered the cheerleaders, all the while Joe was mentally mapping out what he could do with the team.

"They could add more stunt partners, they're not using everyone."

Les elbowed him. "You could make them better."

Joe's glance darted his direction. "I see what you're up to, Payton."

Les laughed. "I'm not trying to hide my motivations."

Joe gave him a long look. The chemistry between them fifteen years ago had been off the charts, but fifteen years was a long time. Things change, people change, and Joe had lived a very different life, but he was still the driven guy he'd been back then.

Les...he moved a little stiffer, a little less cocksure. His blond hair had thinned, a fact that he seemed to ignore considering his mullet. He maybe had a few more lines on his face. Under that shirt, Joe was sure the six-pack was less defined... But Les still had that same warm enthusiasm for life that Joe had initially ridiculed, and then come to admire. And his smile still lit Joe up like a roman candle.

Differences or not, Joe was damn glad to see Leslie Payton.

Barry was talking over the loudspeaker, something about great plans for the future, but Joe was focused on Leslie.

"Can you honestly see me back in Ayre Valley? Fifty miles from the nearest major airport? A hundred and fifty miles from the nearest theaters and shopping—"

"We've got Target fifteen miles away now—"

"Shopping that's *not* at a department store."

"I've got a Cessna out at the airstrip. My pilot will take you wherever you want to go."

Joe laughed. "What about you? Monday Night Football and Postgame Wrap-Up? That's all over?"

Les shrugged. "Brother Barry needs me, Greenvale needs me, I come. Plus I built that big-ass house for my mom, I might as well live in it. She's pretty spry for her age, but you know she's slowing down a little. My brothers keep her entertained, but she's tired."

One of the things the two of them had bonded over was being raised by unique moms.

"That's right. The twins. They live here too?"

Les laughed. "Yeah, they heard I was coming and they decided we'd have a family reunion. They've got a new YouTube series they're going to do, I guess, and they're joining the coaching staff."

"Oh yeah? That should be an adventure."

Les's twin brothers were twenty years younger than him and the epitome of chaos. They both played baseball and football, a matched set of tight ends, and they did fairly well, but they were also entrepreneurs and more than one of their cockamamie schemes made them a fortune.

"An adventure." Les turned to Joe. "Come have an adventure with me. What's the worst that could happen?"

That was a damn good question.

Joe had a lot to think about, but he didn't want to disappoint Leslie. They'd gone to a lot of trouble to bring him here this weekend, it was the least he could do to give it some thought.

"Ask me again later."

Les raised his eyebrows and then the crowd was up and moving to the BBQ and they were swallowed up. There had to be nearly two thousand people at the expo between the students, alumni and townsfolk and there would be twice that here tonight. A decent turnout, but in the Greenvale heyday they'd easily have double that for Spring Fling.

On the way to the courtyard where there was a band set up to play and giant grills grilling several options, Joe was greeted by a few folks he recognized and many he didn't. One that he *did* know chose to make a big scene.

"I'll catch up with you later," Les said to Joe as he was called over to some guys in suits.

"Joseph Jehosephat Judd! Get your ass over here!"

Marti Simmons was captain of the Jackets cheer squad Joe's freshman year. He'd approached her, told her the team needed him, and they became inseparable. She had been the one to convince the others to let Joe—and then several other guys—join the team, paving the way for the transition to coed. She'd been Joe's biggest supporter and critic ever since, and it had been a ridiculous amount of time since he'd seen her.

Joe picked the petite Black woman up with his big hug and they spun around in a circle.

"It's so good to see you, although I probably should have known that you were going to be here."

She crossed her arms over her chest. "Yeah, you *should* have because you should have called and told me you were coming. What the hell are you doing here?"

Joe barked out a laugh and looked around. "Would you believe considering a job offer?"

She blanched. "Here? *You?*"

"Right? That's what I'm saying!"

Marti appraised him for a moment. "They want you to come coach cheer, huh? President Payton was talking about a lot of changes, guess you'd be one of them."

Joe nodded. "Cheer, yes, and he mentioned me starting up a dance program. Like I would have any idea how to do that."

Instead of agreeing with him, Marti narrowed her eyes.

"You do realize that's a fabulous idea and that you'd be great."

Joe sighed. "Not you, too. How can you possibly think—"

"You know your stuff," she said. "You may not be the most upstanding citizen, and you may lack academic status, but you know dance. You know the ins and outs of the dance world better than any academic would, and you definitely have the credibility. Why not?"

"I need protein before I try to unpack all that. Come on, I'll treat you to some borderline toxic meat products and artery-clogging side dishes, and then we can watch kids beat the crap out of each other in the name of victory."

Marti put her arm around him and laughed. "I've missed your cheerful disposition, my friend."

Joe said hi to a bunch of folks he recognized but didn't remember their names. He tried to smile and look engaged, but he really wanted to sit in a corner and brood. Marti's comments hadn't helped.

Joe's life for the past fifteen years had consisted of concert tours, TV and film appearances, and stage productions. He had a modest apartment in West Hollywood for home base, but otherwise he was constantly on the move. He'd achieved most of the career goals on his bucket list, and at thirty-six the offers were fewer and farther between with more choreography jobs than performances these days. *Dance Machine* was his steady gig, he was contracted for the next three seasons for that show for choreography and guest appearances, but then what? He couldn't keep up with the younger dancers considering the injuries he'd been nursing for years. How much longer could he sustain this lifestyle? What if this was his best option?

It was hard not to be depressed by that. Had he really done all he'd set out to do? Was he ready to settle down and be a college cheer coach?

Joe and Marti found a spot and sat down away from the rest and Joe took a bite of his veggie burger.

"Not half bad," he said. "Maybe I could survive here."

"They had veggie sausages too, and bottles of kombucha." Marti held up her bottle and took a sip. "Not bad at all. Things have changed. Modernized some. They're not in the dark ages anymore. My son will be a freshman here next year." She gazed at him with her eyebrows raised. "He wants to cheer."

"That's great," Joe said. "But how is it possible that you have a kid old enough to start college? I swear I was just sending you gifts for your baby shower yesterday."

Marti laughed. "Terrence and I celebrated too thoroughly after graduation? I don't know. We'd always planned to get married and have kids." She shrugged. "Guess we got to it right away. They're here somewhere."

"Well I'm sure the little bundle of joy will be great in college." He laughed. "Terrell is a great kid. He didn't have a choice not to be with you two for parents."

After college, Marti and Terrence had stayed in the Kansas City area, where they were both originally from. Joe had tried to persuade her to take a shot at a career in dance but she wanted to stay home and be mom to her rambunctious kid with more dancing talent than she could keep up with.

"Mm hmm. He's a good boy. He's not ready to get out from under his parents' thumbs. He didn't want to stay home and go to community college so Terrence encouraged him to apply here and he got in. We'll still be close by but he'll be in the dorms. He struggled a bit in school so we wanted him to be in a nurturing environment."

"I can relate." Joe had agreed to attend Greenvale for a similar reason. Perhaps the two of them had more in common than he imagined.

"If he knows you're coaching cheer, I'm sure he'll try out."

Joe winked. "If he's anywhere near as good as you, he'll make it."

Marti had been a flawless performer. She was a compelling dancer with so much stage presence she had to hold back sometimes to keep from overshadowing the rest of the team. She was also a skilled flyer, meaning she had the strength, confidence and technique necessary to be tossed in the air and land precisely where she was needed, or she could stand stock still on a stunter's shoulders and turn herself into a pretzel if she was asked to. The world was at her feet, but she chose marriage with a side of super mom for Terrell and a career teaching at a dance studio.

She grinned at him and then got serious. "I'd love to know he was in good hands."

"I'm sure he will be."

She groaned. "Come on, Joe. Aren't you ready to have something of your own? Remember how good it felt to create the coed team? You've been working under someone else's parameters for so long...don't you want something that's yours?"

Joe had considered it. He'd dreamed of producing his own show someday, that is once he was a washed-up dancer no longer able to perform. Had he really reached that point? His back was telling him an exuberant "Yes, Joe! It is time for you to hang up your dancing shoes." But his heart kept pushing him. *One more show. One more season of* Dance Machine. *One more chance to make something special.*

"Say you'll think about it? What have you got to lose?"

There was that question again.

"I *am* thinking about it."

Eventually Terrence and Terrell returned and Joe was glad to get caught up on their family happenings. Terrell had grown up to be about an inch shorter than his six-foot-tall father, who'd played football for Greenvale. The two Black men had identical athletic builds and confident postures as well as serious expressions, but when you got Terrell laughing, he smiled just as wide as his mom.

Not long after, it was time for the flag football game. Similar to the idea of powder puff, but these kids played flag football to hopefully avoid injuries. There were the usual laughs over the boys donning makeup, pig tails, and pom pons, which Joe loathed, but once the game was on, the competition was fierce. He sat with Marti's family, but his gaze continued to search for Leslie.

He finally spotted him by the snack bar with all three of his brothers and a few other faculty members Joe recognized. Leslie was holding court, laughing and pounding on one of his brothers' shoulders, his eyes twinkling with mischief...and Joe couldn't take his eyes off of him. What would it be like to stand next to the legendary football player, the "nicest guy in the NFL" and share that spotlight, share that warmth and camaraderie? Joe'd wondered for fifteen years. And now he had an invitation, a perfect opportunity, to find out what it would be like. All he had to do was say yes.

At halftime it was customary to introduce notable alumni, and sure enough Barry introduced Joe and Leslie as well as Marti and a few other folks: a woman who'd hit it big in finance, a politician from Kansas, and a former Olympic Men's Volleyball player, who apparently was coming to join the coaching staff. Joe stood and waved when his name was called and he made eye contact with Leslie, who had returned and taken the empty spot next to Joe to watch the "cheer-leaders."

"Did the football players always look this ridiculous?" Leslie asked as he sat down. He handed a can of water to Joe.

Joe smirked. "I can't speak for the *olden* days, but yeah, they did." He held up his can and Leslie tapped it with a smile.

Marti burst out laughing and pushed Joe into Leslie's shoulder, the contact making him hyperaware of how close Les was. There was no awkward adjusting to not brush thighs or to make room for Leslie's shoulders. They just...fit, like puzzle pieces whose curves and ridges were made to go together. *Huh.*

Les laughed at the antics on the field as Joe and Marti groaned. The guys actually managed to do some stunts that looked legit. He and Marti exchanged surprised looks.

"See? When you join the staff, we can fight over kids like those that can do both cheer and football."

Marti's eyes bugged out. "Mr. Payton, you're really planning to come back and coach?"

"I sure am!"

Joe introduced Marti, Terrence and Terrell to Leslie and they all started chatting as soon as the routine was over.

Much to Joe's chagrin.

"Yes, I absolutely think that Joe would be the perfect choice for cheer coach and dance instructor." Marti was definitely not playing fair. She kept looking between Joe and Leslie and her eyebrows could not have gone further up her forehead.

Joe didn't stand a chance.

"I'm certainly going to do my best to convince him."

Joe actually loved that Leslie was not a slick salesman. He was such a nice guy that there was no hard, obnoxious push. That did make him pause and think about how Leslie would be recruiting kids for football. Joe figured that Leslie would tell them how it is and be real with them, which was honestly how it should be done. It wasn't a tough sell anyway, not with Leslie Payton as their coach. Any up-and-coming player would kill to be coached by one of the NFL's top-scoring quarter-backs with two Super Bowl rings.

Leslie turned and placed a hand on Joe's shoulder. "Hey, I've gotta go talk to some more folks but I want to talk some more and I need to get you settled into your accommodations. When do you fly out?"

"Tomorrow afternoon. I have to fly back to LA and pack to go to New York."

"Meet me where we parked after the game? I want to go over a few more things."

"*Do* you?" Joe gave him a sly smile.

Leslie blushed bright red and Joe loved it.

"Yeah. Meet me after."

Leslie's killer smile left Joe wondering if this was all just a way to get Joe alone for nefarious activities. Not that he was against anything even slightly less than wholesome with Leslie. He'd tried to get him alone for years and life had conspired to keep them apart every damn time. Joe's self-imposed celibacy was the stuff of legends among his friends. He'd say he didn't need the distraction, didn't want the attachments, but really he didn't want to be tied down to anything, anyplace, anyone.

If there was to be someone in his life... Perhaps he had kept the smiling blond football god in the back of his mind. Leslie Payton was incomparable and no one Joe had dated over the years had ever come close to being the complete package like him.

And now, he wanted Joe. Well, he at least wanted him as a colleague. Joe couldn't wait to find out if there was more to Leslie's proposition.

FOUR

L eslie

Leslie fought to keep his composure. He wanted to grab Joe and find the first private space, even if it was under the damn bleachers. It had been agony to be so close to him but surrounded by people. He'd thought about this moment since the first conversation he'd had with his brother about this plan to revamp the athletic department.

Fifteen years ago, he'd become infatuated over the course of one night and he'd spent the time since trying to tell himself he wasn't falling in love. One look at Joe Judd in the parking lot earlier that afternoon had confirmed his suspicions.

Joe Judd was the man for him and Leslie needed to handle this right. Joe was easily spooked, resistant to Les's power of persuasion, and still as irresistible as ever.

Oh, they'd been at the same events several times over the years in New York and Hollywood. Les had conned him out of his phone number early on and they would text from time to time, especially if they were going to be in the others' hometown, but their schedules rarely matched up, nor did opportunities for one-on-one time crop up. It was like Fate was determined to keep them apart, so they resorted to texting random thoughts or funny pictures and videos...Les wanted Joe to know that he was still invested, still attracted, and that he was still hopeful one day their separate paths would converge.

God, he wanted this to be that time. He'd waited long enough.

The rest of the game was dramatic. The cheerleaders actually got close to winning, but the football team pulled out an interception at the last minute. *Thank goodness.* Sure, the flag football rules evened the playing field a bit, but still. Football players trained all year for their sport. They ate, slept, and breathed it. To be bested by athletes who didn't, even if they were just as fit? Shameful.

Les made the rounds and caught up to his twin brothers Sandy and Randy, who were serving drinks at the snack bar while entertaining the college girls. The twins were twenty-six and had only been out of college a few years themselves, but they could be a menace. Barry was constantly having to remind them to behave.

"You ready for the after-party?" Sandy asked, handing him a can of water. One of their companies sold canned water as an alternative to single-use plastic, and they donated a portion of the proceeds to recycling programs. They prided themselves on making sure all of their businesses were moving toward sustainability. Sometimes it drove Les nuts the lengths they'd go to, but then he'd turned around and invested a shit-ton of money into their endeavors. They'd all made a fortune and he was proud of the whippersnappers.

"I'll catch up with you later. I've got something I've gotta do first."

"Or *someone* you've gotta do," Randy stage-whispered and then he and Sandy did a complicated high-five/fist bump thing and Sandy nearly knocked over the nacho cheese machine.

Les shot them a stern look and they acted contrite. For a minute.

"We're sorry. We promise not to say a word about Operation: Twinkle Toes."

Les rolled his eyes and cracked open his water. "Give me another one of these, would you?"

"Right, right. You two might work up a thirst—"

"Randy!"

"I'm just kidding, but I'm not. Have fun. We'll see you at the Goal-post later?"

"Yeah, yeah. Maybe." *If things don't go well.*

Les made his way over to Barry and spoke close to his ear. "Keep an eye on Tweedle Dork and his sidekick Tweedle Dweeb. I don't trust them."

"Me neither." He turned to face him. "How'd it go with—"

"I'm going to Phase Two."

Barry nodded and fought a smile. "Well, good luck, brother. Just...don't be disappointed."

"What? Why?"

Barry looked around and waved to some people before moving closer. "I don't want to see you hurt. I know how much you want this to work, but don't get your hopes up."

Leslie had been forced to admit his obsession with Joe Judd to his family a couple of years after he and Joe met. He'd gotten attached to his phone, and would sneak off to text. Then he'd come home after a trip to LA in which he hoped to connect with Joe only to be disappointed when Joe had let him know he'd injured himself at that night's perfor-mance and needed to go to the ER. Leslie had offered to take him, but Joe was proud—read stubborn—and he said he didn't want Leslie to have to take care of him. Leslie was a caregiver by nature and that had hurt. He'd *wanted* to nurse Joe back to health... His family didn't understand his behavior, so he confessed.

He was smitten with a dancer.

And he'd heard about it ever since.

"I'll be fine."

"Uh-huh."

Leslie rolled his eyes and left the stadium, walking briskly toward the parking lot, hoping he wasn't going to be waylaid any longer.

And boy did his heart go *pitter-patter* when he saw Joe standing by his rental car, laughing with Marti. Oh, Les had wanted to kiss her when she'd taken his side on the fight to win Joe's commitment to coach. It would be a major victory for Greenvale and a dream come true for Les.

A chance to spend quality time with Joe and show him that settling down with the right person wasn't settling.

"Hey," Marti said. "I was just giving one last plug for Joe to come here."

"Great." Les beamed. "I'll get your Venmo link later." He winked and Joe barked out a laugh.

"The honorable Leslie Payton isn't above bribery. Good to know."

Joe hugged and kissed Marti on the cheek, and she shook Les's hand before saying goodbye.

"Her husband is a physical therapist who specializes in sports medicine and her son is coming here next year. You know, if you're still trying to build your dream team or whatever."

"Will it help me convince you to take the job?"

Joe sighed, but he was smiling. "What are we doing here, Les?"

"You mean, at this very moment? Barry wanted me to get you set up for the night."

"Uh-huh, and after that?"

Les shuddered at the possibility of after that.

"After that, there's always the after-party at the Goalpost—"

Joe frowned.

"And," Les added quickly. "I'm supposed to answer any further questions you might have." He slid his hands into his back pockets to avoid reaching for Joe. They were still in public, and he certainly wasn't about to make any moves without consent. He'd learned that lesson watching his fellow NFL colleagues make countless missteps that ruined their careers.

"Hmmm, questions. All right. I'll follow you?"

Les did a mental fist pump and end-zone dance. "Yes, sir. Right this way."

They got into their vehicles and Les drove out of the parking lot, down the main road into campus, and then turned left onto the road facing Jackets Pond and he parked in front of the second to last of the six cottages owned by the college. Currently three of them were vacant after several retirements this year. Many of the long-term employees had purchased houses in town, and one of the cottages was always left vacant for visiting professors, but Barry and the board had approved the one most recently remodeled for Joe.

Leslie hopped down from the truck and reached back in for the cans of water. Joe climbed out of his rental and rested an elbow on the roof.

"What are we doing here?"

Les approached and held out the can of water. "This, I hope, is your new home."

Joe had been in the process of opening the can, which sloshed onto his shirt.

"Are you serious?"

"Come on," Les said, holding up the keys. "Let me give you a tour."

Joe stood staring at the house as if it might swallow him whole. He didn't speak. Leslie couldn't tell if that was a good sign. He went ahead and climbed the steps and had the key in the lock when he heard Joe's car door slam. He smiled to himself and opened the door.

Yeah, he'd come over earlier and cleaned up, dusted, and changed the bedding. He put out towels and set up a Keurig and coffee cups, put creamer in the refrigerator... He even brought over a collection of teas in case Joe preferred that in the morning.

He wished he would have had the opportunity at some point over the past fifteen years to find out Joe's morning preference for himself.

Les remained on the covered porch and watched as Joe climbed the steps.

"You should have everything you need, but if you don't, you can let me know. I can run out and—"

"I'm sure everything's fine."

Joe walked in the door and Les flipped on the light. He wanted to see Joe's face. Maybe it would give him a clue whether or not he was impressed, whether he was thinking positively about the—

"Aren't you coming in?"

Joe wasn't looking at the house. He was looking at Leslie.

Leslie was still standing outside. Stepping across the threshold would require an invitation.

"My intention was to show you to your room and say goodnight. I don't want to crowd you."

"Get in here, Les. It's obvious you came here to do more than open a door for me. Come in."

Les stepped inside and closed the door.

"Wow, this is nice," Joe said, finally taking it all in. "This all looks new."

"Yeah, uh, Barry had the vacant cottages renovated. New kitchen, new appliances including a stackable washer—"

"Aw, you mean no more lugging fifty pounds of laundry two miles to the laundromat? How would I survive?"

Les laughed. "Yeah, I made that trek myself when I lived off-campus, but I borrowed a car."

"I didn't have that luxury, thank you very much. I didn't get my license until later," Joe said. He strolled around and peeked in the kitchen and then into the hallway where the bathroom and two bedrooms were. "Nice place. I could have just stayed at Motel 6, you know."

Les cleared his throat. "I know, but I wanted you to see this, see where you could be living if you take the job."

Joe turned to face him. "Is that all?"

Leslie's heart pounded. He hadn't been nervous like this since his last Super Bowl performance, or maybe his first championship game as head coach at University of Kansas City several years ago. As a rule, Leslie wasn't unsure of himself. He knew his strengths and he knew his limits, but when it came to relationships, he'd always felt awkward. And after years of pining after Joe Judd, to be here with him now, he didn't know how to proceed.

"Joe..."

"It's been a long time since we started this dance, Leslie." Joe moved to stand in front of Les and held out his hand. "What are we going to do about it?"

Les hesitated a moment, wondering if he should pinch himself. Was this really happening after all this time?

FIVE

J[oe]

All the near misses, the flirty conversations, and the innuendo-filled texts over the past fifteen years had led to this moment. Joe's head was spinning from all the day's events and that whopper of a decision he needed to make, but tonight, he didn't want to think. He wanted to *feel*, and he wanted to feel the man standing in front of him, the man he'd dreamed about for so long.

As Leslie stared at Joe's hand, Joe was taken back to the Goalpost's parking lot fifteen years earlier.

"Take me with you," Joe had said, breathlessly. "Let's see if we're still this hot without all the conversation."

Leslie had looked at Joe's extended hand then and...sighed. He'd clasped Joe's hand and squeezed.

"I've had the best night with you," he'd said. "And I'm invested, Joe. If I take you back to my hotel, I'm not going to want to let you go, and you've made it clear that you're just getting started. If you really think you are ready to try for something real, let's go. If you need time—"

"But I want you now. Les, I don't know where I'm going, what I'm going to be doing...I can't make you any promises."

"I know that, and I know I'm going to regret this, but it would be too hard to let you go if we take this any further."

Joe had never wanted to be tied to anyone, never wanted to settle down, but damn, if Leslie Payton hadn't been a temptation.

Now they were back in the same position. They knew each other somewhat better now. They'd each had years to search for something or someone else, and now, standing before him, Joe felt just like that college kid staring at the gates of heaven and being tempted to step into the light. Had his circumstances changed? Would Leslie be willing to take a chance on him now?

On this night, Leslie took his hand, letting his much larger fingers slide over Joe's. He turned Joe's hand over and ran his thumb over Joe's palm

"What's changed?" Les asked, his voice husky. "I still feel the same. No, that's wrong. I feel...more."

Goose bumps erupted over Joe's skin at Les's slow, languorous touch. He'd be lying to himself if he said that he hadn't hoped something would finally happen between them when Barry's secretary had asked him to come for Spring Fling. Or when Les had texted him and asked whether he was coming. Or when he'd first seen Les slide down out of his monster truck, looking over the roof of Joe's rental car as if he'd just gotten what he wanted from Santa. Les was the total package, a man with a big heart, sexy as hell in a "he has no idea" kind of way. Joe wanted Les to wrap those arms around him and change Joe's mind, make him give up his running ways. Because he didn't know if he had it in himself to stay put, even with this perfect man as incentive.

"What's changed is that we're both here now. No interruptions, no missing each other. We're both grown-ass men who want this. Right? You do want this, don't you, Leslie?"

"With everything."

Joe pressed his free hand against Leslie's beefy chest and ran it up his right pec, loving the way Les trembled under his touch. He dragged his fingers up Leslie's throat and into his hair, giving the back a gentle tug that elicited a moan.

Leslie's head fell back and his eyes closed. He sucked in a breath and let it out on a sigh.

"Joe."

"All of these years I've thought about how I would kiss you for the first time."

Les slowly tilted his head forward and looked down at Joe, a smile splitting his lips. "How?"

Joe moved closer, pressing his body against Les's much larger one. At 6'4", Les had about five inches on Joe and about fifty pounds. But Joe knew that he was the one who needed to be careful. He might be slighter, but Les let himself be vulnerable with Joe, and he needed to remember that.

Joe moved Les's hand to Joe's lower back and then used his own left hand to run his fingers down Les's cheek. "I thought maybe our first kiss would be wild, like we'd crash into each other and rip each other's clothes off."

Les's hand tightened against Joe's lower back and he balled up Joe's shirt in his fist.

"God, Joe—"

"But now that I'm here—"

"Joe, please. Tell me you'll take the job, tell me you're really here."

Joe froze. "Leslie—"

"I know, I always ruin it by getting too heavy with you, but Joe... It's been such a long time. What can I do to make you stay?"

Joe took a deep breath and let it out, choosing his words carefully.

"I can't promise you forever, Leslie, but say I took it. The job. For a year, to start. Could that be enough for you to see what we could be together? To finally touch me?"

Leslie's eyes flared and he wrapped those strong arms around Joe so tight. It was exactly what Joe was looking for. It was the invitation he needed.

Joe brushed his lips over Les's with his eyes open, wanting to savor every bit of the contact he'd waited fifteen years for. Now that it was happening, his heart was ready to take a flying leap out of his chest and his knees were dangerously close to collapsing.

Les blinked and gazed at Joe like he was a fresh-baked cookie his mom had forbidden him to take but he couldn't resist the taste. He moved his hands to cradle Joe's jaw and pressed his forehead to Joe's.

"It would be a start."

Joe thought of all the romantic overtures Les had made over the years. Once he'd had Joe's hotel room filled with roses when Joe had had a rough show, and there was the time after a particularly bad audition that Joe's ride hadn't shown up and he was about to be late for a flight out of San Francisco. Les had dropped everything to drive him to the airport and Joe was so thrilled, he almost said to hell with the flight and begged Leslie to take him to *his* home. Joe wished he could be as giving, as generous, as loving. He wished he was enough for Leslie Payton. He thought maybe, just maybe, he was closer now...

"Then let's start," Joe said, giving Les the permission he knew Les needed.

And it paid off.

He couldn't breathe as Les consumed him, kissing him so deeply it took Joe by surprise. Les crushed Joe to his chest and made deep swipes with his tongue, leaving Joe breathless. Joe smiled as Leslie dipped down to suck on his throat, thinking Les controlled the kiss the way he orchestrated his offense. He called the shots, he knew where everything was supposed to be, and Joe didn't want to put up any defense.

Leslie moaned as he turned Joe's back to the wall, adjusting his stance and bending his knees to get closer to Joe's level.

Joe was trapped and loving it *because* it was Leslie. If anyone else had him pinned against the wall, he would have fought to be free, but he trusted Les with his life and wanted Les just as desperately as Les wanted *him*.

Joe went to work on the zipper of Leslie's jacket, trying to force the thick down parka over his shoulders, but Les caught his hands and held them in one of his over their heads. He sucked at Joe's lips, further paralyzing Joe in the most delicious way, and Leslie stroked his tongue, leaving Joe panting and ready to combust. He wanted skin, he wanted teeth, he wanted—

"God," Les moaned, pulling back. "That was so much better than I imagined. On all of my sleepless nights I never imagined this would finally happen, that I'd have you like this. You were a fantasy, and now—"

"And now I'm wondering why you're stopping," Joe whined, trying to make below-the-belt contact, anything to relieve the ache...the need.

Leslie kissed him twice, searching his eyes for what, Joe had no idea. Joe could only imagine the wanton picture he made, his lips deep red, his cheeks splotchy from the contact... Then Leslie kissed him a third time and stepped completely away, leaving Joe in agony.

"Why?" Joe finally asked.

Leslie ran his hands through his hair. "Give me a second," he said with a laugh. "I'm having pregame jitters."

Joe snorted. "Really. Big, bad Leslie Payton getting jitters over Twinkle Toes Joe Judd." He rolled his eyes and adjusted himself.

"Stop it," Leslie said in that soft voice, the way he got when he was about to scold. *Don't put yourself down, Joe. Don't ever consider yourself less-than.* "I think I should put the brakes on is all."

Joe wanted to hurl himself at Les, his brain chanting the cheer "sack that quarterback, said sack that quarterback." He was willing to do just about anything to get Les to give up his chivalrous ways and get back to the touching part of the evening, preferably with no clothes in the way.

Instead, Joe ran his hands through his hair and straightened his shirt.

"Wow, didn't realize I was so resistible."

"Joe—"

"No, I get it," he said, holding up a hand as he attempted to compose himself. "I do. You've made it very clear over the years that sex outside of a committed relationship was a no for you. I'm sorry if I pushed you." *And made a fool of myself.* Thankfully he hadn't begged, but he knew, if left unchecked, his now-unbridled libido would have forced him to his knees in front of Leslie.

"Joe, stop it. You did nothing but be honest with me and that's what I appreciate about you. Always have. I just couldn't take it if—"

And that was just it. Joe had run away from him so many times, had panicked and canceled potential meetups. Who could blame Leslie for stepping back?

"I know." Les was the most in-touch-with-his-feelings guy Joe had ever met. Despite his superstardom, Leslie Payton was grounded in a way that Joe had been running from his whole life.

Feelings. *Ew.*

What Joe *would* admit was that if he ever opened himself up to feelings for someone, it would be Leslie Payton. He just hadn't been ready or willing to go all in with the whole picket-fence shit he knew Les dreamed about. And it had nothing to do with wanting to keep his options open, he just didn't want to be that open with anyone. Like Slipknot so eloquently put it, "People = Shit." Joe didn't trust anyone. Well, except Leslie. He'd proved over the years that he was trustworthy. But Joe didn't trust himself either, and until he could honestly say, "I'm here and I'm staying," he had no business hopping into bed with Les.

Dammit.

Six

L eslie

"I'm sorry." And he was. *So sorry*. Sorry he wasn't like most men who let their dicks happily lead them into temptation. Sorry he couldn't go there with Joe when he knew it would be spectacular. Sorry he was too afraid to live in the now and take what Joe was offering him.

"Don't be sorry," Joe said with a sigh. He slid his arms around Leslie's waist and rested his head on Les's chest, tempting Les with the scent of his cologne. Cologne Les had sent to Joe years ago because he'd discovered it at a commercial shoot he was doing and thought it would smell great on Joe. Yeah, he was a sap like that. Joe had sent him back a video demonstration of just how he'd applied it and Les had wished he could climb through the phone and smell it for himself. "You know it's one of the things I like most about you. Your honorable nature."

Leslie barked out a laugh and rested his chin on Joe's head, a move that made Joe squirm in his arms. His squirming, though, brought their bodies into contact in a way that made Leslie's senses hyperaware.

Joe was here. In his arms. And wasn't saying no to the job, which meant they'd have time to explore this thing between them. Leslie would do whatever it took to convince Joe to stay. He knew getting Joe to agree to the job was just the first step, and then he'd be able to work his magic.

"I'm not sorry about that kiss, though," Leslie said, pressing his lips to Joe's hair, inhaling his berry-scented shampoo. "It was worth the wait."

Joe looked up at him. "I'm glad. There's plenty more where that came from."

And it would be so easy, Leslie. Joe's lips were swollen and shiny, his pupils wide and his eyelids heavy. Leslie had a pic of Joe saved on his phone from his second season on *Dance Machine* where he looked similar, his white T-shirt torn and his hair mussed in a bedhead sort of way. He was showing a lot of skin in that picture. Leslie had fallen asleep staring at it more than a few times while on the road.

"Good. I'll be looking forward to it."

Joe sighed and stepped back. "Did you want some..." He looked around and peeked in the kitchen. "Water? Coffee?"

"There's tea in there, too," Leslie said. "I didn't know which you prefer in the morning. I wanted to make sure you had options."

Joe stepped back and wrinkled his nose. "Oh, you're good. But if you want to know what I do in the morning, you're going to have to find out for yourself. Right now, I'm going to go to bed, so if you want to know what I do before bed you're welcome to watch. Join in if you want."

Les shook his head. "And you're dangerous. I'll let you get some rest. How about I take you to breakfast?"

Joe tried to hide his disappointment, but Les noticed the quiver in his chin. "It would have to be early. It's a two-hour drive to the airport."

"Then I'll be here early," Les said. He moved closer and took Joe's hand in his. "I'll take you to breakfast and then we can talk about you coming in the fall. You know, the dates and everything. I can answer any questions you might have, and then I can say goodbye and know it'll only be a short time until I see you again."

"Are you really making me do this?" Joe said, curling his lip. "Becoming a resident of Ayre Valley once more?"

"I'd love it if you would," Leslie said solemnly. "I think it would be a good experience for you, and it would be a phenomenal win for Greenvale." *Please say yes.* He squeezed Joe's hand before reaching for the door. "Sleep on it." He leaned in and kissed Joe's cheek, his lips lingering as if he was losing the battle between willpower and temptation and was going to scoop Joe up in his arms and take him where they both wanted to be...

"Are you taking me to the Tasty Grill for breakfast?" Joe whispered.

Leslie laughed. "There is a new place, an actual chain restaurant even. But if it's Tasty Grill you want—"

"*Yesss*," Joe breathed. "That's the only place that can tempt me from my clean eating regimen."

Leslie bowed. "Your wish is my command. I'll see you..."

"Oh, uh, seven? That too early?"

"Nope. See you at seven." Leslie opened the door and then paused to take a long, long look at Joe. He needed one more dose of Joe's incredible presence before leaving. "I'm so glad you came."

Joe raised his arm over his head and leaned against the door. "I mean, I'm here. And I'm considering this terrible plan you and your brother have concocted. That's something, right?"

Leslie looked around to be sure all was quiet on First Street. The moon illuminated Jackets Pond and the water danced softly with the chilly breeze brushing over its surface. During the day, the fountain would provide a lovely sight and a relaxing sound for those in the area. Leslie remembered looking out the window of the third floor of the McCann Building during class and watching the fountain. He'd dream of his future playing in the NFL, and a special person in his life cheering him on. Then it had come true. Well, the NFL part. The special person needed to agree to the cheering on part. Maybe Jackets Pond had magical wish-granting powers. He'd send a little wish up tonight in hopes the rest of his dream came true.

"It's more than something. Good night." He leaned in and hesitated inches from Joe's face. If Joe closed the distance, it meant he really was considering the plan.

Joe chuckled. "Good night, Leslie."

Then Joe leaned the rest of the way in and made light contact, tentative contact, teasing contact. It was enough. Enough to make Les's lips tingle. He stepped back and laughed as Joe rolled his eyes and shut the door with a huff.

It was a start.

Or at least he'd thought so.

When Leslie pulled up at 6:58 a.m. he growled and slammed his hand on the steering wheel.

Joe's rental car was gone, which had to mean Joe was gone.

"Dammit, Joe." That familiar twinge pulled at his heart as he turned off the ignition on his Lincoln Town Car. He didn't want Joe to have to scale the mountain that was his F-250, so he'd brought his sensible classy car that he used to drive his mom around in. He climbed the steps to the front porch and noticed a rolled-up piece of paper tied with a string.

A note.

My Dearest Leslie,

I texted you, but I figured you might not check before coming.

I needed to think. I'm sorry about breakfast. You've been so patient with me, and I'm going to ask you for a little more of that patented Payton patience.

I've got to make some calls when I get home, first to my agent to see what my schedule is like before I commit to the job. I'd likely have to take you up on the airplane offer a few times to fly out for Dance Machine *filming, but I can probably make it work, even from the middle of nowhere.*

I'm more concerned about you and what me potentially taking this job means. To be honest, I don't know what it means. What I do *know is that I'm ready to be in the same place with you for an extended period of time and to see what happens.*

You and I have been doing this dance for so long. I think we owe it to ourselves to take the next step, even if it means reaching our finale. I'll be going into this with no expectations other than we continue being honest.

I hope I see you in August.

I hope you're ready.

Twinkle Toes

. . .

"He didn't say 'no.'" Leslie beamed. He didn't even care that Joe stood him up for breakfast. He knew Joe was terrible at saying goodbye. Les hadn't exactly counted on Joe being here when he arrived.

God, what would it be like? Them working together? Playing together? Making something of all this after all these years? Was Les setting himself up for heartache?

"I have to know. Either way." He put the car in drive and pulled away from the curb, the fountain in Jackets Pond catching his eye. He made another wish as he drove out of town and toward his family's property.

Fifteen years had been a long time to wait. He could wait three more months.

SEVEN

T hree months later
Joe

"Have you seen the news?"

Marti and Joe had been in constant contact since he'd had a video conference with Barry and signed an employment contract for the upcoming school year. He'd made some demands, though. First, an assistant coach, one Marti Simmons, and Joe had strongly suggested that Marti's husband be considered for the head trainer position, which Barry had enthusiastically supported. Anything to bring Greenvale's best of the best back to the fold.

"I've been watching *Criminal Minds* nonstop on Netflix while packing up my apartment. I can't believe I'm doing this."

"I know, dear, you say that every time we talk. Now turn on the news."

"You have time to watch TV because you guys already moved."

Marti and Terrence had decided to rent a house in town and Terrell would be rooming on campus. They'd be close but Terrell would have his autonomy. And free tuition.

"Joseph Jehosephat Judd, the news. Or better yet, the Weather Channel."

"Are you trying to talk me out of coming? You know the weather is my least favorite thing about the Midwest. Besides the lack of good food."

"Joe. Turn it on."

Joe groaned and flopped down on the couch. "I don't even know where to find that channel. You do realize people in California don't watch the weather channel. We wear layers. Now, what is going..."

Joe clicked on the channel to find on-the-scene coverage of a band of massive tornadoes that had touched down in southern Iowa and were now making their way across northern Missouri.

"Oh my God. Is Leslie—"

"He's fine. His place wasn't in the path, neither was ours. But Joe... the campus sustained damage."

Joe covered his mouth with his hand as the name Greenvale College was emblazoned on the screen followed by images of the gym and football field strewn with debris. A golf cart was on top of the ruined roof of the fitness center. If he would have been standing, his legs would have failed him.

"Is everyone okay?" Joe whispered. He couldn't breathe. He'd hated how everyone treated tornadoes like they were no big deal when he was a student. Natural disasters were nothing to make light of.

"There were no injuries. Everyone's fine. But I wanted you to know what you were arriving into tomorrow."

"I appreciate it. I gotta go, Marti. I need to—" *What are you going to do, Joe?* He stood in the middle of the empty room flapping his hands while trying to decide on a course of action.

"Right. Be safe. We'll see you at the airport."

"Marti, you guys don't have to come get me, I can Uber."

She laughed. "No, you really can't, darling. And it's fine. We're getting our last load out of storage while we're down there. We'll see you when you land."

"Thank you," Joe said, but he was already typing out a text to Leslie, his trembling fingers barely making any coherent words come together.

Please tell me you're alright. I just saw the news.

Joe gripped the phone tightly with both hands and couldn't tear his eyes away from the bouncing three dots on the screen.

We're fine. Just helping Brother Barry assess the damage. Everyone is okay. You finish packing?

Just like Leslie to turn the focus around to Joe. As vain as Joe was at times, he hated that Leslie would often avoid talking about himself and focus on Joe instead.

I can fly out tonight if you—

Joe deleted that text. He wasn't normally the jump-in-for-the-save kind of guy, but with Leslie it felt like the natural thing to do. He wanted to do it.

That gave him pause. God, he was really doing this. Moving across country to Tornado Alley because Leslie thought he'd make a great coach. *Unbelievable.*

Let me see if I can get an earlier flight so I can help—

"What, Joe?" he asked himself out loud, pacing across his tiny living room. "Like you're gonna swing a hammer? Take some measurements and shit?"

I'm sorry I can't pick you up at the airport, and I swear we'll have housing arranged for you by tomorrow night. I'm sorry your place got hit. I was so excited for you to—

Joe's sinuses burned and his pulse pounded in his ears. He couldn't finish the text.

Housing? WTF?

Be safe. I'll see you soon.

Joe had to turn off the TV or he'd go into full panic.

He didn't even try to sleep. He finished packing up his apartment and had the eight or ten remaining boxes next to the door that he'd take to storage along with his car in the morning. Movers had already taken his furniture to storage, so his place was empty except for the flat-screen, which was dated and would be left behind. He had four suitcases and two duffel bags he'd be flying with. That was it. Anything else he needed he'd have shipped. He'd already seen his place and it was fully kitted out.

Or it had been.

Several times, Joe had picked up his phone to have his agent call the whole thing off, but no. He knew he needed to go, for Leslie and for himself. But a *tornado*? Was he really ready for all this?

He could back out and no one would blame him if he had no house to live in.

But he owed it to Leslie to be better. He wanted to be better.

Part of this job was Joe's desire to see what life could be like offstage. He'd been performing for so long...could he actually do anything else? Knowing Leslie would be there to support him had been the final piece falling into place. He might not be ready for love and marriage and a baby carriage, but he and Leslie had provided moral support for each other above and beyond their attraction. He wanted to be more than a performer, wanted to believe Leslie when he said Joe could do anything. Wanted to prove to Leslie that he was right all along.

So he would go. He would put on his big-boy G-string and face whatever was waiting for him in Iowa. He just hoped he was strong enough.

Marti and Terrence picked him up at baggage claim in Kansas City, thank goodness, because he'd had a hell of a time lugging his shit to the skycap at LAX by himself.

"How bad is it?" he asked as he shook Terrence's hand.

"We've got space at our place."

Joe sighed. "Thanks, but Leslie texted me five times this morning to let me know they have something worked out temporarily until it's repaired."

"Uh-huh," Terrence said with a half-smile. "I'm just sayin'."

"And I appreciate you both."

Marti had hugged him extra tight. "I'm so glad you're here, although I'm sorry it's getting off to a rocky start."

"It'll be *fiiiiine*," Joe said and he kept telling himself it would be, otherwise he never would have gotten on the plane, nor would he have made it the additional two-hour drive to Ayre Valley.

"The President called an all-hands meeting for tomorrow to go over the situation," Terrence said.

"You're more than welcome to stay with us and I can take you out there for the meeting, since you don't have a ride?"

"I'm going to buy something. I didn't want to drive mine out from Hollywood." *Because there's no way I could have spent all those hours in the car without a joint or five freezing up.* "The house wasn't too far, I planned to walk—"

"Right, and I guess you thought you'd be having groceries delivered? And what about the snow?"

"Yeah, I was postponing thoughts of weather. It's the only way I could make myself get on the plane."

They chatted the rest of the way, and Joe was wishing Terrence drove faster. He needed to see Leslie. He needed to make sure he was okay. And now he needed to rethink his living arrangements.

His phone buzzed when they were about ten minutes from the exit.

Are you almost here?

Joe grinned.

Where is here?

The three dots hovered for quite a while. They exited I-35 and Joe was ready to tell Terrence to just head to their place when Les's text popped up.

Can you meet me at Higdon?

"The old dorm?" Joe muttered.

Yeah, sure. Be right there.

"Higdon? Wait, did you hear from Les?" Marti turned around in her seat. "That's where he wants you?"

"Yeah, he asked me to meet him at Higdon."

"Oh, right. Yeah, we can do that."

Terrence took a left and then they were on Campus drive. Jacket's Pond was to the right and—

"Oh!"

The row of cute faculty cottages was now flattened with debris strewn about the road and floating in the pond. Giant sycamore trees were split in two and lying on their sides, casualties of Mother Nature.

"At least the school was mostly spared," Marti said. "It would have been devastating to lose the dorms or administration building."

Terrence turned right and drove around the back of the boys' dorm, Booth, and pulled into the small lot between Mesle, where the women lived, and Higdon.

Leslie's big 4x4 was parked out front and he stood next to it with Barry and the twins. They all wore grim expressions and were dressed for getting their hands dirty.

This was not the reunion Joe had been hoping for, though his heart did some fancy footwork in his chest at the sight of Les. Not that he had any clue what would happen between them, but he didn't picture arriving in the middle of a disaster.

"Thank you, Terrence and Marti, for bringing Joe," Barry said.

Leslie didn't speak, but Joe saw a twinkle in Les's eye that let him know, despite the dire circumstances, he was happy to see him. Relieved, maybe. A little nervous. Same as Joe.

"Joe," Barry said, holding his hand out. Joe shook his and the other men's hands, lingering with Les. "I'm so sorry about all this. We had the cottages all ready and then this."

Joe felt sorry for the guy. He assumed Barry would normally be under a huge amount of pressure to get school started smoothly, but throw a tornado into the plans...

"We hadn't gotten around to a full renovation of Higdon Hall yet. That was going to be next year, but we do have two vacant apartments downstairs. The upper floors are used for student housing and there are RAs assigned on those levels. The second floor is for visitors, but the first floor has the head resident's place and two additional units with kitchenettes and private baths. It's not as nice—"

"I'm sure it will be fine."

Joe might have come off as a diva on *Dance Machine*, but he didn't want Leslie or any of the Paytons to think of him that way. He'd made the choice to make this move, and he was determined to be a team player.

"You sure? I—thank you for understanding," Barry said, relief evident as his shoulders lowered. "Leslie will show you the units. You can pick which one you'd like and we can get maintenance in to clean—"

"It's fine. I can take care of cleaning. I know you have much bigger issues to deal with."

Everyone looked at him in surprise. What, like he didn't know how to use a mop?

"Thank you, Joe. I really appreciate it. Let us know if there's anything you need or if anything isn't in working order."

There was an awkward silence and then everyone launched into action. Barry and the twins left in a golf cart, Marti and Terrence each grabbed a couple of Joe's bags, and Joe and Les stood staring at each other.

"You're really here," Leslie breathed almost as if he didn't intend for Joe to hear him. "Thank you. For being so understanding. Barry was very worried. He knows what you are giving up to be here."

"Giving up? Oh, you mean the tour. Yeah, it's not a huge deal." *It most certainly is.* Going out on tour with Lady Gaga was definitely a big deal, but Joe wasn't sure his body could handle the grueling schedule. It was better that he focus on other endeavors before everyone else knew that he couldn't do it anymore. "Besides, I already agreed to come. A measly tornado wasn't going to keep me away." He gave an exaggerated eye roll that made Leslie laugh.

"Did you want to give us the key?"

Marti and Terrence were back and had grabbed the last of Joe's things. Time had a way of standing still when Joe was with Leslie and everything else around them went on unnoticed.

Leslie fumbled with the keys while his already ruddy cheeks burned redder.

"I've got it, sorry."

Joe followed him and took a deep breath, trying to hide his anxiety about this change in plans.

Higdon Hall, built in 1899 after the administrative building was finished, hadn't been used for housing while Joe was a student. He recalled a Halloween social being held in the dark and creepy lounge on the second floor at one point, but the building hadn't been needed back then as the population of students had been smaller than at its peak. He did like all of the old-fashioned dark wood and figured it should be quiet enough.

As he glanced around the large lobby with high ceilings and wood floors, his heart grew considerably lighter. It was a great space. A wide staircase ascended in front of the doors and there was a common room behind it with a large bank of windows.

"The two apartments are down this way," Les said. "They're identical in layout so I suppose it would depend on if you want the morning light or you want to be on the side of the student entrance."

"Maybe not the entrance side?"

Les nodded and turned left halfway down the hall. "It'll be bright in the mornings. We can order some heavier curtains if you need—"

"I'm sure it will be fine," Joe said, getting a kick out of Les fussing over him.

"We're going to take off," Marti said. "Let me know if you need anything."

She and Terrence smiled at Joe, but it was obvious they were concerned. Marti sometimes let her supermomming bleed over to Joe and he wasn't always mad about it. Right now, though, he wanted to be a real grown-up in front of Leslie.

"Thanks," Joe said, leaning in to kiss her on the cheek and give her a quick hug. "I know that was a long trip in one day."

Terrence shook his head. "We stayed in KC last night. Not a problem at all. See you soon."

Joe didn't miss his knowing smile as they shook hands.

Marti had known that Joe and Les had history, and after he took the job, of course he'd let her in on the true depth of his fixation over a Facetime call his last week in New York.

"Joe," she'd said with mock seriousness. "I'm your best friend and that's why I'm putting it to you straight. You know the man wears a mullet?"

Joe had burst out laughing. "And I seem to recall Terrence still wore his *Fresh Prince of Bel Air* look when we were in school complete with the overall strap hanging down."

"He did not," she'd protested, but she'd laughed at the honest truth.

"Okay, his fashion might be dated, but he makes up for it in other ways."

"And I intend to find out about Leslie Payton's other ways." He'd imitated her shocked expression and listened as she lectured him about workplace romances and boundaries blah-blah.

Apparently, she'd filled Terrence in as well.

"See you tomorrow," Marti said as she tugged on Terrence's sleeve. Terrence, who continued to smile between Joe and Les.

"Ah, here we are."

Leslie had been fumbling with a wad of keys during this exchange. He waved to the Simmonses and then unlocked the door so Joe could get a look at his new place.

And he coughed.

"Boy, the dust mites sure are productive here in Ayre Valley." Joe joked to cover up his terror at the massive dust cloud swirling in the dim light. And were those cobwebs?

"No, No, there's no way. Look, Joe, I've got extra bedrooms. Several. You can stay with me."

"Les, it's fine. I'm not afraid of a little elbow grease." He *was* afraid of whatever made those cobwebs. And his stomach turned at the possibility of other creatures who might have made this building home.

"But Joe—"

"I can't stay with you, Leslie. For several reasons."

They had yet to talk about whatever was going on or would go on or might possibly occur and the weight of that hung heavy between them.

"Just tonight, then. Until I can get a cleaning crew in here."

"As long as you point me toward some cleaning supplies, I've got this. Oh, and I'll need to grab some groceries—"

"You've got full privileges at the Buzz. They've got vegetarian options, though I'm not sure what all you can eat on your regimen. Barry wanted me to tell you."

"Oh. Okay. That will work until I can get to the store."

"And I can have the terrible two bring over my Lincoln until we go to get you a car. My friend Tim has a dealership in Leonard. I thought we could start there. When you're ready."

That was the one thing Joe had asked Les for, help finding a car. He knew Leslie would help him choose the right vehicle for driving in Midwest conditions.

"That's great, but I know you're busy helping Barry—"

"Stop it." Les smiled and shoved his hands in his pockets. "You're really here."

"Yeah." Joe grinned back and then he sneezed.

"Aw geez, Joe—"

"It's fine! I swear. Let's see what I've got to work with."

Joe needed a moment to collect himself so he darted around the living space turning on lights and opening drapes. The windows were up higher, which would give him some privacy as Higdon happened to be smack dab in between both dorms and the path to the Buzz went by right outside his window.

"When do the kids arrive?"

Leslie had moved to the kitchen and was pulling open cabinets, sending more puffs of dust into the air.

"Some are here, and the rest are supposed to come throughout the weekend. We might have to push back the start of school by a couple of days to be sure all the debris is cleaned up, but the dorms will be safe enough and the Buzz is ready for them." He opened a small closet next to the door. "Aha! Okay, we've got surface and glass cleaner and Lysol for the floors and bathroom. There's an old mop here; let me go hit up the head resident, and see if he's got some sponges and rags and we can get to work."

Joe stepped in front of him. "*You* stop it." He winked, having fun using Les's line. "I know you need to get back to Barry. I don't need to be supervised. I'll go introduce myself to my new neighbor and borrow a cup of flour or whatever it is you're supposed to do with Midwest neighbors."

Leslie let out a huge sigh and let his shoulders fall. "This is not how I wanted to welcome you, Joe. I hate it a lot."

Joe stepped closer, brushing his chest against Les's. "How did you want to welcome me?"

Leslie dropped his arms to his sides and shoved his hands in his pockets.

"You know what I want," Les breathed. "But you made me promise we'd talk first."

Joe placed a hand on his chest. "I did say that."

It would be so easy to let go.

"I'm so glad you're here. I can't wait—"

"Okay, but you're gonna have to wait. A bit." Joe patted Les's pec and let his hand rest there...longingly. Then he sighed. "Go help Barry. Let me start cleaning so I can get settled in. If you get a break later, call me."

Les searched his eyes and Joe saw his hands twitching as if he wanted to grab Joe and toss him over his shoulder.

The cave man routine might not be a bad thing with Leslie Payton, as long as Joe was in charge.

Les leaned down and Joe was transfixed by his lips. A kiss would be alright, wouldn't it? Before they laid out their expectations of how they would work and exist together in a small town where everyone knew everyone and everyone talked—

"Hello? Has my new neighbor arrived?"

Les stepped back reluctantly and his blush warmed Joe down to his toes.

Warm. It was muggy, and Joe hadn't even noticed. *Huh.*

"Hey, Matt. This is Joe Judd."

The big, beefy Iowa-corn-fed white dude bro with his hat on backward trotted forward and shook Joe's hand.

"That's awesome. Can't believe we've got not one but *two* celebrities on campus this year. Excellent."

"No celebrities here," Joe said, quick to nip that in the bud. "I'm just Joe. Nice to meet you, Matt. I was about to come find you to introduce myself and see if you had some cleaning supplies I could borrow?"

Matt grinned. "Abso facto. Got keys to the supply closet as well in case industrial strength is what you're after." He snapped his gum and Joe forced himself to keep his eyes steady and straight.

"Thank you!"

He turned to Leslie. "I think we've got this handled. I'll check in with you later?"

He cocked his head to the side and raised his eyebrows to be sure Leslie understood this was not a dismissal but a necessary break.

"We're talking sooner rather than later," Les growled close to Joe with his back to Matt. Then he turned, nodded at the kid, and filled up the entry on his way out.

Joe chuckled. "Yes, sir, Coach, sir," he called after him.

Les snorted as he turned the corner.

"Wow, I can't believe he's here," Matt said. "He's totally my hero. I feel, like, honored to have shared space with him, you know?"

"I can see that." He couldn't even make fun of the kid because he was right. Being around Les was awe-inspiring, but it was different for Joe. He didn't worship Les for his football prowess or his post-NFL career. He admired the man for his humanity, his optimistic outlook on life. Okay, and he was incredible to look at, and to touch...

"Cool. So, you known him long?"

"Uh, well we met here at Spring Fling when I was a senior." He wasn't about to tell this dude bro that he'd wanted him ever since. Nor would he admit that Leslie Payton had ruined him for all other men before they'd even touched. "We're acquainted." There. That should suffice.

"Awesome. So let's go get you some cleaners. This place hasn't been used for the two years I've been here and while I do inspections once a month to make sure there are no leaks or infestations, no one's cleaned. Sorry, bruh."

"No worries." Joe almost believed his cheerful reply.

This was going to take him a week to get cleaned.

You could be in Leslie's bed.

No problem. A week. He could do it.

EIGHT

L eslie

It was well after dark before he could finally get away and instead of heading back to Higdon to check on Joe, he'd had to have Randy drive him home so he could dose himself with migraine medication. He'd gone to bed with 64 oz of water and some crackers, furious that he was once again laid up because his body was beat to hell.

Joe hadn't answered his past few texts, and even though he knew the likelihood was low, he couldn't help being afraid that Joe would have hired a car to take him back to the airport and back to LA. Leslie almost wouldn't blame him.

What a clusterfuck! The athletic center had sustained significant damage and the football field was toast. The gym with its indoor track only needed repairs to the roof, but the fitness center and offices were destroyed. There was insurance, of course, but their first game was next week. Now they'd have to find a new space.

The strategic plan for this year had been that Joe and Leslie would rally their troops, bring in spectators and interest so they could build their programs with ample resources. Now, Leslie was going to have to tell Joe that the lucrative budget they'd been promised was mostly going to go to cover whatever insurance wouldn't. They'd be starting from scratch. Hell, the football field turf needed to be replaced, the bleachers had been wrecked, the scoreboard shot. Les had a meeting with the admin at Ayre Valley High School in the morning to see if they could use their field for some games and the rest they'd have to travel to or reschedule.

No one had been hurt. He had to keep reminding himself: It could have been worse.

Barry had told him more than once how sorry he was, how much he appreciated him being there, and how hard he would work to get repairs done as quickly as possible. But Barry wasn't a miracle worker, and even with Leslie's connections, they'd be lucky to have a field before the season was over. And Barry refused to take Leslie's money to get the ball rolling.

"You have already done so much for the school. You donated the funds for the athletic center! The field is named after you! You need to hang onto your money."

Barry worried that Leslie was going to need all of his resources as he got older, and while Les appreciated his concern, his accountant assured him that he and his family would be taken care of...for generations.

Before the medicine pulled him under, he tried texting Joe once more. Then the phone rang, the ring tone sending sparks of pain through his head.

"I can't text, I'm up to my elbows in Lysol."

"Jesus, Joe."

"And Mary," Joe said and laughed at himself. Music blared in the background.

"Right. I wanted to make sure you ate."

"Mmm-hmm, sure did. Matty brought me vegetarian lasagna from the Buzz. We ate and then he watched me clean while he talked about the pranks his dorm mates pulled on each other. It was a riot."

Leslie ran a hand down his face, but the contact stung and it hurt to even smile.

"Look at Twinkle Toes making friends. Bless your heart."

Joe cursed under his breath and Les couldn't hold in a laugh, which he regretted a moment later.

"Hey, you okay? You sound tired."

"I am. It's been a long couple of days. I'm just...dammit I wish..." He sucked in a breath at the stabbing sensation at the top of his head.

"Les? Are you okay?"

"Just a migraine. Took meds. Going to sleep but wanted to apologize."

Joe shut off the music.

"You have nothing to apologize for. This sounds like a bad one. I wish I could do something for you."

"It'll pass. Just wanted to say I'm glad you're here."

Joe's soft laugh reached through Les's fog and did a lot to ease his pain.

"I'm glad too. I'm mad that I don't have a car or I'd come take care of you."

"Stop it," Leslie whispered and Joe laughed softly.

"Go to sleep. I want to see for myself that you're okay in the morning."

"Yeah. Nite, Joe."

"Good night, Leslie."

Joe's voice echoed in his thoughts until the darkness took over and he fell dead asleep.

He nearly missed his alarm the next morning. Sandy's shower sing-along got him moving.

Sandy's room was at the other end of the upstairs and his voice carried that far.

The new medicine Leslie's doctor prescribed for the migraines definitely helped and he didn't feel as hung over that morning as he usually did. He even found himself humming along to the song Sandy was belting out: "Tube Snake Boogie" by ZZ Top.

Wow. Yeah, the Payton brothers were all stuck in the past when it came to music and they had their father to blame. Rick Payton had been a football legend and his legacy was a mixed bag. Yes, he'd blessed his four sons with athletic prowess and skill. He'd also left them a slate of painful memories featuring addiction, violence, and loss. Research on concussions in football came too little too late for the Paytons. Too late for their father to get the help he needed before he passed at a young age of fifty-two, too late for their mother who had to watch her broken beloved turn into a monster, and too late to avoid a lot of the physical damage done to Leslie. Thankfully, Sandy and Randy benefited from the findings and then made the decision to finish playing after college. They had their sights set on making money and making a difference all while having a blast along the way.

Leslie made it downstairs by seven and found his mother cooking up a massive breakfast spread that had his mouth watering.

"Mom, how many times do I have to tell you that you don't have to do all this? We can hire a chef."

Agnes Payton stuck her cheek up as Leslie leaned down to kiss her.

"The same amount of times I have to tell you that I love cooking and I particularly love seeing people enjoy my food. As long as that's happening, I will keep doing what I love." She patted his cheek and got back to stirring the pancake batter. "I baked cinnamon rolls for you to take with you to the meeting. They're already packed up in those tins," she said, pointing with her chin.

Leslie chuckled as he wiped flour off of her forehead.

"I'm sure everyone will appreciate it."

"Yes, and more importantly, did Joe make it in alright and when are you bringing him home for dinner?"

Randy sauntered in right then, plopped down at the counter and rested his chin on his fists.

"Yeah, Leslieeee. When are you bringing your *boy-friend* home?"

Les picked up an egg and went to throw it at his brother but Agnes reached over and covered his hand with hers, not even skipping a swirl in her pancake batter.

"Enough, Randy. Leslie will bring his *friend* and *colleague* over when he is ready, isn't that right, son?"

Leslie palmed the egg and knew the satisfaction he'd have at hearing the crack against his brother's fat head and watching the yolk ooze down his forehead would be short-lived when Agnes took that wooden spoon out of the batter and smacked him with it. He might have been forty-five years old, but he wasn't too old to get smacked. And most of the time he deserved it.

"How did Mr. Dancing Machine take it, moving into Higdon?" Randy's snark had disappeared a bit. They'd all been worried Joe would walk away from the whole thing, and while the college would have survived, none of them were sure *Leslie* would, considering the amount of pining he'd done over the guy.

"Really good, actually. He got to cleaning immediately and kicked me out."

Agnes smiled. "Good for him. Maybe you don't have anything to worry about."

Leslie's phone rang and he groaned when he realized that Sandy had messed with his ring tone again. The dulcet tones of "All The Single Ladies" piped out of his phone and he dropped it twice as he tried to answer it and hush the song.

"Les Payton."

And a familiar face popped up on the screen.

"Good morning, Mr. Payton, it's Malcolm Darling from *Time* magazine. We had a video interview scheduled for this morning?"

Leslie pressed a fist to his forehead. "Right. Sure. Sorry, I'm a little distracted this morning."

"That's right, I saw that Greenvale had some damage from that big storm on Saturday. Do you need to reschedule?"

Leslie accepted a plate from his mom and went to sit on the back patio to avoid any interference from his brothers. Days after migraines, it was hard enough to focus as it was.

"I have some time this morning, and maybe we can finish up another time if you need more."

Malcolm was a soft-spoken, serious-looking biracial guy who Leslie often had a hard time reading. Thankfully, one-on-one, he sensed that Malcolm genuinely wanted to work closely with him. "I appreciate that," Malcolm said with a smile. "This is a cover article, the main spread for the magazine, so yeah, we might need more than a few minutes."

"Right," Leslie said. The only reason he'd agreed to do this was the possibility that the article could help his brother Barry and Greenvale, and he'd worked with Malcolm in the past so he trusted him as much as one could trust the press. "Yeah, well, I'm happy to do what needs doing."

"Excellent. I'm going to record this, if that's okay?"

"Sure," Leslie said. "And I'm going to scarf down my breakfast before I head off to a meeting, if that's okay."

Malcolm chuckled. "Absolutely. Can you talk a bit about your decision to leave the network for a college coaching position? And rather than a top-ranked NCAA Division One school like you've done previously, you left for your alma mater, Greenvale College, which is in the NAIA?"

Leslie sighed. That had been a shock to everyone but his family. "Look, I love football, and I loved my time at UKC, but everyone who knows me knows that family is everything to me, and the opportunity to work with my brothers and be close to my mom felt like the right thing to do at this point in my life. I love the network and I loved coaching at the university, but Greenvale is a program with great growth potential where I felt I could really make a difference. With my brothers coaching with me, it's going to be great. We'll bring our philosophy of the Three I's to Yellowjackets football."

"Right. Inclusion, Integrity, and Ingenuity. I've heard you mention this before. Care to elaborate?"

"So many of the kids recruited for college teams, especially at the Division One schools, it's all about stats and who looks most attractive on paper. I want to find those athletes that are great at problem-solving, who come from different backgrounds, and who know how to improvise and support the team rather than try to be a hero. There are three I's in team as far as I'm concerned."

"And those strategies paid off for you during your time at UKC. Your standout players there were often never heard of before they played for you. Your coaching brought out the best in them and made a mediocre team on the books into a powerhouse."

Leslie laughed. "Why, thank you, Malcolm. Maybe you should be writing my CV since I'm rejoining the academic world."

"Come on, Les. You could take your skills virtually anywhere, including back to the NFL. You're known as the thinking man's quarterback. Why hide out in small-town middle America? Did you lose a bet with your brother?"

Les chuckled, but Malcolm's words stung. He knew people felt that way, but Les made this move for his own well-being and to spend time with his family, especially his mom, and he told Malcolm as much.

"Right, your mother was very sick for some time."

"Crohn's Disease is very painful and requires constant monitoring. Agnes Payton isn't one to sit down and relax. She's busier than me, so sometimes she needs a nudge to remind her of her age and fragility."

"Kind of like her son?"

Les froze, although he'd known the question would come up. He'd missed a couple of weeks of the last NFL season due to his migraines. He wasn't about to lie.

"I wouldn't call an affliction that millions of Americans live with daily being fragile. Yes, I'm being monitored by doctors, but I'm perfectly fine. Well, as fine as a forty-five-year-old former quarterback in need of a double knee replacement can be." He tried to laugh it off, but inside he was trembling. Admitting there might be more to his headaches than migraines was a terrifying prospect. He dreaded being compared to his father.

"Of course not. I have to ask, you understand. There will be questions. You coming clean about your TBI could go a long way in forcing the NFL to address the suffering many of your counterparts are experiencing."

"I'm not doing this article to beat up the sport that's given me an incredible life, Malcolm."

Malcolm held up his hands. "Fair enough. Let's talk more about this dream team of coaches your brother has lined up."

The smile plastered on Les's face couldn't be avoided. He still couldn't believe Joe was actually here, and that he hadn't been scared off by the tornado.

"So far, we have the Payton brothers on football, plus Randy will be coaching baseball along with an unbelievably good candidate I can't name at this time. We're also bringing back US Olympic medalist Bryce

Danner for men's volleyball and we're interviewing candidates for women's softball and coed wrestling."

"That's great, but you know I want to hear how you nabbed celebrity dancer Joe Judd. To be honest, he's even more of a shock than you."

Tell me about it. "Joe is a legend at Greenvale. He was the driving force behind Greenvale's first coed cheerleading team and he was on the first championship squad at Nationals. We're grateful he's agreed." Especially after the tornado.

"Will he be sitting out this season of *Dance Machine*?"

"Apparently he's already choreographed what they needed from him, and he'll fly out for a couple of the live shows." Which Les was trying not to think about. Not that he wanted to keep Joe hostage here, but Leslie was counting on this time to implement his campaign to win Joe's heart. If Joe was going to be gone a lot, and still have his foot in his dance world, would it even be possible to convince him to stay?

"Leslie?"

"Sorry, what was your question?"

"It's fine. I wondered how the tornado will affect your big plans this year? From what I understand, the sports programs were the most impacted."

"That's what we'll find out this morning. In fact, I'm about to be late for our meeting with the adjuster. Can we schedule a follow-up?"

"Sure," Malcolm said. "How about I call your brother? Manager? What are we calling Sandy Payton these days?"

"A pain in my—uh, my manager is good. Thank you."

"Thank you, Leslie. This has all the makings of the feel-good story of the season."

"Wish us luck."

They disconnected and Les shoved the remainder of his cold food in his mouth. He left his dishes on the counter and kissed his mom.

"I'll be back at some point."

"Remember! Let me know when Joe is coming for dinner."

"Yes, ma'am."

Les slid his wallet, phone, and keys into the back pockets of his black Levi's and got a little pep in his steps out to the truck. "Today I get to see Joe. At work. The first of many. And today is one day closer to the day I can call him mine."

Then he hit his head on the side mirror of the truck, and stomped around the garage cursing for a moment. When the pain subsided, he climbed inside and started the truck with a huge grin on his face.

NINE

J^{oe}

The sound of thunder woke Joe and sent him sprawling out of bed and into the bathroom.

"Bathtub, right? That's where you're safest in a thunderstorm." He thought about calling Marti, but he'd left his damn phone on the bedside table. He crouched next to the edge of the tub, trying to decide if he needed to be in it. Maybe he should have grabbed the mattress. Did tornadoes hit the same spot twice? Within a week?

The unmistakable sound of male laughter filtered into Joe's apartment and he frowned. Should he go tell them to run for cover? He was about to head for the door since he was supposed to be all responsible and shit now when he realized—

"Fuck."

The sun was shining brightly through the bedroom window, meaning that rolling thunder he'd just heard was the hoofbeats of a student herd. God, was this going to be his wakeup call every day?

Sound carried in this old building, apparently, right into Joe's bedroom. Maybe it wouldn't be quite as noisy in the other apartment...but no, then he'd get the slamming of the doors all day and night.

Joe questioned his life choices while he did a quick round of stretches. He took a lengthy hot shower, and was about to hit start on the small blender he'd packed in his suitcase for his morning protein smoothie, when his phone buzzed.

I'm grabbing coffee, can I get you some?

Joe smiled down at his phone, his irritation gone at the sight of Les's text.

I told you, you're going to have to be here in the morning to see what I prefer.

Not that Leslie Payton would be spending the night with him in his current housing situation. Not with what was likely his whole football team upstairs. He thought he'd remembered Matty telling him that many of the athletes lived in Higdon House and that a lot of the football players had been there for two weeks already.

Stop it. See you soon?

Joe asked him where they were meeting and Les texted back the administrative building, conference room on the main floor.

Joe hadn't spent much time in the ad building as a student, and now he was about to attend his first meeting as a faculty member of a college.

Who thinks this is a good idea?

Joe had struggled to put together an appropriate wardrobe for working at a college. Lots of button-down shirts and khakis, a nice stretchy blend that he could move in. He hoped the material would be cool enough during the muggy months and warm enough for winter with the proper undergarments.

That made him snort. Long johns were not exactly what he would have considered desirable undergarments to have. He'd much prefer something that showed off his hard-earned physique, the one he worked endlessly to maintain. His main *asset* was world-renowned. It had a reputation of its own as the male equivalent to the JLo booty, according to the more salacious corners of the press.

And his ass was running late. He downed the rest of his protein shake, and changed his shirt three times, settling on a slim-fit light-blue collared shirt. If he had a deodorant fail, it would be less likely to show.

The football players were long gone by the time he made it out to the lobby. He paused to take in the potential of the common room. It was a good-sized room. Perhaps in a pinch it could work for a studio. He had his first cheer meeting tomorrow with the returning kids, then it was time to recruit.

Music blared as Matty opened his door wearing only a pair of pink plaid pajama bottoms. And Crocs.

"Oh, hey, Joe! I can call you Joe, right?"

"Yeah, that's fine."

"Cool. I forgot to warn you, it gets a little loud when the kids come down en masse like that."

"I figured that out a few minutes after I thought another tornado was coming through."

"Oh, ha! That's funny. Nah, you'd have heard the sirens in town if there was a tornado headed this way. You need some coffee? I made some extra just in case. My mom sends me a craft brew from Seattle. It's tasty."

If Joe was going to take coffee from anyone, it would have been Leslie. Better to keep him guessing.

"Thanks, I'm okay. I'll see ya."

"Later on, man." Matty shut his door and turned his music up even louder.

It was country.

Alrighty then.

Joe was stiff and sore from cleaning the day before and wished he would have had the energy for an Epsom soak, but he didn't have a tub here and he'd been so tired. Thankfully, he'd packed a set of his favorite sheets and after a shower he fell into bed. The place still needed a lot of work, and he needed groceries, some less harsh chemicals for cleaning in the future, and some goddamned house plants. He needed some oxygen, or maybe it was the small town already suffocating him.

His feet carried him on autopilot to the ad building and he took the front steps slowly to avoid that stabbing pain in his knees that nearly knocked him on his ass. He pushed open the front door and spotted

Leslie down the hall talking to Barry and another guy, none of whom looked happy.

He'd sounded terrible the previous night. Joe had talked Leslie through some migraines in the past, but he didn't recall them being so bad. Joe had asked him about them but Leslie had blown it off. *"Stop it. You keep after me and I'll get the wrong idea from you."* Truth was, there *was* no wrong idea. As much as Joe fought against settling down, settling for anything, he knew that being with Leslie would be so good. But Joe had always been selfish, putting himself before Leslie's wishes time and again. *Leslie* deserved better than that, better than a guy who was more worried about how many shows he had left in him than about being a good partner. Leslie was more than Joe deserved.

"Good morning," he said as he approached the men. Leslie's smile, while not as intense as usual, was still enough to make Joe giddy.

"Thanks for coming," Barry said. "Joe, this is Jacob Wright. He's the publicist for the school."

Joe shook his hand and figured that the way this guy was looking at him he was thinking about how he could use Joe to gain attention for the school. Joe knew that was part of the reason for being there, but he didn't like that kind of attention.

"Let's hear from the adjustor and then I have some ideas," Jacob said and he gestured for them to all come in and sit around the big conference table.

Barry introduced a bunch of folks and Joe tried to remember them all.

The news was bad. Joe let the numbers pass over his head but they were looking at months, not weeks, before there would be an athletic center of any kind for the teams to use. That meant they were out a training room as well. Terrence sat quietly with his arms crossed over his beefy chest during the discussion. The other coaches had on their best poker faces as well.

"The damage to the structures will be covered, but there likely will not be enough to cover the costs of replacing the fitness equipment as most of what was in there was dated. As for the field, that will take top priority and should be ready in about three to four weeks, if the weather holds, that is. The bleachers can be easily replaced as well."

Joe looked to Leslie, but other than a slight line in his forehead, he wasn't giving anything away.

"Now, what this means," Barry said, standing up at the head of the table, "is that a lot of our plans will need to be pared down or even postponed until we take care of this. We've made arrangements with the high school to use their facilities as needed, and we are also in talks to reschedule some events. There are PE classes to consider. All of your jobs are secure, that's a different pot, but things are going to be...tight. My office will work on budgets with you. We're open to discussing any and all ideas."

No one spoke. A few of the coaches traded looks.

"May I share my thoughts?" Jacob chimed in.

Barry gestured for him to take the floor.

"Thank you, President Payton. I think we have the real potential to appeal to the alumni and community at large to respond to this disaster. Greenvale is certainly not the first college to experience a natural disaster, and we need to pull upon our strengths and connections and get the media involved. I think it's a valid way to call attention to our plight."

Jacob clasped his hands and looked at Les. "One thing to consider, and I know you weren't crazy about this idea, Coach Payton—"

"You're right. It'll be a distraction." Les scowled at the PR guy.

Joe frowned. What could be so bad?

"I think we're all going to have to get comfortable with distraction this fall at the very least. I don't think a camera crew would be any more distracting than crews working on the felled trees or the construction workers repairing the gym and athletic center."

Joe's ears perked up. "Camera crews?"

Jacob grinned at Joe. "We've had a request to do a miniseries reality show on the attempts to rebuild the college. There are networks who are very interested in you and Coach Payton being hired, as well as some of the other more notable staff. Networks that would spend good money to obtain the rights to this phenomenal story."

"That's not going to happen," Leslie said. "I told you we don't need that kind of distraction. I have a brand-new team I'm going to be putting on the field and many of these kids have very little experience. They need all of their focus to be on the game."

Joe, on the other hand, was intrigued by the idea. A reality show? It was definitely in his realm of experience. But then he also knew how much Leslie needed to be out of the spotlight to recuperate at times.

"How about a competition?" he asked with a shrug. "Each of the teams fundraising to rebuild the program as a whole. That could bring in larger donors once they see the kids are willing to take it upon themselves to work hard for what they want, and the team with the most funds raised gets bragging rights."

Everyone looked from Joe to Barry and there was murmuring around the table.

"That's not a bad idea," Jacob said, a little more excited than was called for. "Cheerleaders vs Footballers, Soccer vs Softball, we could run it like a tournament bracket, get the student body involved, call in the local media—"

"Now, wait a minute," Leslie said, and Joe was surprised by the frustration in his voice. "When are my players supposed to be fundraising? They have classes starting in a week and practice, which we're already going to have to get creative with since we don't have a field."

Barry walked over and put a hand on Leslie's shoulder. This was a whole other side of Les than Joe had ever seen. His always-look-on-the-bright-side attitude had become overcast this morning.

Leslie held up a hand.

"I'm sorry. I'm sure we can find a way. Everyone else is willing to do their part, so football will participate. And win." He smiled and the other coaches laughed.

"Hold on a second," Joe said, leaning forward with his elbows on the table. "What makes you think football will win?"

Whispers circulated all around the table.

Leslie's eyebrows rose, and whatever overcast remained was gone. Back was the twinkle in his eye.

"Sheer numbers. And determination."

Joe barked out a laugh. "I'm willing to bet that *cheer* will win."

Leslie leaned forward and laced his fingers on the table in front of him. "How do you figure, Twi—Coach Judd?"

Joe pressed his lips together to keep from laughing at Leslie's slip.

Using his pet name for Joe in the middle of a meeting was sure to raise eyebrows.

"Cheerleaders are experts at fundraising. Unlike the rest of the sports programs, we're used to having miniscule budgets and having to fight for every crumb necessary. Do you know that when I was a cheerleader here, there was no NAIA cheer competition? We had to raise money to fly to competitions sponsored by USA Cheer and United Dance Association, Varsity Sports… We had to buy our own competition uniforms, especially because there were none for the men and no budget for them. Marti and I even fought with NAIA to get them to recognize it as a championship sport. That didn't happen until the 2016–17 school year. So yeah, I may not have a college coaching background, Coach Payton, but I know how to hustle. You can guarantee cheer can raise more money than your team despite the number of participants."

Joe leaned back in his chair and crossed his arms over his chest.

Gauntlet thrown.

Mic drop.

Boom.

Electricity passed between him and Leslie, and he became aware of the fact that if anyone else in the room picked up on it, their secret correspondence all these years was about to be public.

"I love this idea," Jacob said, clapping his hands together. "What do you say, Coach Payton? It seems to me Coach Judd has challenged your team. Do you accept."

Leslie pressed a hand into the table. "You've got a deal, Coach. May the best team win."

Heat rushed through Joe's body and he shifted in his seat. Oh, this was going to be fun.

"And I'm sure you won't mind media coverage of fundraising events, Coach? I'll do my best to keep your players shielded from reporters—"

"If it helps the cause, I'll allow it. The sooner we raise this money, the sooner we get back to playing football."

The other coaches agreed to participate and shared some of their own ideas about raising funds for their teams, including community sports camps on weekends and after school for local kids during off-season.

Meanwhile, Joe was vibrating with the desire to climb over the table and into Les's lap. He was sure hot when he was competitive.

"I know you all have a lot to do to prepare," Barry continued. "As for facilities, Leslie, the football team will need to share the gym with the cheer squad for the time being for workouts, and practices can be held at the high school field—"

"Actually, Barry," Joe said. "What about the common room at Higdon? There are great wood floors in there. If you wouldn't mind me clearing the furniture out, maybe purchasing some full-length mirrors and barres?"

Barry glanced around the table and shrugged. "That's not a bad idea. We can let the students know that the area is off-limits and they'll have to use the common areas on their floors. You won't have a lot of privacy—"

"That's fine. Cheerleaders know how to work through distractions." Joe almost winked at Leslie, who cleared his throat.

"So confident," Leslie said, shaking his head. "And to keep things honest, I won't donate any money to the cause from my own pocket."

"Same." Not that Joe's pockets were anywhere near as deep as Leslie's but he wanted to keep at least that much of it fair. Joe did have a few favors to cash in, and he was sure Leslie would do the same. It was for the kids, after all.

"What's the wager?" Terrence asked. He'd remained fairly quiet through the whole process to this point.

"I think I'll determine the wager to keep things fair," Barry said thoughtfully. "Whichever team raises the most money by the end of the fall season is in charge of Spring Fling. How does that sound?"

Joe seemed to recall back in the day that there was a lot of hype about which student group organized the annual event. Clubs and teams requested the honor and the President's committee chose the best proposal. The winning organization also received the funds raised throughout the event to go toward the charity of their choice.

"You're on," Joe said, not even caring what he'd get if his team won.

It would just be fun to see how far Leslie would go to in the name of a friendly wager. He waited anxiously for Leslie to answer.

Leslie was a little hesitant to accept, but he finally nodded.

"I'm in."

"This will be great!" PR guy clapped his hands. "We can definitely work with this rivalry between the teams. The media will eat it up."

"Thank you, Jacob." Thankfully, Barry cut him off because Leslie looked ready to pummel him. "I appreciate all of you being flexible during this difficult time. Let's all be thankful no one was hurt and that Greenvale College will be able to start fall semester on time!"

There were a few cheers at that sobering reminder, but Joe and Leslie continued to size each other up across the table. Joe shook hands with a few folks and then he grabbed Terrence and Barry.

"Where is the training center going to be located?" Joe asked.

Terrence raised his eyebrows and waited for Barry to answer.

"Well, there is some space in the health center, but it'll be tight and it's far from the gym."

"I had a suggestion," Joe offered. "How about the empty apartment across from mine in Higdon Hall? If we're having cheer practice there in the common room and most of the players are living there, it could work?"

Barry looked to Terrence. "Whatever you want. I may be able to get a temporary trailer close to the field when it's ready, but this might be a good option for now."

Terrence shrugged. "Sounds good. Terrell and I are going to see what we can salvage from the old facility as soon as they clear us to enter."

"I can help," Joe offered, but then asked himself once more: What could he possibly do? "I can...clean, I guess?" He hated this feeling of being out of place, unprepared, over his head.

"I think we've got it covered, Coach, thank you. I'm sure you have more important things to do," Barry said and turned back to Terrence.

Joe stood there for a moment, fully getting that he'd been dismissed and unsure what to do about it. Once again, he wondered what he actually had to offer this place.

Barry and Terrence continued discussing options for the training center, and Joe decided to find Leslie. After their little back-and-forth, Joe wasn't sure if proximity would solve anything, but Joe's body was on autopilot trying to get another hit of whatever passed between them as he left the conference room.

Maybe his biggest fan could help him figure out what the heck he was doing there.

Ten

L eslie

"Coach Payton?"

Leslie had been talking to the school's financial officer, who'd been in the meeting, when Joe came up behind him. Acting like they were just colleagues.

"I'll catch you later, Bob."

Bob waved, gave Joe a glance, and then went back inside the ad building.

"What's with the 'Coach Payton'?" he asked, but Joe was walking away, down the sidewalk and around the back of the building. Leslie nearly had to jog to keep up with him.

"Hey," he said when he caught up to him, hands on his hips, chest heaving with breath. "What's wrong?" Leslie asked him. "What happened?"

"Tell me again whose idea it was to hire me."

"Where's this coming from? Did my brother say something?"

"No, not really. It's just, I'm not afraid to work hard, and I want to help out. I'm afraid people think I'm some prima donna—"

Les reached out suddenly and placed his hands on Joe's biceps, causing Joe to flinch. Les stepped back, realizing he'd overstepped his bounds. Joe had said more than once that he sometimes had issues being physical with people, especially ones he didn't know well. Les hadn't thought that applied to him. "I'm sorry, Joe, I just want to make sure you know I don't feel that way. I know how hard you've worked to get where you are. I wouldn't have encouraged you to be here if I didn't believe in you."

Joe blinked up at Les. "That means a lot to me. I couldn't stand it if you felt that way."

"No way, Twinkle Toes," Les said, stepping closer again but keeping his hands to himself. "I'm sorry if touching you is out of line."

"It's not," Joe said, and then he laughed. "Well, except for the fact that now we're supposed to be some big rivals. That certainly changes things."

"I'm not happy about any of this," Leslie said. "I was hoping..."

Joe stepped closer and looked up, shading his eyes from the sun. "You were hoping?"

"I wanted us to have this time, you know, to see where things, how things—"

"I know. I want to see how things play out, too."

"I really want to kiss you," Leslie breathed. "It's all I've been able to think about since April." He leaned a little closer, feeling Joe's breath, warm and minty, against his face. "I want to bring you home with me. I want to pamper you, spoil you. I want long talks and longer kisses. I guess I thought we could have all that—"

"In the middle of football season? Really? Not that I don't love where your mind is at."

Les ran a hand down his face. "I guess you're right. So what do we do?"

Joe sighed. "We do what your brother brought us here for. We coach. And now? We fundraise. And if you aren't totally sick of me in, say, November, maybe you take me out on a proper date."

"*November*?" Leslie shouted and Joe pressed a finger to his lips.

"Someone's going to find us," Joe said with a laugh. "I know, it's only August. At least we get to see each other every day. It's better than texting while hundreds or thousands of miles apart, isn't it?"

Les groaned. "I don't know. To see you and not be able to touch you might be worse."

"I promise it will be worth the wait," Joe said in a husky voice, winking at Les.

Les didn't think he could withstand temptation, not with perfection right there in front of him.

His first sight of Joe that morning had nearly buckled his knees. Those slacks he was wearing highlighted the fact that Joe was in top shape, that he'd just come off a show. He filled them out so well, Les wanted to curl himself around Joe and feel their bodies pressed together in all the right places. He wanted to finally explore all of Joe's topography with his own hands. Of course, if he tried to tell Joe how he felt it would come out in grunts and growls at this point. He lost his cool whenever he was near Joe.

"Or, I mean, we could always sneak away to the Motel 6 on the highway."

"Stop it," Les said. He planted his hands on his hips and let out a bit of his tension by laughing at Joe's suggestion, however tempting it was.

"Soon you won't be telling me to stop it," Joe said. "Until then, we're rivals, and I do intend to out-fundraise you, so I hope you're ready to bring it."

Les was ready to fall to his knees and *give* it. *All.* "You're enjoying this a little too much."

"See, Leslie Payton, this is the part where the two of us get to know each other better, and this is me. I'm competitive to a fault. I wasn't kidding before. I've had to scratch and claw my way to everything I've ever had or done, and I'm willing to do it now."

Leslie wondered if Joe would ever fight that hard for him, or if this was all another avoidance strategy, but he had to clear that out of his mind. He needed to focus on the task at hand, and now wasn't the time to get all intense and scare him away.

One of their near-misses had been in Hawaii. Leslie had been on an extended vacation after what turned out to be his last season in the

NFL, or so he'd said to the public. In reality, he was having extensive medical tests run to determine the extent of his brain injury. The last few concussions he'd suffered had been worse than the previous ones and his personal physician had been concerned that he'd passed the point of no return. When the tests showed that indeed he had a serious TBI, he'd let the team management know that he would be retiring. They'd fought him, said he had a few good years left in him to play, but he'd insisted and bought out the remainder of his contract.

After telling his family, Leslie had texted Joe and it turned out Joe was in Hawaii doing a photoshoot. Leslie had told him about his impending retirement and asked Joe to meet him, offered to send his private jet to pick him up from Oahu after his engagement and fly him to Maui where they could hang out for a couple of days at the Payton's home there. Joe had agreed, but then at the last minute he'd texted that he'd been called back to LA. It hadn't been the first time, but that rejection in particular had stung.

Was Leslie setting himself up for that again?

The team had their first official practice that afternoon. Some of the players had come two weeks early for conditioning, but this was the first time the whole team was together. They met in the gym where at least they'd be out of the elements. The power had just been restored to that side of campus and the kids were hyped up.

Once they were all seated on the floor, Leslie stood before them, his brothers behind him, and he chose his words carefully. Normally he was completely at ease with his players, but these were extraordinary circumstances and he needed the kids to be in the right mindset going into the season.

"Welcome to Jackets football. I'm your new coach, Leslie Payton. Behind me are Randy and Sandy Payton, who will be taking care of special teams and drills, as well as keeping you on your toes. You'll understand what I mean soon enough." *Lord, these kids better be ready for the twin terrors.* "We also have Damontae Marcus as defensive coach and Terrence Simmons is our head trainer." The men waved at the kids.

"Those of you who know me know that I have a different approach to the game than many coaches." There was a lot of shuffling and smiles. Yeah, these kids knew exactly who he was and for many of them, he was the reason they'd chosen to forgo lucrative scholarships or acceptance at bigger schools for the chance to work with him. Leslie knew he was a good coach and knew he had a lot to offer players at all levels, and he wanted all of his players to be there for the right reasons.

"My philosophy is based on the notion that there are three I's in team. Integrity, Inclusion and Ingenuity. I believe all of you have the potential to learn those qualities and skills. As long as you keep those three I's at the forefront, we'll get along just fine. You'll also learn that I love to *talk* about the three I's, so get used to it."

Randy groaned quietly and Leslie shot him a look. The little shit grinned at him.

Sandy elbowed his twin and the two of them put on serious faces. Leslie hoped they weren't going to require more babysitting than the players.

"Some of you may have noticed we had a little redecorating done on the east side of campus."

A few kids snickered, but most of them looked rightfully concerned.

"As a result, this is going to be a year of the three F's for Jackets football." He smiled. "Yeah, I just made that up. The three F's will now stand for flexibility, focus, and...fundraising."

More shuffling, a few uncomfortable coughs.

"Flexibility means we practice where and how I say, no matter what that entails, and no questions asked or complaints tolerated. The weight room is toast so we're going to get creative. Focus means there's going to be a bunch of distractions on campus like construction and, well, members of the press. Ignore it. You're here for two purposes: learning and playing. Learning comes first, always, and we will be having conference three times a week. What is conference, you ask? It's our time to practice mental toughness and to tackle any academic struggles you're having. It's more than study hall, more than tutoring. It's transformative time, and it's mandatory to attend if you want playing time."

This time there were a few more grumbles. *Too bad.* One stern look from Leslie and they quieted down real quick.

"And the last F is a necessary evil. Fundraising might seem like a time suck, but listen up. The college's insurance will cover the building repairs and the field, but not all of the equipment. If we want a world-class weight room and training facility, we're going to have to earn it."

"Can't the cheerleaders do the fundraising?"

"And why would you suggest that, Thomas?" Sandy asked, stepping closer to the kid who'd asked the question.

The kid's eyes were wide and he sat up a little taller. "Because the cheerleaders at my school did all the fundraising? The football team was too busy with practice, I guess?"

"That is not our way," Leslie said. "We all work for what we get here. Cheerleaders work just as hard. Many of you are fully aware that life is more likely to give you lemons than lemonade and that you have to work for the things you really want." He paused, Joe's words coming back to him. Yeah, he was willing to work for it, and to wait for it.

"Some of you may have heard that we have a bona fide VIP here on campus this year, Mr. Joe Judd from *Dance Machine*."

"Is it true he'll be coaching the cheerleaders?"

Leslie nodded and crossed his arms over his chest, maybe to keep his heart from pounding too loudly while talking about Joe. "Indeed he is. And Coach Judd has placed a bit of a wager on what's going to be a fundraising tournament of champions. See, all of the teams will be competing to see who can raise the most money. I've assured him that we will be victorious, but he seems to think cheerleaders know more about raising money."

That got the desired effect. Joe wasn't the only one who was competitive, but he was more interested in the wager.

"Yeah, no way we're getting showed up by a bunch of—"

"Don't finish that thought," Randy said, stepping forward. "You have no fucking clue what those athletes are capable of."

"And whoever wins gets bragging rights and dibs on Spring Fling."

That got a lot of attention. Leslie was glad to see that the kids still cared about the event as much as they had when he was a student. It was considered the best weekend of the year and everyone participated.

There were snickers and a few outright laughs. That gave Leslie had an idea.

"If y'all need a reminder of how hard cheerleaders work, then perhaps we'll have to have some combo training sessions. What do you think, Brother Randy?"

"I think that's a splendid idea, Brother Leslie."

The snickering stopped.

Another reason to work closely with Joe. Another competition.

This could be fun.

"Today's practice is going to be administrative tasks. Forms, uniforms, etc. Tomorrow, we run, and every day after that. Coach Randy or Coach Sandy will sign you up for morning or evening runs. And like I said, be ready to be flexible. We have no field at the moment, so stay tuned for the location of our first game. Any questions?"

Leslie dismissed them, feeling like he should have given more of a pep talk or done something inspirational. But then he realized this wasn't a football movie and he wasn't expected to be Denzel Washington or Jim Caviezel. He figured the tornado had them all shook up, though, as there wasn't a whole lot of reaction from them.

"That went pretty well," Sandy said. "Not too many complaints."

"Listen, I want the two of you to promise me something."

The twins' attempts to look serious were comical. They were capable of it, but sometimes it took a while before they settled down.

"What is it?"

"I appreciated that you said something about the cheerleaders, Randy, and I'm going to want you to continue. It's about time we drill the toxic masculinity out of these boys. I ran a tight ship at UKC when I was there, but we still had a couple of instances of sexual assault and I'm tired of the sport I love being associated with that shit. So we're going to do our part to get through to this team that not only do we expect them to be on their best behavior on the field, but off the field as well. You hear them acting up, you put it down. You feel me?"

Sandy and Randy stood in the identical pose with legs spread shoulder-width, arms crossed over their chests, heads tilted at the same angle.

"Sure, boss," Sandy said. "That's easy. If you were going to tell me to stop calling soccer players drama queens, I don't know..."

"I am telling you that if it has anything to do with who's more manly, you cut that shit out."

"All right, all right," Sandy said, his hands raised. "I hear you."

"And I guess when Joe finally comes over, we can't ask him about his tights or anything—"

"You *especially* can't say that shit to Joe."

Leslie knew Joe had a few run-ins with football players and he'd had his fill of the jokes. He only put up with Leslie calling him Twinkle Toes because he knew how much respect Leslie had for him.

"What's the deal with you two, anyway? I thought you'd be inseparable once he got here."

Leslie had hoped as much. "It's complicated, and now with this fundraising shit... That Jacob guy expects us to have a rivalry going, so I guess we're going along with it." Leslie's shoulders slumped and he sighed. If there would have been a rock in front of him, he would have kicked it.

Sandy and Randy looked at each other and did that twin thing where they communicated without speaking.

"Come on, big guy," Sandy said, patting him on the back. "Time to go have Mom's cooking. You'll feel better once Agnes gets ahold of you."

Leslie smiled. He was hungry. But he had a feeling nothing would feel quite as good as being with Joe. And didn't that suck?

Eleven

J oe

"It's time to put your thinking cap on, Ms. Simmons. We've got work
to do."

Joe had left the meeting and immediately called Marti. She'd met
him at his apartment. She took one look at his new accommodations
and once more offered their spare room.

"It's fine. It's bigger than my Hollywood place. We have more
serious things to discuss. We are going to out-fundraise the other teams
and I have just the idea how to do it."

He and Marti had been huddled around his laptop ever since,
creating spreadsheets, emailing a number of useful people, and sched-
uling social media posts.

"Okay great! Now, we have a start. What do we have by way of a
team?"

"I got the list of students from Barry and did some digging. We've
got a solid six girls and two boys. Only two of the kids are returning.

The others tried out in spring, more than half are incoming freshmen, including my son."

"So you're saying we need ten to twelve kids. Easy peasy. Don't make plans for Friday night."

Marti frowned at Joe. "What do you mean?"

"We're going out, hon. Flyers will be open and we're going scouting. Now—"

"Whoa, Flyers? Scouting? At the club for the college kids?"

"Yes, ma'am. I have a plan. We're not looking for cheerleaders necessarily, Marti. You've seen what I can do with the untrained. I kind of got famous for it."

No longer was Joe limited by choosing the qualified candidates for a team like he'd done for three years as captain here at Greenvale. No, he'd spent the last twelve years associated on and off with TV's longest-running dance reality show, first as a contestant and then as a coach and choreographer. He'd learned all the styles from the best in their fields, and then he taught B-boys, ballerinas, and bebop dancers how to dance whatever style he wanted them to. The fans and producers loved him. The dancers thought he was a hard-ass. They cringed when they were assigned to work with him because they all knew how hard he pushed himself and that he pushed everyone to dance as hard as he did.

"Hold up. So you plan for us to go...dancing?"

"Is there a problem, Coach Simmons?"

She burst out laughing. "Oh, well, I don't have a problem with it. Terrell isn't going to like it. His mama at the club?"

"Hmmm, you're right. Well, we can stick to the shadows. Maybe we should wear disguises."

The two of them laughed at their options until they were out of breath. Then Marti got serious.

"Am I out of line to ask you about a certain football coach?"

Marti knew they'd kept in touch over the years, but he hadn't come clean with her about his feelings for Leslie.

"What do you want to know?" She raised her eyebrows and he laughed. "We were going to kind of see what would happen, you know, if we were in the same place."

"And now?"

Joe shrugged and wrinkled his nose. "The only thing happening now is that we're going to beat him at fundraising. He's promised not to use any of his own funds, I've agreed to do the same, and if I win, cheer gets Spring Fling."

"That's great!" she said, clapping her hands. "Remember we had it my senior year. So much fun."

"It was. So that's our wager. As for anything else between us..."

"I see. Okay then. Let me get to work on this list. I'll get a few things scheduled. The rest of the kids move in Thursday and Friday and we have our first meeting with the team on Monday."

"I'll also recruit kids for the team through my dance classes. Also, I'm going to be teaching a PE class."

Marti clapped her hands together again and laughed. "I love it. Joe Judd goes legit. This is epic."

"Hush, now. I'm going to teach some alternative strength-building workouts including barre, Pilates, and light weights. If anything, it will help keep *me* in shape."

"Like that's a concern. Speaking of, what shape is your kitchen in?"

"If you opened one of those cabinets and spoke into it, you'd hear echoes. I was going to..." Yeah, he wouldn't be having Leslie take him grocery shopping now. It wouldn't do for them to be chummy over in the produce section and then smack-talking each other. Joe wasn't sure he trusted himself to do something so domestic with Leslie anyway. He did need to arrange for Leslie to take him to see his friend the car dealer so he wouldn't be reliant upon others to get his necessities, but other than that, it was probably best if they kept their interactions on campus. Not any fun, incredibly frustrating, but probably best. Probably best sucked.

"Let's go grab you some groceries and...flair. This place is morbid as is. Then we can do some more planning."

Their shopping trip to Des Moines took five hours round trip as they hit up Target, Bed Bath and Beyond and Mattress Discounters. Joe would be getting a new bed delivered the next day because his body was his temple and if he was going to be a prima donna about anything it was that he needed a good mattress. He'd be of no use to anyone if he couldn't move. Marti dropped him off and helped him carry all of his goods into the dorm, pestering him to join them for a real dinner.

"I'm sure whatever the Buzz is cooking is going to be fabulous." He didn't have the energy to meal prep tonight so Buzz food it was. He got there just as they were starting to put away the food, but they dropped everything to help him. There was a way about the staff, how they rushed around, hushed voices, making sure they fawned all over him. He didn't want to be treated like that. He didn't like that part of being a celebrity, especially not here. Here, he wanted to be Coach Judd, and, well, someday Coach Payton's plus one.

But what would that even look like? Could Joe see himself doing this college gig forever? Staying in Ayre Valley?

Joe brought his dinner back to his apartment and scarfed it down before flopping down on the surprisingly comfortable couch a previous resident had left behind. He closed his eyes and let his mind drift to that place he'd go when he imagined his future.

For the longest time that place was filled with all of the items on his bucket list. Winning an Emmy for *Dance Machine*, having one of his Broadway appearances lead to Tony recognition, being head choreographer for a film or Broadway show...well, one of the shows had won a Tony, although he hadn't been a lead, and he'd been nominated for an Emmy. All of that had been great, but the more he got to know Les, the more the man invaded his daydreams. He began picturing Les being his plus one to the Hollywood parties, having Les accompany him to Europe, and the two of them doing some of Les's favorite activities, which always made Joe laugh to think about; he couldn't really picture himself going hunting or snowmobiling, but he'd been willing to try them if it meant being with Les. But when Les had invited him to spend time with him in Hawaii...things had changed in that daydream. Then he was picturing what their house would look like and where, having drinks on the beach, hiking the ruins in South America, all things they talked about wanting to do someday. Had someday really arrived? Joe was a little jumpy thinking along those lines. Someday was someday. He was too young for someday to be now. Right?

Joe knew once he had that kind of someday with Leslie, he wouldn't want to leave. But he was terrified that he'd hurt the man who'd come to mean so much to him.

As if he'd sensed Joe's thoughts, Leslie texted him.

I'm sorry I didn't text earlier. Did you eat?

I did. Buzz food is mmm mmm good.

Stop it. Can I get you anything?

A date for our car shopping trip. Marti took me to Des Moines and I've got all the basics but I need my own wheels, and ones with GPS. I still don't know how y'all navigate around here with all of these random roads.

Let's go tomorrow. I have time after morning practice. We'll be doing double days, but practicing in the evening at the high school field. Without the weight room, I'm going to have to get creative.

Mmm creative. Let me know if you need ideas.

I like your ideas.

Joe watched the three dots floating for several minutes and then he laughed.

· · ·

Let me come pick you up. You can show me your ideas.

A thrill ran through Joe's chest. They'd be sneaking around, it could be fun, but he was a little old for that, wasn't he?

I need beauty rest tonight but tomorrow would be great. You can show me what I should be driving.

You did that on purpose.

Joe covered his mouth. **I can't help it. You're so easy.**

I could be. For you, I'd be anything.

Joe rubbed at his chest. How was it that with just a few words Leslie made him feel cherished, special. Important.

You are too good for me.

I could be bad for you.

Joe barked out a laugh and his skin heated.

Oh, I'd like to see you try. Text me when you're ready tomorrow. I'm going to take a cold shower now, thanks. I'm glad I'm here, Leslie. Closer to you. Soon, okay?

. . .

Soon. See you tomorrow.

Joe did exactly what he'd said. Took a cold shower and allowed himself more of those daydreams where he went to bed with Leslie every night, shared morning routines, went to school functions. Could that be his someday?

Joe climbed onto his soon-to-be-replaced bed and checked his email. His agent wanted updates on everything and let him know that he'd gotten several calls about him. There were still opportunities for him, which made his current situation feel all the more temporary. If the right show came along, could he resist temptation to hit the road again?

No, he'd made a commitment and he needed to fulfill it. He'd always wanted to be a part of something bigger, to do something that meant something. He had a chance to do that here.

Joe woke to the dulcet droning of tired football players trudging down the steps with less gusto than the previous day. He figured Leslie had tired them out and they weren't anxious to find out what he had in store for them bright and early. All Joe had on his agenda was car shopping with Leslie, but he couldn't sit still and wait around. He had his morning shake, did his stretches, and then made his way into the common room.

It really was big enough for everything except stunting, so he decided to make himself comfortable. He took measurements of the walls and ordered mirrors and barres after getting email confirmation from Barry that there was money to pay for that. Then he set about moving the furniture into the hallway, which he was doing when Matty came out in low-slung holey pajama pants and a T-shirt so ripped on the sides that it was basically a neckline with cotton fringe.

"Hey there, Coach. Need a hand?"

The proud part of Joe wanted to say, "I've got this," despite the fact his back was already killing him, but the saner side prevailed.

"That would be great, thank you. We're going to be using this space for practices and classes, so I apologize in advance if it gets a bit noisy in here."

Matty smirked. "That's where noise-cancelling headphones come in handy, bruh." He gave Joe a hang loose sign and Joe tried to hide his judgy thoughts.

"Where are you from, Matty?" he asked as they both picked up the ends of a long coffee table built solidly sometime in the 1960s. He fully expected Orange County or Florida.

"Denver," he said and Joe nodded, hiding his smile. "Originally. But I did live in Guam, Germany, and the Philippines as a kid."

"Oh, well, that sounds like quite an experience." Interesting.

They set the table down and Matty stretched out his back, rubbing his six pack. If Joe didn't know better, he'd think Matty was trying to flirt with him.

"Yeah. Dad was a military contractor. Thankfully, I was already graduated from high school when he moved to Iraq. Mom stayed in Denver."

They moved a few other big pieces, including the couches, and once the floor was cleared, Joe was pleased with the space.

"This is going to be great," he said. "Thank you for your help."

"Absolutely," Matty said, clapping him on the shoulder. "Means I can skip lifting today. I'm headed out for my run before the weather gets too hot. That's one thing I can't stand about this place. The humidity." He shook his head, gave a little salute, and then headed out the front doors, leaving Joe to stare at the nasty floor. College kids were not known to be the cleanest, but the amount of gunk that had been hiding under the furniture was unbelievable. And probably dated back to his time as a student.

An hour later he heard the door open, but he was focused on the second to last patch of truly disgusting wood. He figured it was Matty so he didn't bother getting up off his hands and knees.

"What the hell are you doing, Twinkle Toes? We've got people to do that."

Joe pushed himself up and sat painfully on his haunches.

"And where are those people? Preparing the school for the kids, right? It's fine."

It *so* wasn't fine. He hadn't paid attention to how long he'd been in that position, and when he tried to stand up, his lower back seized up and his knees gave out. So he stayed on his hands and knees hoping Leslie wouldn't notice he was stuck.

"Joe for real, come on. Let me at least have the Terrible Two come over."

"It's fine," Joe answered through gritted teeth, breathing through a spasm. He turned his face away from Leslie and counted to ten, hoping the spasms would stop. When they eventually did, he straightened his legs and kept a downward dog position for a few minutes to stretch out his legs and then slowly rolled up, grateful his back had loosened up. He put on his biggest showbiz smile and flicked his bangs out of his eyes. "Are you done with practice already?"

Leslie frowned and looked at his watch. "It's almost noon. I tried texting you, but you didn't answer. Now I know why." His eyes softened. "Have you been working this whole time?"

Joe rubbed the sweat from his face with his forearm and laughed a little harder than was called for to be sure he didn't cry. "Time flies when you're having the best time of your life."

"Right. Listen, if you want me to stay and help you, we can get your car tomorrow—"

"No way. Let me just take a quick shower and I'll be ready. Come on in, I'll be quick."

"You sure?"

Joe breezed past him, afraid if he stopped moving he'd stiffen up again, and not in any sort of pleasurable way.

"Yeah, I'm almost done with this floor," he said as he walked into his apartment, Leslie hot on his heels. "And I bought some heavy-duty floor wax, so once I get the rest of the fossilized gum off the floor—I really hope that's all it is. I'm afraid to think of what else might've been under those couches—anyway, I can get a nice coating down on the floor." He pulled off his shirt and grabbed his jug of ice water, downing half of it. He set the metal bottle down hard on the counter and was going to continue telling Leslie his plan, but Leslie's jaw was nearly resting on the counter.

"See something you like?" He couldn't resist, but he should have. "Sorry, I'm just going to—"

Leslie reached for him, but let his hand pause in midair. "You know I do. You're killing me, Joe."

It was killing Joe, too, the tension, the inability to reach for what he wanted, what was right in front of him. Once they crossed that line—

As if on cue to remind him of exactly where he was, shouts filtered into his apartment from the lobby. Most likely Leslie's football players.

"I'm sorry," Joe whispered. "That wasn't—It's not fair of me. Let me go shower."

Leslie swallowed hard and then smiled weakly. "Make sure you come out of that bathroom in more than just a towel?"

Joe nodded, should have said more, but took the easy way out of this awkward interlude. He closed himself in the bathroom and exhaled.

So not fair. Why couldn't they be naked in Joe's bed right now? Oh, right, because for the foreseeable future he'd be living in a student dormitory that likely had thin walls, he had to pretend to be Leslie's rival, and he needed to be all upstanding and shit. That meant no more stripteases in front of Leslie, who looked as if he might have popped a vein in his neck fighting the urge to grab shirtless Joe. It wasn't fair to play with Leslie's emotions like that. Joe knew just how much Leslie cared about him, that he was attracted to him. He didn't need to rub it in his face.

Quit being a dick.

Joe showered, shaved, ran his fingers through his hair with product and let his curls dry natural. He dressed in tan cargo shorts and another short-sleeve collared knit shirt, this one black, and put on a pair of Sauconys. He figured this would count as reasonably covered. He entered the living space of his apartment as Leslie was ending a phone call.

"Everything okay?" Joe asked. "Did you need to be elsewhere?"

Leslie looked way too proud of himself. "Nope. I just called in the janitorial service for the network studios in Des Moines. They are sending a crew down to redo these floors, paint, hang those mirrors you bought—yeah, Barry told me—and do some maintenance in this building."

Joe's chest deflated. "Les, I was going to do it myself." His voice sounded muffled in his own head so he could only imagine how it sounded to Leslie. "You didn't have to do all of that. I don't want you to feel like you have to swoop in and save the day."

"I just want things here to be good for you," Leslie said.

"They are good, or they will be. You gotta give them a chance to be."

"I'm sorry, I thought you would appreciate…I just wanted—"

"You're making a fuss over me. Do I seem like I need to be fussed over?"

"No, Joe, I just—"

"Would you have done this for anyone else?"

"Joe—"

"Like, would you have Barry's office floors refinished and walls painted?"

"I want you to be happy here, Joe. I—" Leslie's face turned beet red and his forehead crease deepened.

"I'm fine, Leslie—"

"I want you to want to stay."

Leslie's words hung in the air between them like the crowd shouting at a football game might cut out when their team missed a field goal and lost the game. Even though they'd spoken quietly, their words seemed to echo off the walls of the apartment.

Joe opened and closed his mouth a few times, he shifted his weight, he brought his hand up to gesture, although what the gesture was going to be he had no clue. Would he have slapped Leslie like Cher in *Moonstruck* and told him to snap out of it? Would he have grabbed him by the collar and shaken him? Or kissed him?

"Leslie," he began, his hand sort of floating in front of him. "I just got here. All right? Give me a second before you start assuming I'm going to leave."

Leslie exhaled and shoved his hands in his pockets. "Maybe this was a bad idea."

"What? Coming over this morning? Taking me car shopping?

Swooping in like some superhero to save the day? Which part?" Joe made sure the teasing in his voice was loud and clear.

It worked. Leslie gave him a shy smile. "I just...I can't settle down." He barked out a laugh. "I'm like a damn puppy, ready to fetch your slippers or bring you the paper or some shit." He brushed his hair back, the baby-fine golden strands looking like silk, and Joe wished he could press his face against it and inhale, wondering if his hair smelled like the sunshine it always reminded him of.

"Les—"

"I want to know it's going to be okay, that I'm going to have the time with you."

Joe's eyes blurred for a minute and he blinked them to clear his vision. This was new for him. Or at least, he hadn't allowed himself to really think about whether someone would want him to stay. He was always on the move—that was the career he'd chosen, the life he'd chosen.

"I'm here, Leslie. You can settle. As for what kind of time we have together, that remains to be seen. Now, let's go find me a car so I can sneak away occasionally and visit some smokin-hot upperclassman living off campus." Joe winked at Leslie.

"Smokin' hot." Leslie rolled his eyes.

Joe raised his eyebrows. "God, don't you know?"

Leslie shrugged and shook his head, kicking at something on the floor as his cheeks burned red. "Stop it."

"It's true. Now. Unless you plan on hanging out here at Higdon with me and my new buddy, it's the only way I'll see you other than at games, and there we have to be all rivalrous, or rivaly, or however you would say that."

"Your new buddy?"

"Hmmm? Oh yeah—"

"Hey Joe? Are you done with the—Oh! Hey, Coach Payton. Outstanding to see you."

Apparently Matty was determined to wear as little as possible in the dorm as he was now in a pair of gray sweat shorts and no shirt with a pair of pink Crocs on his feet.

"If I'm interrupting—"

"Not at all. Coach Payton is taking me to the car dealership. I need more than pedestrian transportation."

"Oh, right," Matty said, pointing to Joe's feet. "That's funny. Dude, you should totally get something with all-wheel drive or front wheel, you know, for the weather."

"I got this," Leslie said, gesturing for Joe to go ahead of him. "Thank you..."

Matty offered his hand and gave Les a complicated two-handed shake. "How funny! The football coach and the cheerleading coach going to drive." He did a little air-steering and then laughed his way out of the apartment. "You know, because they, like, drive the other team... get it?" But he was already gone before Joe could even begin to question what the hell he was talking about.

"He seems friendly."

Les said friendly like someone describing a slimy fish complete with a nose wrinkle.

"Yeah. He offered me coffee the first morning."

Les turned on him. "Now wait a minute, I—"

"Relax, Coach. He doesn't know my morning preference either."

Joe grinned as he pushed open the front doors, laughing as Leslie muttered under his breath.

"That's fine, make fun. Keep it up, though, and I won't invite you over for my mom's cooking."

Les's smile evaporated as if he realized what he'd just said, and that threw Joe even more than just him saying it.

"I'm sorry," Leslie offered, reaching for Joe's shoulder. "I didn't mean to bring up a painful topic."

"It's okay. It's been a long time. I can talk about her now."

Unlike Agnes who doted on her boys, Jenna Judd was content to be a dance mom to a point, but whichever man was in her life at the time usually took precedence. When Joe returned home after college graduation, which she hadn't attended, he found her living with the latest in a string of con men, and sick. Within three years, she was gone. Ovarian cancer. It took Joe a long time to be able to handle any sort of mom stuff. He'd wanted to move in and take care of her, but she told him to take the first of many traveling jobs, not to stick around where he wasn't needed. He was with her at the end, but he'd been bitter. She'd chosen her latest boyfriend over him as her caretaker, just as she'd done most of his life, when all he'd wanted to do was take care of her. His best hadn't been good enough for even his own mother.

When she died, Joe had wanted to call Les with a yearning he didn't understand at the time. Later he came to realize that it was because Leslie was the most nurturing person he'd ever met, and the most solid and dependable. Joe could call him anytime and Leslie would genuinely be interested in what he had to say.

He'd been the perfect *un*boyfriend then. What if he could be the perfect boyfriend now?

Twelve

Leslie

Les had brought the Crown Vic in case Joe wasn't ready for the full Iowa 4x4 experience. He stayed quiet at the beginning of the drive while Joe processed whatever he was thinking and assumed it was about Joe's mom. Man, had she been a piece of work. The one and only time Les had spoken to her, she'd asked if he could get her boyfriend tickets to the 49ers/Rams game. Of course he could, and he did. But the more he got to know Joe, the more he'd understood Joe's "I am an island" routine. He really had been for most of his life.

Leslie figured taking Joe to the Ford dealership in Leonard would be a good bet. Tim Caldwell was a former teammate and good friend. Tim had a great sense of humor and handled all the jokes about being a cliché former NFL player-turned-car salesman. He would give Joe a low-pressure sales pitch. Les had no idea how much money Joe wanted to spend; they hadn't really talked that much in detail. Joe had simply asked for Les's advice on the best vehicle to handle the Iowa weather and Leslie had jumped at the chance.

"You asked me to come with you today but I don't know what you're thinking."

Joe turned to face him. "What I'm thinking?"

Les smiled. "About a car? Besides being good in weather, is there anything else?"

"Hmmm," Joe said. "Well, I'm used to my Porsche. I've had it for twelve years. It just didn't seem like the right car for out here."

"Not exactly, unless it's one of their crossover models. They probably have all-wheel drive."

Les snuck a glance at Joe when he didn't answer. "What?"

"You know, I don't mind admitting when I don't know much about a topic, but there's something about being male in this country that if you don't know cars, you're less of a man. You say all-wheel drive and I think 'yes, I'd like all of the wheels to drive, thank you.' So when I asked you to come, my intention was that you would help me avoid total emasculation."

Leslie gave Joe a very obvious once-over, taking his time as one can do on Iowa highways where nary a car is in sight, as was the case today. His gaze lingered on Joe's thick thighs, which pulled the fabric of his mid-thigh-length Bermuda shorts tight, the way the light dusting of dark hairs on his legs seemed to accentuate the cut of each muscle. Then his gaze landed on the sizeable bulge in the front of Joe's shorts that was not merely the curve of the zipper. Leslie had yet to see all of Joe's incredible body unclothed, but there was little mystery about what he would find behind his fly. Leslie's eyes went back to the road and he sighed.

"What was that?" Joe's tone had an edge to it that hadn't been there moments ago.

"That was me mentally cataloging all the ways you are the epitome of masculinity." Leslie's eyes wandered over Joe's corded forearms and long, graceful, thick fingers, also faintly sprinkled with dark hair. Joe Judd was the quintessential example of male beauty and perfection. Les had always thought so, and Joe had only become more so with age.

"Whatever. Ogling me is not helping the situation. I need you to tell me what questions I should ask so I don't sound ignorant and you don't look like my daddy buying me a car."

Leslie choked on that word. "I know I'm older than you, but I highly doubt anyone would consider you my...*Ohhhhh.*"

The back of his neck burned as he caught Joe's knowing smile.

"Come on, man. We've never been that way with each other. That's not...you know."

"*We* know that, but if we go in there and you do all the talking for me while I just stand there looking fabulous, it's going to be obvious."

Leslie barked out a laugh and shook his head.

"It just so happens that the dealer is a friend, not just someone I played ball with. He knows I'm gay, but more than that, he knows *me*. He's going to be curious, but I let him know you are new to the faculty and in need of reliable wheels. I don't think it's going to be awkward."

Joe turned sideways in his seat. "Fine, but shouldn't I know about torque and horsepower? And how many wheels drive I need? God, it was so much easier when my agent just bought my car for me. I told him I wanted a Porsche, and he bought me one with my signing bonus for the second season of *Dance Machine*."

Les reached over and squeezed Joe's knee. It was instinctual, but then he lifted his hand as if he'd touched a hot surface and looked at Joe for his reaction.

Joe grabbed his hand, laced their fingers together and sat it back on his knee. When Leslie just stared, and swerved the car a little, Joe exhaled.

"Okay, watch what you're doing, Payton. It's just holding hands. It's not like I reached for your fly."

"Stop it," Leslie said, putting on his blinker to make the turn onto a state route that was a shortcut to Leonard. "I'm sorry, I just don't know what's okay with you. I want to respect you."

Joe pressed his free hand to his chest. "You better respect me, gosh." Leslie couldn't understand how Joe could be so worried what people would think one minute, and then flippant about something so intimate and familiar.

"What I *mean*, Twinkle Toes, is that we've been in this holding pattern for so long, is it okay to touch you? When we're alone, I mean?"

Joe ran his finger over their joined hands and looked down at them thoughtfully. "I've never been much of a hand-holder. It's nice. Yes, holding hands is okay."

Leslie pressed his lips together. There was so much he wanted to do with Joe. Alone. In person. No more phones or prying eyes.

"Touching your hair?" Les's voice cracked, making him feel like a young man again. "Can I touch your hair?"

Joe squeezed his hand and licked his lips. "You can touch me wherever you want, Leslie Payton. I know we have to wait to go public, but in private? Let me make it clear that have my permission to touch me however you like."

Leslie wanted to pull the car over in the middle of the cornfield and take Joe up on his offer, but he'd never been one for brave spontaneity. Instead he squeezed Joe's hand back and kept driving, his heart racing faster than the car. No, he was too polite to maul Joe in a car in a cornfield. Really, he was. Despite his current salacious thoughts.

He'd been the perfect date for girls in high school, always the gentleman; they always knew they were safe with him. In fact, they sometimes fought over him. Moms approved because the prom pictures would always turn out great and he had a reputation for being "the nicest guy." He never touched the girls he went out with. Never touched *boys* either, not until college, but he had been focused. Football always came first, so there was no time for dating or carrying on. He used that as an excuse for a long time.

The first time he'd met Joe Judd, it was like the moment their knees touched under the bar it unlocked a desire in Leslie so strong it made him think, *football who?* And though he wished Joe would have been his first, he made up for lost touching time for a few years. He was careful, but he decided to come out publicly just in case pictures got out or paparazzi caught him with his pants down.

"Oh-kay. I guess I'm going to need to up my game a little," Joe said with a laugh when Leslie didn't respond to his offer.

"Sorry, but if you up your game anymore, I'm going to embarrass myself." Leslie shifted in his car seat. "This is not me resisting you. This is me wishing to have you the way I want you the first time. I'm willing to wait to do right by you. I told you I don't want to have to sneak around."

"Oh, but sneaking can be fun, too."

Suddenly the car emerged from the cornfield and came to an abrupt stop, jarring them both out of their banter.

"Where the hell are we?" Joe looked around. "It all looks the same here. How do you know where you are?"

Leslie shrugged, looked both ways, and turned left onto the highway. "I grew up driving these roads with my brother. You'll get used to it."

But would Joe? Would he get used to the roads, the weather, the lack of culture?

"We're here."

He pulled into the lot and found Tim standing outside with one of his other salespeople, his daughter Tamara.

"Leslie Payton." Tim's booming voice rang out and he moved as swiftly as a white man in his fifties with two blown-out knees and a bad back could, and he pounded on Leslie's back.

"Good to see you, man." Leslie had always liked Tim. They played for a few years on the 49ers together, then a few years as rivals when Tim went to the Cowboys, and when they retired, they'd both returned to their home state and set down roots. Their families had gathered for cookouts and he and Tim had supported each other through their respective health issues as only brothers in pigskin could do. "Hey, Tamara!"

"Coach, and it's a pleasure to meet you, Mr. Judd."

"It's *Coach* Judd, Tamara. Joe's working at Greenvale this year, coaching cheer and teaching dance." He knew the pride came out in his voice. He couldn't help it. He could take no credit for Joe's phenomenal career, but he'd been there in the shadows, watching and cheering Joe on through it all.

"That's so great! My little sister is starting there this year. She always loved to dance, but she's too shy to go out for cheer."

Joe smiled and shook Tamara's hand. "Tell her it's not scary. I'd love to have anyone with experience come to fall tryouts."

"That sounds great," Tim said. "Now, I hear you're in need of a vehicle."

"Yes, I am," Joe said, sucking in a breath. "I want something that I won't have to worry about the weather while I'm here. Something that handles well but is fun to drive, too." He nodded when he finished and then snuck a look at Leslie, who nodded back. Joe was doing just fine.

Tim looked around and leaned closer to Joe, speaking in a low voice. "I might have just the thing for you. It's kind of a secret. If people knew I had this baby, I'd have to beat them off with a stick. Come on over this way." He made another covert glance around and guided Joe toward the back of the lot.

"Daddy," Tamara said. She rolled her eyes and turned to Leslie. "He's so dramatic."

"That's what made him a great tight end, sweetheart." Leslie squeezed her shoulder and she laughed.

"Now, Coach Judd, what I'm about to show you is—"

"A twenty twenty-two Bronco Outer Banks model, two-door, with a Sasquatch package in Rapid Red," Tamara said, cutting off any more of Tim's antics. She launched into a very detailed but not overwhelming spiel about the car before they even laid eyes on it. Once they did, Leslie was in love, but even better, Joe and Tamara carried on a lively conversation. She walked him around the car and pointed out all of the practical features as well as the fun aspects of the car.

"So, how's it going?" Tim asked Les. Les had told Tim about Joe years ago when it seemed as if nothing would ever come of their correspondence. Tim was his closest friend outside of his family and he trusted his discretion.

"It's too soon to tell, but I'm trying to be hopeful."

Tim looked him in the eye and held up a fist, which Leslie bumped and then they joined Tamara and Joe around the front of the car.

"So I'll be okay in snow and ice in these tires? I won't have to do anything else?"

"No, these tires are more than capable of handling anything Iowa throws at you, and since this one came in with a hard top, one of the few, you don't have to worry about the cold. The marine-grade vinyl is easy to clean and if you do decide to take it out into the wilds, there are rubberized floors and drain holes for easy cleaning."

Joe was looking at the sticker and Leslie thought for sure he'd seen a twinkle in his eye.

"Joe? You want to look at the trucks or an Explorer?"

"I've got some certified used selections—"

"This is perfect. I'll take it."

Leslie couldn't blame him for being enamored with the Bronco. His dad had one back in the 80s and he'd loved it. Randy had a 1968 model he'd restored as well. If Les didn't love his truck so much, he'd buy one of these babies...maybe he would anyway.

"This was a canceled order or else we wouldn't have any in stock," Tim said, once again the conspirator. "They're selling as fast as we get them off the truck."

"Will you be financing?" Tamara asked.

"I'll be paying cash, thanks," he said, winking at her.

It probably wasn't often that she made a deal that good. She stumbled over her words a bit as she explained the price was slightly over MSRP and he smiled and nodded, but Leslie could see his excitement, which was probably just as much about him handling the sale himself as the car.

"Great, Coach Judd. We'll get started on the paperwork then," she said, gesturing for him to follow her inside, but he held up a finger and walked over to Les.

"Hey, you can take off," he said, glancing between Tim and Les. "I know you have practice."

Well, look at you, Leslie thought.

"Would you excuse me?" Tim asked, giving them privacy like a good wingman.

"Are you sure about this?" Les asked him. "I mean, I couldn't have picked out a better car for you, but this part can be aggravating."

Joe shrugged. "I'm okay. I can't thank you enough. You told me what I needed to know and this whole process was smooth because you were here. If I couldn't afford it, that would be another matter. All the money stuff can be overwhelming, I hear."

"Right, and don't let them sell you a bunch of extra shit. Extended warranties and all that."

Joe bumped him with his shoulder, but kept his hands behind his back. "Now I can sneak off campus," he said in a low voice. "And we can...hold hands." He wiggled his eyebrows.

Leslie laughed with his whole self, crossing his arms over his chest.

"Definitely hold hands."

"Soon?" Joe asked.

"Very soon," Leslie answered.

He could so get used to this, this rapport, this connection they had.

"I'm so glad you're here," he said, hoping it didn't break the spell of the day.

"Me too," Joe said. "Really glad. Now go on. Go run those poor kids into the ground. Make them do burpees until they puke or whatever you football types do."

"You've got practice starting soon too. Somehow, I think you'd run a helluva tough practice."

Joe raised his eyebrows. "You'll have to see for yourself. Doubt you could handle it."

"That's not saying much," he said with a laugh. "Some days I can barely get off the toilet."

"Whatever," Joe said, but he squeezed Leslie's arm. "Seriously. I can't thank you enough for making this such a good experience. Everything's better with you, isn't it?"

"That's what I've been trying to tell you," Leslie said, enjoying the teasing.

"I'll see you back at school," Joe said, backing away.

"You sure you can find your way? I should have left you bread-crumbs or something."

Joe kicked his chin up. "Tamara said it comes with navigation. I'm all set. See you later."

Oh, Leslie liked this way too much. Later. But hours this time, not weeks or months like they'd always been separated before.

Try as he might to protect his heart, it was too late. He was in it to win it...win Joe all to himself. Nice guy Leslie Payton was at first and goal with victory in his sights.

THIRTEEN

J^{oe}

Marti rolled her eyes at Joe's ridiculousness. "I can't believe I let you talk me into this."

"But you did." He danced a little cha-cha in front of her.

"I can't believe I'm going to a club. Without my husband."

"But you are."

"I can't believe we're doing this."

"Oh, we are *doing* this."

Joe had picked up Marti in his new baby and she'd rolled her eyes while he gave Terrence the whole tour.

"I'm not too proud to say this is way too much car for me," Terrence said. "Which means it's probably too much for you."

"I think I'll be fine, thanks. First order of business is taking your wife out on a date, so now who's the better man?"

Marti loved it when Joe and Terrence fought over her. Terrence knew there was no question who she preferred, but Joe loved to mess with him.

"Yeah, well, I'm also not too proud to say you're a better dancer than me and to step aside and let my wife have her fun. Just be careful driving her in that beast."

"Don't worry, I'll have her home by mid—next week."

Terrence groaned and Joe gave Marti a boost up into the cab.

"You had to go and get a big tall vehicle like these men out here. You sure you aren't trying to compensate for something?"

"Hey, when in Iowa," Joe said with a shrug. "You think maybe I'll blend in a little better?"

"Huh. In a big red Bronco that no one has seen on the road. Right. You wouldn't know how to blend in if you were foundation."

Joe snorted. "I blend better than a sponge from Sephora."

"The fact that you even said that means you won't blend in here."

Joe tapped his thumbs on top of the steering wheel and sighed. He'd never blended in anywhere, but could he fit? "You're probably right. Okay, are we all set for tryouts next week?"

"Yes, sir," Marti said, pulling out her phone. "I've got three coaches coming in from nearby schools to judge. Our returning team will be coming to make posters on Monday."

"You're so good at this," Joe said, elbowing her. He pulled onto 2nd Street and parked, the bass from the college-run nightclub rattling the windows of his new ride. "You think they'll play decent music in there?"

Marti pulled down the visor and reapplied her lipstick. "Depends. If they have a real DJ or if they are relying on whoever the current activities director is to play today's top hits." She rolled her eyes and pressed her lips together. "Either way, it's not going to be the kind of parties you're used to." She opened the door of the Bronco and slid down to the street, squealing when her skirt slid up her hips.

"And what kind of parties am I used to? I barely ever go out."

"After-parties, before parties. Hollywood parties. You had to go to some?"

Joe shrugged. "I guess, but I'm getting the feeling you have a very different idea of what my life has been like."

"You were short on details," Marti said as she rounded the back of the car. "All you ever really told me about were the shows you were in at the time. I have no idea if you were dating half of LA or what."

"Uh, no. If you saw me out with anyone it was all arranged. I went to the mandatory events, but I spent the majority of my time off rehearsing, working out, or sitting in a hotel room reading or watching Netflix while applying ice or heat to my injury du jour and don't you dare let that get out." Joe turned to walk down the side stairs to the club, but Marti grabbed his shirt and pulled him to a stop.

"Joe?"

He huffed and rolled his eyes. "I found out real quick that I needed to avoid toxic people, and guess what? There were plenty. I talked to you, I talked to Leslie...I had a few folks around to keep me sane, but yeah, I wasn't in it for the social life, that's for sure."

"But Joe—"

"Let's go party like it's two thousand seven and you're about to graduate and leave me."

He tugged her by the hand, his heart pounding at making those admissions. He'd been great at ducking her questions and redirecting the conversations to safe topics for years. He hadn't wanted to answer questions about why he hadn't been with anyone and what he'd put his body through.

She finally allowed him to lead her down the steps and into the dark entrance of the club. A kid with a flashlight asked for their IDs, and Joe and Marti flashed their staff cards. Joe had laughed hysterically when they'd taken their pictures in the office.

"Guess it's for real now. Let's see how long it takes them to recognize their mistake and revoke it."

The club was in the basement of the movie theater, which was also run by the college. The decor hadn't changed much. The walls were still painted black, there were rows of high-top tables along the back wall elevated above a decent-sized dance floor. Same disco ball, same colored lights, and same DJ booth. The only difference was that they'd added a snack bar, which seemed to be popular with the kids. The place was about half-full, which made sense since this was the first official weekend that students were moving into the dorms.

Joe was overcome with joy, recalling the nights he'd spent on this dance floor with Marti and their fellow cheerleaders. He'd reigned supreme even then. He could clear a dance floor in three moves or less, and it was that adulation and praise that had fed him, that and the feeling he got leading the crowd in cheering on the Jackets sports teams and competing with his team. Then it was his years dancing behind pop stars in front of tens of thousands of fans, and the votes from fans who watched him bare his soul each week and push his body beyond its limits. Maybe it wasn't the healthiest way to live one's life, but it had sustained him, more or less.

Marti gestured to him rather than shouting over the music that they should grab a table toward the back so they could have a good view of the dance floor. She'd been intrigued by his plan to scout out any unconventional talent on campus. He wanted to be sure they had a healthy turnout for tryouts, and he wasn't above conscripting students if he thought it would help him create magic with this year's team.

The music was loud, but they could still chat. She pointed out a few girls that she thought had potential, but Joe's attention was caught by a group of AAPI young men who were standing together, egging each other on. One of them went up to the DJ and argued with him before going back to his crew. Joe had an idea what that was about and he figured he'd watch them and see if he was right.

Then a banger came on and Marti gave him a look.

"Oh yeah."

She took a last swig on her water and the two of them strutted out to the dance floor. Most of the groups of kids were still in the talking stage of the night, so the floor was pretty empty, but once Joe and Marti started moving it didn't take long before they had the attention of everyone in the room.

"Oh my God, is that—?"

"He's really here? Holy shit!"

"Out Out" filled the room and Joe let the bass reverberate through his body and take over. Marti still had it, and though her moves may have been a little dated, it didn't take long before the two of them were moving in sync through some of their old routines until they were both laughing hysterically. They both gestured for all the kids who'd been standing around to join them and soon the floor was full and everyone was in the zone.

Marti left him for a minute and came back dragging Terrell. Marti was one of those moms that kids didn't mind having around. Terrell may have rolled his eyes when she started dancing, but it wasn't long before he joined them in showing off. The kid was a total ham on the dance floor, making fun of their old-school moves by doing them exaggeratedly. When Lady Gaga came on, he and Joe started doing some of the moves from Joe's last tour with the diva. Dancing for her and for Jennifer Lopez had been his favorite gigs he'd done. Terrell asked him what he should be doing if he wanted to dance on tour like that. Joe agreed to mentor him as long as he tried out for cheer. He liked the kid and was happy to give back to Marti's family after all the times she'd been there for him.

Joe moved closer to the group of boys. He noticed a couple of them trying out some B-boy moves, which gave him an idea. He made sure he had enough room and then went up behind one of them and tapped him on the shoulder. Joe jumped at the kid with his arms out, did some fancy footwork and then did a standing back flip that really didn't feel good but he was too into it to feel the pain.

Later, pain.

The boys all erupted into movement and came toward him as he backed up, gesturing for them to follow. The kid he tapped hopped around a bit holding onto the front of his pants until he got his flow and then he dropped down and lifted both feet off the ground and over his head while holding himself up with one hand. Then another came forward with some spins and a full-twist flip and Joe knew he'd found some conscripts. He bumped Marti with his shoulder and she nodded in agreement.

Joe got carried away and did a few more moves he'd be paying for as soon as he left, but he needed to get lost a bit in the one thing he knew how to do without fail. He'd felt out of his element since stepping foot back on campus, but here? This was his place and he knew it.

The music cut out and a student took the mic.

"Welcome, Jackets! I just have a few announcements, but let's hear it for our new cheer coaches, Joe Judd and Marti Simmons."

It had been Marti's suggestion that they share the details of tryouts at the club to get the kids thinking and Marti had gone ahead and shared the info with the DJ. She told the crowd that clinics started Monday afternoon in Higdon and that if anyone had questions between now and then, Coach Judd would be available to answer them.

He noticed some of the kids had phones out and he knew for sure his moves would be plastered on social media before long, but he couldn't be bothered to care. People were going to find out what he was doing soon enough and then he'd start getting calls and messages. His agent agreed to field as much as he could as long as they had weekly check-ins and that Joe answered his calls within twenty-four hours.

His phone buzzed and he thought maybe his grace period was up.

My players are posting pictures of you doing flips on Instagram.

Joe smiled at Leslie's text. His small world was now miniscule.

Yeah? How'd they look?

You have to ask? How much longer are you staying?

Why? You gonna come dance with me?

Tempting, but I was actually wondering if you were ready to sneak off campus.

Joe's breath left his chest as if he'd been hit and he staggered back. Could this be it? Was he finally going to—

"Is that who I think it is?"

Joe pulled his phone into his chest.

"Caught you. I'm going to say bye to Terrell and then I think I should leave him to his friends without parental supervision. Mind taking me?"

"No problem. Let's go."

She grinned at him and clicked her tongue against her teeth.

"Uh huh, don't mean to rush you."

Joe was already heading toward the door. He waved to the three B-boys and made a stop at their table.

"You guys should come to clinics. I'd love to work with you."

They laughed. "You're kidding, right? I don't think I'd look good in a skirt," the leader said.

Joe flicked his chin up. "What's your name?"

"Ivan. Ivan Trinh."

Joe held out his hands and looked down at himself. "You see me in a skirt? Cheerleading is a whole lot more than pom-poms and pigtails. Come to clinics Monday and Tuesday. Tryouts are Wednesday. I think I can change your mind."

The boys looked at each other, their eyebrows raised. One of the others nodded at Joe.

"We'll check it out."

Joe waved and then trotted up the stairs, only then starting to feel the warmth leaving his muscles followed by a tightness that he'd regret later.

He dropped Marti off at home and put up with her teasing before pulling his phone back out.

Where am I going?

Leslie answered with an address, which Joe promptly plugged into the Bronco's navigation system, making sure to add it to his "favorites." Thank goodness for navigation; from the map, it appeared that he'd never find Leslie's place in the dark.

It took him about fifteen minutes to get there and he was sure some creatures of the night would spring out of the cornfields and attack at any time. He missed two turns and had to backtrack before driving through a tree tunnel. His insides were doing pirouettes as he finally pulled up in front of a massive two-story-plus brick house with pillars in the front. The driveway curved around and Joe saw Les's truck, an old Bronco, a Jeep, and the Crown Vic.

Les stepped out from behind his truck as Joe put his car in park and he screamed.

"Jesus, you scared me! Haven't you seen *Children of the Corn*? You can't *do* that!"

Joe started to climb down from the Bronco and Les stepped in front of him.

"No, stay. You look good in this car." Leslie stepped forward and with the Bronco's height, they were eye level. Les snaked his hands around Joe's ass and pulled him forward, caressing Joe's thighs that had split to accommodate Les's hips. He reached up to touch Joe's hair and Joe pulled back.

"I'm all sweaty."

"I don't care. I want to kiss you."

Joe reached for Les without hesitation and pulled him in for a fiery kiss that had him wrapping his legs around Les's torso. Les's arms were so massive as he held Joe to him. It was almost too much. Joe had a moment of panic, but then he realized this was Leslie and he had nothing to fear. Leslie would let go immediately if Joe hesitated.

"Hey, where'd you go?"

Joe stiffened a little. How did he tell Leslie, the sweetest man he'd ever known, that this was new for him, this kind of intimacy? That he hadn't always been touched as lovingly as Les always touched him. How did he explain the flare-up of his fight or flight reflex?

"Nothing...aren't you worried about someone seeing?" he reached up and turned off the map light.

"Who? My brothers? Please. The worst that could happen is the two of them singing the sitting in a tree song while they make kissing noises at us. They're children—you realize that, don't you?"

Joe laughed and rested his head on Leslie's shoulder. "They're fun though, right?"

"Fun, yeah. Like jock itch maybe. Athlete's Foot."

Joe pinched his side and Les grunted.

"Fine, they're fun, but I don't want to think about my brothers right now." Les pressed a kiss to Joe's neck and Joe shivered. "Did you have fun tonight?"

"Hmmm, I'm having fun right now," Joe said and he chuckled, running his fingers through Les's hair. *Yep, just like sunshine.* He inhaled and moaned. "But yes, dancing was fun."

"I love watching you dance," Leslie said, pulling back with a smile. "I could watch you for hours."

"I could *kiss* you for hours." Joe tugged on Les's hair and captured his lips, loving this height advantage. He let his hands wander over Les's T-shirt clad torso, amazed by the length of his biceps, his massive deltoids, the divots in his back where his lats inserted into his scapulae. His enormous hands nearly spanned Joe's waist, and when they cupped his generous ass, Leslie groaned.

"God, Joe."

"I know, right?"

Leslie pulled away from the kiss and laughed, resting his head on Joe's shoulder.

"I can't believe we're making out in a car," Leslie said, shaking his head. "I promised I'd wait—"

"Wait for what? You know, I don't want to wait anymore. Life isn't going to wait for us forever. Besides, we have a lot of time to make up for. Seems silly to keep putting it off."

FOURTEEN

L eslie

"You're right," Leslie breathed. Joe had assured him he wanted to explore this thing between them. No time like the present? Why couldn't Leslie just relax and take what Joe was offering? "I don't...I don't know what...where to start."

Joe's smooth hands on his face were cool from the air conditioning in the sultry summer evening. He ran his fingers over Leslie's cheekbones, dragging a thumb over Leslie's lips. Floodlights danced in Joe's dark brown eyes as he pursed his lips.

"Tell me what you imagined would happen. How did you think of me over the years? What did you wish to happen?"

Joe continued to touch him lightly, exploring, and by the time he reached Leslie's chest, he was panting. How did he ask for what he wanted? Leslie ran his thumbs over Joe's pelvic bones and tried to find the words.

"Hey," Joe said, using his finger to lift Leslie's chin. "You can say anything to me. I'm always going to be honest with you. I've told you before that I have issues around sex, so anything you tell me is going to be between us and I'm going to understand."

Leslie exhaled, his chest loosening up a bit at Joe's confession. They had talked about Joe's issues. He had a hard time with being touched, hard time trusting people, but he'd sworn he trusted Leslie to the fullest. They'd known each other a long time, although the context was unusual.

"Things are different with you," Leslie began, "but I put so much pressure on performance and worrying that sometimes I just...can't."

"You know that doesn't matter to me, right?" Joe asked him, his finger tracing Les's waistband. "We could just kiss all night and that's all I'd care about."

Leslie smiled. "You've always been so understanding. I remember when I told you, after I retired, that my testosterone levels were low and you knew exactly what to say to make me feel better. You always do."

Joe ran his fingers lightly over the fly of Les's jeans and Les shuddered, pressing his face into Joe's neck.

"Seems like you're in a can-do mood tonight," Joe teased, his fingers more insistent as they stroked him over his jeans.

"But I...I wanted it to be," he gasped. "Right...when we finally got to do this."

Joe held Les's face in his hands and made deliberate eye contact.

"It *is* perfect because it's *us*. It's perfect because it's you and me, Leslie, right here, right now, and that's all that matters to me."

Joe kissed him and licked at his lips until Les opened for him. Les clung to Joe's shoulders as Joe unfastened Les's Carhartt's and slid his hand inside, gripping Leslie's very cooperative erection. Joe's hands were smooth, warm now...so strong and attentive—

"Oh God, Joe, be...God...be careful."

Leslie moaned as Joe stroked him slowly, insistently, with just enough pressure. Leslie's legs shook so hard, he was so overwhelmed with the sensation of Joe's soft hands running over his tender flesh, he...lost...it.

"Oh my God," he said, pulling his hips out of Joe's reach. "I...Joe—"

"Come back here," Joe said, tugging at Leslie's hand, which had a death grip on the Bronco's oh-shit handle. "Come here, Leslie." Joe wiped his hand on the bottom of his shirt as he pulled him closer.

Leslie let Joe support his shaking body in an embrace and he sighed. "I told you, I wanted it to be perfect—"

"And it is, to me. *You* are, to me." Joe stroked his back and held him close. It wasn't awkward, it was perfect, just like Joe said it would be.

Leslie laughed softly. "Just more evidence as to how tied up you have me. I'm not too proud to admit it."

Leslie had never been so open about his body's failings with anyone else. The sexual experiences he'd had with other men were always a little uncomfortable, and nothing compared to how being touched by Joe had made him feel, and he'd gone and embarrassed himself. His chest burned. He'd wanted this for so long. Would Joe ever want to touch him again? A broken-down middle-aged man?

"I haven't been with anyone in years, Les. I'd probably be the same."

"*Years*?" Leslie's head jerked up. They'd never talked about exclusivity. How could you ask someone to commit to something when you hadn't even had a date? There was no saving themselves for each other, no expectations, but he'd assumed Joe had an active sex life. On Leslie's end there had been a someday hope, but he'd been careful not to push Joe.

"Surprised? Yeah, years. It wasn't intentional at first, but honestly, Les? The more you and I talked, texted, whatever...that satisfied that need for me. Knowing I could call or text if I wanted to talk, knowing you'd be there with a corny joke or football metaphor was an intimacy I didn't know I wanted in my life. I had my years of hookups, tried dating a few times, but I never had that kind of a connection with anyone else. You've always been here." He placed Leslie's hand on Joe's chest and his other hand he placed on Les's cheek. "And now you're here and that's what matters to me."

Joe's smile made Leslie think about the cocky kid he'd met fifteen years ago, the one who'd captivated him and also made him wary. He knew Joe needed to spread his wings and fly, which he'd done to the ends of the earth. The smile on his face now was that of a worldly man who'd gained wisdom and maybe a little heartache along his journey. It was honest, open, vulnerable. Leslie wasn't the only one exposed out here.

"And I'm not done kissing you. Come here."

Joe pulled him in and Leslie kissed him hard, loving the scrape of Joe's stubble against his lips. He couldn't get enough of the contrast between the soft and wet and rough all at the same time. It was intoxicating and he wanted more, his mouth craving those contrasting sensations of hard and soft at once.

He broke away from the kiss and searched Joe's eyes. He touched Joe's waist band, fisting the material there. "May I?"

Joe grinned and leaned back against the center console, spreading his legs in invitation. "By all means."

Leslie's hands were shaking so bad he couldn't figure out the clasp of Joe's black slacks and he worried he would tear something in his fumbling.

"Need assistance?" Joe breathed.

Leslie's cheeks flushed and he nodded, no longer frustrated with his clumsiness. Joe made it all seem okay.

Joe took his time unzipping his pants while Leslie teetered on the edge of control. He opened his fly and then Leslie pushed his hands out of the way, preferring to seek out Joe's cock with his own hands, and his mouth.

"Fuck, Leslie," Joe groaned and tangled his fingers in Leslie's hair as Leslie found what he was craving and enthusiastically said hello.

Joe slid down further in the seat and Leslie heard Joe's hands grasping for something, anything to hold onto. His feet lost purchase on the floor and the ledge and he moaned, but Leslie was in his own version of heaven with his nose pressed against Joe's pelvis, breathing in the scent of his cologne—God, the cologne Leslie had bought for him— mixed with his natural scent, tasting the salt on his skin as Joe's hips bucked. Leslie wished they were somewhere he could strip Joe of these layers and be skin to skin with him, but he was strangely beyond caring that they were out in the open, that he was in a very compromising position with a man, something he'd never allowed...

"Les, it's so...I'm coming I'm..."

Joe's body jerked and he tried to slide his hips back out of Leslie's grasp, but Les held on tight, his big hands overflowing with Joe's powerful ass. Joe's arms flailed as he came in a rush, his whole body tensing. And then he smacked the horn.

"Oh shit," he said, cracking up. He sat up hurriedly and fixed his pants, pushing his hair out of his face. "I can't see, Les. Jesus. There were stars!"

"The stars are brighter here, you know. No city lights to drown them out." Leslie wiped at his bottom lip, so pleased with how Joe responded to him.

Joe flopped sideways against his seat and laughed, his head falling against the headrest. "That's not what I meant, and you know it." He reached for Leslie's hand and squeezed while he fought to catch his breath.

"You lasted longer than I did," Leslie said and Joe smacked him lightly in the chest.

"Come on, we're not going to be competitive about that, all right? And barely. You ran a full blitz there, a total assault. I had no defense."

Leslie burst out laughing so loudly, Joe shushed him. "We're being sneaky out here, shhh."

"Says the guy who hit the horn."

The porch lights came on and the front door opened.

"Shit. Sandy. Hey," Leslie yelled. "Sorry, it was just us."

"Uh-huh," Sandy called out. "Well, keep it down. And tell Joe he needs to run the defroster before he tries to drive home. Good night!"

Sandy shut the door and they burst out laughing.

"Busted," Leslie said, shaking his head.

Joe pulled Leslie into an embrace again. "Look at us, acting like a couple of kids. This was fun."

Leslie nibbled on Joe's ear and Joe shivered, clutching Leslie's shoulders tighter.

"Mmm, it was. I wish I could hold you right, though. I want to spend the night with you."

Joe kissed Les's neck, sucking and biting as he went, and Leslie thought *yes, more. Leave your mark.*

"I want that, too. Soon. But for now, I need to go. I need to be ready for tomorrow, for the first step in winning that wager."

Joe's grin had Leslie feeling lightheaded. Real-life Joe was so much hotter than fantasy Joe. Leslie had lost count of how many times he'd dreamed about finally being intimate with Joe, and now that he'd actually had his kiss, had his spend, he was insatiable. He'd waited so long, and now any more waiting seemed unbearable.

"Did you hear me?" Joe said, running his tongue over Leslie's bottom lip.

"Hmm? Sorry, all I can think about is when I can touch you again."

Joe pulled back, that cocky grin faded and his eyes widened, softened, went a little glassy.

"Was it okay? I want that too, Les. I'm just..."

"You're right, it's perfect, Joe, because it's us. Go ahead, get some rest. I'm glad you came."

Joe's eyebrows raised and wiggled. "Me too."

"Stop it." Les chuckled as his cheeks heated. "Goodnight. See you Monday."

"Or tomorrow," Joe said as he fastened his seatbelt and started the Bronco. The porch lights began to flicker rhythmically and Joe laughed. "I think someone is waiting up for a postgame report. Be sure to tell them I was fabulous."

"I'll do no such thing," Les said, stepping back and shutting Joe's door. The window was down so he leaned inside. "I don't want to encourage them. Wait...tomorrow's Sunday."

"Mm-hmmm," Joe said. "Time to start the fundraising challenge. We'll be up bright and early to get a head start." He winked and put the car in gear.

"Joe, you know football is going to win. You might as well sleep in tomorrow. We've got this."

"We'll just see about that. Have sweet dreams, baby."

"You're trouble." Leslie stepped back and Joe blew him a kiss before backing up and driving away, bass thumping as he headed around the curve and down the private tree-lined driveway. Leslie watched him go with conflicted feelings.

Tonight had been an awesome surprise...a bit overwhelming, but also...he was confused.

Everything had happened so fast...

"Aw man. I wanted to see his Bronco."

Les turned to find the twins pouting on the front porch.

"No. We're not doing this."

"Aw, come on, Leslieeeee," Randy whined as Les pushed past him to get in the house. "We just want to get to know your *boyfrieeend*."

"Follow him on Instagram. Leave us be." Leslie swung the door closed but Sandy put his hands out to stop it.

"Wait. Hold up."

Sandy and Randy looked at each other.

"Hold up, wait a minute." And they started bumping, grinding, some sort of dancing that Leslie had no time for. He needed to find out what Joe was up to and he needed to put his own team's fundraising plans into motion. Greenvale College. That was why he was there, back living with mom and the twins, working for his brother in their hometown.

Priorities, Leslie. He scolded himself as he climbed the steps to his suite of rooms at the end of the hall. His focus had been torn away from football this week between making sure Joe had what he needed and the storm cleanup, which thankfully a crew was taking care of and he didn't have to be involved. He'd had more migraines lately than he'd had in a while and he didn't want them to become a daily occurrence. Before going to bed, he'd make sure to mark them in his journal for his next doctor's visit, which was coming up.

He'd been so preoccupied he hadn't noticed the twins had followed him. Randy cleared his throat and Leslie turned to find them standing together like they used to when they were wee lads about to get punished for their latest prank.

"What is it now?"

They looked at each other and Sandy spoke.

"We're sorry we interfered with your date."

Leslie frowned. "It wasn't a date."

"Okay, visit then. Anyway, we're sorry if we interrupted. We just... we had an idea for the fundraising challenge."

"I'm listening."

Sandy grinned. "Cool. Okay, how about a celebrity calendar? You could make each month cover certain players or positions, and then hit up some of your NFL pals from the corresponding positions to join in."

That was actually a good idea. One thing the twins got that Leslie hadn't was that brain for business. They always had big ideas and were great at making things happen, even if they weren't always great things.

"I like it. Get on it. I'm sure you're aware of all that needs to happen, getting releases signed, etc. Feel free to use my contacts, and let me know if I need to make phone calls." Leslie rubbed at his head and sucked in a breath.

Randy had his hand up.

"Yes, Randy?"

"Um, we need to talk about workouts. I've got tractor tires being delivered later this week and heavy ropes, we've got pads, but do you have any other ideas? I'm going to have to get creative without a weight room. I can't just have them running all over Ayre Valley."

Leslie smiled. Oh, he had ideas all right. "Let me handle that." He winced as another pain stabbed him in the top left side of his brain.

"Do you need me to call Doc?" Sandy asked. "Need any medicine refills?"

"I can handle it, Sandy. Thank you." Sandy had acted as his personal assistant over the past couple of years. He'd struggled to keep his appointments and schedule straight after a particularly difficult few months of migraines. Sandy had set up his phone so he only needed to add voice memos to his phone and then Sandy used various programs on his phone to set reminders and complete tasks for him. Now that they were in the same house and working together on the team, Sandy fell all over himself to make sure Leslie's needs were taken care of. Most of the time, he and Randy were just smart-assed twentysomethings who liked to annoy their older brother, who had actually done a lot of their child-rearing. Their father died when they were so young, only nine, and Barry was already married, so it fell to Leslie to help their mother raise the boys. Men. They seemed to grow up overnight, though, like their college graduation seemed to be just yesterday instead of four years ago. Since then, they'd started three businesses and sold them, making a shit-load of money each time, but through it all, Sandy had continued to handle Leslie's life: his plane tickets to the network; his medical appointments and medications, which had thankfully remained out of public eye; and he'd managed Leslie's social calendar, making sure he remembered the birthdays, weddings, births, etc. of Leslie's wide network of friends. His memory wasn't great, so Sandy acted as his stand-in brain when he needed it.

Sandy's motivation was purely out of love and devotion to his older brother. Also, he was just a whiz with technology and gadgets.

Randy was more like Leslie in that his charm opened doors for him and he had the interpersonal skills to create a huge network of friends, investors, and influencers.

Together, his brothers were his dream team for this fundraising challenge. Joe didn't have a chance, and while that should have tickled Leslie from a competition standpoint, he had to admit that he was thrilled at the prospect of winning the wager. Because truthfully, Leslie would be the ultimate winner whether his team beat the cheerleaders in fundraising or not. He had Joe here and that was everything.

"You should get some rest," Sandy said softly as if he were ready to have his head bitten off. Leslie wasn't an ogre by any means, but he sometimes took out his frustration over his physical limitations at home and he hated that about himself. He'd had a terrible example from their father and though he'd worked hard to be different, sometimes the apple hugged the tree roots.

"Yeah, I'm headed to bed. Listen, guys, this thing with Joe—"

"You don't have to say anything," Sandy said quietly. "We just want you to be happy."

Well, that was the thing. Why couldn't he be happy? Joe was here, they were having fun, why couldn't he just relax and enjoy the spoils of the last fifteen years? He'd been patient, he'd bided his time, hoping that the foundation he'd built with Joe would blossom into something real, more permanent. Now that it was actually beginning to be...something, Leslie was trying not to panic. Would he have enough time to truly enjoy Joe? Would he have enough time?

FIFTEEN

Joe

It was a good thing there was no drought in Iowa, because Joe planned to spend the next several hours standing under a hose. It was the only way he was going to survive the brutal heat.

Marti'd had the brilliant idea to do a car wash on Sunday, when the college kids were moving in and literally everyone in town would have to pass by the town's only gas station on their way to the three churches. "They'll see us on their way and come back by after service. It's not supposed to rain for a few days. It's perfect!"

And of course Terrell had helped modernize the car wash by posting it all over the college's social media, tagging everyone he knew in Missouri who wouldn't mind driving a couple of hours on a boring Sunday to get their cars washed by hot guys, gals, and nonbinary pals. Joe capitalized on his massive social media following by running a live feed and a crowdfunding link. Folks could get autographed pictures or personalized video messages for making donations. He could answer a thread of "ask me anything" questions while shirtless in the hot sun while lovingly washing cars.

An hour into the car wash, they had a line of cars as far as the eye could see. Traffic on the two-lane main road through town was at a standstill. The deputies were trying to reroute through-traffic onto residential streets to go around the mess, and three news vans, TMZ, and Buzzfeed had been dispatched. Joe ended up doing more interviews and signing autographs than washing cars, but then he got to work and let Marti take over schmoozing with folks. Around noon, a minivan showed up carrying three of his former mentees from *Dance Machine* ready to join in the fun. They lived within a four-hour-drive radius and Joe promised them hotel, food, and personal coaching at a later date in exchange for their appearances. They came dressed for washing cars and the cameras ate up their hamming around, splashing each other, and flirting with customers. A few lucky standersby even got dance lessons.

Joe kept the sunscreen on, passing bottles around and reminding his ten squad members and fifteen hopefuls that stunting would be painful with sunburns. He stayed hydrated, ate a couple of protein bars, and tried to conserve his energy.

Until Leslie showed up in his giant truck around noon. His completely mud-covered monster.

"So this was your brilliant plan," Les said, grinning and shaking his head as he slid down out of the cab.

"Like I said, cheerleaders have been fundraising forever. We got this."

"Really. All right, I admit it's a nice idea. You might make a grand today—"

"We're up to thirteen thousand eight hundred, Coach Judd." Terrell came over and handed Joe his phone. "Your manager just texted you with numbers from the online fundraiser." Terrell turned and acted surprised to see Les. "Oh, hi there, Coach Payton."

"Simmons," Les shook his hand. "My offer is still open. I got your stats from your high school coach. Seems a pity to not have you on my defense this year."

Terrell kicked up his chin. "I told my parents after high school I wanted to pursue dancing. No offense, Coach, but I never felt real comfortable on a football team."

Leslie's smile faded and he took on a terrifying expression. Terrell took a step back, bumping into Joe.

"I do not tolerate that kind of nonsense, son. I think you understand why."

"Y-yes sir," Terrell said. "And I appreciate that. But if it's all the same, sir, dancing is my passion, and I'm afraid that a football injury could kill both potential careers."

Joe caught the shift in Leslie from fierce to frightened and he intervened and he breathed easier. He'd never considered Leslie scary at all, but then he'd seen the soft gooey inside that no one else got to see. It was sometimes easy to forget that Leslie was raised on one of the roughest and most violent sports on the planet.

"Thanks for the update, Terrell," he said, squeezing the kid's arm. "Can you go share the numbers with your mom?"

"Sure, coach. And thank you, Coach Payton."

Leslie nodded, tried to look pleasant, but his jaw muscle twitched.

"I can't believe you would try to poach one of my prospects, Coach Payton." Joe tried to lighten the mood, and it worked. Either his joke or the way his wet trunks cling to his pelvis. Or the fact that he was shirtless. There was no way he was going to chance getting a farmer tan.

Leslie groaned. "You're trouble." Then he sighed. "How much would it take to get Coach Judd to climb up there and personally wash my...pickup?"

Joe's eyes flared and he barked out a laugh. He glanced around and leaned in closer. "After last night? I'd wash it for free. I'd be glad to do it."

"Stop it," Leslie whispered, his cheeks beet red and not from the heat. "You're getting me all worked up over here, and I actually have something serious to discuss."

Joe ran a hand in front of his face to wipe away his smirk. "Yes, Coach Payton. What can I do to you...I mean for you?"

Leslie attempted a reprimanding look, but all it did was make Joe grin wider.

"You can run training for my players tomorrow. Hard training, like the kind that will make them walk funny afterwards."

It was Joe's turn to laugh. "Are you serious? What do I know about training football players?"

"You know about training bodies in flexibility, agility, balance, and strength. That's what I want. Plus I've got a few boys that could stand to be taken down a peg, if you know what I mean."

Joe crossed his arms over his chest, which he sensed was in the beginning stages of a burn. "So you want me to put up with a bunch of homophobic douche bags and teach them a lesson."

"I do. Look, Terrell's right. Football as a whole could use a little education and I can't think of a more qualified person."

Joe loosened his arms. "You know I'm going to make them all suffer. I'd do no less for my team."

Leslie inclined his head. "I'd expect nothing less. Sandy and Randy will be there to supervise. I've gotta fly out for *Monday Night Football* or else I'd be there..."

"No, it's fine. I've got this. What time? And where should we meet?"

"Tomorrow afternoon? How about the high school gym? Should be big enough?"

"You're on." Joe gave a confident smile that didn't reach all the way inside. He wasn't sure he was quite ready for this much of a challenge to his authority—to his masculinity—so soon, but he also didn't want to let Leslie down. "No problem. As long as you know what shape they'll be in Tuesday morning."

"Sounds great. Now, about washing my pickup..."

Joe leaned a little closer. "You couldn't afford me. Besides, I'd insist on doing it naked and, well, this town ain't ready for that on a Sunday afternoon."

"I don't think I'm ready for that," Leslie said, his voice hoarse. "I'll have the, um, kids wash it then."

"Probably safer for you that way. I'll just be over here reapplying sunscreen." He took out the bottle and squeezed some in his hands, rubbing it slowly between his palms, coating them generously.

Leslie's eyes bugged out and he cleared his throat. "Coach." He walked swiftly away and toward Marti, who he handed a wad of bills before walking over to chat with some of the townsfolk waiting for their cars.

"That was cruel, even for you," Marti said as she joined him. "That poor man."

"You saw that, did you?"

She clicked her tongue against her teeth. "You're bad. Now, you want the totals?"

"Give it to me. Oh, and guess who's leading football practice tomorrow afternoon?"

Marti's eyebrows raised dramatically. "Oh, oh...oh, this is priceless. That's what he was asking you for?"

"Mm-hmm, I get to torture footballers for two straight hours. I think I've died and found heaven in a cornfield."

"Man, I'd love to be there, but I've got clinics tomorrow from four to six. But you could take Terrell? You know, if you needed an assistant."

"That's a good idea. Can you believe Payton was trying to poach him?" Joe shook his head.

Marti laughed. "I can believe it. My son made up his mind. His dad and I fully support his decision. I have to admit I'm relieved, although you're going to have to hold my hand through all the auditions and shit. A career in dance is a roller coaster I never wanted to ride on."

"He's going to be great. How could he not? Look at who raised him."

The two of them plotted the best exercises Joe could give the team to really make them suffer. Joe promised to make it to clinics for the second half and the two agreed that it was good for her to have some time alone with them. They'd been afraid that some of the kids would just be trying to show off in front of him rather than truly trying to make the team. They called Terrell over and he was hesitant to go to the football practice, but he agreed when Joe told him about the whole torture part.

By four o'clock, the cheerleaders were toast and they'd made over $3,000 in cash and another $20,000 online. Joe was pleased, it was a good start, but they had a long way to go to break through the level he knew Leslie would reach with his contacts.

By the time Joe got back to his apartment, he found a cooler outside his door with a massive salad, homemade bread, and granola. On top was a note.

You worked so hard today, I wanted to feed you myself, but I have to prepare for tomorrow night's game. I wish I could take you with me to Dallas. We'd have a hotel suite after the game...

Anyway, my mom made this for you and would like you to come to dinner one night soon. It would mean a lot to her, but I understand if that's not comfortable for you and she will too.

Your kids did a great job on my truck. Nice work today.

Les

Food from Agnes? Running away for a work function overnight? Jesus, this was really happening, wasn't it? Secret or not, he and Leslie were dating. And Joe didn't feel the urge to run.

Wait.

He did a mental inventory.

Nope, he wasn't anxious about it at all. Could it be that he was ready to stop running? Could he really settle down with a wonderful man like Leslie?

Joe swayed on his feet. He couldn't tell if it was the hard work and sun and lack of food or if it was the thought of settling down that had him shaky. He went over to pick up the cooler and when he stood up his vision went fuzzy and he got a little lightheaded. He was able to get inside his apartment and set things down. He poured himself a huge glass of water and ate his delicious salad standing up at the counter. His mouth had found true bliss. Agnes Payton was a genius and it was obvious the food had been prepared with love. He just knew it, from everything Leslie had told him about his mother, Agnes was the kind of mom Joe had always dreamed of. He desperately wanted to meet her, and was terrified at the same time. What if she didn't approve? What if he was his usual asshole self and she didn't think he was good enough for her son?

Joe took a quick shower and he fell into bed still wet and wrapped in a towel. He needed a good night's sleep if he was going to torture the footballers tomorrow.

That thought made him smile and he dreamed sinister dreams…

Joe and Terrell drove together to the high school and on the way, Joe ran through his plans. Terrell remained quiet.

"So what do you think?" he finally asked Terrell. "You're awfully quiet over there."

Terrell crossed his arms over his chest and scowled. He got that scowl from his dad. It used to intimidate Joe a bit back in their Greenvale days until he realized it was genetic, not an indicator of his mood.

"I think…this is going to suck."

Joe pulled the Bronco into a parking spot and turned off the car. He turned to face Terrell.

"Tell me."

Terrell sighed. "I thought it would be different, you know, coming here and no one knows I played football, there would be no expectations. Already some of the guys in the dorm are hassling me for not coming out for the team, saying I'm not man enough to play for Coach Payton. I know it's bullshit—"

"It *is* bullshit. Just wait until we're done with them today. They'll be singing an entirely different tune." Joe held out a hand and Terrell hesitated a minute before he slapped and shook it.

"All right then," he said.

By the time the players began filing into the high school gym, Joe and Terrell were properly warmed up and ready to do battle. He'd texted Leslie to remind his players to bring water and dress in clothes they could move in, preferably not super baggy. It was important that Joe be able to see their form and whether or not they were performing the techniques correctly to avoid injury.

The kids came in mostly quiet and looking as if they were headed in to see the dentist or get vaccines. None of them looked comfortable. Only a few gave off attitude and had that cocky vibe about them. Maybe this wouldn't be so bad?

One of them bumped shoulders with Terrell and made an exaggerated apology. That kid was going to earn Joe's wrath if he put one more toe out of line.

Terrell stood against the wall with that Simmons Scowl and Joe nodded at him.

Randy and Sandy came in behind them and one of the boys asked, "Coach? You providing ballet slippers?"

His friend snorted. "Or maybe a tutu?"

Right. *You asked for it.*

"Good afternoon. I'm Coach Judd and this is my assistant, Terrell. Enough with the niceties. Spread out in straight lines with your arms out to your sides. Be sure there's at least a foot between your fingertips."

While the kids continued to grumble, Joe walked through the lines to where Randy and Sandy were standing at the back.

"I'd like for you two to stand on either side and monitor. If any of the players are struggling, give me a nod. If any are fucking around, shake your head. I will deal with any misbehavior. Is that understood?"

The twins pressed their lips together and tried to pull their faces into solemn expressions but Joe could tell they were delighted to see him at work. They probably thought he couldn't handle these kids. They had no idea how much experience Joe had with men just like these.

"I'm going to be instructing you to do things your bodies are not used to doing—"

"Cuz I'm not gay," one of the boys muttered. Shame for him Joe had been standing close when he said it.

"Do I need to remind everyone in this room about the tolerance policy of the school? Hmm? Do I also need to remind you that some of your straightest football heroes have taken ballet to supplement their training for football? Or remind you that one in ten people is on the queer spectrum, so that means some of you in here, definitely players you've stood next to, people you've admired and respected? This is such a tired argument. I'd love just once for a puffed-up jock to be honest and say, 'you know, I'm afraid of trying something new, but I'm here and I'll do my best.' I'd have a helluva lot more respect for that than for someone who thinks calling something gay is an insult. Please. If you have a question, ask it. If you want to laugh because it feels funny, go for it—"

"And," Randy said, stepping forward to address the crowd. "If you want to make homophobic comments, you can leave right now and say goodbye to playing football at Greenvale College. Coach Payton's rules. Any questions? No? Then I suggest you focus."

Joe appreciated that Leslie had that rule, but he had this under control.

"I'm going to ask you to all take your shoes and socks off for the first part. I ran a disinfectant over the floor when I got here. The warmups we're going to be doing will require careful articulation of all of the bones in your feet and it will also help you with balance."

The kids mumbled a bit as they removed their shoes and put them on the sides of the gym and then they lined back up.

"All right. Let's do this."

Joe led them through a series of thorough stretches. A few of the players chuckled and more groaned at the unfamiliar muscles. Terrell stood with his back to the crowd so they could see both views. He was bigger than quite a few of the players, and Joe knew he was fast, agile, and flexible. A few of the players whispered and pointed, obviously curious about him.

"Okay, have any of you ever heard of barre classes?"

A couple of hands went up.

"Good. Barre is low-impact, high-intensity work aimed at increasing your muscle endurance, improving posture and balance, and it is guaranteed to make you want to cry." Joe turned on the music, a mixture of old and new dance tunes that had a few of the kids bopping their heads.

"Is barre like ballet stuff?" one of the boys asked.

"Barre incorporates ballet technique, yes."

"Man," the kid said. "My mom made me take ballet for a while. That barre shit is hard."

Joe smiled. "It is, but it's good for you. And hey, at least you're not out in that fun Iowa afternoon heat, am I right?"

An hour later, the players were all sprawled out on the floor panting, crying, sipping water, and sweating. They probably *wished* they were out in the Iowa heat right about now.

Joe waved to Terrell to join him and they walked over to Randy and Sandy. "Have they had enough?" he asked, nowhere near ready to stop.

Randy cupped himself. "I don't know, man, but I'm in pain just watching."

Terrell laughed and then covered his mouth. Randy assured him it was okay.

Sandy shuddered. "When you guys did that plié thingie and bounced like that forever? Damn."

Joe smiled. "The first time I took a barre class I thought I'd died. I couldn't walk right for a few days, and I had been dancing for years already." He looked around. "If you think they can take it, I had a few more things planned."

Randy and Sandy grinned at each other and Randy gestured to the kids. "Be my guest. If they're still breathing, they can keep going."

Joe looked to Terrell who had broken a sweat but shrugged. "I'm just getting started."

Joe clapped him on the shoulder. "I love that attitude."

Terrell blew out a breath. "Or I just know better than to say I've had enough. You *do* know who my mom is."

"Point taken," Joe said, then he addressed the group.

"Okay, break's over—"

"Coach Judd? You or your assistant ever play sports?"

Joe's throat tightened and he tried to swallow around it. "Not me. I wasn't exactly interested in extracurricular activities that required me to stay out of trouble and get good grades," Joe answered. He raised his eyebrows at Terrell, who sighed.

"Yeah. I played football."

The room got quiet.

"But...you're a dancer."

"Right. And I made that decision after trying to fit in and gain respect by playing varsity football all four years. I was a tight end, held my high school's record for receiving over and above the receivers. I was also out, which made me a target on the field and off. After one too many hits—on the field and off—I said fu...screw it. It wasn't worth it. No matter how hard I worked, I never had the support of my teammates."

"That's bullshit." A few of the players shared that sentiment. Others looked at the floor.

"Well, it's the truth. For a lot of folks," Joe said. "I've had my share of people assume things about me because I'm a dancer, who happens to be gay." He looked around, challenging any of them to even have a ghost of a smirk. "I hope none of you ever have to experience the feeling that your friends, teammates, or coaches don't have your back. And I hope no one in this room ever does the deserting."

The room was dead silent and Joe's gut clenched, that feeling of dread he'd get before casting announcements were made.

"Terrell?"

One of the kids, one who had been making smart-assed comments when they came in, had his hand up.

"Yeah?"

He tilted his head to the side. "Your team should have been there for you. On and off the field."

Terrell cleared his throat and nodded, then looked to Joe.

"You're right," Joe said. "Make sure none of your teammates go through that." He looked around and saw a little more respect going around. "Now, we're not finished here, so everyone up."

"Man. Is this the kind of shit cheerleaders do at practice?" One of the players who had been groaning the whole time and who had gotten louder as the practice went on, stood with his hands on his hips. "This blows, man."

Joe and Terrell looked at each other. "Want to show them what else we do at practice?"

Terrell nodded. "Yeah, Coach."

Coach. That title still felt odd to Joe. He'd been called an asshole, a diva, and by Marti, a brat. The idea of him as a leader was just...ridiculous. But then he thought of Leslie and the faith he had in Joe's abilities, and he stood a little taller.

"Let's start with jump drills."

Terrell nodded and the two of them proceeded to do ten perfect toe-touches in a row. Then they did herkies. The footballers all made appreciative sounds and had shocked expressions.

"What's next?" Joe asked Terrell, only slightly winded and grateful his knees were cooperating.

"Tumbling runs?" Terrell said.

"Good call. Hey, will you guys grab two of those mats, please?"

Five of the footballers hurried over and unrolled the nice mats the high school had tucked in the corner. Terrell stretched out his wrists first, then his forearms. Joe spoke close to his ear.

"I'll follow your lead."

Terrell's eyebrows went up. "Anything in particular?"

Joe looked around at the waiting faces. "Start out slow. Then wow them."

"Yes, Coach."

Joe rolled his eyes and then gestured for Terrell to go first. Terrell did a perfect handstand and then proceeded to walk on his hands the length of the mat. The players whooped and hollered. Joe followed Terrell knowing that his handstand was definitely not as steady but grateful he made it the length of the mat. At the other end, Terrell did a back walkover and then continued doing them back across the mat. *Fuck.* Not one of Joe's favorites, but he wasn't about to admit his back was hamburger meat. He followed Terrell and made it most of the way across the mat.

"You warmed up?" Joe asked him and he nodded. "Then try a couple of tumbling runs."

Terrell nodded, rubbed his hands together, and then pushed off his toes. He did a roundoff, two back handsprings, and then a back tuck. That got a whole series of cheers and applause from the entire gym. He tried to hide his smile but Joe saw the pride in his eyes.

"How the fuck do you do that?"

"How do you stay in a straight line? I'd be on my ass."

"Can you do that, coach?"

Fucking fuck. "That's the plan," Joe said, and the players all laughed. Joe glanced over at the twins who were watching him with terror on their faces. Probably Leslie made them promise to get Joe through the practice in one piece.

Here goes nothing. Joe took off at a jog and then hit his roundoff and prayed he had enough momentum to carry him through two fulls and two back handsprings, ending with a twist. He landed hard and his left knee spoke up a bit, but he was just damn glad he didn't end up on his ass.

"Holy shit! Where did you learn to do that?"

"Trial and error," Joe admitted. "Truly. Once I joined the cheer squad here, there were a few girls on the squad who had been gymnasts and I made them teach me."

"I want to learn how to do that!"

"Me too!"

The guys were all clamoring for lessons and Joe had to raise his voice.

"Come on, come on, chill out. Look, your bodies have been through it already and we have a couple more drills to do. I tell you what. I'll be having tumbling clinics for the cheer squad, and any of you that are serious about learning can come and join us. But beware, if you show up and you're any good, I might conscript you for our competition squad."

"But...football?"

"Competition is separate than the games. We'd have to talk to Coach Payton, though. He might not allow moonlighting."

Joe glanced at Randy and Sandy, who were shaking their heads. *Huh*, Joe thought. *He might do it for me.*

They spent the next hour doing jumping drills and Joe taught them dive rolls to help them get to their feet faster from a fall. Terrell was the hero when he did standing back tucks and a standing full twist. Some of the players started to do parkour and Joe knew it was time to end practice before someone really did get hurt.

"All right, let's do a cool-down exercise."

They all lined up and he led them in some slow stretches and breathing techniques. At the end of the two hours, the attitudes seemed to be gone. Joe wanted to believe they were gone. As he packed up his things, he heard some of the guys inviting Terrell to hang out with them later and it made him smile. He wanted Terrell to have a great college experience and not have to deal with the bullshit he had.

Joe dealt with homophobic bullshit for his first two years, but after they won their first championship, it got a little easier, and he learned to avoid situations where it would be bad, like when the football players were in the gym en masse, or the locker rooms. If it was a couple of them, they left him alone. But when they had an audience…

"Nice job," Sandy said, squeezing his shoulder. "That was definitely different than anything I've ever done with them and they are going to hurt in ways that I'd never dreamed to inflict on them."

Joe laughed. "Thanks? Happy to help out."

The twins stood staring at him and Joe began to be concerned.

"Is there something else?"

Sandy cleared his throat. "Brother Leslie is really glad you're here."

Joe stood a little straighter. *Oh boy.*

"Yeah. Me, too."

They continued to stare. It was eerie having identical eyes gazing at you, especially when they were taller than you. They weren't as big as Leslie, maybe a couple inches shorter and not as muscular, but they were a tad intimidating, or they would be if Joe didn't know Leslie would literally murder them for fucking with him.

"Like, he's *really* glad. It means a lot to him."

"Yeah. Me too." Joe set his bag down and faced off with them.

"Like *a lot.*"

"I get it. Look, if there's something you want to say—"

"No, no," they said, backing away with their hands up. "We just wanted to be sure, you know. That you knew."

"Coach?" Terrell said, approaching them with a questioning look. "You good? My ride is here."

Joe raised his eyebrows. "Oh, I was going to take you—"

"It's cool. I've got a thing."

"Ohhh…go on then," Joe said, giving Terrell a hug. He loved being a mentor to this awesome kid. It took balls for him to address the group they'd had tonight. Joe was damned proud of him. "Don't, uh… Well, have fun." He wasn't about to get all parental on him. He liked being the cool adult.

Terrell said goodbye and walked away, but the twins continued their posturing. *Was* it posturing, though? They weren't giving off asshole vibes. Just…weird.

"So we're going to the Goalpost to watch the game."

Joe raised his eyebrows. "The game?"

"*Monday Night Football*? Brother Leslie's broadcast?"

"Oh, right. Cool. That's…cool."

"We thought you should join us."

Because that wouldn't be weird at all. "Uh, sure? Maybe for a little bit? I need a shower—"

"You do know the farmers go there after a day's work and rarely clean up first," Randy said.

"Yeah, and they also come over after the livestock auction. I think you're fine for a game at the Goalpost," Sandy added.

Joe looked at his watch. *Shit.* Clinics. "I need to go back to school for the end of clinics. What time will you be there?"

"Game starts at seven."

"Great. I'll, uh, I'll try to stop by?"

"Do that."

What a weird conversation. It was weirder because they were trying so hard to *not* be weird, but Joe only knew of them what he'd heard from Leslie. He hadn't had cause to hang out with them before and wondered what he might possibly have in common with them.

Joe grabbed his things, assured them he'd be by, and then he drove alone back to campus.

What a bizarre day! He couldn't wait to tell Leslie what they'd accomplished. That thought gave him pause. He was thinking of the two of them like a team. What was next? His morning smoothie at Agnes's counter going over game schedules, ideas for training, meal prepping together? And he was going to have drinks and football with Randy and Sandy?

What is this life?

SIXTEEN

Leslie

It had been a whirlwind day, the kind Leslie was going to have to get used to. The network needed him to fly out to Dallas for this interview and he agreed to do commentary for one last game before diving into his season with the Jackets, which started next week. By the time the game had wrapped, he was ready to crash, but he had been dying to find out how practice had gone that day.

He texted Joe as soon as he got into his hotel room and then set his phone down while he struggled with his tie and buttons. He had just pulled off his dress shirt when his phone started rattling and jumping on the glass-topped table. He dove for it to find Joe calling. On FaceTime? He clicked accept and nearly dropped it when he found Randy's face on the screen.

"What the hell are you doing with Joe's phone? Am I going to hate the answer?"

Randy held up his hand. "Now, it's not my fault that he doesn't have proper security on his phone, which he left in my capable hands while he plays pool against Sandy."

"God, I hope there was no betting. I'm guessing you didn't tell him your brother has a reputation as a pool hustler?"

"Noooot really, no I didn't, but we didn't bet money. I bet him he has to let me take his Bronco off-roading if he loses."

"Absolutely not. Is he available to talk?"

Randy put his hand over the phone like it was a regular call and shouted over the din of what Leslie assumed was the Goalpost, and then laughed.

"He said he can't talk now, he's gotta concentrate on beating Sandy. He's actually doing really well. Hey, how's Dallas?"

"Hot. I'm glad this is my last network event for a while. How did practice go?"

"Brutal," Randy said, shuddering.

"What do you mean brutal? Is Joe okay?"

"Oh, *he's* fine. Your offensive line is going to be crying tomorrow and a few of the guys landed on their heads trying to do flips, but otherwise it was awesome. Joe's amazing, Brother Leslie."

Leslie sighed. "Yes, he is."

"Hey, listen, we came up with a little fundraising event plan and I thought you'd probably want to approve it."

"Hit me."

"A jogathon. All athletes together. They all get their own pledge sheets and then whatever they raise goes on their team's leaderboard."

"Sounds good. Joe agree?"

Randy grinned. "It was his idea."

Leslie laughed. "I never thought he'd get into it this much."

"Oh, he's into it. He ever gives up this Twinkle Toes shit he'd make a helluva football coach."

"I'm sure he would. May I speak to him now, please?"

"I mean, I'll try, but he's pretty into his game here. And that kid Terrell? Man, you missed out persuading him to join the team. Sounds like he was done dirty by his team in high school and now he wants to dance? That's pretty cool Joe and Marti stayed friends all these years. Did you know—"

"Randy. The phone?"

"Oh, right. And don't worry, Brother Barry is our designated driver. He's coming in a little while to pick us up. You were great tonight, by the way. I think Joe thought so too. He was real quiet when you talked."

"Stop it. Give him the phone."

"So pushy. Gosh."

Yeah, Randy totally regressed when he'd been drinking and judging by his current slurred speech, he'd had at least a couple of drinks. The screen got all shaky while he walked across the bar and Leslie could hear shouts and laughter.

"Here he is. I told him you were playing. He's your problem now." The screen went all wonky and then Joe's smiling face appeared.

"I was just about to make Sandy wish he'd never messed with Twinkle Toes. How are you? You were great tonight."

"Hey." Leslie melted into the chair in his hotel room and sighed. "It's good to hear your voice. And see you, although, you've got company."

Sandy was behind Joe, jumping up and down trying to wave to Leslie. Joe turned around and laughed and then walked outside the bar.

"There, is that better?" he asked.

"Hi."

"Hi."

They grinned at each other like a couple of lovestruck teenagers.

"So, the last show, huh? Are you going to miss the network?" Joe asked him.

Leslie exhaled and rubbed his forehead. "Yes and no. I like being connected with the league still, but no, I'm happy with my little team. I have a lot of work to do with them. It's not going to be a picnic. I can't keep on gallivanting off to Dallas or LA or New York in the middle of football season."

"Hmmm, but maybe you could gallivant with *me* next month to LA?"

Leslie sat up straighter. "With you? To LA?"

Joe grinned. He looked around. "They need me for a *Dance Machine* special live performance. We have a bye week so I thought maybe, if you weren't busy—"

"*God* yes, I'd love to come with you."

"Good. Great. It's a date."

Leslie had a herd of wild horses running through his chest. "Are we doing this? Joe?"

Joe bit down on his lip and grinned. "Let's do this. I mean, we can't *do* this, like, at Greenvale, but like I *want* to do this. Let's *do* this."

All this talk of *doing this* had Leslie's slacks feeling snug, but also his chest was so full, he was ready to make declarations, which was a bad idea while Joe was likely tipsy in the Goalpost parking lot with Leslie's creepy brothers lurking nearby.

There was some commotion behind Joe and the screen went black but he could still hear him.

"Yeah, I'm going to take off. Thanks for the drinks. No, thanks. I walked up here. I'm going to walk back. No, I don't need an escort. Goodnight." The sound of footfalls and the phone scratching against the material in Joe's pocket. Joe singing to himself. Then he pulled the phone out. "Oh, you're still there. Good. You can talk to me while I walk home like a responsible little faculty member. Geez, I can't believe I was out drinking on a school night. What would your brother say?"

"That you should not be hanging out with the youngest Payton brothers if you don't want to do foolish things?"

Joe smiled and looked around him in the bar's parking lot. "I'm just going to stay here for a minute and talk to you. I want to see you and I don't want to trip and fall if I'm watching you and walking while tipsy."

Leslie really liked his profile from this angle. It was still dimly lit outside at nine o'clock and the streetlights illuminated his face. He smiled into the phone and Leslie was glad he had this moment, this connection with him. Joe's smiles were infrequent and Leslie cherished every one of them.

"Yeah. I only had two beers but I'm a lightweight. And your brothers are kinda sweet. Like, they were trying to look out for you without being obvious but being *totally* obvious that's what they're doing."

"What did they do now?" Leslie groaned. Was he going to have to forbid them from talking to Joe? Most of the time they meant well but they were loose cannons...without alcohol.

"Nothing bad, I promise. But, if I listened to them, I might think you were kind of sweet on me."

Joe glanced down at the screen for a few beats, and Leslie saw that vulnerability he craved, when the dancer, the reluctant "out" spokesperson in his field who put up that wall to keep anything from possibly hurting him allowed Leslie to gaze inside at the beautiful man behind the anger.

"You know I am, Joe. I have been for fifteen years. Since that night in the Goalpost parking lot, right where you're standing. All of these years, all of our texts, phone calls... Yeah, I think sweet on you is an understatement, but it's a factual statement."

Joe covered his mouth with his hand, but his eyes crinkled at the corners.

"You're making me blush, Leslie."

"Good," Leslie said, chuckling. "I like you blushing."

"I like *you*," Joe murmured. "You have no idea how many times you reaching out was exactly what I needed to get me out of my head, out of my... You were there for me so many times, whether you knew it or not. I always knew I could show you the shitty side of my life. I didn't have to be perky or perfect with you."

That confirmed one of Leslie's theories, that the pressure put on Joe as a part of *Dance Machine* was more than he let on.

"You can tell me anything, Joe. You know that. Don't you know I get it? I know our lives have seemed different, but are they really? We're both under a microscope all the time, everyone watching, waiting for us to make a misstep and be the one to screw it up for other out athletes and artists." They'd both been in a place where people were okay knowing they were gay as long as it wasn't in their faces. His crush on Joe had been safe in a lot of ways.

"I know you get it. But, Leslie? Why do we only do this over the phone?"

"That's a good question," Leslie said, hoping Joe would fill in the blank.

"It *is* a good question. I guess my not-so-good answer is that I needed you, needed our connection, and I was terrified of what would happen if my lifeline was gone, if you decided you were done listening to my bullshit, tired of a long-distance whatever the fuck we're doing." Joe laughed and ran his hand through his wavy hair. "I don't know what I would do without you in my life, Leslie Payton, and I'm terrified I'll fuck it up face-to-face."

The air left Leslie's lungs. Joe had never been this open with him. He wasn't telling Leslie anything he hadn't thought was probably true, but he'd never said it, not this boldly.

"I hate it that you feel that way, but I'm glad to hear you say it. I always worried you didn't...that it wouldn't be a big deal if we drifted apart, you know? Like, one day you might change your number, tell me you'd...found someone."

Joe shook his head vigorously. "No, Les. No. It's always been you. It was only ever going to *be* you." His eyes widened. "God, Leslie, say something. I can't believe I'm telling you all of this standing alone in a damn parking lot while you're thousands of miles away."

Leslie looked down at himself. He was still mostly dressed. "I could see if they could fly me home now. I could be there in a couple of hours. I could—"

"No, babe. You need to get some rest. You've got a big job when you get back. Your players, man..." He rolled his eyes and whistled, shaking his head. "Out of shape. They need work."

Leslie threw his head back and laughed. "I've only had the whole team for a couple of practices. Don't worry. They'll be in tip-top shape for our first game Friday. Question is, will your team be ready to cheer them on to victory?"

"Oh, we'll be ready. We've got tryouts Wednesday. We'll likely just be in T-shirts for Friday's game, but we'll be ready to bring it."

"And soon we'll gallivant."

Joe grinned. "Soon we'll gallivant. A for-real date. I can't wait."

"Me neither. You need to get home before some wayward tractor runs you over or something random like that."

Joe looked around. "It's beyond dead out here. I think maybe four cars have passed the whole time we've been talking. Fine, I'll start walking. Stay on the phone with me, though. You know, in case I get lost."

They both laughed at that. Ayre Valley was tiny. A main street with one stoplight and a population of approximately three thousand five hundred people, not including the students living on campus, which made up another thousand. Joe had to jaywalk across the main road and walk about a half mile through houses before he'd be on campus, and then it was about a quarter mile to his apartment in the dorm. They traded jabs about each other's teams and Joe filled him in further on practice that afternoon.

"Your players reached out to Terrell, but I really hope they cut him some slack about his choice to focus on dance rather than football. It's a sensitive subject for him."

"I get it. I will nip it in the bud if I hear anything. I'm not going to tolerate any homophobic bullshit, you know that."

"Yeah, and Randy made that clear. Some of the players changed their tune after hearing they would be off the team. I'm so glad. I hoped it wouldn't be a big thing, you know? That they'd just shut up and work, and they did. But for Terrell, he had some incidents. Kids trying to rough him up, you know..."

"No, I didn't. I can't believe his teammates—"

"They never came right out and beat him up, but they got physical. To test him. Some fucking guys just have to push."

Joe was holding the phone out in front of him and watching where he was going, but Leslie could see the set of his jaw in the streetlight.

"You talk like you know from experience."

Joe groaned. "Old news. I told you I hated football players when you met me, remember?"

"I do," Leslie said. "I remember you saying we were all 'homophobic misogynists playing a homoerotic sport with homo erectus brains and homogenous stupidity.' Am I leaving anything out?"

Joe snorted. "No. I think that was about right. And yeah, you changed my mind about certain football players, but Les, you have to admit many of your brethren are notorious for bad behavior."

"I cannot argue with that," Leslie said, picking up an edge in Joe's voice.

"You can't because it's true. I can tell you, it's true."

"Since we're being open and honest while thousands of miles stand between us," Leslie said, hoping he wasn't pushing his luck. "Did someone hurt you, Joe? I've always wondered."

Joe blew out a harsh breath as he came to a stop, looked both ways, and continued to walk, this time a little more forcefully, it seemed.

"Yeah, Leslie, I've had to fight off the unwanted advances and tests of my manhood by more than one professional athlete. And before you ask, yes, I was successful in evading them. But how many guys like me aren't? How many gay men have been bullied and abused by other men who are so frightened someone will think they're not macho enough, nor as straight as they purport themselves to be? It fucking pisses me off to no end. You know, that's part of the reason I took this damn job. Marti reminded me of the shit Terrell had been through and was worried about him starting college and having to go through the same shit."

Leslie cursed and pressed his fingers into his forehead just above the eyebrows. "It's gotta stop. I'm not going to let anyone get hurt like that, not on my watch."

"You can't be everywhere, though. All you can do is lead by example and when someone fucks up, show them no mercy. If more of these assholes had limits set for them when they were younger, who knows? Maybe things would be better."

Their beautiful conversation had turned dark, but Leslie counted it as a win that Joe was finally opening up to him. He just wished he was there before him, beside him, to walk with him and show him how serious this was to him. All of it.

"You know, talking with you all of these years changed me in a lot of ways, but probably the most important was that you gave me the motivation to confront toxic masculinity and stop letting it get past me. There's gotta be a way to change this terrible dynamic in our corner of society or at least make a dent."

Joe sighed and smiled, still not looking at the phone. "If anyone can do it, it's you. Dammit Leslie, you've changed my mind from thinking it will never get better to having hope. Why do you do this to me? Before I met you, I was content being this pessimistic ogre and you make me see things can be better. Why, dammit, why?"

Leslie burst out laughing, which made Joe laugh, and the tension was gone.

"You make it to campus yet?"

"Almost. I'm near Jacket Pond. Man, that little house was going to be fun," Joe said. "I love that you had it all ready for me."

"I hate that it was ruined. I heard from Brother Barry that they're going to have to rebuild all three cottages from the ground up. Too much structural damage."

"Oh. Man. Oh well. The dorm isn't so bad. I don't have to set an alarm, I have the shortest commute ever, and I don't even have to cook if I don't want to continue eating clean."

"Look at you, all positive and shit," Leslie said with a laugh. "We'll figure something out if you want to get off campus. Maybe there's a house for rent—"

"It's fine," Joe said. "At least I can sneak off campus, right? And gallivant."

Leslie flushed and his slacks were real tight now. He thought about Joe's last visit to his house, and he thought about what might happen if he actually came inside next time. What if he spent the night? What if he...moved in?

But he was getting ahead of himself and he needed to slow down.

Slow and steady wins the race, Payton.

"Okay, I made it to Higdon. Oh, sounds like Matty's got some friends over. God, I hope I can get past without them noticing—Oh hey, what's up? No, thanks, heading to bed. Good night." He slammed the door and Leslie laughed. "Phew, that was a close one."

"You're hilarious. Listen, I'm glad my brother called tonight on your phone, but you might want to change your password—"

"I don't have it password protected. It's old."

"You might want to check your pictures then."

Joe frowned at the screen and then his eyes went wide. "Oh my God, is that his nipple?"

"Probably. Randy is notorious at planting gems like that on unsuspecting phones. I'd suggest you add some security if you're going to be out drinking with my brothers."

"Duly noted. Hey, I hope that wasn't too weird. I was trying to be, um, what's the word? Congenital? Congenial? Collegial?"

"Right. You sure you only had two beers?"

Joe rolled his eyes. "Listen, my old-ass unprotected battery is about to die, or I'd take you to bed with me and make you talk to me until I fall asleep, but that would be selfish since you need to rest. What time are you going to be back tomorrow?"

"Early. I've got to go over films with my coaches before practice. We've only got three days until the game and they start classes Wednesday. Plus, we've got fundraising to do."

"Right. We've got a head start on you guys. You need to catch up."

Les grinned. "Already working on it. Get some sleep, Twinkle Toes. I'll see you tomorrow."

"Goodnight, Leslie. And thank you."

"For what?"

And Joe's phone either died or he hung up, Leslie wasn't sure. What he *did* know was that they'd had a major breakthrough. Not only were they going to have a getaway weekend, but Joe agreed to give this thing between them a real shot.

He was about to score in all the ways that mattered: a winning team and the guy of his dreams. He drifted off to sleep believing there was no possible way he could lose...and that maybe he believed that because the alternative was unacceptable.

Seventeen

J^{oe}

Joe fell asleep with a smile on his face and woke up with a scowl. It was his last day to sleep in before classes started and his phone started ringing off the hook as the sun rose in the sky.

First had been the director of *Dance Machine* calling from his apartment in New York, forgetting Joe was an hour behind, confirming Joe would appear for the October weekend. Joe had kept his tone light and friendly while he was growling inside. He let him know he'd be flying in that Saturday morning and that he had to leave directly after the show on Sunday so he could be back in time for school, which led to a whole conversation about his decision to put his career on hold for this job. Not the subject Joe wanted to discuss bright and early on a Tuesday morning.

Next was Marti asking about football practice the night before since they hadn't had time to chat when he'd stopped into clinics. Fifteen new kids had showed up to clinics—including the B-boys from the club the other night. It was a great start. More would likely show up today and then tryouts tomorrow would be a breeze.

"Your son blew the players away."

Marti chuckled. "He is pretty incredible, isn't he?"

Joe's heart tightened a little at the warmth in her voice. If he would have had a mom like her...

"He is, but he'll be trying out like all the others. Can't have his head getting big."

Marti laughed. "Without a doubt. See you this afternoon."

He moved to get out of bed and groaned. Yeah, he was definitely paying for his showboating the day before. He was about to start his morning stretches when his phone buzzed again.

"Hello?"

"It's Arthur, Joe. How are you?"

He flopped back on his bed. He wasn't sure he had the energy to talk to anyone else this morning much less the rest of the week.

"Hey, you're up early. How's California?"

"It's lonely without you, is that what you want to hear?"

Joe barked out a laugh. Arthur Frye, Joe's long-time manager from Slade Artist Management, was almost as sarcastic as he was. Almost.

"Sure. I want to know you're suffering without me."

"My sleep certainly has. You talked to Duncan about the October *Dance Machine* appearance?"

"I did, he was call number one this morning. I'm all set."

"How will you be arriving? I understand you're out in the middle of nowhere. Do you need me to take care of your flight?"

"No, I can handle the flight. Either Leslie and I will be flying out of Kansas City or—"

"Leslie?"

Oh. He'd said it out loud. He'd wanted to try it out. "Leslie and I." He wasn't sure Arthur was the best person for him to inform of his change in status from perpetually single to possibly in a relationship of indeterminate definition, but it was out and he figured all he could do now was go for it.

"Mm-hmm. Leslie Payton. He's coming with me. If you can book our hotel room, that would be great."

Tee hee. He was relieved this conversation wasn't happening on video call as his face was burning. Joe Judd, thirty-six-year-old man giggling about his new boyfriend.

"Leslie Payton the, um, quarterback?"

"Former quarterback. Currently the head football coach at Greenvale College."

"*Riiiiight.* He's coming with you to LA because...?"

Arthur was great at his job and he mostly kept his opinions on his clients' personal lives to himself, but Joe was sure he'd shocked his manager and friend with this revelation.

"I invited him." Yeah, he was being coy. He couldn't help himself.

"And I'm only booking one room? Uh, Joe? How long have you been in Iowa?" Arthur's voice went way up at the end of that question.

"A week? But, uh, Leslie and I have known each other for a long time."

"Ah."

"Like, fifteen years long time."

"Ah—*Oh.* Okay. You sure you're ready for this? You know the press is going to go wild."

The press. Joe wasn't sure how he felt about it. He definitely wasn't sure how Leslie would feel. They'd both kept their private lives out of the media for the most part. Not that Joe had much of a private life to speak of. There had been rumors about him and a couple of his co-stars in the past and he'd dealt with it by making flippant comments. He figured if he didn't take it seriously it wouldn't get to him. But was it fair to Leslie to expose him to the wolves at the beginning of his first season with the Jackets? And what about this fundraiser battle? If they ended up all over the news as an item, how would that affect their football vs cheer competition?

"You make good points, Arthur, once again reminding me why I hired you."

"You did, and as your manager, and I will do what you ask, but I can't control the media. On a personal level, I'm happy for you and I wish you well. But maybe this isn't the best time to go public. I also have something else to discuss with you."

Joe climbed out of bed and stretched. "Thanks and yeah, hit me."

"Guillermo Diaz called me."

Joe's ears perked up. Guillermo was his producer from the limited run of *West Side Story* over the summer. Joe loved working with him. He had a fantastic eye for detail and was really supportive of the dancers.

"And?"

"He was curious about your job at the college because he's got you in mind for a new project."

Joe stood a little straighter. "I'm listening."

"He's going to be auditioning principal dancers for *Kinky Boots* and he wants to see you. This could be huge, Joe."

"*Kinky Boots*?" His heart pounded in his chest. "Give me the details."

Joe stalked around his apartment the rest of the day until clinics. He left Leslie's texts unanswered as he brooded.

Not only was he going to have to tell Leslie that he was hasty in inviting him to LA, but he also had some difficult decisions to make. Arthur's call reminded him that taking this coaching job likely meant the end of his dancing career, a move he wasn't ready to make, not really. His mind ran through any possible scenarios where he could do the show...

"Hey, Joe, where you going with that gun in your hand?"

Matty gave him finger guns as he approached, singing the off-color song off-key.

Joe smirked and waved. He wasn't in the mood for shirtless Matty and his flirty finger guns.

"I take it it's going to be loud in here?"

"Yep. Really loud." Joe didn't care if he came across as an asshole. He needed to set a boundary with this guy. "I'll give you the practice schedule, but until we have the athletic center rebuilt, this is what we've got. I'm sure you understand."

"Rah rah," Matty said, pumping a fist. Joe started to protest but Matty held up his hands. "I'm just kidding. Cheer on, dude."

Joe waved and entered the lounge, instantly feeling better the moment the bright sun hit his face through the large windows. The air conditioning worked really well, surprisingly, in Higdon, sometimes leaving him with goose bumps. He set down his things and lay on the floor on his back, just letting his body melt into the wood before running through some easy stretches. The sun felt great on his skin and the warm spot on the floor helped loosen his stiff and sore muscles and joints. It only slightly melted his foul mood.

"Hey, Coach."

Joe turned his head to find an upside-down Leslie.

"Oh," he said, scrambling to his feet. Too fast, apparently. "Head rush. Hang on."

Leslie put a hand under Joe's elbow and for a moment, Joe wished he could fall into Leslie's arms and be swept away.

"You need to sit. Have you had water?"

"Yeah, I'm fine." He couldn't help smiling as he gazed into Leslie's worried eyes. "I'm...hi."

"Hey," Leslie said, grinning. "I had a few minutes before practice. I wanted to—"

He let go of Joe's arm just as the door swung open and the cheerleaders and hopefuls began trickling in.

"Clinics," Joe said, putting his hands on his lower back. "Tryouts are tomorrow."

"Right. I, um. I just wanted to touch base..."

Joe sucked in a breath as all the things he needed to say to Leslie flooded his brain.

"Absolutely. I'll have to give you a call."

"Hey, Coach," Terrell said as he came in. He let his bag slip to the floor. "Your team walking okay after yesterday?"

"I'll find out soon, I guess?" he said, then he frowned, likely in confusion as Joe was doing a terrible job of playing it cool.

"Right, well, let us know. We'll try harder next time." Joe grinned at him but it slipped the moment hurt passed Leslie's face.

"Sure. Sorry to keep you. We can catch up later." Les waved to the kids and started to leave.

"Oh, uh, I'll walk out with you. Terrell? You'll get them started?"

Terrell nodded and strolled over to turn the music on.

Joe slipped out the door and followed Leslie.

"Hey, sorry." He smiled, but Leslie still looked confused.

"What's going on? I thought—"

"You thought right," Joe said and exhaled. "I'm sorry. It's been a day. Can I swing by later?"

"I'm going to be working late. It seems MidAmerica have a new quarterback and I have no film on him so I've got Sandy doing research. We'll probably be at it all night. I can call—"

"It's okay. I know you're busy. We'll catch up...sometime?" Joe laughed nervously.

Leslie turned and attempted to block the view of oncoming traffic. He started to speak and was interrupted.

"Coach Payton? We're meeting on the soccer field?"

"Yeah, Danny. I'll be right there."

The kid's eyes lit up when he saw Joe. "Thanks for the workout last night, Coach Judd." He waved and trotted out the door.

"What's going on?" Leslie asked. "Did something happen?"

Joe opened his mouth to speak—though he wasn't sure whether he would have come clean—and a larger group of footballers came pounding down the steps.

"Coach!" they all yelled.

"You're all about to be late. You better hope you beat me there."

The kids paused for a nanosecond and then ran like hell.

"Wow, they sure move fast"

"I'm sorry, I've gotta go."

"It's okay," Joe said, backing away. "I'll catch up with you soon." He stumbled over a football straggler and Leslie laughed.

"I...I'll see you later."

Leslie turned and left without looking back.

Fuck. Fucking fuck to the fuckedyth power. How the hell was he going to make Leslie understand their weekend escape was a bad idea? Without hurting his feelings?

Joe returned to clinics grateful he had something else to focus on because this whole unraveling sensation was terrifying.

"Hey, the kids all here?"

Marti startled him and he pressed a hand to his chest.

"You look like you've seen a ghost," Marti said, her brow furrowed. "Are you feeling okay?"

"Fine. Yeah, I'm sorry. It's been a morning. I just, my director for *West Side Story* wants me to audition for a show. Broadway."

"That's..." She reached out and put her hand on his forearm. "That seems like a lot. I thought you were committed here for the year."

He exhaled and planted his hands on his hips. "But what if I can make both work? Not during the fall, of course, but like a summer show..."

"Joe, FOMO is real, I get it. But can you give your all in both places? And *Dance Machine*? The kids need you here, especially since you're teaching courses."

Was it fear of missing out? "Right...I know. I just...I feel like this is it, then, you know? My dance career is over."

She gave him a sympathetic smile and then the music got louder inside the common room and Joe realized he needed to face the music, in more ways than one.

He'd taken the job because he felt obligated to the school and the kids...and Leslie. It meant finally having time and proximity with Leslie to see if their relationship would blossom, which was very important to him. He'd thought he could find a way to keep one toe in the dance world. A lot of college professors did that, right? They still played music, or had their art in gallery shows, or wrote books... Sure, Joe's art required him to be away at times. He wasn't ready to close the door completely, especially not if it was Broadway. If auditions were in March, rehearsals in May, maybe they could be pushed to late May for Joe, the show would open in June and run for ten weeks. It should be plenty of time. Joe could stay in shape on the off-season with his workouts with the kids. It could work. Arthur seemed to think so. He would need to discuss it with Barry, of course.

And Leslie.

Shit. His expression had seemed so confused earlier, which would make sense after the candid conversation they'd had the night before. Joe had meant everything he'd said. He really *did* want Leslie, wanted that intimacy they had to grow, wanted that familiar comfort to be a daily part of his life. Did that necessarily have to mean giving up his career?

He was right back where he'd been the night they'd met. Running. That wasn't fair to Leslie.

Joe stepped inside and was faced with thirty-five kids looking to him for leadership, support, and knowledge. It hit him suddenly just what he'd taken on by coming here. This job wasn't another gig, wasn't a notch on his belt. It was his chance to give back to the community that supported him during a tumultuous time in his life, that had given him the foundation he needed to launch a successful career.

It was a big responsibility, one that had sounded plausible over the summer as he'd pondered it, but now, with thirty-five sets of eyes—including Terrell and the daughter of the guy he'd bought his Bronco from—waiting anxiously to see what he'd do next, he was humbled. No one was expecting him to be a superstar here; they wanted to *learn* from him. They didn't care how his makeup and hair looked, if his body was the right size and in the best shape... They only cared that he cared about them and that he provide for them the level of support he'd had when he was a student.

He could do this. Nothing else mattered right now. This was important work, bigger than himself. Maybe that was the phase of his career he needed to ease into next. Broadway would have to take a backseat.

"All right, Jackets! Show me what you've got."

The whole group lined up and ran through the three cheers Marti had taught them the day before. They looked good. Only a couple of weak links in the group and they were mostly guys. Today they would be working on some simple stunts so Joe could get a sense of their strength and dependability.

"Great job, everyone. Take a seat."

The kids sat together, smiling eagerly up at him, hanging on every word.

"I want to share with you my philosophy. From what I can see, and from my experience, any of you can learn the cheers we have to teach you. Most of you can pick up the dance routines, and some of you will become proficient in tumbling and stunting. But what's more important to me than any of that, is that I have to know I can trust you. That your teammates can trust you. For you to make it on this team, I have to know that if I put you as a spotter, you're not going to let one of the flyers hit the ground, not even one hair on their head touches the mat. I have to know that if we have an away game, you're going to be there with your uniform clean, pressed, the right shoes, and even the correct bow in your hair. Ability to cheer and dance is not the end all be all. Integrity is important. Creativity is important. Attitude really is everything. I will not jeopardize any member of my team by allowing someone to compete who I can't rely on, that the team can't rely on. I'm asking you to put cheerleading first after your studies. I'm asking you to be willing to miss parties, and I'm absolutely asking you to be on your best behavior. You will be representing Greenvale College twenty-four seven. There is no room for bad behavior on my team. That may sound harsh, and if so, thank you for your time and there's the door. If you need to ask what I mean about bad behavior, I'm happy to discuss it with you, but it absolutely means being sober during the season. At all times. Even if you are of age. Now...are there any questions?"

A few of the kids looked around as if they were thinking of bolting, but Joe was pleased to see that most of the kids just seemed excited to get started. They all gathered around waiting for instructions. The B-boys, however, moved away from the group and muttered to themselves.

Joe looked to Marti to start discussing stunting roles so he could head his prospects off at the pass.

"Hey," he said to them. "Be real with me, which part of that speech did you guys have a problem with?"

The three boys looked at each other and Ivan sighed. "Look, Coach, we've got a DJ business going and we were hoping to book gigs on weekend nights when we didn't have games."

That was not at all what Joe was worried about. "Okay, so we go over the schedule together and you make sure it doesn't interfere."

They looked at each other and David cleared his throat.

"We, uh, can't guarantee there won't be certain—"

"Substances?" Joe figured he'd help him out. "I'm not asking you to control other people, but if you can agree to stay away from substances yourselves and to avoid trouble with the cops, I'm willing to compromise."

David shrugged, Ivan nodded, and Gino answered for them, "Yeah, Coach. We can agree to that."

"Cool, now...I'm going to go over stunting with the group, but I want you guys to show me some of the partner stunts you do in your dance battles. I'd love to get creative. I don't want to only use the tired old stuff for our competition routine."

The guys shrugged. "You got it, boss."

Joe chuckled and then the guys broke into a flurry of movement that captivated the entire group. Joe stood next to Marti and they pointed out moves they thought they could work with. When the boys started to flag after just a couple of songs, Joe laughed.

"And this, my friends, is why you can expect to spend hours conditioning with me. You'll be in the best shape of your lives this season. I can promise you that." There were a few groans. "Now, let's get an idea of what we have to work with. How many of you have experience as flyers?"

Five of the returning girls and four of the incoming girls raised their hands.

"Good, that's good. How many of you have had experience as a base?"

The five returning guys raised their hands as well as Terrell, but that was it.

"All right, then. Let's head over to the gym and see what we can do."

Joe and Marti spent the next two hours pairing up different kids together. Terrell shared some ideas that the group seemed to get excited about, and Joe found himself thrilled with the prospects he had to work with. He was tempted to take them all so he had reserves. He'd seen other colleges do that, have stand-ins available in case of injuries. They could have separate teams to hit all of the sports on campus so no one was overwhelmed. Barry had said he had carte blanche, and though the budget was lacking this year, he could work with it. They'd raised nearly thirty-thousand dollars in one day, and funds were continuing to roll in from his friends and colleagues. They were *so* going to beat the football team.

Oh, Leslie, winning will be sweet...

Joe was excited...for the first time in a long time. It was different than nailing a performance, or looking forward to a show. It was an act of creation he was joyful about. The only thing close to this had been when he watched the performers on *Dance Machine* land the routines he taught them. That made him happy, too, but this was on a whole other level. It felt organic, not forced. It was real, this life, this job, not something fabricated for network television. These cheerleaders were nothing like the dancers he shared the stage with on Broadway or on tour. They were naive and innocent and had no idea the potential they possessed.

He wanted to call Leslie and talk to him about it. No, he wanted to see him face-to-face and discuss his feelings while holding hands. Maybe even cuddle on a couch somewhere while giving Leslie a foot massage.

Say what now? That was some domestic shit he'd never envisioned himself enjoying before. Not true, he'd had some fantasies about playing house with Leslie in the past. But this was real. He could actually do this.

Joe got through the rest of the clinic, flying high despite his body's protesting the demonstrations he'd done with a flyer named Krista and the three or four times he'd caught a kid's full weight because the spotters were just learning how to get in there and catch. By the end of the night, the kids were pumped and left chattering excitedly about the tryouts the next day and how much they wanted a chance to shine.

"Damn, Joe. I didn't think you could still do all that."

He grinned at Marti and clenched his teeth.

"I wasn't sure I could. I'm definitely not sure I can sit down and be able to get up again."

Her smile disappeared. "What do you need? Ice? Advil?"

He waved a hand at her. "Nah, I'll be fine. I'm just going to stretch out a bit and then hit the shower."

"Don't forget dinner."

Joe looked at his watch. It was already 7:50, meaning The Buzz was closed. He hadn't made it to the grocery store and there was no food delivery in town.

"Ah...yeah. I'll figure something out."

Marti rolled her eyes. "Don't let this be the start of your downfall, Joe. We're no spring chickens. We need to take care of ourselves. I'm going to say goodbye to Terrell and get home unless you need anything?"

"Hey, Marti? What do you think about keeping them all, having alternates, special teams?"

She grinned. "Already a softie. I've seen it done, and it's not a bad idea. I'll back whatever you decide. Let's talk again tomorrow morning. Good luck with your first classes tomorrow."

"Thanks." He cringed a little remembering he had a basic flexibility class in the morning for the PE department and a beginning dance course the kids could take for fine arts credit. Barry had suggested they start slow when they talked last spring, and so Joe agreed three classes plus the cheerleading would be best. On the alternate days, he'd teach Hip Hop. All three of his classes had waitlists. The hope was there would be enough interest to offer more the following year and to start a degree program.

Which was the kind of long-term planning Joe wasn't sure he was prepared for. The only plans he wanted to make at the moment included how he could see Leslie and apologize for their earlier conversation. He pulled out his phone and texted before he chickened out.

I've been told we do have to eat at some point. Have you done so?

Joe was heading out of the common room after stretching a bit and packing up his things and about to give up on a response when his phone buzzed.

Mom packed us spaghetti. There's some left if you have time to come by my classroom.

Joe did a little victory dance and rapped, "Palms are sweaty. Mom's Spaghetti." He asked where and when. Leslie answered they'd be taking a break soon, giving Joe enough time to shower and hopefully unclench the muscles in his lower back. By the time he jogged across campus, he felt like he might make it. He felt like he was winning today and Leslie was his victory prize.

Eighteen

L eslie

"You could drive a goddamned semi through that line. What were they thinking? And how did he miss that block? Oh, come on!"

Randy was at that point in the night when he was up and pacing and shouting at the screen. Sandy was at his point in the night when he was alternatively pulling his hair out and plugging his ears shouting, "Shut up, dude. I can't even think when you do that!"

Leslie balled up a piece of paper and chucked it at Randy's head. "Simmer down over there. Let's just get through this last film and call it a night."

"But seriously! How are these kids going to protect him when they are too busy doing the cha-cha or whatever the fuck they're doing is that's *not* holding the line?!"

"Pipe down," Leslie shouted, chucking more paper wads at Randy, who ducked.

The wad bounced off Joe's forehead and he caught it in his fist.

"Wow. Am I interrupting?"

Randy cursed, Sandy told him to shut up again, and Leslie paused the film on the screen.

"Actually, I think you just saved me," Leslie muttered. He pushed himself up to standing and switched on the lights. "You two get out of here. I'll see you at home. We'll finish in the morning."

"Uh, classes start tomorrow. You have conference at nine and one on Wednesdays, remember?"

Leslie's cheeks heated and he ran a hand through his hair. "Right." He really wished Joe hadn't been there to hear that. "Thank you." He leaned his weight onto his elbows on the table and sighed, his hands clasped in front of him.

"Okay, we'll see you at home." Sandy got the hint and practically dragged Randy out of the room. Joe stepped aside as they passed and waved at them.

"I'm sorry, I didn't mean to interrupt—"

"You want some of this spaghetti?"

"No, thank you. I grabbed a protein bar after my shower. I just…Les, I'm sorry about earlier."

Leslie held up his hand and shook his head. "Stop it. It's fine. I know we have to be careful in front of the kids." He dropped his face into his hands. "I'm just tired."

"Hey," Joe said, moving swiftly through the tables. "Are you having a migraine?"

Leslie just grunted. He'd been trying to ignore it all afternoon. "I was trying to push through it. So much to do today."

Joe stepped behind him and shushed him. He placed his hands on Leslie's shoulders. "Shoulder rub, or want me to focus on your head?"

"You don't have to—"

"Not here? Okay, shall I drive you home, or are you coming back to my place? Because I'm not leaving you alone."

Leslie had spent all day in a funk. First, he'd had a bumpy flight home from Dallas and then he was unsure what had happened between the previous night's conversation and seeing Joe this morning. And then he cursed himself for letting it affect him. He had huge responsibilities on his shoulders at the moment and he couldn't afford to let his personal life put him in a foul mood. He'd seen firsthand where that road led. What if he lashed out at someone? What if that someone was a student?

"Leslie?"

"I'm okay. You don't have to take care of me." He stood up and towered over Joe, but Joe didn't back down.

"I don't *have* to do anything, you big lug. I want to. Now, either you let me try a couple of things here, or we go back to my place, or I drive you home. But you're not getting rid of me until my sunshine's back."

"Sunshine?"

"Mm-hmm. I have come to require a dose of Leslie Payton sunshine daily. I haven't had any today, and I know you wouldn't want me going to bed without my daily requirements." Joe wrapped his arms around Leslie's torso and sighed as he pressed his cheek to Les's chest.

Leslie chuckled and hugged him back, thinking there was something to this daily requirement. Joe's damp hair brushed his chin and Leslie inhaled deeply, loving the Joe Judd cocoon treatment.

"I like doing this. I wouldn't be at all opposed to doing it daily. But seriously, you don't have to drive me home. I'm okay, just tired."

Joe looked up with a frown. "It takes a fibber to know a fibber. I know you're used to covering it up when you have a migraine. I get it, you don't want people to worry or think you're a mess, but Leslie, I'm not people. I'm Joe. I'm here for you, at least I want to be. Won't you let me take care of you?"

Leslie dropped his head until their foreheads were touching. "I don't ever want to be a burden on you, Joe. You or anyone. Having said that, I would love to feel your hands on my head for a little while."

"Then let me drive you home, babe."

Leslie wanted to argue but he wanted more time with Joe and damn his body for not cooperating. He looked around at his classroom and figured he'd be here early enough to get it set up. He put an arm around Joe's shoulders and allowed himself to be led out the door.

"My car's in the Higdon lot. How about I drive you in yours? It's closer."

Leslie handed him the keys. He didn't have it in him to argue. Joe stood behind him as he climbed up into the cab of his truck and he chuckled as he sat down.

"You look so small down there, Twinkle Toes."

Joe rolled his eyes. "Watch your feet, Sasquatch."

Leslie barked out a laugh, but it ricocheted around his brain, making the pain more intense. He reclined the seat back and let his eyes fall closed. Joe made a crack about mountain climbing before shutting his door and starting the truck. Leslie was so tired, he muttered his address, but he wasn't sure if he said San Mateo, which was his home during his 49ers years, or if he said State Route 2, which was his current home. Regardless, the next thing he remembered was Joe pulling open his door.

"Now don't squish me, Sasquatch." Joe caught his weight as Leslie slid out of the cab and stumbled a bit.

"I should probably drive the Lincoln for a while, especially if you're taking me home. Could you reach the pedals?"

Joe poked him in the side and pulled Leslie's arm over his shoulders. "At five-eleven, I am taller than the average male, for your information."

"How tall is the average male?" Leslie asked. "I would have thought six feet."

"Nope. It's five-nine. I checked. My manager kept telling me I was not getting parts because I was too tall, and I thought for sure I was short."

"So two inches makes or breaks a dance career, huh?"

Joe snorted. "Two inches makes a big difference, Leslie. Size does matter."

Leslie groaned as he pushed open the front door.

"Mom will be in bed; who knows about my brothers. I'm upstairs and to the left."

He led Joe to the massive staircase that took up the middle of the first floor. There was a library and dining room off to the left and to the right was the formal sitting room and the master suite where Agnes stayed. The kitchen, family room, and game room spanned the entire back of the house. Leslie and Joe made their way slowly up the stairs giggling about inches and sizes until they reached the top. The door to the twins' wing was shut and Leslie shushed Joe when he heard their voices.

"Let's not invite trouble."

And then he knocked into a table and a glass of water fell over, spilling all over the rug. The twins' door flew open and they barreled through the opening together.

"What the—"

"Shhh, you'll wake Mom."

"Boys?"

Agnes came into view at the bottom of the stairs and Leslie sighed.

"Sorry, Mom."

"Oh, I didn't know we had company." She raised an eyebrow expectantly and pulled her robe shut to cover up her Motley Crüe T-shirt. Her long silver-streaked blonde hair was piled up in a messy bun and her bright smile lit up the room. At sixty-seven, she was so beautiful, so incredibly beautiful...and happy. Happy as she'd been when Leslie and Barry were boys and Rick Payton was in his prime with the San Francisco 49ers. Happy as she'd been when Rick retired and she'd looked forward to their life together really starting. He liked to see her happy, but it also reminded him of the times she wasn't. When Rick started having headaches, when his mood changed and he became violent. When he had been diagnosed with Parkinson's and early onset dementia. When he died at the age of fifty-two from a stroke and what turned out to be complications of Chronic Traumatic Encephalopathy.

Leslie teared up at how beautiful and happy she looked in that moment, that she could be happy still after what she'd been through. His stomach clenched at the terrifying thought that he could put her through that again.

When Leslie didn't speak, Joe stepped forward with a smile.

"Sorry, Mrs. Payton. I was just seeing Leslie home. I'm Joe."

"It's great to finally meet you, Joe! I look forward to chatting with you. Soon. Leslie was supposed to invite you to dinner."

"Sorry, Mom."

God, he was a forty-five-year-old man living with his mother and just got caught sneaking his boyfriend up to his room.

"It's fine, honey. I'm gonna get back to *Criminal Minds*. Good night!"

She trotted back to the bedroom and shut her door and the twins broke out laughing.

"Busted."

"Don't worry," Sandy said. "We'll get this cleaned up. You should get some rest." His smile melted as he apparently recognized the fact that Joe was supporting Leslie's weight and this wasn't a social call. "Do you need anything?"

Leslie frowned. *Don't say anything*, he tried to telegraph to his brother. Joe knew he had migraines. He didn't need to know anything else.

"We're good."

"Good night," Joe said and he looked up at Leslie expectantly.

Leslie gave one last warning look to his brothers and they scattered. Then he led Joe toward his suite of rooms and opened the double doors. There was a family room of sorts in the middle, a small kitchenette and half bath off to the right, bedroom off to the left with a full bathroom en suite including a jacuzzi tub. Which sounded great right now, but not as great as Joe's hands.

"Please forgive the mess, please forgive my brothers, and for the love of God, please forgive the fact that I live with my mom."

Joe burst out laughing and then covered his mouth. "Oh, I'm sorry. Wait, you're serious about that?"

Les rolled his eyes and stepped away from Joe. "Have a seat, I'm going to...um, I'll be right back."

"Is there a bathroom?"

"Yeah, there's one around here or in my bedroom."

They stared at each other for a minute and Joe pressed his lips together, fighting off a smile. "You look like you're about to drop. The only thing that's happening in your bedroom is me tucking you in tonight, got it?"

Leslie's cheeks heated—he was an open book for Joe. "Right."

Joe walked around the kitchenette to the half bathroom and shut the door.

Leslie hurried to the cabinet where he kept his nighttime pill box, and started popping pills as fast as he could get them down. He guzzled three quarters of a bottle of water trying to get through them all and was just closing the lid when Joe came out. Leslie tried shove the pill box into a drawer but it kept catching. He smiled and tried to look innocent, but Joe raised an eyebrow.

"You really keep your trophies in the bathroom?"

Leslie barked out a laugh, left the drawer open and turned off the light in the kitchen on his way around the counter.

"Seemed appropriate. Look, Joe, I'm sorry you had to come all the way out here. I can get Sandy to drive you back."

Joe held up Leslie's keys. "I can get back when I'm ready. I came here to take care of you. Now where would you like your Joe Judd Migraine Special?"

Oh, yes, please. "Um, here? I guess?"

Leslie led Joe over to the overstuffed leather sectional and they sat next to each other. Joe turned his body, kicked his shoes off, and tucked a leg up under him.

"What do I need to do?"

"May I touch you?" Joe asked, his voice low.

Leslie whimpered and then cleared his throat. "Yeah," he said, his voice raspy. He rubbed his sweaty hands on his black khakis. He'd decided on the black khakis, white polo shirts with the blue and gold Jackets logo for the coaching staff and Sandy had outfitted them all. He preferred a uniform to having to pick out dress shirts and ties, but he loved his band tees and denim or Carhartt work clothes around the house. Right now, he just hoped Joe couldn't see the telltale signs he was nervous.

Joe waited for him to settle and then held out his hand. "Give me your right hand; we'll start there."

Leslie rubbed his pants again, hoping his hands weren't as clammy as they felt.

Joe simply smiled and began moving his joints around gently, bending his fingers, feeling around the major knuckles and minor connections between bones.

"Relax and let me do the work, okay?"

"What are you...*ow.*"

Joe pressed his thumb into the space between Leslie's index finger and thumb, up against the bone.

"Acupressure. You ever try it?"

Leslie shook his head and sucked in a breath.

"I refuse to take pain medication," Joe said, his eyes trained on Leslie's hand. "My doctor sent me to a holistic center and I learned all about pressure points. There are several places in the hands and feet that can help mitigate the effects of a migraine. Let me work on these and I want you to close your eyes for me, okay?"

Leslie complied. He didn't care what Joe was doing, acupressure, witchcraft, satanic rituals, as long as he kept touching him. His hands were soft and nimble. And strong. They weren't as big as Leslie's, but he had enough strength to really apply pressure.

"Have you ever done guided imagery?"

Leslie shook his head and let it fall back against the couch. "Like meditation? I tried but it felt silly."

"I get that. But I think it does help to find your special place to go to when you're in pain. A place with no pain. Want to try?"

"I'll try anything you say, Joe, just don't stop touching me."

Joe chuckled. "Okay, then. All right, I want you to picture a blank movie screen in front of you. You're sitting in the seats—"

"Holding your hand?"

Joe sighed. "Yes, dear. You're holding my hand. Your eyes are focused on the screen and you're looking forward to the pictures appearing. When they do, you see light followed by deep, intense green. The green splits into leaves of all textures and shapes. The leaves pull away to expose a private slice of sand leading to crystal blue water before you."

Leslie's skin grew warmer and the pressure in his head dissipated as he literally felt the heat from the sun blanket his skin. He sank further into the couch and moaned. Joe had moved to his other hand and was making small circles with his thumbs in certain areas: his thumb, the pad between the index and middle finger, the palm of his hand...

He heard Joe's voice continue, but in his mind, he was already on that beach. Without knowing, Joe had taken him to his family's Hawaiian getaway, his father's first extravagant purchase after signing with the 49ers. Leslie and Barry spent a lot of time there with their mother while Rick Payton got knocked around on a football field. It was a place for them to escape and explore as boys, and then as they got older, it became a refuge when their mother needed space from their father's tirades.

"You're tensing up."

"Mmm sorrr..." Leslie could barely make his mouth work to form words. He was too far away, wishing that the two chairs in the sand with a large umbrella between them were occupied by him and Joe. He wanted to see Joe there, splayed out on a towel on a lounge chair, his golden skin covered with fine dark hair. Maybe he wore swim trunks, or if it was just them, maybe he was covered only by a sarong. Maybe he'd pull it off and Leslie would chase him into the water where they would cling to each other in the surf and—

"Feeling better?"

"Mmmm?"

"Shhh. Don't open your eyes all the way. I've turned the lights down. Let me guide you to your bed. I'll have you lay down with your head at the foot of the bed so I can work on your neck."

Leslie did as he was told, leaning on Joe while they moved through the dark. His mind remained on that beach, in the sun, with the warm breeze caressing his skin. His shoes were tugged off and he imagined digging them in the sand, remembering how he and Barry used to bury each other up to their necks, how much he loved having that weight on him from the cool, damp sand in the hot Hawaiian afternoons. Hawaii was definitely a place of memories...

"Why didn't you come meet me in Hawaii, Joe?"

The beach faded to the dark room as he opened his eyes and the support of the sand on his neck changed to two points of pressure under the base of his skull—Joe's thumbs.

"Where did that come from?" Joe had paused his movements but now he began his thumb circles again, this time with a little less fluidity.

"My happy place is there, well, the place I went was my place in Hawaii. I wanted you to meet me there, but you said you had to go back to LA. You never told me why?"

Joe was quiet for a long time and the pressure began to be a bit much for Leslie. One thumb circle hit a particularly sore spot and Leslie winced, sucking in a breath.

"I'm sorry, babe. Here. Breathe in through your nose, out through your mouth, slowly and deeply." Joe began applying gentle pressure strokes over the top of Leslie's skull, somehow magically finding all of the tender spots and lovingly easing them.

"That feels so good."

"I was afraid to come meet you. No, keep your eyes closed. No, I can't talk to you about this if they're open, you're too close."

Leslie placed his hands over Joe's to still them. "I'm sorry. It's okay, whatever it was. I just always wondered."

Joe exhaled and sat back on his haunches. "I was afraid, Les. I knew if I came to you, I wouldn't want to leave."

Les smiled up at him, but kept his eyes closed. "Would that have been so terrible?"

"No, it would have been amazing. But Les, I wasn't ready. I knew if I went to Hawaii, spent time with you, it would be great...but it also would have been the end of my dance career. I wasn't ready for that."

"But I would have supported whatever you wanted to do. You know that. I just thought...well, *I* was ready. It's okay that you weren't—if you're not. I just wondered if it was something I said or did, if it was someone else."

"Well, it was Lady Gaga, Les. Come on. Do you blame me for running off to join her tour? That's what excuse I used to go back to LA. It was Lady G. I 'had' to go. That tour led to me doing the Super-bowl gig with her, remember?"

Les shuddered. "Yeah. I remember it well."

Joe sighed. "Really, though? I was afraid. I'm mostly not afraid anymore."

Les held Joe's hands still and he turned his face to kiss the inside of Joe's left wrist, then the right one. "You're here now. I'm so happy you're here now."

Joe leaned down and kissed his forehead. "I *am* here, and I'm not going anywhere, but I'm supposed to be helping you relax and go to sleep."

"Fine," Leslie said, dropping his hands. "I still want to take you there. To Hawaii. I want to show you my secret hideaway."

"I'd love to see your secret hideaway. Now go back there in your mind. You were almost rid of this tension."

"Thank you," Leslie sighed. "Thank you for taking care of me. Everything is better with you here."

Joe snorted. "You say that now..."

But he kept up the pressure and Leslie went back to the beach and frolicked in the waves with naked Joe and they kissed and touched each other until a really loud buzzing sound—

"What the?"

Leslie sat upright and found his five o'clock alarm going off. He was so confused. He was still in his clothes and socks, but he was laying on top of the duvet with a throw blanket tangled in his legs and...

Oh, Joe.

Joe had been there. He'd been helping Leslie manage his migraine, which was totally gone. He'd even placed a pillow underneath Leslie's head and covered him with a blanket. There was a note on his bedside table.

You are so peaceful when you sleep. So handsome. I hope the Joe Judd Migraine Special helped.

I'll see you later today. You'll have to come get your monster truck keys from me at some point.

Always,
   Joe

Leslie beamed through his workout and shower, grinned through his morning meds, smiled as he cheerfully greeted Agnes for breakfast, and even laughed at his brother's antics.

"What crawled up your ass and made you happy this morning? Wait...don't tell me—"

"Randall Lee Payton, you watch your mouth." Agnes lightly smacked Randy upside the head. Then she laughed when he found egg in his hair and stomped back upstairs to clean up again.

"You seem much better than you have most mornings lately. You have a good time last night?" she asked, wiggling her eyebrows.

"You're just as bad as him. Joe drove me home, did an acupressure treatment for my migraine, and then he tucked me into bed. That's it, you pervs."

Sandy chuckled over his coffee and morning spreadsheets. "I didn't say a word. I wish you would have told me you weren't feeling well before we took off last night. It's a good thing Joe was there. I think from now on one of us should drive you home at night—"

"Oh, come on. Let me enjoy a morning of wellness before you start mothering me." He saw the look of hurt on Sandy's face and went right to his side. "Hey, thank you, Brother Sandy. I appreciate everything you do for me, but I don't want to be a burden on you guys. I hate that, you know? It was bad enough Joe had to see me like that."

"He knows, though, right?" Agnes had lost her teasing smile and was dead serious. "About the TBI? You told him, didn't you?"

Leslie's smile deflated. "He knows I have migraines. That's as much as I've told him."

Agnes tapped a long manicured finger against her spatula several times and stared.

"What? If things get worse or we get more serious, I'll tell him. I promise." His eyes burned and his chest squeezed. "I just want a little more time." *Time to make Joe fall in love with me and stay, time to get this under control, time to live my life before I'm not me anymore.*

"Just be fair to him," she said, looking down at her scrambled eggs. "Most likely, he's not going to care. If he knows what's good for him, it won't matter. Just be fair." She set down the spatula and walked out of the kitchen.

"Fuuuuuuu," Leslie said, leaning against the counter.

"What'd I miss?" Randy said, coming back in the kitchen tucking in his Jackets coaching polo. "I'm not sure white was the best color, dude. I better stock up on stain remover."

"You ready for today?" Sandy asked Les, his gaze unsure.

"Yeah. I'm ready. I feel good. Steady. No funky lights or auras, not even a stiff neck. I feel really good. Let's go start our semester, huh? Go Jackets!"

"Go Jackets!" his brothers shouted. They all high-fived and Randy caught the end of the spatula, flipping it up until it splatted against his chest.

"Dammit! That was my last white one! I'm not going to be matching you guys." He pouted as he pulled it off over his head.

"Fine, grab one of mine," Sandy said. "But you better throw all of the dirty ones in the wash before we go."

"Yeah, yeah," Randy said, stomping out of the kitchen.

"You're really okay?" Sandy asked. "Joe stayed a long time. I saw him leave around one. He was smiling."

Leslie's grin was back. "Victory is within my grasp."

Sandy looked him up and down. "Your shoelace is untied."

"Huh?"

Leslie looked down at his bare feet.

Sandy shrugged. "Made you look."

NINETEEN

J^{oe}

Joe absolutely adored his first day of classes. There was something so organic and joyful about seeing kids push past their limits and discover new possibilities. The students had been bright-eyed and willing to try anything he asked, and man, was it fun. No attitudes, no challenges to his authority. He could learn to love this.

He was still on a high when it was time for cheer practice. He'd texted Marti that morning and said, "Call the judges and cancel. We're taking them all." She'd texted him back a thumbs-up.

He grabbed a quick dinner to go at the Buzz and ate it while standing up in the corner of his makeshift classroom. The common room had proved to be a great space. The floors would be professionally waxed this weekend by Leslie's network crew from Des Moines, but it was already close to perfect. Cheer needed a gym, though, when they started doing stunts. They needed more headroom.

Joe had his laptop on a bookshelf he'd moved out of his apartment and into the common room and was watching some recent championship dance teams while sucking down electrolytes not quite fast enough to replenish his system with as much as he'd sweated that day. Marti came in and set down her bag and he immediately scooped her up and lifted her over his head.

"I see someone is still running on adrenaline." She batted his hands away and laughed. "Terrell said you were a little…zealous in your instruction today."

Joe did a series of pirouettes and a leap without spilling his drink and Marti laughed at him.

"Pure adrenaline. I'm sure I'll crash soon. You think we're good, taking them all?"

Marti nodded, crossing her arms. "I suggest you come up with some policies and put them in writing, including how they can earn their spot on the competition squad."

"You're right. Good plan. Let's do that." He snapped his fingers and clapped his hands together, then did a little spin. "See, this is why you're here."

"Wow, this is easier than I expected. You can tell me later what's got you in such a good mood."

He wiggled his eyebrows at her, unsure where all of this energy was coming from, especially considering the fact that he'd not had much sleep the night before.

Oh, Leslie.

If Joe was being honest, his high had just as much to do with taking care of Leslie as it had his teaching day.

Caring for Leslie came so naturally. Being in his space felt…right. He knew he couldn't give it too much weight since Leslie had been pretty out of it, but when they'd walked into his rooms? Apartment? Joe felt so comfortable walking through the door with Leslie's arm around him. He hadn't been weirded out about meeting his mom or anything. Even seeing Sandy when he left hadn't been awkward. The twin had thanked him for taking care of Leslie, although he'd seemed sad.

Joe planned on asking Leslie about the frequency of his migraines and what sort of medication he was on. He'd been surprised when Leslie seemed to be hiding the fact that he was taking medicine when Joe came out of the bathroom. Was it because Joe mentioned not taking pain medication? Did he think Joe would think less of him? That was so not the case. Joe knew Leslie's body had taken a beating as a football player. Even though he'd had a great defensive line that worked hard to protect him, Joe knew he'd had a few bad hits. They hadn't known each other as well during Leslie's years playing with the 49ers, but he'd seen a few montages of Les's greatest plays, and worst hits. It was terrifying to watch, especially when all of the information came out about concussions and their lasting impact on NFL players.

Joe had breathed such a sigh of relief when Leslie confided in him that he'd be announcing his retirement soon and he'd wanted Joe to be the first to know outside of his family.

Of course, he'd also panicked. Because Leslie had started talking about where he was going to settle down, and what did Joe think about it, which meant Joe ran away from Hawaii instead of finally consummating their…whatever it was. He knew it was a shitty thing to do. One he wasn't proud of. One of the many times he wasn't pleased with his behavior when it came to Leslie, but the previous night? He'd done everything in his power to make it up to the man he admired so much, cared for so much, and he'd do it every night if it meant having Leslie in his life.

That thought scared him less than he thought it would, which made him smile.

"All right, Jackets! I have good news and bad news for you. The bad news is we're not having tryouts tonight."

The kids slumped a little and murmured amongst themselves. Joe counted and there were twenty-six kids there, meaning a few hadn't shown up; probably they'd changed their minds after his chat the night before. Good.

"The good news is that we're taking all of you who showed up today! Now," he said, holding his hands out to quiet the excited chatter. "That doesn't mean you'll all perform at every game, nor does that mean you'll all be on the competition team. You're going to have to earn your spots, but having reserves is good for us in case of injuries or emergencies. We'll have contracts for you to sign tomorrow, if you agree, and we'll get measurements. Then on Friday our returning cheerleaders will lead us at the game. The rest of you are there to learn. We'll have ten more games for the whole team to perform together. Regional Competition is in November, and depending how we place, Nationals are in February. Any questions? No? Then let's get to work!"

They spent the next two hours going over basic cheers and Marti and Joe let the previous year's captains, Sidney and Franklin, lead the group. Joe and Marti made their way around the room helping out where kids needed help, but mostly just watching.

Joe was happy to see his dancers Gino, David, and Ivan keeping up. They made a few faces at each other and it was obvious they felt out of their element, so Joe pulled them aside. "I have plans for you, don't worry."

They nodded and gave him a secret handshake which he tried not to totally screw up, then he directed them to pay attention with a mock frown.

When he got up next to Terrell, he leaned in. "You got this?"

Terrell smiled at him and didn't lose a beat doing the cheer. The kid was such a natural. Since childhood, he'd taken dance lessons at the studio where Marti had worked, which started out Marti's idea but the kid took it to the extreme. He played football, too, city league, which Terrence coached, and then high school. He never stopped moving, worked hard, and soaked up choreography like a sponge. A coach's dream. Thank goodness he'd picked cheer.

Joe and Marti met up at the back of the group and shared a fist bump.

"Everything ready for the next phase of fundraising?"

"We're doing the joint jogathon, but I have a feeling the football team will beat us."

Joe groaned. "We'll give them their sheets tomorrow to start getting pledges and then guess who will be dipping into their personal numbers for the kids to call? 'Yes hello? Is this Jennifer Lopez? I'm calling from Greenvale College and Joe Judd is my coach. He humbly asks that you support our team in our fundraising event? See, our college was hit by a tornado—'"

Marti hip-bumped him. "You are terrible. Brilliant, but terrible."

He bowed to her, feeling a twinge in his hip. Ugh, that damn tendon was acting up again. He doubted there was an acupuncturist anywhere closer than Kansas City or Des Moines, though. He was going to have to suck it up.

At the end of the night he shooed all the kids out, making them promise to drink lots of water, and be ready to work the next day.

And that became his life for the next month...

At the end of their fifth football game, these were the stats:

The Jackets had won four and lost only one.

Cheer had become so popular that the high school stands were full every game, and the crowd shouted right along with the team.

Okay, *maybe* it was equal attendance for football and cheer. The two ends of the track were full of standing-room-only spectators as well. Joe's "hype squad" of Gino, David, and Ivan were a smash, joining the cheerleaders and then running around with a bullhorn and busting out some sick moves. It was so much fun Joe couldn't believe this was considered work.

Construction was nearly complete on the Jacket's field and Leslie was hoping it would be ready for homecoming in three weeks. Joe's house, however, hadn't been touched, which wasn't a problem. He barely had any time in his apartment unless he was showering or sleeping. He mostly ate at the Buzz with the other coaches and faculty. Evenings and Saturdays were for practice. He'd been over to Leslie's for dinner once, but the Brothers Payton had had to eat and run, leaving a happy Joe with Agnes, helping her do the dishes while she dished on Leslie's youth. It was epic.

The competition routine was choreographed and it was just a matter of working on stunts, which was a tricky process. They needed the right combinations to pull off the intricate pyramid and skills. He'd hit the jackpot with tumblers so he tested them on all the runs they could manage.

Everything was going well. Even the fundraising, although Leslie's damn celebrity charity calendar had put the football team over cheer. Joe had one hanging in his bedroom...with Leslie's picture out even though it was May's feature. The jogathon funds were still being counted, but Joe was going to have to get creative if they were to regain the lead. He was getting a little tired of Leslie's comments.

Not true. He loved Leslie's little victory shuffle dance he'd do as he passed by gloating, something he did with gusto whenever he had the chance.

Which wasn't often enough.

Leslie hadn't been kidding when he said he would be slammed during football season. They hadn't had time to do more than call each other every night and whisper sweet nothings until they both fell asleep. It seemed Leslie was feeling great, energized by his new team, and that made Joe happy, and relieved.

But he missed him, and the weekend trip to LA for the show was a week away. He hadn't made up his mind whether or not he should bring Leslie.

The decision was made for him three days before.

"Joe I really hate to do this," Leslie said during one of their late-night calls. "I have an emergency this weekend and I can't go with you to LA."

"What's wrong? Everyone okay?"

"Yes, and no. My old coach, Carl Thompson, he's got cancer and he's been put on hospice. I really need to go and see him in Atlanta. A couple of my teammates and I are going out—"

"Oh, no. Of course, Leslie. Honestly, it's probably better. I'm not sure how much time we'd actually get together and my manager wondered if it was a wise move, us springing us on everyone like this."

Leslie cleared his throat. "Us springing us?"

Joe sighed. "You know, going public. The press? We haven't talked about any of that. I kept meaning to bring it up, but you know, it's been a little hectic."

Now that they were talking about it, Joe was really disappointed. He wanted to spend the night with Leslie. He wanted no interruptions. There'd been a couple more kisses over the past few weeks, but they'd been quick and sneaky. They were never alone. Either students were around, or Leslie's brothers, and neither Joe nor Leslie had had the energy for drive-by make-out sessions at Leslie's, which totally sucked. Enough was enough.

Leslie covered up the phone and said something to someone on the other end, groaning when he returned. "Sorry, that was Sandy. The only flight he can get me is a red-eye out Friday night."

"What about your plane?" Joe asked him, realizing he hadn't made his travel plans either and he'd told Arthur he'd take care of it. Oops.

"Plane needs maintenance. My pilot said he'll get it all set up, but he's dealing with family stuff. I don't want to put him out."

"God, Les, you truly are the nicest guy in and out of the NFL." And Joe meant it.

"Stop it." Leslie chuckled and then he sighed as if he were settling into bed. "Let's talk about it then."

Joe imagined him in that giant king-plus-sized monster in his room, naked, hair messed up...

"Talk about it? Fine. But all I can think about is whether you're naked in bed right now."

Leslie's full-bodied laugh made Joe smile in the darkness of his apartment. He stripped out of his clothes, too tired to shower before bed; besides, he'd already decided tomorrow was laundry day.

"I am nearly naked in bed with an ice pack, so no, not completely naked."

"Ice pack?"

Leslie growled. "Yeah, I ran with the kids today. I'm fine when I do it on my treadmill, but I hit a damn rock and tweaked my knee. I hate this bullshit."

"Tell me about it. I gotta try to squeeze in a visit with my chiropractor when I get to LA to see if she can pound this rib back into place before rehearsals for the show. Every time I throw a stunt it's like it's stabbing me in the lung."

"Joe, you need to be careful," Leslie breathed.

"Says the guy out running with teenagers. How far and how fast, huh?"

"I made just under 5K before I had to tap out," Leslie rasped. "Did it in about twenty-five minutes. Shameful."

"That's so hard on your body. You try swimming? More effective but with less pain after. I've been thinking of checking around for pools since ours is out of commission." The Greenvale pool hadn't been damaged, but the roof needed to be replaced due to a few leaks found after the tornado. Nothing major, but it would have to wait for the field and the gym/athletic center.

"*Ooo*, swimming. You want to come swimming? I have a pool, but Sandy fired the last pool service company. I'll have him get someone else out here and we can go when you get back from LA."

"That sounds awesome," Joe murmured. "I'd love to swim with you. But I can't afford tan lines. Are suits optional?"

"Not for you," Leslie growled. "It's indoor, though. And if you aren't wearing a suit, I'll drown. I couldn't handle it."

Joe grinned. "You're too good to my ego. But Leslie, what about the whole us springing us thing? We need to talk about it before we take any more chances of being seen together, clothed or not."

"Personally, you know, I don't care about the press, but this is bigger than us. If the media comes sniffing around for any other reason than us raising funds for Greenvale right now, it'll be yet another distraction for the kids. Man, I can't believe I'm saying this because I know I've been the one pushing things, but maybe we should wait until football season is over, at the very least?"

Joe pouted and kicked at the clothes he'd left on the floor, nearly stubbing his toe on a chair. If Joe didn't know Leslie, didn't trust in him to be true to his word, he might take this as a rejection. But he knew how important the football team's success was to him. It was one of the things he admired about Leslie, how dedicated he was. Joe was tired of waiting for that dedication to be directed toward him.

"I know you're right, but this really sucks."

"It *does* suck. Joe, I want you."

"God, I want you, too."

"This is worse than before," Leslie said, his voice cracking. "Before you came here, it was always 'what if,' then 'why not,' and now it's 'be patient' and dammit, I'm tired of not being with you."

"Just hearing you say that makes me feel better. But, Leslie? You better be ready, because when I finally get you alone, I'm going to use your body in all the ways I've dreamed of over the years."

Several loud cracks came through the phone followed by Leslie's swearing.

"Hello?"

"Yeah, babe, I'm here. What happened?"

"God, Joe, you've got me a mess over here. I dropped the phone. You can't say things like that—"

"Oh, I'm going to say those things, and so many more things until I get to put my hands on you."

Leslie panted on the other end and Joe felt a thrill. If this was all they had right now, he was going to see how far Leslie would go with him.

"How about we try a little of that guided imagery? See if we can't work some of that tension out over the phone."

Leslie groaned. "Please, Joe. Wait, hang on. Let me lock the door before I have unwanted visitors." He was gone mere seconds. "Okay, baby. Tell me where to put my hands."

"You're such a quick study."

Joe whispered his not-quite-sweet somethings in Leslie's ear for the next hour, bringing him to the edge and then coaxing him to pull back, over and over. Leslie begged for more, loved every move Joe choreographed from his bed several miles away, and the two of them dragged out their orgasms until they were both covered with sweat, legs shaking, out-of-breath sated.

"We're pretty good at that," Joe said, moaning softly. His skin was sensitive all over, his muscles loose and relaxed. "I'm going to sleep like a baby."

"Joe? Is it weird that I'm glad we did that over the phone?"

"Not at all," Joe said, taking a sip of water. "If it's all we have, it's what we'll do, right?"

"No, but I mean...I don't want it to be over so quick next time we're together, you know? I want to make it good for you."

"Babe, you need to stop worrying about that. I love that you're so open with me. Your honesty is so hot, you've got me in a pool of happy over here. I could spend hours, days, telling you all the things I want us to do together."

"Good, because I want to hear them all over the next damn month and a half we gotta wait."

Joe laughed at Leslie's impatience. "Glad you're feeling like me."

"Oh, more, Joe. Seriously, how many more nights?"

Joe opened the calendar on his phone. "Last game is November thirteenth. That's like thirty-something nights."

"Mmmm, well, we're just going to have to continue being creative." Leslie chuckled.

"Guess so. For now, get some rest. I'll see you tomorrow." Joe really didn't want to disconnect but it was after midnight and they both needed their rest.

"Yes, you will. And thanks, Joe."

"For what?"

Leslie was quiet for a minute. "For being you, for being here...for being patient with an old man."

Joe snorted. "You're mine, *old man*, so no need to thank me."

Leslie moaned softly. "Say that again. Call me yours."

Joe ran a hand over his torso and sighed. "You're mine, Leslie Payton. Now go to sleep so it'll be closer to the night I can finally claim you in every way."

"God, that sounds incredible. Okay, I'm hanging up, but Joe?"

"Yes, babe?"

"That means you're mine, too. And I've been holding back, trying not to put too much pressure on you. That's not going to last when you put your hands on me. I'm going to be using words and making pledges and shit...you might want to start preparing yourself."

Joe laughed. "Bring it, Coach. I'm looking forward to it. Maybe *you* should do some extra stretches. Wouldn't want you to pull a hamstring."

"You'd take care of me if I did."

The amount of trust and love behind Leslie's words floored Joe. There was that vulnerability. And he was right. Joe would take care of him.

"You know it. Good night, Leslie."

"Good night, Twinkle Toes."

Joe rolled over and plugged in his phone, his heart thudding hard in his chest.

His emotions were all over the place. He wanted Leslie, and not just for sex. He still wasn't sure how he felt about staying in Ayre Valley permanently, but man, he wanted a life, and he felt like he was *this close* to having one. Moving and setting up the program and the classes, all that, had been overwhelming, but there was a light at the end of the tunnel. And it had been fun! Way more fun than he'd thought. And there was so much more to do, more he was looking forward to.

But thoughts of all he needed to take care of to be ready for the weekend, including booking his flight, packing, going over the routines he needed to perform for the weekend, yanked him out of bed and it wasn't until two hours later that he actually grabbed a measly three hours of sleep.

The rest of the week flew by. Cheer practices surpassed his hopes, the kids giving him their all every night. On Friday night, the kids were extra chatty and Joe was too distracted to really get on them.

"Coach? Can I ask you a question?"

Terrell sat near the front of the pile of kids hydrating and doing cool-down stretches.

"Sure. Hit me."

Terrell looked around at the kids as if his question was an uncomfortable one. "What's it like, dancing on tour? Do you get to meet cool people?"

Once he spoke, the rest of the kids went for it.

"How do you go from place to place? On a bus?"

"I bet the after-parties are wild!"

"Where's the coolest place you've been?"

The questions and comments flew fast and furious.

"So that's a lot to address, um," he said and the kids all laughed. "It's been an adventure, to say the least. It's exhausting and exhilarating at the same time. You want it to stop and you never want it to end. Its surreal dancing for tens of thousands of people three or four nights a week but all you hear is the singer's voice in your head, or the stage manager. You experience pain like you've never felt before, and yet you can't wait to do it again. You see the world but also a lot of hotels and venue bathrooms. You look your best, you're in your best shape ever, and you've never been more of a mess in your life." He looked to Marti and she shrugged with a sad smile.

"Would you do it again? Like are you doing anymore shows or are you staying here?"

Joe's mouth went so dry his throat cracked like a drained riverbed when he tried to speak.

"I've signed a contract for this year at Greenvale, but I will do some traveling because of commitments I had before I took the job." *And now I've made a really big commitment!* Had he been hasty the night before? He couldn't help it. He was all-in with Leslie whenever they were together. It was only when he was away from his sun's gravitational pull that he started to doubt.

"But you'll be back next year, right?" Terrell frowned a bit with his question.

"That's the plan," Joe said. "But that's a long way off. For now, we need to get busy with our next fundraising project."

"I can't believe football went to the Kansas City game and worked in concessions. That made them a ton of money. How are we ever going to catch up?"

"They're going to win because there are so many of them."

Joe looked around at these kids who were willing to follow him to the ends of the earth and he wanted to do right by them.

"We can catch them, but it may mean stepping out of your comfort zone."

They all leaned in, and that was exactly what he'd been hoping for.

TWENTY

L eslie

"Run it again. I don't care how many times we have to run it, you'll run this play until you figure out how to get out of your own way. I've got all day."

They were finally on their own turf. The new field had been completed and the team was having practice for the first time. They'd opted to go with artificial turf and the bleachers would be in before the game next week.

Sandy stood on one side of him, Randy on the other, and they started doing the snake and snapping their fingers while singing, "Run this play. Get out of your way. I've got all day."

"I *don't* have all day for you two," Leslie growled.

"We're just singing your latest hit," Randy said, throwing in a very goofy attempt at the running man.

"What you should be singing about is how to fix this damn hole in our offensive line because if we lose again next week, there goes my year-one plan, Brother Randy."

Leslie had taken their one and only loss last week hard. He absolutely knew there would be growing pains taking over the new team, but they'd won their first four games with a comfortable lead. Last week, however, his offensive line had fallen apart and his quarterback had been sacked twice. He wasn't having that.

The twins quit dancing, looked at each other, and then started doing this weird shimmy thing on either side of him. "Yes, Coach."

"Coach! Have you seen this?"

Damontae brought his phone over and handed it to Leslie.

"What am I looking at?"

Randy and Sandy crowded in and they tried to shade the phone so they could see.

"It's on Instagram and TikTok live and they're doing stunts. They've got their crowdfunding link up and if they get to certain levels, they'll keep doing more difficult stunts."

"Aw, how cute," Randy said and Leslie elbowed him. "What? They aren't going to catch us after the calendars and the concessions in Kansas City."

They'd really hit the jackpot with the charity calendar. He'd gotten twelve of his former NFL pals to send him shots and so each month featured different Greenvale players and the NFL player. It helped that one of Leslie's pals at the network shared early pics with the morning show and a deluge of pre-orders had come in. Sandy was trying to keep on top of the printer to make sure they could meet demand. It also helped that the players had gone all out. Some were in formal dress with tuxedos and sports cars, others shirtless with kittens and puppies, all the sprinkles of awesome that would ensure its success.

"They've already got fifteen thousand dollars raised. They're also doing dance routines for each ten thousand raised. Coach Judd said if they get to fifty thousand in the first twelve hours, he'll dance."

God, Leslie would love to see that. Watching Joe's YouTube channel was his secret obsession. If Joe ever found out how many times he'd watched certain videos on there, he'd probably question the claim he'd made the night before.

Leslie would have been fist-pumping thrilled after their late-night session, but he still couldn't believe Joe was really going all in. He worried about Joe leaving for the weekend. It was different for Leslie; he could meet his NFL and network obligations knowing full well his place was at Greenvale, and he was happy about that. But what if the job offers came pouring in for Joe? He was younger, still in great shape, could still do his sport/art. Leslie was physically done, a situation that was getting more real each day.

He'd met with his doctor over video conference the day before and his doctor had confirmed it was time, that he couldn't put off the knee replacements any longer. He was young for a full replacement, but the tweak he'd done the previous week put bone-on-bone and the doctor feared he'd fracture it if he didn't take care of it now. They were going to schedule it after the first of the year, before he needed to start working on the next year's team. He was forbidden from running, so it was definitely time to get the pool back in order. Leslie didn't have the body he'd had when he was playing, but he hadn't let himself go. He liked being in shape, but wasn't willing to work as hard as he'd need to for an eight pack...or even four or six...or those V lines...

Which led his thoughts back to Joe.

His cheeks got red just thinking about what they'd done the night before. Leslie wasn't a total prude when it came to sex even though he'd been raised under pretty conservative beliefs about sex and relationships. He had a vivid imagination and desires like a lot of people, but the act was often hard for him. He worried so much it affected his performance, but not with Joe. Joe had this way of talking him through everything that didn't feel weird or forced, it felt natural. Like his own personal sex coach.

Leslie laughed out loud and then realized his coaching staff were all staring at him.

"We gotta do something. If they win—"

"They're not going to win," Leslie said. But he was having a hard time not whipping out his credit card to make a donation in order to see Joe dance. Would it count if he used his own funds for the cheerleaders and not football? God, he was a mess.

"Hey, how about we do an all-sport Olympics?" Damontae asked. "Like a series of events like push-ups, races, tug-of-war, an obstacle course... We get sponsors and the money goes to the winner's team for each event."

"Sounds great. Really great, actually. Damontae, would you be willing to work with Sandy to get it set up?" Leslie asked. Because as much as he wanted to win the fundraising challenge, he wanted his damn team to win their game next week. He was trying to have perspective about the trip he had to take this weekend...he didn't have any more focus to give to fundraising. He'd had to learn how to delegate when he took his first coaching job, and now that knowledge would serve him well.

"Sure, Coach. Whatever you need."

They shook hands. "Sandy will handle the sponsors, won't you, Brother Sandy?"

Sandy blinked. "Suuuure, Brother Leslie. I'll get right on that as soon as you give me some ideas."

They shared a look and Sandy appeared to want to say more.

"If there's nothing else? Can we get back to getting this team ready for next week?"

Randy frowned at him too, but Leslie didn't have time for any more distractions. He moved away from them on the sidelines to watch his special teams working out, and his phone buzzed in his pocket.

"Hello?"

"Coach Payton? It's Malcolm Darling, *Time* magazine. We had an appointment today. Is this a good time?"

Leslie chuckled. "As good a time as any, I suppose." *More distractions.*

"Great. I wanted to check in first and see how things are going with the team? Great start to your season but a rough week last week."

Leslie pinched the bridge of his nose. "Yeah. When you've got a young team, you have those off nights. These kids have been giving their all despite all of the chaos on campus and we just couldn't score last week."

"Your quarterback particularly suffered from the lack of offensive coverage. Was he injured?"

"Brandon is fine, thank you for asking. We had our trainer do the concussion protocol with him during the game and after and the next day and he's fine, no worries. He'll start next week against Baker University."

"That's good to hear. I wonder if seeing him get hit like that brought back any memories for you."

Leslie's hearing hollowed out. It *had* brought him back. His last game as a starter for the 49ers. He'd been hit so hard by two defensive tackles from the Steelers it knocked him out of his cleats, knocked his helmet off. He'd had his bell rung for sure, but he'd stayed in and finished the game. It wasn't until after the game that he started vomiting. Sandy had taken him from the stadium to his personal physician, who confirmed his suspicion that he had a serious concussion. He let the team know and he spent the next month recuperating in Hawaii... and deciding his career was over. He'd been sad, but he'd also been relieved. It hadn't been much of a choice. He either quit or he was most assuredly going to end up like his father, which was unacceptable. He couldn't let his family go through that again.

"Yeah, I had my share of hard hits. We're focusing our practice time on correcting this weakness."

"Excellent. And how is the cheer/football rivalry going? I heard from President Payton's office that the teams are in tight competition but so far it appears football is in the lead."

That damned publicist. Well, at least he was doing his job. "Yes, sir. It's been fun seeing the teams join in the fun, but I'm pretty confident we'll win. The campaign will run through the end of football season and then we'll crown the winner for the first season. The kids will keep working throughout the year."

"And how's the repair process coming?"

"Good. We're finally on our new turf. The team is excited."

"And the cheerleaders will be performing a pretty spectacular half-time next week from what I understand."

"That I hadn't heard," Leslie said with a laugh. He could only guess at what Joe had in store.

"Let's talk a little about your personal life. You've been out for a long time—"

"Since my second year in the NFL."

"Right. But no serious relationships? No Mr. Payton in the wings?

Is part of your decision to return to Ayre Valley a desire for a social life and perhaps dating?"

Leslie barked out a laugh. "Malcolm, have you been to Ayre Valley, Iowa? I wouldn't say it's a hopping place for a social life. But yes, I want to spend time with my family and I'm hopeful to have a family of my own, whatever that looks like at my age."

"That's right, your father was close to your age when your brothers were born. How did you feel about having the new additions to the family?"

Leslie smiled thinking about the conversation with his parents.

"You're kidding, right? Shouldn't the two of you be enjoying your retirement?"

Agnes had laughed. *"At forty? No way, I'm so ready for this."* Of course she hadn't known then that it was twins. That had been a whole different matter. But Rick had just smiled in a distant kind of way that became more and more frequent. And then there were no smiles.

"I have always been close to my brothers, but a lot of time it felt more like I was parenting them along with my mom. Especially when they hit middle school. Now? They take care of me. They're invaluable to my coaching staff and they keep me on my toes."

"Right. I heard they nailed both you and President Payton with the cellophane across the doorway prank this past week."

"Man, you got spy cameras around here? Yeah, they need better supervision, I suppose. It's great, really. I love spending time with them."

"But the social life is lacking?"

Leslie froze, knowing full well he couldn't answer that truthfully, and since he didn't know for sure when the article would come out, he couldn't divulge anything.

"I can't answer that right now, Malcolm. Ask me after football season."

"So there *is* something to the rumors."

Leslie clenched his fist too tight around his phone and it nearly popped out of his palm. "Rumors?"

"Oh, nothing concrete, only that there's a reason you've been single for so long."

Leslie was ready to blow his top. Who had he trusted when he shouldn't have? Who'd been running their mouth? Or who had seen him and Joe? Had they been caught? God, what if someone had seen them outside his house?

"Well, I would appreciate that you not speculate in your article. I'm under enough pressure here as it is." If Malcolm printed anything salacious about him, this would be their last conversation.

"Hear you loud and clear. Off the record, whoever it is, whatever the situation may be, I wish you the best, Coach. You're a great guy, a fantastic coach, and an excellent representative of all the good your sport should be. If we had more players like you, perhaps the league would be in better shape. They could be leading the movement for equality and social justice instead of trying to protect their assets."

Warmth spread through Leslie's chest. That was all he'd ever wanted: to play football and do what he could to leave the game with the league better than it had been before. If someone like Malcolm Darling thought he'd done a good job, that was something.

"Thank you, Malcolm. I've always appreciated your integrity."

Malcolm chuckled. "Then I should probably be transparent and say that I pitched this article as a cover and feature article, which will be out shortly, but my gut says there's more to the story here. Coach, I'd really like to write your biography. Have you considered telling your story?"

It was Leslie's turn to laugh. "Ready to tank your career? Come on, Malcolm. Who needs another washed-up quarterback story?"

"You honestly don't believe that, do you? Not only did you have one of the most impressive careers in the last twenty years of the sport, but you surpassed expectations laid on you for being the son of a player with an impressive career, and that's without even considering you were also the first publicly out quarterback and a spokesman for LGBTQ athletes. How can a book about you *not* be a bestseller?"

Leslie felt pressure behind his eyes, but not from an incoming migraine, thankfully. He didn't trust his voice to speak. As he gazed out over the rolling green landscape of Southern Iowa illuminated in pinks and oranges at dusk, the land that had crafted his father, been his home for a large portion of his life, he thanked his higher power for the blessings in his life, including this job, what was left of his health, and Joe Judd.

"I'm honored you would think those things, Malcolm," he said with a hoarse tone. "Let's talk."

"Wonderful. We have one more appointment scheduled next week and then I should have enough for the article. Let's talk then. Thank you, Coach. Have an excellent day."

Leslie disconnected and blew out a shaky breath.

Was his story important enough for publication? Would it maybe help other athletes? Would it inspire people?

What would Joe think? He looked at the time. Practice had another half hour and then he needed to hurry home, pack, eat, and pick up Tim, who would be going with him to the airport in Kansas City for their red-eye to Atlanta. Maybe he'd ask Tim about the book.

He'd definitely ask Joe. They were going to have a come-to-consensus meeting when he got back from Atlanta. Correction, when Joe returned from LA. They had a lot to discuss, especially Leslie doing something as invasive as inviting a journalist into their lives. He'd need to ask his family as well since they were a huge part of his story—

A whistle pulled him from his thoughts.

"What the fuck was that?"

Randy stormed onto the field and grabbed one of the defensive linemen by the facemask, spinning him around.

"What did I do, Coach?"

Leslie ran out onto the field after Randy, ignoring the pain in his knee.

"What did you do, Casey. What did you do? I want you to think about how you just hit Tyler. Do you remember how you hit him? Do you? I want you to show me right now how you think you hit Tyler."

Randy let go and the kid stumbled away, getting back into line looking a little dazed.

"Run it again."

"What's going on?" Les asked him as they walked off the field.

"I'm not going to tolerate this shit," Randy growled as he stalked over to the sidelines. When they were off the field, he blew the whistle. "Watch that kid."

The quarterback called out the play, the ball was hiked, the players sprang into action, and—

"Holy hell."

The kid Randy had scolded tucked his head under and rammed the center, trying to break through to get to the quarterback.

Randy blew his whistle and waved the kid to come over. "You tell him, Brother Leslie. You tell him while I take a time-out so I don't do something stupid."

Randy stormed off and Sandy looked between his brothers, unsure where he was needed most.

"I got this," Leslie said.

Sandy nodded and trotted off after his twin brother who was kicking cones and equipment as he went.

The kid stood before Leslie, his eyes wide as saucers, his hands trembling. He pulled off his helmet. "Y-yeah, Coach?"

Leslie rested his hands on his hips and sighed.

"It seems my brother took offense at the way you hit that kid. Do you know why?"

"I don't, Coach. I'm sorry, whatever I did. I'll fix it."

Leslie patted him on his shoulder and squeezed. "Son, lowering your head like that before a hit can cause a catastrophic spinal cord injury. Didn't your coaches teach you about that?"

A tear rolled down the kid's cheek. "No, sir."

"It's all right, we'll work on it. A hit like that also increases your chances of concussion, and that's a big deal in our family. Do you know about my father?"

He nodded. "I know he had some problems..."

"That's putting it mildly. But now we know how to avoid that, right? So we hit with our shoulder or chest, we don't hit with our heads, is that understood?"

"Yes, Coach. I'm sorry."

"Don't apologize to me, son. But let's have this conversation with the whole group before my brother loses his shit, all right?"

"Yes, Coach."

Leslie sighed and patted the kid on his back. He followed him out onto the field thinking yeah, his story might be important. No time like the present to start sharing it.

Twenty-One

J oe

Joe's flight landed in Des Moines on Sunday night at 9:00 p.m. and he limped off the plane with his two carry-ons. He took small steps, practiced his breathing, and tried not to panic. The Bronco was right where he left it in the daily parking lot and he fumbled with his backpack to get his keys out, cursing under his breath the whole way. It took several tries to lift his roller suitcase and backpack into the backseat. When he lifted his right leg to set his ass on the front seat, he cried out. Luckily, he was the only one in that section of the lot. He ended up having to use a combination of the "oh shit handle," his left leg, and a head duck to climb into the four-wheel drive beast. Fuck, he hadn't thought about his hip flexor when he bought the damn car. What normal thirty-six-year-old man worries he might not be able to lift his leg off the ground to climb into his own car?

He managed to get seated, fasten his seatbelt, and start the car. And then he cried. Deep, bone-shaking sobs that made his voice hoarse and blurred his vision so that he couldn't start driving yet. He sat for several long moments before he could pull himself together enough to catch his breath. Then he put the car in reverse and nearly screamed when he moved his right leg from the brakes to the gas.

"Pull your motherfucking self together, Judd. You've gotta get home." He blew out a breath, backed out of his spot, and made his way out of the lot.

The weekend had gotten off to a rough start. After missing a connecting flight Friday, spending the night in the Denver airport, and then arriving in LA with only three hours until rehearsal, he'd only had time to go to the hotel, clean up, shave, and Uber to the venue. Everything went fine in rehearsals, but there was a complicated tangle of bodies kind of lift move toward the end and something in his hip snapped during the performance, the hip that had been bothering him for the past year. He'd managed to finish the routine, but had to improvise with a leap and cut out a tumbling run. He played it off, but he'd had to tell his stage manager, who got him to the production's trainer.

They'd wanted to take him to the hospital, but Joe swore he'd ice it and take anti-inflammatories instead. The next morning, however, he could barely lift his leg. He'd gone to a private clinic where he'd been once before and had X-rays taken, which thankfully showed no stress fracture. The doctor had given him muscle relaxers, painkillers, all shit Joe likely wouldn't take, but he'd also told him this could be a career-ending injury if he didn't rest it. No activity, no dancing, period, for at least three to four weeks. Joe had gritted his teeth and lied through the appointment that of course he'd stay off it. The doctor had told him he should use crutches and he'd nodded—of course he'd get some when he got home. He'd called Arthur and let him know.

"Joe, I'll do whatever you ask, you know that. But don't ignore this, don't ignore his advice. There will come a time when you can't just act your way out of a situation like this. You won't be able to just bounce back like you used to, and I know you don't want to be done yet."

Arthur knew about Joe's toe still dangling in the dance career door, that Joe wasn't ready to close that door.

"*Fuck fuck FUCK!*" Joe slammed his fist against the steering wheel and cried some more. Why couldn't his stupid body cooperate?

The drive home from the airport was a white-knuckle experience, but focusing on driving took his mind off the pain for a bit. Leslie's name kept appearing on the screen every few minutes, first texts and then calls. By the time Joe pulled into the Higdon lot, it was after ten and all was quiet. He texted Leslie: "I'm home. Talk tomorrow," and then he hobbled into the dorm. Matty's country music was blaring so Joe hoped he wouldn't run into him.

"Hey, Coach Judd! You were so great last night!"

He turned to find a couple of the football players and Terrell coming down the stairs.

"Oh, thanks. You guys watched?" Why couldn't he get the damn door unlocked? Oh right, his hands were shaking.

"Of course we did. They put it up on the big screen in the lounge upstairs. The whole dorm was watching. I think they had it playing in the student center too. Man, that was amazing how you—"

"Thanks, guys, really. I gotta get to bed—"

He dropped his keys and tried to bend over to grab them, but he had to stand up and let out a breath so he wouldn't scream.

"Coach? You need some help?"

Terrell picked up his keys for him. When Joe reached out to grab them, he gritted his teeth and tried to smile, but Terrell pulled the keys back. "Hey guys? I'll catch up with you later."

The players waved and headed out the front doors.

"Terrell—" Joe warned.

"Let me get you inside. Then you can tell me what's going on before I call my mom."

Joe cursed and let Terrell open the door. He started to walk but he couldn't put weight on his leg, so he used the handle of his suitcase to hobble into the apartment and Terrell took his backpack from him.

"Thanks, man, but I'm okay. Just a little strained tendon in my hip. I'm going to shower and then ice it and go to bed. I promise I'm fine."

Terrell put his backpack down. "I'd believe that if I hadn't seen your face. So who am I calling? Because you are not okay."

"You always been this much of a pain in the ass?"

"Coach? I'm not playing."

Joe groaned. He made it to the counter and leaned on it to catch his breath. "Look, I'm going to go into the training center across the hall and take an ice bath, then I'm going to go to bed. If you would be so kind as to just make sure I get over there without falling on my face, I'll be fine. I don't want to bother your parents—"

"Coach."

Joe's phone buzzed again and he pulled it out of his pocket. "Oh, great. Coach Payton. Awesome. The last thing I need is him showing up over here. Give me a hand, would you?" When Terrell raised an eyebrow at him, Joe said, "I'm not too proud to beg here, Terrell. Please. I went to the doctor; I have medicine. I'll be okay, I promise."

Terrell mumbled something about adults and hypocrites, but he let Joe lean on him as they hobbled out Joe's door and across the hall. Joe used his keys to unlock the training room door and breathed a sigh of relief when he saw the low tub that he could get in and out of. Hopefully. That was the plan.

"You're gonna need help—"

"Just help me fill it with water and ice. You're not going to be in here when I do this. Keep your phone handy, if you want, in case I get stuck, but I promise I'll be fine."

Terrell set up the tub and grabbed some towels, then he turned on Joe with a scowl.

"I'll be up in my room. Keep your phone and call me if you need me. If I don't hear from you in fifteen minutes, I'm coming back in. Let me at least call my mom?"

"I promise I will call her if it gets worse. I'm going to see her in the morning. I'll tell her then. Thank you."

Terrell was a good kid and Joe was not proud of roping him into his mess. He also had his mom's feistiness so Joe knew he wasn't going to just let this go.

Dammit.

Joe stripped out of his nasty airplane clothes and mentally prepared himself for sinking into excruciating pain.

Why the fuck do I do this to myself? He questioned all of his life choices as he set the timer for fifteen minutes and stepped into the tub. He used his upper body strength, grateful his shoulders weren't fucked since he'd had cortisone shots a few years ago, and he lowered himself into the bath. He gasped and cursed and the tears fell involuntarily as his ass hit the bottom.

Why? Why did he have to torture himself? Why did this stupid career, the only thing he'd ever been good at in his entire life, have to hurt so fucking much?

He sat there sinking deeper and deeper into self-flagellation, jabbing at his soul's deepest fears and beliefs, until he mentally gave himself a slap. Then he concentrated on breathing, counting between inhales and exhales, focusing on being there rather than feeling his body. His phone buzzed and he assumed it was the timer so he picked it up only to hear, "Hello? Joe?"

Leslie. Joe crumbled. His teeth chattered and the tears started up in earnest.

"Joe?"

"Hi," he finally said. *I miss you. I need you, please Leslie.* He wanted to cry out, wanted to beg for Leslie to be by his side, terrified of being alone with his thoughts and his pain, but the shame kept his mouth shut.

"Joe! Where the hell are you?"

Joe heard banging outside and realized that, shit, Leslie was at his door. He was there.

"I'm in the training room," Joe said weakly, "I'm here."

Two beats later the door burst open and Leslie filled the doorway, blocking out the dim light from the hall.

"Oh my God, what happened? Joe, I've been trying to call you."

Joe's buzzer went off for real this time.

"I'm sorry, Leslie. I came straight here."

"Yeah, Terrell texted me. Said I should check in with you."

Joe let his head fall back. Damn kid. He couldn't blame him.

"How was Atlanta?"

"Jesus, Joe—"

"Don't forget Mary."

Leslie planted his hands on his hips. "Your lips are blue. Let me get you out of there."

"I can—"

"Stop it. Babe. Why didn't you...never mind. I'll yell at you when

I'm sure you're not going to die of hypothermia. You'll appreciate me for it later."

Joe took Leslie's hand and let the much more powerful man pull him up from the bath. He'd left his boxers on, thankfully, because he didn't need complete humiliation tonight. Once he was standing, Leslie carried his weight as he stepped out of the tub, then he wrapped him in several towels.

"If you just let me lean on you—"

Leslie pulled his arm over his shoulders. "Where does it hurt?"

Joe gazed up into his blue eyes and his bravado melted.

"Everywhere." His chin quivered and he cursed as a sob escaped.

"I'm going to carry you." It was not a request.

Joe bit his lip and gave a slight nod before Leslie scooped him up effortlessly. Joe groaned and tucked his head into Leslie's neck as Leslie guided them out the door, across the hall, and into Joe's apartment. He spoke to someone before the door closed behind them, but Joe was fighting too hard to keep it together to care who saw them.

"We need to get you moving around and then get you a hot shower and then some sleep. I'm going to put you down and let's try to walk. Slowly. Lean on me."

Leslie set him down gently and thankfully the ice had numbed the area enough that the slicing pain had eased. Numb was better than pain tonight.

"I'm s-s-sorry I d-d-didn't answer when you c-c-called. It t-t-took everything to d-d-drive." Joe was shivering so much he could barely get the words out. Ice baths were a suffering athlete's accomplice and torturer at the same time. Joe used them sparingly, but tonight he'd been desperate for relief. The hours on the plane, the lack of sleep—he'd reached his limit, he truly had, and if Leslie hadn't been there...

"Shhhh. Just walk. We need to keep you moving for just a bit more and then I'll stretch it out. Is it your hip?"

Joe nodded. "Right hip flexor. It's torn. S-sn-snapped d-d-during the p-performance. I can't...Leslie, I can't..."

"It's going to be okay, I promise. We'll get through it. I'll do therapy with you. I'll take care of you, Joe, God, why didn't you... Sorry."

Joe put his hand on Leslie's chest to stop him. "Didn't want to fall apart on you. Fucking hate crying."

But when Leslie wrapped his arms around Joe and pulled him in tight, Joe let it all go. He cried. He bawled. He was a snotty mess and he didn't care. Neither did Leslie. He stroked Joe's back and hair and whispered assurances to him, so calm, so patient. So loving.

Once he had it out of his system, he stepped back and accepted the tissue Leslie handed him. He blew his nose, took off the towel and wiped at his face.

"Let's get you on the bed and I can stretch you out a little, just a little. Don't want to overdo it. Did the doctor give you the severity?"

"Grade two," Joe said, wiping away the last of his tears and sniffling. "And I really want to shower first." He dropped the rest of the towel and started to pull at his wet boxers but he couldn't bend over to pull them off. "Les?"

Leslie sucked in a deep breath and nodded. He crouched behind Joe and slid them carefully down. He lifted Joe's right foot, pulled it off, and then he tried to lift the left and Joe cried out but he freed his foot.

"I'm so sorry, Joe. I've pulled my groin but not the hip flexor. I'd imagine it's a lot worse."

"I'd kill for a pulled groin right now," he gasped.

They hobbled to the bathroom together and Joe leaned on Leslie as he got the shower running. Joe stepped in and reached for the soap, but Leslie cleared his throat.

"How about...can you just hold onto the wall and I'll... Let me wash you, Joe. I don't want you to fall."

Joe put his hands against the wall and laughed. "Bet this wasn't on your list of perfect nights."

"Stop it," Leslie said. He lathered up the soap and ran it over Joe's neck, shoulders, and arms, making sure to scrub each finger, each joint. "You know nothing about my perfect nights list then. Taking care of you, being needed by you, tops my list every time."

Joe's eyes burned and he sucked in a shaky breath, thankful he was facing away from Leslie. "Now, *you* stop it. I'm tired of crying."

Leslie chuckled softly and then moved to Joe's legs. He was so careful and gentle, it wasn't a sensual act at all, and for that reason Joe had a hard time relaxing. He must have tensed up because Leslie placed a hand on his lower back.

"Are you okay?"

"Yeah? It's just...I'm glad it's you, but it's...I've never had someone bathe me." He'd never showered with someone in a sensual way either. It was different like this, different than sex, and he just felt so...exposed.

"Before I met you," Leslie said, rinsing the soap from Joe's body. "My first year in the NFL, I had a bad game in Detroit. I ran the ball from the thirty-yard line and when I got hit, I kind of went up and over the two tackles, dropped the ball, and landed on my hands before tumbling over. They rushed me off the field, worried I'd broken both my wrists, and since it had been raining the whole game, I was covered in mud. The trainer had to strip me down and shower me before we could go in for X-Rays. Aw-kward. But honestly, he made it fine, talked to me the whole time about his kids and his husband and the time his husband broke his wrist gardening and how he wished he had a much cooler story to explain his injury. Anyway, I don't want this to be awkward for you. I just want to take care of you. Always. Whatever you need."

As Leslie talked, Joe let himself sink into his touch, let Leslie's voice lull him into a state of relaxation, and finally, he stopped resisting. He was hurt, he was injured, he would get better if he did what the doctor told him to. It would suck, but he would survive this, and his dance career would have to wait. All he could do was focus on the here and now. With Leslie.

"Everything is better with you," Joe slurred, his limbs growing weak and his head too heavy to hold up. "Wash my hair? Please, baby?"

"Yeah, I can do that."

Leslie turned him under the spray, giving Joe a chance to get steady on his feet and then he tipped Joe's head back, supporting him with one arm. Joe stumbled a bit and winced, but he managed to remain upright until Leslie was done.

"Stay there. Let me grab towels."

Joe pointed to the cabinet where he'd put the ones he'd bought on his trip with Marti and then he sighed as Leslie wrapped him in soft fuzzy towels.

"I got you all wet," Joe said as Leslie picked him up and carried him to his bed. He was too tired to fight.

"I'll dry. Here, lay back. Let me stretch this leg."

Joe held his arms up. "Please, Leslie. Just...please?" He wiggled his fingers. "I can't keep my eyes open. Can you stay for just a little while?"

"Yeah," Leslie said, his voice cracking. "Whatever you want." He looked down at himself and pulled his soaking shirt away from his chest. "I don't want to get your bed wet."

Joe groaned. "Just take it off and get in here." He rolled onto his side and grunted as he tucked his body pillow under his right leg. "Climb in here behind me."

TWENTY-TWO

L eslie

Leslie took Joe's request as consent, stripped down to his boxer briefs, and climbed in behind Joe, keeping space between them. He used a towel to dry Joe's dripping locks and then ran his fingers through the silky mass. "What else can I do, Joe?"

"Tell me a story," Joe mumbled into his pillow. "I want to hear your voice. Relaxes me."

"Okay...what kind of a story?"

"Tell me the story of the night we met."

Leslie laughed. "You were there, too, you know. You kinda already know what happened."

"Just tell me. Please. And keep doing that. Feels good."

Leslie had been running his fingers lightly over Joe's back, wishing he could take Joe's pain away. He was such a strong man, stronger than anyone Leslie had ever known, and to see him in so much pain and yet so trusting of Leslie, was truly humbling.

"So a cowboy rode into town—"

"Thought you were a miner."

"What?"

"Miner 49ers, right? Dallas is the Cowboys."

Leslie let his head fall against the pillow. "Right, how could I forget? Anyway, a miner rode into his hometown looking for glory, carrying untold riches in his, uh, bag. His saddlebag. After a day of accolades, flashing cameras—"

"Did they have cameras back then?"

"Joe, this was two thousand eight."

"No, when the miner rode into town on his horse."

"Well, it was a Ferrari. They've got a horse on them."

"Whatever happened to your Ferrari?"

Leslie rubbed at his face, his eyelids feeling heavy. He, too, had had a long, painful weekend, but his pain was of the emotional kind. Seeing Carl so frail and weak...it had been difficult for Les and Tim and the other players who'd gathered. They'd gotten drunk at their hotel that night together, talking about the old days, and Leslie had thought about Joe, how he couldn't wait to get back home to him, how time was so fleeting, and how he was going to convince Joe they shouldn't wait anymore to be together. Because life made them no promises about how much time they had left, and the team and college community would just have to deal with it, wager or not.

Joe shifted and the towel slid off his hip, leaving him completely naked. At any other time, Leslie would have felt blessed to see Joe's most famous asset. Now he felt blessed that Joe trusted him enough to be so vulnerable with him.

"Keep up the tickle scratch, Payton. Now, what about the Ferrari?"

"The twins wrecked it." Joe gasped and Leslie laughed. "It wasn't their fault. They *had* taken it without permission, though, and they were being careful on the backroads, but some guy came flying out of a blind intersection and T-boned them. Thankfully no one was hurt, but the car was toast. They were terrified to tell me, but they handled it way more mature than I thought them capable of being at fifteen years old. Anyway, I never drove the thing anyway. It was a vanity purchase, one I thought I was supposed to do with stupid money. I took the payout and ended up donating it to the college."

"You're such a good man," Joe said. "I would have made them suffer, though."

"Oh, their terror was enough punishment. I kept them guessing what it would be. Ended up making them go volunteer at the Veterans Home with me. Giving sponge baths and changing out pee bottles actually turned out to be less of a punishment than I'd thought. It led to their first invention, their first business, and their first million when they sold the patent to a medical supply company."

"Wow," Joe said. "Okay, I want to hear more about them another time. Right now get back to our story. So the miner rode into town..."

Leslie sighed. "At the end of a day where the whole town, it seemed, was blowing smoke up the miner's ass, he waltzed into a bar and was immediately surrounded by coeds wanting his autograph, giving him their phone numbers, but one kid, cocky as hell, stared him down, shook his head, and then went back to his drink and a conversation with the bartender."

"I wasn't about to compete with your adoring fans."

"Of course not. So when I—I mean the miner—could finally break away, he went to the bathroom just so he could walk by the cocky kid and assess the situation. It was then he realized that the cocky kid had been the one who'd played such a mean game of flag football, he'd nearly bested Greenvale's actual football team. So the miner did his business and then on his way back into the bar, he took the empty seat at the corner of the bar, hoping that he could perhaps talk to the cocky kid."

"You said, 'where'd you learn to play football like that?' And being the asshole I am, I said to you, 'buy me a drink and maybe I'll tell you.'"

"I didn't even know if you were of age. I refused."

"You did until the bartender assured you I was old enough. He was helpful that way. Anyway, continue your story."

"The, uh, miner, he eventually caved and bought the cocky kid some fruity disgusting drink and when he handed it to the kid, the bar got super loud because the band started up, so the miner pulled his stool closer—"

"And their knees touched under the bar," Joe murmured dreamily. "The cocky kid was intrigued by the miner's attention and thought he'd flirt for a bit, enough to get another drink since he was a broke-ass college student cocky kid and the miner was loaded. But the cocky kid realized the whole 'nice guy' image wasn't an image. It was really true."

Joe rolled over onto his back and scooted his upper body closer so he could snuggle against Leslie. "Keep going." His eyes drifted closed and he sighed.

Leslie ran his fingers down the center of his chest. "The miner got so lost talking to the cocky kid that before he knew it, it was closing time. He didn't want the night to end, though, and the cocky kid also seemed hesitant to leave."

"Oh, the kid wasn't hesitant to leave. He wanted to go with the cowboy, I mean, miner. He wanted to have an adventure. But the miner was being all honorable and shit."

"That's right," Leslie breathed, nuzzling Joe's hair. "The miner was ready to take his fortune and settle down on the homestead, make home and hearth. But the cocky kid was ready to fly."

Joe sighed and turned gingerly on his side, facing Leslie. He tucked his left thigh in between Leslie's and snuggled up against Leslie's chest.

"Well, the cocky kid wanted you, still wants you, and really wanted this. He wanted to be close to you. And now he has you right where he wants you." Then he wiggled. "But he wants closer." He pulled on Leslie's arm until Leslie wrapped it around him.

Leslie's hand shook as he pulled Joe flush against him...for the first time, skin to skin. He wanted to weep at the wonder of having the man he loved, with all of his heart, so close to him. He let out a shaky breath and squeezed his eyes shut, not wanting to blow the moment by getting all sappy.

"Finish the story, Leslie," Joe said, and then he pressed a kiss to Les's pec, sending goose bumps across his torso. "How does the story end?"

Leslie took a breath for courage. "The miner eventually convinced the cocky kid to come home, and once he had him in his sights, he was determined to love him forever."

Joe sighed. "Mmm, forever. That sounds wonderful. I want to love you forever, Leslie."

They held each other for a long time, just breathing. Leslie ran Joe's last words through his mind several times, wondering: *Did I hear him correctly? Is it possible he feels exactly as I do?*

"Thank you for bringing me home and taking care of me."

"I wish you would have called me, Joe. I'll always take care of you."

Joe lifted his head and pressed his palm against Leslie's cheek.

"I didn't want you to know how bad it is, because if I tell *you*, that makes it real. I don't want it to be real. The injury."

"I know," Leslie whispered. "God, you know I get it. And I'll take care of you, Joe, seriously. I want to. I want this. Us."

"This," Joe said, running his hand over Leslie's torso. "This is real. Us. Kiss me, Leslie."

Leslie gazed into Joe's troubled brown eyes and smiled. "No matter what, okay?" He brushed his lips against Joe's and they both moaned. For a moment they were lost to the magic they'd created, this space where tornadoes, fundraisers, football, cheerleading...none of it mattered. It was just the two of them curled together in the dark and nothing could break their connection.

They touched and kissed for the longest time and it was everything Leslie had ever wanted. Joe slid his fingers under the waistband of Leslie's boxer briefs and tugged at them until Leslie took over and removed the last barrier between them.

"Joe, you're hurt—"

"And you're going to take care of me." Joe grasped Leslie's hand, held it up to his mouth and Leslie groaned as Joe licked his palm. "Take care of us, Leslie." He guided Les's hand to his cock straining against Leslie's own. "Make the pain go away for a little while."

Leslie wrapped his hand around both of their erections and let desire take over, let his worries fade away, only keeping the slightest concern that he'd hurt Joe. That was enough to keep him focused on drawing out their pleasure, taking it slow until Joe was quaking against him, and it allowed him to keep enough control over himself that he finished when he was damn good and ready, when Joe had finished and was sated, that he'd enjoyed himself, and only then did Leslie allow himself to come. Under any other circumstances, he would have shouted a victory roar. Instead, he had a quiet moment of success where he nuzzled Joe's hair and pressed a kiss against his head.

Joe murmured loving words and then slumped against him and fell deep asleep draped over Leslie's body. Even if Leslie could have moved, there was no way he would miss out on this moment, on the trust Joe had placed in him. Instead, he covered them with the blankets and he basked in the peace and quiet interrupted only by the sound of pipes and creaks in the old building and the gentle rain blown against the window.

At some point in the night, Joe rolled over and Leslie woke in the wee hours curled up to his back. He wanted to stay with all of his heart and wake up with Joe, but he had concerns:

What if things were awkward between them?

What if all the talk of love and forever had been a fever dream?

What if they were caught?

He didn't want to leave, but the responsible part of his little mental committee thought those were all valid concerns. He left the warm cocoon of Joe's bed and pulled his clothes on in the dark. He couldn't resist kissing Joe's forehead before he left.

"Leslie? Thank you."

"You're welcome, Twinkle Toes. Get some sleep."

Joe grabbed his hand and opened his eyes wide. "I love you. I said it. I meant it. I want you to leave here knowing that."

Leslie dropped to his not-as-bad knee and pulled Joe's hand to his lips, kissing it.

"I love you so much, Joe. I wish I could stay."

Joe smiled and closed his eyes. "You just want to see my morning routine, don't even lie."

Leslie laughed and his body flooded with warmth. "I do want to see your morning routine. I want to be part of your morning routine. I want so much with you, but mostly I want you to feel better. Call me if you need me and I'll be right here."

Joe kissed Leslie's hand and then let go. "Everything's better with you."

When Joe didn't say more, Leslie figured he'd fallen back to sleep. He stood and moved quietly as possible through Joe's apartment, only grunting once when his shin connected with a low table. He soothed himself with thoughts that in the very near future, he'd convince Joe to move to Payton Manor where Leslie wouldn't have to worry about leaving in the middle of the night, where he knew the placement of all the furniture, and where there'd be no sneaking around.

Where they'd be a permanent team. In love. Forever.

TWENTY-THREE

J oe

Homecoming weekend was a big deal for Greenvale College. The Jackets football team were playing their biggest rival, Culver-Stockton, Friday night and were favorites to win. A win would clinch a playoff berth and Leslie was determined that would happen. Joe was so thrilled for Leslie that the team had come together. Watching him lead the young players this far was so inspiring. Joe hoped he could do the same.

The cheerleaders would be performing their competition routine at halftime of the football game. Saturday morning, the Jackets cheer team would be headed to Kansas City bright and early for the Heart of America Conference cheer competition. Placing in the top three meant a bid for nationals in March, which Joe was counting on. The kids were unbelievably talented and driven and had come together as a solid team with a fighting chance.

President Payton would also be introducing the new faculty to the alumni and families joining the school community at homecoming, which meant Joe would have to act all collegial and shit, which had grown increasingly difficult. Ever since Leslie had found Joe in the ice bath, they'd become a bit daring. Joe spent almost a full night at Leslie's, Leslie had come over to Joe's when he was less likely to be seen, and they'd even made use of the athletic office storage closet because Joe hadn't been able to wait until later that night. All of it flustered Leslie, but he loved every minute. Since the athletic center reopened, the teams were both using the facility. Proximity had made it more difficult to remain professional and they'd been nearly caught making out more than once.

Joe's hip was much better. He'd come clean to the team, told them he'd been injured, and asked for their help in reminding him to set a good example by letting it heal and not working out with them.

Leslie had been instrumental in his rehab, working him out in private, pushing him as far as he could take it and no further. After three weeks, he'd been able to give up the cane and lead stretches...carefully. He figured after another three weeks he'd be able to start dancing again, easy at first of course, but he was determined to be okay.

The football team was ahead in the fundraising, but Joe cared less about that than he should. How bad would it be to lose the wager? He had everything he wanted, including Leslie, and the team was doing great. He and Marti continued to brainstorm more ideas, but his heart wasn't in it.

The night of the homecoming game, Joe was getting ready in his apartment, finally dressing warm because they'd had their first chilly weather that week, when his phone rang.

"Hey Joe, it's Arthur. Listen, *Dance Machine*'s producers called. They want to do a nationwide tour. They want you to choreograph it and they want you to star."

Joe's chest tightened. On the one hand, he was elated to be asked. On the other, he was frustrated that he was being asked.

"This puts me in a tough situation, Arthur. What are the dates?"

"They're still in the planning stages of booking the shows and the talent. They want the winners from each season, but they want you as the headliner. They're talking spring and summer."

Joe exhaled and dropped his chin to his chest. "You know I can't do that. I've got the job here through May. Choreography, maybe, but I can't be gone more than a few days. The kids need me."

And he needed the kids. He'd come to love the practices and his classes. He'd worked with the dean of instruction to outline a degree program, done the research to see what other same-sized colleges had done, and was working on a proposal to share with Barry and then the board. The more he worked on it, the more excited he got, and the more excited Leslie got.

Because Leslie wanted him to stay. Because they were in love. And Joe wanted a life with Leslie.

How could he even consider being away from him?

The running away he'd done for all those years seemed so foolish now. All he wanted to do now was run *to* Leslie.

"Are you there, Joe? They said they're willing to discuss your schedule because they want the Joe Judd stamp on the production. I can tell them the tour would have to be in the summer, but rehearsals..."

"Yeah. Look, thank you for taking care of this, Arthur. I've gotta get to the game."

"As your agent, I'll say this is important, but as your friend, I'd encourage you to consider sitting this one out. With your injury—"

"I hear you. And thank you. I'll let you know after this weekend. If we qualify for Nationals tomorrow, it will be tough for me to get away. Let me think on it."

"And talk to Leslie."

"Yeah," Joe answered. Leslie's feelings mattered in all of this. He didn't want Leslie to think for one minute that he wasn't serious about staying and committing to a life on the homestead with him.

Joe walked at a brisk pace to the field and caught up with the Payton brothers outside the gates.

"Coach Judd, care to join in on the wagers for the game?"

Joe raised his eyebrow. "Who's betting against your team?"

"No, no no no, it's not like that. We have more important things to bet on. Like, will Brother Leslie swear? Will Brother Randy throw down his clipboard?"

"Ah," Joe said to Randy. "Of course. Put me down for yes to both."

Leslie turned on him with mock shock. "I can't believe you'd bet against me." He blinked his big blue eyes and Joe wanted to kiss him until his pout went away. He didn't really need an excuse to want to kiss him, though. He never thought he'd be so sappy as to want to kiss all the time, but he really did. He loved kissing Leslie...

"You could always add to the bets whether or not Coach Judd bites his nails during the team's performance."

"Ooo, I'll put fifty on that," Randy said, pulling out his phone and typing into a spreadsheet.

"You guys are like bookies here."

"Yeah, but it's all harmless," Sandy said. "It's all in fun."

Joe turned to Barry who was shaking his head. "And you allow this type of Paytonfoolery?"

He shrugged. "The alternative is them pulling pranks. Like the time they filled Leslie's water bottle full of saltwater, or the time Randy kept dropping wads and wads of chewed gum on the ground so Leslie kept stepping in it."

"That was funny. He was like stomping around the sidelines, wiping his feet on the grass—"

"It was not funny! I got that shit everywhere. Ruined my shoes."

The brothers continued laughing about it as they walked into the stadium together, but Joe and Leslie hung back.

"You all packed for tomorrow?" Leslie asked. They walked close together and spoke in low voices.

"I've still got room in my duffle if you want to come with," Joe said with a wink.

Some kids came running through and knocked into Joe. Leslie's arm came around his back to steady him. Joe smiled up at him, but then he noticed a couple of his kids from his beginning dance class watching the two of them wide-eyed. Joe raised an eyebrow as if to say, "carry on" and they giggled and skittered away.

Leslie noticed it too and removed his hand.

"I'm sorry."

"I'm not," Joe said. "I'd walk in here right now holding your hand. Hell, give me your varsity jacket. Wait, what's the college equivalent of that?"

"I don't know, Joe," Leslie said in a mocking voice. "Since we aren't college students—"

"Ooo, I should wear my number thirteen Payton 49ers football jersey. I love that thing. It's huge on me."

"Stop it. You do not have one of my jerseys."

Joe giggled. "It was an impulse buy. I was with some dance friends in San Francisco and we went to the 49er team store at Pier 39 and I just *had* to get it." He leaned closer and spoke next to Leslie's ear. "I also bought one of those ladies crop top versions, the mesh ones? Somewhere there's a whole photoshoot of pictures of me in that and barely there trunks."

Leslie stumbled and turned to glare at him. "You can't tell me that right now!"

Joe smiled sweetly at him. "Love you."

And Leslie's cheeks turned that lovely shade of pink that Joe adored.

They may not have been college students, but he felt the internal butterflies like a young person in love. The way Leslie looked at him, not even trying to hide how much he felt for Joe, made Joe feel like he was flying. He hoped the flight was smooth and not careening out of control.

"I gotta head into the locker room and make sure everyone is all set," Leslie said. "Will I see you after?"

Joe wrinkled his nose. "I've gotta be up by four. Bus leaves at five. But I'll call you before bed."

Leslie's blue eyes, so bright under the stadium lights, sparkled just for Joe.

"You do that. Oh, and by the way, we have a surprise for you."

Joe frowned, but Leslie strolled away, being as the big coach was needed on the field, of course. Joe wanted to march down there after him and demand he explain, but then Joe was surrounded by cheerleaders tugging him toward the field as it was time for a pregame huddle.

Joe and Marti met them down on the track as the team stretched and warmed up as a group.

"You got your pep talk memorized?" Marti asked him.

"Pep talk? Uhhh..."

"Hey, Coach?" Terrell asked. "Sorry to interrupt, but Genesis is worried about our partner stunt. Can you talk to her?"

"Sure. But let's huddle first."

Joe didn't think he'd ever get used to the kids looking to him for leadership and guidance. It was different than working with contestants on *Dance Machine* or choreography for group numbers. They were there to learn the routine and move on. These kids wanted to learn from him, were inspired by him, and that was a whole new ballgame.

"I don't know why y'all look to me to motivate you. You've got everything you need to go out on that field and nail not only your job as cheerleaders, but to nail your competition routine. I can give you the outside perspective, show you what you can't see yourselves, but each and every one of you has worked your asses off to be here, and it shows every time you take the field. It shows every time you show up to practice. I see it, your teammates see it, and tonight, the crowd will see it. Tomorrow, the judges will see it. You're going to be amazing, and that's all I have to say. I believe in you. If you make a mistake, keep going. Make sure not a single hair touches the ground. Anything else, Marti?"

She smiled at him like a proud mama and his cheeks burned. "No, Coach, I think you summed it up. Now, finish your stretches. Game starts in fifteen minutes."

Joe checked in with Genesis and confirmed that it was just nerves, that she was okay, and then he fist-bumped her and Terrell.

Joe and Marti waved at the kids as they climbed the steps to the bleachers. They sat up a few rows from the bottom and to the left of the squad so he could see them, watch their lines, etc., but they would be on their own. Joe knew it was best to give them the autonomy to make their own decisions during the game.

It also freed him up to watch Leslie, which was actually his favorite sport.

Leslie was a physical coach. He moved up and down the field, he used gestures, he acted out his instructions...he was constantly in motion. They'd talked a few nights prior about his coaching style after a rehab session. In Leslie's giant bed. With Leslie stretched out over Joe's naked body.

"You know you've lost weight, right?" Joe had asked him. "Probably close to twenty pounds." He'd run his hands over Les's ass, under his boxer briefs. "Does this happen every season?"

Leslie had laughed, sucking in a breath when Joe's fingers dragged between his glutes. "Yeah. I don't eat as much and I move way more. And I work out more because I work out issues while I'm exercising."

"A kinesthetic learner, huh?"

"Yeah, I'm real hands on," Leslie had murmured as he'd held himself in plank position above Joe and kissed him...everywhere. Then he'd done push-ups, kissing Joe on the down position.

"I love hands on," Joe had murmured as Leslie finally lowered himself between Joe's thighs and demonstrated his love of hands-on work. Lips and tongue-on work as well.

"Before I lose your attention completely," Marti said. "We need to talk about tomorrow."

"Hmm?" Leslie had bent over to tie a player's cleats and Joe had a perfect view.

"You two are a hot mess, you know that?"

Joe sighed and smiled at her with his chin resting against his palm. "We are, but I've never been this gobsmacked before." He pressed his lips together and his eyes burned. "I love him, Marti. I can't believe I waited so long."

Marti squeezed his thigh. "You waited until the right time, that's all. And I'm happy for you. But does that mean you're staying permanently?"

Joe's dreamy smile slipped. "I think so. But I definitely feel like that moment when you're mid-stunt and you look down only to realize that no one is there to catch you."

"That's normal, Joe. Once you give your heart to someone completely, there's an adjustment period. And even still, sometimes you'll wonder whether you're as steady as you think you are, you'll wonder what if...but deep down you'll know you're solid, that your person isn't moving, and they won't let a hair touch the ground."

"Great. I feel so much better."

Marti elbowed him and they both laughed as the announcer started the evening's production. The cheerleaders held up the poster for the team to run through and they cheered as the team ran out two at a time.

The seniors were introduced and had a moment to wave to the stands. Then the senior cheerleaders were introduced and Marti and Joe shouted loudly for them. Leslie's coaching staff was honored while the crowd cheered and Joe and Marti stood up and waved when their names were called. Joe and Leslie made eye contact across the field and Joe placed a hand over his heart. Leslie nodded and smiled before joining the team's huddle on the sidelines.

Once the game started, Joe's attention was on his team...unless they were in between cheers, and then it was on Leslie.

Who did swear.

And Randy threw his clipboard on the ground.

The cheerleaders kept the crowd engaged and on their feet. The Jackets had a slim three-point lead at halftime as the football team ran off the field and Joe and Marti descended the steps to check in with the team captains before the cheerleaders performed.

"Make sure everyone's shoes are tied and fix your shirts. Everyone better be tucked in. Brittany, fix your ribbon. Ivan, you and the hype team, make sure you keep those megaphones going and nail those twists at the end."

"We got you, Coach."

The team gathered together, Marti and Joe stuck their hands in and they all shouted "Jackets." Joe and Marti moved out of the way and back up to the bleachers to watch the performance, both of them trying to appear calm, cool, and collected. Joe brought his thumb up to his mouth, and then he shoved his hands in his pockets, looking around to be sure no Paytons were still out.

That's when he saw the team coming out of the locker room. They trotted over to the sidelines and lined up in the endzone.

Then they started to cheer. "Hey, Jackets?" They stepped and clapped, mostly staying in rhythm.

The cheerleaders had lined up in their formation, but they gawked at the football team.

Finally Terrell yelled, "Yeah?"

"Hey, Jackets."

"Yeah?"

"Introduce yourself—"

The cheerleaders got with the program and answered back the football team's "introduce yourself" cheer with "right on" and then the football team did their part...and ended with a bunch of them doing standing back tucks. Like Joe and Terrell had taught them.

See, the team realized how much they could improve with more workouts like Joe's and so he'd been their guest trainer several more times, and several of the players had indeed come to tumbling clinics.

He clapped for them and pumped his fist, but their surprise wasn't over. Joe looked to the goalpost closest to the locker rooms and found the coaching staff standing there clapping. Then the football team all took a knee to watch the cheerleaders.

In all of Joe's years being involved with cheer, he'd never seen a football team support their cheerleaders like this. It was exactly the type of thing he and Leslie had said they wanted to see: the teams working together and supporting each other.

Mission accomplished.

God, he really needed to get some allergy pills or something. This burning in his sinuses had his eyes watering. That had to be it.

The music started and the squad exploded into action. Joe was thrilled to see everything go off without a hitch and the crowd went wild. He and Marti held hands the whole time, praying everything went smoothly so as to not jinx their performance the next day. They were perfect.

As soon as the squad hit their final stunt and finished with a bang, Joe and Marti raced down the steps—well, Joe was as careful as he could stand to be—and they ran out to meet the kids. There were hugs all around and high fives, the team all congratulating each other and squealing with elation.

Until Joe saw Terrell and Genesis.

"What's wrong?" he asked as he reached them. Genesis was crying and apologizing over and over.

"It's okay," Terrell said, but he held his hand against his stomach. When he looked up, his chin was quivering and his eyes were wide open.

"Let me see," Joe said and Terrell held out his hand.

"Oh my God," one of the kids said, echoing Joe's thoughts. There was a tomato where his thumb had been before.

"I'm so sorry, Terrell. I came down wrong and caught his thumb—"

"Let's go." Marti led Terrell away from the group and over to the trainer's table where Terrence immediately went to work. Terrell was quickly going into shock so it wasn't long before Marti and Terrence made eye contact.

"Leonard ER," Terrence said. "I'll be there as soon as the game is over."

Marti nodded and turned to Joe.

"Go," he said to her. "I'll take care of everything."

"But competition," Terrell said.

"We got it, man. Just go get looked at. Your mom will message me."

Marti whisked Terrell out of the stadium and Joe sighed. Then he turned to face the team.

"And this, my friends, is why we have reserves. William, you know Terrell's part, right?"

William nodded, looking a little shell-shocked.

"Okay. For the rest of the game I want you, Genesis, Sidney and Franklin to go work through the changes needed. Take whoever spots that part. Make sure you and Genesis can nail the stunts, and if not, we'll try something else. We will be fine, got it?"

They nodded and trotted off a bit away from the rest of the squad, who were standing around trying to figure out what had happened.

"Coach Judd? What happened?" David asked.

"What happened could have happened to anyone. Accidents happen and sometimes a missed foot in a stunt means a broken thumb, other times it's no big deal."

"But what are we going to do?"

"We'll work William into the routine and if that doesn't play out, we'll go to plan B." *Whatever that is.* "Plan to stay after the game. We'll go over to the gym and do some run-throughs."

Joe was surprisingly not losing his shit. Losing Terrell was a big deal. William could do the stunts, but Terrell was front and center for the tumbling runs. They'd work it out. They'd be fine. And Joe would take them on the bus tomorrow. He had all the forms they needed, all official and shit, and he would handle it like the college had trusted him to do. It would be fine.

The second half started and Joe's mind was whirring with all the things he needed to take care of. His phone buzzed.

I heard from Terrence. I'm so sorry.

He smiled down at his phone.

Thanks. It'll be fine. Especially if I keep telling myself that.

Want me to come with you? Tomorrow? A second set of hands? I was going to drive down anyway.

Joe slumped a little in his seat. Yes, he very much wanted Leslie to come with. But would that be a sign of weakness? He didn't care if it was. Leslie had gotten him into this mess in the first place, the least he could do was be there to hold him up.

Bus leaves at five. You sure?

He held his breath while the dots floated. Several plays went by on the field and Joe figured he was busy doing coachy stuff. When the Jackets lost control of the ball and defense took over, the dots reappeared.

See you then, Coach Twinkle Toes.

Joe held his phone to his chest and exhaled. *Everything is better with Leslie.*

Twenty-Four

L eslie

He slid his phone back into his pocket and cursed when Culver-Stockton scored a touchdown, eliminating their lead.

"Dammit," Randy growled and threw his clipboard down again. "I told Tyler to cover 88." He went over to the wide-eyed kid and got in his face, shouting orders while also managing to be encouraging.

Leslie laughed. Randy may have been excitable, but he was a damn good coach. Watching him grow this year had been a pleasant surprise. Sure, he still pulled all of his goofy pranks, but he was laser-focused at practice and at games. Leslie began to think about eventually handing over the reins. Sandy had other goals, other things he wanted to accomplish including graduate school, but Randy loved football almost as much as Leslie did and he'd fully immersed himself in the sport and learning to coach. Leslie's body likely wouldn't hold up to the pressure of college coaching forever, but if he imparted whatever wisdom he had to his younger brother over the next few seasons, he could make a graceful exit.

And focus on a life with Joe.

After the Wildcats scored their extra point, it was time for special teams to take the field and Sandy rallied them. The Jackets' kicker was a loan from the soccer team and the kid was amazing. He'd routinely done both sports in high school and had earned a scholarship from Greenvale to do both. When he jogged back over to the sidelines and began to do his cool down exercises, Leslie thought about his baby team, and then he thought about Joe.

Joe had done a tremendous job coaching the cheer team. That half-time performance had been flawless, even with the injury. Leslie's heart had been full to bursting when he'd seen Joe's reaction to the kids' performance. But Leslie knew Joe had been struggling with what taking this job meant for his dance career, especially after his recent injury. Could he do both? What would that look like? Leslie had been worried that Joe would want to leave Greenvale, but he saw how attached Joe had been to the kids, how excited he'd been about the dance degree program he was working on, and how much he'd fit right in with Leslie's family. It was hard not to get ahead of himself.

Joe and Agnes had become besties from the get-go and there'd been additional trips to the Goalpost with the twins. Agnes loved having someone to try out vegetarian recipes for and someone to talk about dance with. It had been a long time for her. She had girlfriends she took weekend excursions with, cruises, etc., but after her mother passed away, she hadn't had as many tight connections to the Greenvale community. She and Barry's wife, Evelyn, worked on fundraisers for the college and special events, but Evelyn was shy around the rest of the Paytons.

Agnes and Joe had spent more than one Sunday doing yoga together, watching reality TV, and gossiping about celebrities they both knew while Leslie and the twins went over game films. Agnes even took Joe's side in silly arguments. It meant the world to Leslie that Joe fit so well with his family, and he wanted to broach the subject of making him a permanent member.

Leslie had asked Agnes how she'd feel about Joe moving in with them and she'd paused. "I love Joe. But does he know what that would mean? To you?"

Leslie still hadn't talked to Joe about his long-term medical concerns. He hadn't had another migraine since the night Joe had taken such good care of him, perhaps because Joe had continued to offer his healing touch, spending late-night hours massaging Leslie's head, hands, neck while they talked and laughed together. Leslie had a CT scheduled for the upcoming week in Des Moines to determine whether or not there had been any changes, although diagnosis of CTE was difficult to determine premortem and the science was still new. He'd told himself he would tell Joe just as soon as he'd talked to the doctor. Agnes only looked sad when Leslie explained his plan.

"Coach," Damontae approached. "Brandon wants to run something by you."

Leslie waved his quarterback over. "What's up?"

"Coach, Bryce's family is all here and he didn't say anything but I want him to get play time—"

"Send him in," Leslie said.

"I know we're down—"

When the kid started to explain himself, Leslie held up a hand. "No need. I get it. But you tell him he better play without distractions."

"Thanks, Coach."

The kid ran to grab his backup and Leslie turned his attention back to the game.

Sandy bumped his shoulder.

"What?"

"What happened to the playoffs? Bryce isn't nearly as accurate."

"Some things are more important than the playoffs. Did you know that Bryce lost his grandfather right before school started? He's kept a positive attitude and is excelling in his classes, but he shared in conference last week that he really wished his grandfather could have seen him play college ball. Some things are more important than winning. It's all about integrity and the I's in team, right?"

And sure enough, Bryce went in, played his heart out, and ended up throwing two completed passes and ran the ball to get the Jackets in scoring range before Leslie put his starter back in. The team scored, putting them back on top with just a quarter to go. Leslie felt a little floaty as the pressure mounted on his defense to keep the Wildcats from scoring, and when Brandon threw an interception that nearly resulted in another touchdown, he started to see some flickering in his peripheral vision. He handed Sandy his tablet and walked away from the team a few steps, applying pressure to his hand in the places Joe had told him to and tried to focus on his breathing. After a few short minutes, the aura was gone and he prayed that meant he dodged a bullet. When he returned, Sandy handed him the tablet without turning.

"Okay?"

"Yeah. I think so."

"Good thing you have the weekend to decompress, it's been a long week."

"I'm going with Joe to the competition tomorrow."

Sandy's head spun around. "But Leslie—"

The Wildcats fumbled and the Jackets recovered, carrying the ball sixty yards, putting them in scoring distance again. Leslie was proud of his players for their hustle. With two minutes left, the Jackets scored again, the defense was able to hold the Wildcats off, and with that, Leslie's baby team made the playoffs. He'd achieved his first-year goal with his alma mater. He'd lived up to the expectations his brother had asked of him when he took the job.

He thought back to his conversation with Malcolm Darling about the biography. Maybe Leslie's story was more than being a washed-up quarterback. Maybe he wasn't done making a difference. Maybe he did have time left to do some good.

The game ended and the team was elated. They ran out onto the field, hugged each other, hugged the cheerleaders, hugged family members who rushed out of the stands to help them celebrate. Leslie stood with his brothers and they smiled at each other.

"Feeling good, Brother Leslie?"

"Absolutely. Couldn't have done it without you two."

Randy and Sandy beamed at him and then joined in the celebration. Leslie shook hands with Damontae and dodged the Gatorade barrel, letting it hit Randy instead.

The Jackets hadn't made it this far in the twenty-five years since he'd transferred to Cal to gain experience before being drafted to the NFL. His father had insisted and he'd gone along with it, even though he'd loved playing for Greenvale. The Jackets long-time coach retired a year later and since then they'd had a string of coaches who hadn't quite been able to tap into the magic of the small, tight-knit community in Ayre Valley.

What would Rick Payton think of the player and coach Leslie had become? How would he feel about the choices Leslie made in his career? Leslie often wondered, and knew that he wouldn't change a thing. Rick had supported Leslie's decision to come out; it had been one of the last things they'd agreed on before Rick's condition deteriorated so much he could barely function as father and husband.

Barry found him in the throng of well-wishers and gave him a big hug.

"We did it, Brother Barry," Leslie said as he hugged him tight.

"*You* did it," Barry said, pounding on his back. "You did exactly what you said you would and I'm damn glad for it. So is everyone else in this stadium tonight."

"Well, our baby brothers did a lot to make this happen as well. Make sure to give credit where credit is due."

"Speaking of," Barry said, looking around. "The cheerleaders were phenomenal. Regardless of what happens at their competition tomorrow, Joe has more than lived up to your high praise."

Leslie grinned. "He's something, isn't he?"

Barry's smile faded. "You going to do something about it?"

"I intend to. As soon as we get through with the season, I plan to ask him to move in. Scandal or no scandal, Brother Barry, he and I are going to go public."

Barry nodded. "I'll support the two of you. Not sure how your teams will feel, but they'll get over it. By the way, the board seems to be pleased with his preliminary proposal for the dance degree. They're a little unsure about his lack of experience in academia, but I'm sure we can work on it."

"Good, because I'm hoping it's enough of an incentive."

"You mean besides settling down with you."

Leslie smiled but it was pained. Because he was still unsure whether he could ever be enough for Joe to want to stay.

Barry started to speak but they were engulfed with well-wishers and the carrying on lasted for what felt like hours. Then there was press for him to talk to. Sandy led him into the newly reroofed athletic center where there were about twenty reporters waiting for a word from the famous Leslie Payton. But he was distracted by the sounds of the cheerleaders.

Leslie walked to the doorway of the gym and caught the team doing the last phase of their massive pyramid that ended their routine.

Joe stood in front of them with one hip cocked out, his arms crossed in front of him, chewing on his fingernail. When the team hit their final pose, he pumped a fist.

"Excellent. Now, go home, rest, ice, and make sure you're packed. I ordered breakfast sandwiches from the Buzz for you all. You'll be great tomorrow."

Leslie's chest swelled with pride hearing Joe address his team. Such a good leader, a great coach. He entered the conference room and faced the press with a confident smile.

Sandy dropped Leslie off at 4:45 a.m. in the darkness outside the athletic center with strict instructions to meet them at the convention center by eight. He wanted Joe to have all the support he needed, and Sandy was thrilled to be needed.

Joe was waiting with a thermos.

"Morning." Leslie smiled broadly, over the moon excited to be Joe's plus-one even if it was for a cheer competition.

"Hmm, morning, yes. I wouldn't say a good one."

"Why not?"

Joe's dark eyebrows nearly met in the middle with the depth of his scowl. "I forgot how much I loathe these crack-of-dawn bus rides. I made coffee, that's how much I despise being up this early."

Leslie laughed, wishing he could pull Joe against him and hold him close, warm the chill he could tell Joe was feeling...but then the kids started trickling in, yawning and dragging their bags.

Joe greeted each one and asked about their sleep, whether they had everything they needed, how they were feeling. He was so thoughtful and engaged with each kid. Once they left him, they had a little more pep in their step and Leslie could tell they wanted to do their best for Joe Judd the coach, not so much Joe Judd the dancer. Joe had told him he worried that some of the kids might only try out for the cheer squad to get in front of him hoping he could help their career or so they could say they danced with Joe Judd. That was absolutely not the case anymore.

The bus arrived and Leslie stood back while Joe made sure all of the kids got on the bus with all of their things and then he turned to Leslie.

"You ready for this?" Joe asked from the door of the bus.

Yeah, he was asking whether Leslie was ready to get on the bus and drive two-plus hours in the frigid fall morning, but Leslie wanted to believe Joe was asking him if he was ready to take his hand, take the leap, and ride off into the sunset together, spending their happily ever after as one.

"I'm so ready."

Leslie climbed onto the bus behind Joe and waited for Joe to get settled before taking the aisle seat across from him, to give him some space. The driver asked him if they were ready and Joe told him they were clear for takeoff. Joe had his phone out and was furiously typing before he exhaled.

"What's up?"

Joe sighed again and then he stood up to address the kids.

"Friends, Terrell is okay. I heard from Marti. He has a fracture in his thumb at the base and he sprained his right wrist. The doctors said it's not terrible and he should be okay in four to six weeks."

"Does that give him enough time if we make it to Nationals?"

Joe nodded. "It does. And I want to thank William for stepping up to take his place today. William, we are grateful, and Genesis, both of you, thank you for your flexibility. Let's also thank Coach Payton for coming with us to be my assistant since Marti needs to be with Terrell today."

"Thank you, Coach Payton," the kids all said together, with Joe leading them like a conductor, and they all laughed.

"Now, get some rest, we'll be there in two hours."

He turned around and sat back down, then frowned at Leslie. "Why are you so far away?" he whispered. None of the kids had sat anywhere near them; they'd all headed to the back of the bus, leaving the front three to four rows empty.

"I don't want to crowd you," Leslie said.

Joe pouted, then his phone started buzzing again. He pulled it out, read the text with a frown again, then his eyebrows went way up. He tapped out a response and then turned off his phone and put it away.

"You'd never crowd me." He scooted over to the aisle seat and leaned toward Leslie. "I'm happy you're here."

Leslie leaned in. "Me too."

"That way if anything happens, we have an actual grown-up with us."

Leslie rolled his eyes, wishing he could reach over and take Joe's hand. Joe was fidgety and had been frowning all morning, which even at this early hour was unusual for him. Maybe it was Terrell he was worried about?

They chatted about the game and the other teams that would be at the competition. Some of the kids moved forward and asked Joe questions, then they turned their curiosity on him.

"Coach Payton? Were you nervous before football games?"

"Of course I was," Leslie answered, turning around in his seat. "I would often have...intestinal distress, if you get what I mean."

The girl who had asked, her eyes went huge. "You mean—"

"Yep," Leslie said, choosing not to use more descriptive language. "I'd start feeling the rumbly tumblies, then I'd hear the telltale gurgling sounds, and if I didn't get out of that headspace, I'd be running for the nearest facilities."

She covered her face and squealed. "But was it ever too late?"

Leslie barked out a laugh and gestured for her to lean close. "Only once, and after that I always kept extra pairs of pants with me. Just in case."

Joe tried to hold in his laugh and he ended up snorting.

"For real, I pooped in my dance trunks once," one of the senior girls said. "It's true. I had to go out in my underwear. Which were pink and green polka-dotted, and you can bet that wasn't our school colors. After that, I only wore school colors on my drawers."

The kids had a fit of the giggles and Leslie saw them loosening up, maybe getting a little pumped up for their competition.

"How about you, Coach Judd?"

He stopped laughing. "I've never shit myself. Ever." His serious face had Leslie gawking.

"You lie," he said.

"It's true," Joe said. Then he smacked his lips together. "I did vomit onstage before my first *Dance Machine* performance, but never did I shit myself." He smoothed a piece of hair back. "They were able to edit it out before the TV audience knew what happened."

The group of kids at the front had grown to most of the team and they all howled at the stories Leslie and Joe told about nerves getting the best of them before performances.

"The whole picturing them in their underwear thing did not work for me," Joe said. "I once pictured the host of *Dance Machine*, Robin Flanders, in a leather harness and G-string getup and I couldn't look him in the eye after that. Still can't."

Leslie had a stitch in his side from laughing when the bus finally turned into the convention center parking lot and soon the team was swallowed up in a cloud of hairspray and pom-poms. The only way he could even keep track of anyone was their bright green and gold hair bows and the guys' gold sparkly shorts. Leslie had asked whose idea they were and he'd shrugged.

"They wanted to stand out."

The team would be competing last in their division and so Joe made sure the kids stayed loose but not too much. He talked them down when their nerves were getting the best of them, and they walked through the routine a gazillion times so William the stand-in could be sure he was comfortable.

Leslie was in awe of how much work went into their two-minute routine, how intricate each movement was, how much each of the members had to rely on each other to be in the right place at the right time to make all of their stunts go off without a hitch. And the tumblers had to know their exact path so they wouldn't run into each other. It was exhilarating and terrifying to watch all at the same time.

When it was finally time for the team to perform, Joe told Leslie to go stand in the coaches' area and wait for him while he gave them one last pep talk. When he finally emerged from backstage, Joe's dark eyes were so serious. And he was chewing on his thumb.

"You're going to bleed if you keep that up," Leslie said, gently moving Joe's hand from his mouth.

Joe turned on him and snapped his teeth together. "I'll bite *you*."

Leslie put his arm around him and squeezed, then he pulled away quickly. "I'm sorry."

Joe hip-bumped him and remained close. "Don't be. I'm so glad you're here." He looked up at Leslie and smiled.

The Jackets cheer team was announced and Leslie held his breath. Joe leaned against him and Leslie felt the tension running through his body. Joe, on a good day, was wound tight, but today? Leslie knew Joe felt this was a test of his mettle, a way for Joe to show the college community that they'd made the right decision in recruiting him, and to show himself that he was where he was needed. They'd spent hours talking about this over the past couple of weeks and Leslie had done all he could to reassure Joe.

The squad ran out cheering, doing kicks and jumps, and the crowd clapped appreciatively, but it was obvious folks weren't sure what to make of the Jackets team. Joe had explained to Leslie that they were now competing in a different division as they had more male-identifying students and that not only were they dressed differently than the other teams, but their music was different, their moves would be a bit more edgy, still regulation but just...more. Joe had choreographed a unique routine that could be a smash hit...or a flop. There was no doubt that the team was skilled, that they had perfected their routine, but there was always a chance the judges could think it was too out there.

The music started and it was a rock song, a tune from Nothing More called "We Don't Stop," which already made it stand out from the rest of the EDM/techno crowd. The Jackets also had clips from the Beastie Boys "Whatcha Want" and the dance classic "Sexyback" from Justin Timberlake. There weren't the firework sound effects and zips and airhorns like the other groups who had gone before, but it definitely engaged the crowd.

Joe gasped as one of the stunts wobbled and he reached for Leslie's hand, which he held with a death grip for the rest of the routine. But there was no need. The kids stuck their landings, the tumbling went off without a hitch, and Joe's three-man hype team even had a few moments to show off their B-boy moves. Leslie wasn't a judge, of course, but he knew quality when he saw it and the Jackets' routine was a cut above everyone else that had performed that day.

"Here we go," Joe breathed as the team went into their final pyramid. He squeezed Leslie's hand even tighter and his knee bounced.

Leslie couldn't even comprehend how to orchestrate such a complicated, intricate structure but these kids nailed it. Every flyer was solid, the bases all stood strong, and when the music ended, the cheerleaders exploded out of their stance and screamed and hugged and jumped. Every person in the crowd stood from their seats, clapping with expressions like "what did I just see that I loved so much?"

Joe turned on Leslie and leaped into his arms, wrapping his legs around Leslie and shouting an exuberant "*Yes!*" Leslie hugged him with all his might and laughed as Joe shouted. Joe put his hands on Leslie's face and gave him a big smooch and Leslie wished he had a picture of the joy on Joe's face because he was too shocked to really take it in. Then Joe wiggled to be put down, grabbed Leslie's hand, and the two of them ran to the backstage area.

They found the team surrounding Terrell and Marti, who had apparently arrived in time to see the performance. Sandy was with them as well. He grinned at Leslie and gave him the metal horns, his sign of approval.

"You guys were perfect," she said as she hugged the bouncing women and high-fived the men.

Terrell's hand was wrapped in a brace and in a sling, but his smile was genuinely thrilled for his teammates.

"You nailed it," he said, and he was carefully hugged by all of the team.

Then Joe was swarmed by his beloved Yellowjackets. He was scooped out of Leslie's reach and picked up over the heads of his team.

Leslie winced and hoped they were as steady with their coach as they'd been with each other.

"They better not drop him," Leslie muttered as Sandy joined him.

"That was probably the coolest cheerleading I've ever seen, Brother Leslie. Twinkle Toes has set a new bar and those folks out there are quaking in their ballet slippers."

Leslie chuckled and patted his brother on the shoulder. "I love it."

I love him. And he couldn't wait for the world to know.

It was another three hours until the results were announced so the team gathered together and shoved pizza in their faces as fast as they could. The cheerleaders packed away as much, if not more, than their football counterparts would have. Leslie loved their energy. He hadn't spent a lot of time around female athletes and they were a trip. There was more burping and talk of bodily functions than Leslie had thought possible.

And the team all gazed dreamily at their coach as if their souls were trying to express their gratitude for his leadership and he didn't even realize it. Leslie would remind him of this moment later, when they were alone, and could properly celebrate, because even if the Jackets didn't win, they were triumphant.

At four o'clock, the teams went back out onto the mat and lined up to hear the results. The Jackets, straightened up after their pizza orgy, maintained the proper sportsmanlike behavior as Joe and Marti had threatened them with hundreds of push-ups if they acted like fools. They cheered for the other teams as they went through the other divisions. When it got to them, Joe leaned closer to Leslie again as if he could siphon off strength. He could have it. Leslie would give him the world. And he intended to. When this day was over, Leslie was going to ask Joe to move in. They were going to make a plan to go public. Leslie was tired of waiting. He was as giddy as the kids standing onstage waiting to hear if they'd won.

"And now for the Large Coed Category. In third place we have MidAmerica Nazarene!" Everyone went nuts. The Jackets didn't lose their composure. "In second place, Missouri Valley!" The team remained stock-still with well-rehearsed smiles on their faces. It was down to them and the team from Kansas, who'd put on a clean performance as well. Joe had explained they were the Jackets' main competition, but after their performance, where one of their stunts had fallen, he thought they might have edged them out of contention, but then he had said the Jackets also had a mistake that he wasn't sure the judges picked up on. Leslie hadn't seen anything, but Joe would know.

"The winner of this year's NAIA Heart Of America Conference Cheer Championships is...Greenvale College!"

Joe froze and exhaled, letting the tension drip from his body. Leslie squeezed his shoulder and Joe turned to him, burying his face in Leslie's chest.

"You did it, Twinkle Toes," Sandy yelled, slapping him on the back.

Joe smiled at Sandy and high-fived him, but then he turned to Leslie, his eyes wet.

"I can't breathe."

Leslie laughed and gave him a squeeze. "Congratulations."

Joe blinked and then pushed up on his toes. And he kissed Leslie like no one was watching, like nothing else mattered. "Thank you for believing in me," he whispered against Leslie's lips. When he stepped back, he wiped at his tears and laughed at what was probably a stunned expression on Leslie's face.

Then the chorus of "Oh. My. God!" filtered in and the gasps of the cheer squad pulled them both out of the moment.

Leslie and Joe both turned to find the entire squad gawking at them with their jaws hanging open, Marti laughing and Sandy shaking his head.

And then the questions started pouring in.

Twenty-Five

Joe

"Is Coach Payton your boyfriend?"

"How long have you two been—"

"Are you two like—"

"Does President Payton know?"

Joe allowed a few questions and then he held up a hand. "If you'll all calm down and get your shorts out of your ass and hang on." Everyone laughed, but they continued to bounce up and down as if they were waiting for confirmation that Santa Claus had come. "Yes, Coach Payton is my boyfriend," he said and he winked at Leslie. "We've only just made it official but it's been going on for a loooong time, and yes we're in love." He turned to Leslie. "Does your brother know?"

"He does," Leslie said.

"There. Happy?"

A chorus of cheers rang out in the echoey room and hugs went all around.

"I knew it," Terrell said, smacking his leg and shaking his head. Apparently, Marti hadn't told him, which was probably for the best.

"This is almost better than winning," Sidney squealed. "Almost."

Everyone laughed and then tried to catch their breath.

"Does this mean you're staying?" Terrell asked. "Are you guys, like, getting married?"

Joe glanced at Leslie and let out a nervous laugh. Why did he have to get asked that right now when he'd been dodging texts from Arthur all day?

Leslie's cheeks were red but he seemed to be just as invested as the kids in Joe's answer.

"Um, there's a lot going on, so, I can't really say about next year, yet. I don't even know if they want me back next year, and I'm still working out some situations, but now we focus on Nationals, right? Go Jackets." He pumped a fist and the gesture fell flat.

Wow, that was such a mature way of saying, "I don't know."

The kids' smiles faded a bit, as if someone just told them "Santa already came" and they realized they didn't get what they'd asked for.

"The bus is here," Marti said, placing a hand on his back. "Okay, everyone, make sure you've got all of your stuff and let's go."

The kids chattered excitedly as they headed out to the bus.

"I'm glad you made it," Joe said as he hugged Marti. "I'm glad Terrell could be here. He doing okay?"

"Prognosis is good. You guys be safe. I'll see you Monday," she said.

Leslie walked behind him, and when Joe snuck a glance, he saw that Leslie was arguing with Sandy. Leslie made eye contact and Joe's stomach crashed to the ground like a fallen flyer missed by spotters.

Shit.

Joe had a lot to explain to Leslie. He'd been asked to fly out two more times for *Dance Machine* live shows, the *Dance Machine* producers wanted an answer on the national tour, and there was the audition for *Kinky Boots*. If Joe hadn't taken the position at Greenvale, he could have done them all, no question. Okay, maybe not both the Broadway show and the traveling *Dance Machine* tour... Arthur was great at making things work, and he would since Joe was committed here through May. But Joe had wanted to talk to Barry about next year before he made any decisions and there hadn't been time.

The last of the kids hopped on the bus and Joe turned to see Leslie say one more heated statement to Sandy before he walked over, his forehead creased, his heavy brows low.

Joe waved to Sandy, who nodded, gave a half-hearted wave, and then he headed toward his Jeep.

"Ready for your thrilling and luxurious bus ride home?" he asked Leslie. All he wanted to do was curl up in a seat together, no longer required to keep his hands to himself. He was so grateful Leslie had been by his side when his team won. He couldn't wait until they could celebrate together.

Leslie paused a few steps from Joe. "What was all that?"

Joe blinked. No, they couldn't do this now. Not when they had a two-hour drive ahead of them.

"All what? I was kind of running on adrenaline."

"Next year, Joe. What was that?"

Joe stood a little taller. "The truth, as much as I can say right now. I'm a temporary employee, Leslie. I'm not on the tenure track or anything. I don't even know if I'll be offered a contract again—"

"You're still not sure about this. About us."

"Leslie! How could you think that? I love you." And he did, with all his heart, and he was determined to make it all work: Leslie, the shows, everything...somehow. But he knew Leslie had a different future in mind.

Leslie nodded and gave Joe a half smile as he climbed onto the bus.

Joe climbed on behind him and had hoped Leslie would sit next to him, but he sat on the aisle like he had the last time with his body turned away, facing the window.

His body language read, "leave me alone."

Joe sat in the seats where he'd been before and blew out a breath. The driver asked if they were all set and Joe told him they were ready to go. The bus pulled away from the convention center as rain started to pelt the windows. It had been a clear morning, but the clouds had moved in during the day and the chill had Joe pulling his coach's jacket tighter around him.

Leslie closed his eyes and Joe noticed him squeezing the spot between his thumb and index finger.

"You okay, babe? You need me to—"

"I'm fine. I'm just going to rest my eyes."

There was no invitation, no welcoming smile.

"Let me know if there's anything I can do."

Leslie nodded and closed his eyes, resting his head against the seat back.

The bus ride was the longest two hours of Joe's life.

He debated with himself what he should say, how he could fix this. But then what was he supposed to do?

You committed to Leslie, that meant to him that you were going to be here. Even if you weren't hired back by the college for some reason, he wants you with him. You could still dance, you could commute back and forth to LA. But if the college doesn't hire you back, what happens when the dancing dries up? Where will you work? What will you do? You can't exactly let Leslie take care of you financially. That's not how it is between you, and you certainly haven't put away enough of a nest egg to retire at thirty-six. At least if you lived back in Hollywood there are studios, choreography jobs...

But you want Leslie. You belong with Leslie. Somehow, you've gotta make this work.

The noise in Joe's head was so loud it drowned out the noise from the kids and he didn't realize they were calling his name. He turned around in his seat and they waved him over. Leslie was asleep so he shushed them as he scooted down the aisle to where his hype squad was sitting.

"So tell us more about Nationals."

Joe smiled. "Nationals are in Ypsilanti, Michigan in March. We'll be competing against the finalists from all of the NAIA conferences."

"Michigan? In March? I thought it was in Florida and we were going to get to soak up the rays!"

Joe smiled. "Florida is UCA championships, and they're in January. We'd be competing against NCAA teams if we went there. Unfortunately, Greenvale has only been competing in NAIA for the past ten years and there aren't enough funds for us to go to both competitions. Plus we need to get permission from the administration."

"But all the fundraising? Didn't we raise like a shit-ton of money?" Gino asked. "No offense?"

"Yeah, we did, but some of that money is going to replace the fitness center equipment. We've raised enough to meet our goal, but I still want to beat football." Joe grinned. "If we win Nationals, that will make a big difference for next year. The team will be able to request that they participate in both competitions."

David, Ivan, and Gino stroked their nonexistent goatees. Joe's rules meant a clean-shaven squad.

"So you're saying if we work hard enough, next year we can escape the Midwest chill in January and compete in Florida?"

Joe barked out a laugh. "Sure, it's possible."

"And you'll get us there, right?"

All three young men leaned in, waiting for an answer.

"I'd like to. I'm going to be submitting my plans to the president for the dance degree program next week and we'll see. If they like it, maybe they'll keep me around. But you guys have me for this year. We'll go to Nationals and we'll crush it."

He put out his fist and the guys fist-bumped him.

"And we've got basketball season, right?"

"Right," Joe said, pleased his three conscripts were so enthused. They kept their heads together brainstorming actions for basketball season and soon the bus was turning into the Athletic Center parking lot.

"Clean up your messes," Joe said, springing into action. He hurried to Les's side and gently nudged him.

"We're back, babe."

Leslie's eyes fluttered open and he winced at the light.

"Migraine?" he asked.

Leslie nodded and Joe went down the steps in front of him to support him if he needed it.

"Thanks," he said once they reached the lot.

"Let me send these kids back to their dorms and I'll drive you home."

"No, Joe. I'm fine."

"Leslie, please. Wait a few minutes?"

Leslie sighed and Joe did a once-over of the bus, picking up a couple of stray wrappers but otherwise proud of the kids for being neat.

When he got back, Leslie was waving goodbye to the last of the kids. It was chilly but not raining yet.

"Leslie, what happened?"

"What did you hear from your agent?"

Joe shifted his weight. How could he bring the opportunities up without Leslie panicking? And was that even his job? To protect Leslie's feelings? He'd been honest. The whole time.

"*Dance Machine* wants me to headline a national tour next summer. Ten cities in five weeks. I just got the details today. Rehearsals would start end of May. I'd be done end of July."

Leslie nodded. "For the summer then." He planted his hands on his hips. "You sure you'll be okay? With your hip?"

"I think so." He needed to go all in. "They also need me for two more weekends for live shows. And the director I worked with for *West Side Story* wants me to audition for a principal in *Kinky Boots*. That would start rehearsing in August."

Leslie let his gaze drop to the ground in front of him. "You want to go."

"I want to work, yes. Barry can't give me a for sure on next year yet, not until after my evaluations at the semester and the budget. Leslie, I *have* to work. I *want* to work." He stepped closer but was afraid to touch Leslie. Afraid of how he might react. He couldn't take a physical rejection from Leslie, not now.

Leslie didn't speak for several beats and then he exhaled harshly. "I wish I was enough for you."

"*What?* Leslie, are you kidding me? You're *everything* to me. How could you say that?"

"I worried you'd have one foot out the door the whole time you were here. Were you ever planning to stay? Or did you just say that to placate me?"

"That's not fair and you know it! Leslie, you've reached the pinnacle of success in your sport. You won multiple Super Bowls, for god's sake.

You've achieved everything that a football player could ever dream of. *I haven't done that.*"

"And look where it got me," Leslie said, raising his voice for the first time in Joe's presence.

Joe stepped back, a shudder running through him. He'd never seen Leslie angry, not like this.

Leslie's eyes flared at Joe's retreat, and he cursed.

"I'm sorry. But if you weren't planning on staying, I wish you never would have come."

He stumbled a bit and then he turned and walked away, leaving Joe dumbfounded.

"Leslie! How can you...Leslie?"

Sandy pulled up and Leslie climbed into the Jeep, leaving Joe standing there. In shock.

What had just happened? Leslie hadn't seemed himself, but the hurt in his words had come through loud and clear.

Leslie had never walked away from Joe. But then maybe this was what Joe deserved for all the times he'd run from the person he loved most in the world.

Joe felt the first few drops of rain slap his cheek. As the taillights of the Jeep turned out of sight, he started walking back to Higdon.

By the time he reached the dorm, he was soaked to the bone.

Twenty-Six

L eslie

This one was a doozy, this migraine, but Leslie wasn't sure what hurt worse, his head or his heart.

Or his pride.

He'd acted a fool, walking out on Joe like that, but what was he supposed to do? He knew if he'd stayed, it would have gone from bad to worse.

He'd lashed out at Joe, and didn't he feel like an ass for it. But dammit, Joe said they were going to do this. He was going to stay. And now he was talking about not being here next year and taking on jobs that meant endless traveling and...

Had he ever intended to stay?

Sandy remained quiet on the drive from the school to their house and he stood by to lend a hand if Leslie needed it as they headed out of the Jeep and into the house.

"Thanks for coming all the way out there," Leslie said. "I know a cheer competition is not exactly your idea of a good time on a rare Saturday off."

"I wanted to support Joe and the kids," Sandy said.

They went up to Leslie's rooms and Sandy stood there while Leslie took his medication. Sandy didn't speak for a long time, so long Leslie finally turned around to look at him. "What's wrong?"

"Joe's right, you know. He cares about you."

Leslie opened his mouth to speak and then he shook his head. "I can't do this now. I need to rest."

"You can't hold onto him so tightly. You've gotta let him go do what he needs to do if you want to keep him in your life. He'll come back to you. He loves you. And getting upset about it before you even know what's going to happen? It's not fair to him, Leslie, especially since he doesn't know everything about you."

Leslie blew out a breath. "I was going to tell him. But now...if I tell him and he does stay, he'll be staying because he feels obligated."

Leslie felt like a broken man on a good day. Today, he felt destroyed. Stabbing pain in his head, aching back, knives in his knee. Every movement tore him down a little more. The roar of the crowd today at the cheer competition really set off his migraine. It had been coming on since the night before, but he'd thought he could dodge it. The acupressure Joe taught him seemed to work. Sometimes. But when the screaming continued and got louder during the award ceremony, that had been it.

Maybe he had been harsh with Joe, but he was just facing the inevitable. Joe wasn't going to stay with him. Leslie wasn't enough to keep Joe in Ayre Valley. Fifteen years had been a long time to wait for his chance, and it seemed as if it had been in vain. If Joe was leaving in May, Leslie might as well just let him go now.

"Fine. Rest. We're seeing Dr. Taylor Monday. Remember, you've got your test results to go over. And then you need to talk to Joe. Tell him why you're in such a damn rush to be with him."

"I'd hardly consider fifteen years a rush."

"He's been here for three months, Leslie. That's it. That's not enough time for you to expect him to drop everything."

But did Leslie have much longer to wait? The migraines had been so much worse these past few months. Sure, he'd been under more stress—some of it self-imposed—but he was worried. It was a vicious cycle. The more he worried, the more his head hurt, the more he worried.

There was no way to diagnose Chronic Traumatic Encephalopathy, the disease that killed his father, until after death. At forty-five years old, Leslie was nowhere near the level of concern his father had been. By his age, Rick Payton had already started to have major mood swings and aggression. He'd become violent with his family. He had majorly impaired cognitive function, couldn't remember people he'd played the sport he loved with, couldn't remember his childhood. Couldn't remember things from Barry's and Leslie's childhoods.

Leslie wasn't anywhere near that, but the headaches and their frequency terrified him.

The doctor had done a PET scan, MRI and CT scan and could find nothing out of the ordinary. They were going to meet with him in Kansas City to start looking at other causes for his migraines and other treatments. The doctor had been hopeful that they could get his pain under control.

"I'll see you in the morning," Sandy said. "But you should call Joe."

"I don't think so," Leslie said. "Let it go, Sandy. Let him go."

This time it hurt so much more than Hawaii. He knew he'd gotten his hopes up too much then that the two of them could start something real. But now?

Leslie trudged to his bedroom, vaguely aware that Sandy was still talking to him.

He undressed, showered, and fell into bed, his ears ringing and pain scrambling behind his eyes for purchase.

His phone buzzed and he picked it up, the light searing his retinas.

I'm sorry. Please say we can talk about this tomorrow?

Leslie didn't know how to answer, didn't even know what to say.

· · ·

Talk later. Sleep now.

It was all he could do to keep his eyes open long enough to hit send before he dropped his phone on the floor.

The ruckus the next morning—it could only be described as a ruckus—roused Leslie from sleep and into misery. His door opened and he threw an arm over his eyes to keep the light out. It sounded like twenty people were shouting, but only one came inside. Leslie swore as the door closed, and then a weight settled on the bed next to him and he felt soft hands on his forehead.

"You big infuriating man."

Joe. Why was he here? Questions flooded Leslie's mind but he heard Joe shush him.

"Don't talk. I'm mad at you. You just lay here and let me take care of you, Sasquatch."

Leslie wanted to laugh, but tears stung his eyes, adding to the misery. He couldn't imagine why Joe was there, but he didn't want to fight. He sighed and scooted over, giving Joe enough space to slide in next to him. He focused on Joe's healing touch, the gentle pressure over his forehead, cheekbones, and cranium easing him into comfortable sleep.

Each time he woke over that day, Joe was there to give him water, to make him eat bits of soup and bread he recognized as being Agnes's creations. Joe whispered softly to him, but the words were meant to ease, meant to keep Leslie relaxed, allowing his body to shake off this latest impairment.

He woke sometime in the evening pain-free and found Joe snuggled up to him, breathing deeply and evenly. Leslie got up to use the bathroom and rinsed off in the shower without waking him and when he returned, he tried not to disturb Joe, but Joe flung an arm and a leg over Leslie.

"How are you feeling?" he asked in a hoarse voice.

"Better. Everything's better with you."

Joe smiled and pressed a kiss into Leslie's jaw, and Leslie couldn't resist kissing him back. What started out as light, breezy kisses grew needy and desperate. There was a lot that needed saying, but Leslie didn't want to think about all the reasons he should stop, should tell Joe to go. He didn't want clothes to stop him, didn't want anything between them, especially not more angry words. He wanted Joe and if this was the end, at least he'd have this memory to cling to.

"Leslie?" Joe asked as Leslie untied Joe's joggers and slid his hands underneath, cupping Joe's ass over the fabric of his trunks. "Baby?"

"Will you let me have you?" Leslie asked.

Joe gazed up at him, questioning him, probably wondering how Leslie could have said one thing yesterday and now...Leslie didn't have the words, but he had the feelings, and he needed to show Joe how important he was, why he'd been holding on so tightly.

Joe answered his question by removing his shirt and sliding out of his trunks. He held out his arms to Leslie and Leslie covered his body, sliding in between Joe's open thighs.

"Do you have—"

Leslie reached over to his bedside table and pulled a bottle of lube and a condom out of the drawer. He moved on autopilot because if he thought too much about what they were about to do, it would be over before it started. A crease formed on Joe's forehead as if he were unsure.

"Tell me when you're ready. I don't want to hurt you," Leslie said, his voice cracking. Joe nodded and reached for Leslie's hand, guiding it to his opening. Leslie tried to be careful; he was as gentle as he could possibly be as Joe fought to relax and let Leslie's fingers in. Joe's breath caught and he moaned, his whole body shaking. He let his legs fall impossibly wide open and Leslie moved down to place kisses on Joe's pelvis, on his sac, on his shaft. Leslie draped Joe's legs over his shoulders and bent down further to use his tongue to help relax Joe. He loved being this close to him, this intimate. He loved how open Joe was with him, how he writhed against Leslie's face, how he cried out Leslie's name over and over, how he held onto Leslie's left hand with a death grip.

"I'm sorry I'm not... I haven't even waxed." Joe groaned and Leslie laughed.

"I love your hair. Don't ever wax on my account. I love it."

Joe placed his hand on Leslie's cheek, forcing him to look into Joe's eyes.

"I love *you*, Leslie Payton. So much. Please know that."

Leslie moved up and smiled at Joe. "I know. I know you do." He wouldn't allow himself to dwell on thoughts of "but is it enough?"

Leslie slid on the condom and held his cock against Joe. Joe nodded. "Yeah, come on. Be in me."

Leslie's bad knee ached and his body was tired, but he shut it all out as he pushed himself past Joe's tight opening. They both cried out at their joining. They had yet to do this. All of their previous nights together they'd either been too tired to do more than just hold each other and kiss, or they'd spent hours discovering all the ways the other liked to be touched, kissed, licked, and bit and then they rode that edge as long as they possibly could.

But tonight was something else, at least for Leslie. If it was the last time he could be this close to Joe, he wanted it all. In the morning he would go to the doctor, find out what reality he was facing, and then he would tell Joe the truth, being fully prepared that if Joe had any inclination to say goodbye, the news that Leslie may have a degenerative brain disease that would rob him of his faculties would most likely push him over the edge, and the truth was, he was a selfish bastard for keeping that information from him, especially now. So much for being the nice guy. Leslie turned off the part of his conscience that was ringing alarm bells and he let himself get lost in Joe's body.

Leslie rocked his hips against Joe's, memorizing every curve of his body, every sound he made. He focused on Joe, keeping his movements small, tight, and gentle. He wrapped one hand around Joe's straining cock and stroked it in time with his movements, using Joe's precum to make his hand glide over Joe's velvety soft flesh.

"Leslie, baby, I love you. I love you so much. I'm yours, baby. I'm yours." And Joe came, his body curling up off the bed as his cum landed on his chest. His head fell back and he swore, his body loose and sated. He reached up to cup Leslie's cheek as Leslie's body wound tighter and tighter, his balls heavy, his spine tingling.

"Joe...God...Joe." He moaned as his body shuddered, his hips losing their rhythm as they slapped against Joe. Joe dug his fingers into Leslie's ass, pulling him even closer, holding him tight as Leslie let go. He jerked, cursed, gasped, and growled. Tears filled the corners of his eyes and he blinked them away. He dropped his head onto Joe's chest and Joe wrapped his arms around Leslie, turning them on their sides.

Joe caressed his back and whispered to him, smoothing his hair, and Leslie wanted to believe all he had said.

I love you. I'm yours. I'm yours.

Leslie kissed Joe once and then faded into a deep sleep, much deeper now that his head was no longer killing him, and he prayed that when he woke, he could make Joe understand, could make him want to stay.

Joe left at some point in the middle of the night, which Leslie discovered when Sandy woke him and rushed him out the door. He'd overslept and they were barely going to have enough time to get to Kansas City. Agnes and Randy joined them, making the outing a Payton Family Adventure. They asked about the cheer competition and Leslie filled them in.

"I've never seen anything like it," Leslie said. He turned to Sandy, who'd been driving while silent. "Wasn't it great?"

"Yeah," Sandy said. His knuckles were white where he gripped the steering wheel at ten and two. He didn't say another word the entire drive.

Dr. Jonathan Taylor had been a long-time friend of the Payton's. As a young neurologist, he'd been hired by the 49ers to treat Rick's bizarre and terrible symptoms, and after Rick passed, Dr. Taylor had worked with specialists around the world to discover whatever they could about CTE and how to avoid it.

He started off with a long list of questions, which Leslie answered with ease, but doubted himself the entire time, wondering if he was right. Then he went over Leslie's imaging and blood test results. Besides his cholesterol being a tad high—and of course the knees—he was perfectly fine. As fine as he could possibly be.

"There's still no cure, Leslie, and there's no way of diagnosing CTE until after the patient has passed, but I honestly don't think that's what we're dealing with. Your cognitive function is frankly not anymore affected than patients I've worked with who suffered one or two concussions. Yes, there are some elements you struggle to deal with, like the overstimulation you experienced this weekend, the difficulty remembering appointments, etc., struggles with mathematical computation and abstract reasoning. But Leslie, these are all very *very* manageable symptoms. As for the migraines, I want to refer you to a specialist who has had great success treating them through lifestyle changes in concert with medication. Over twenty-nine million Americans deal with migraines every day and they live mostly normal lives."

Leslie exhaled at the doctor's prognosis, and Agnes squeezed his hand. "You mean, I have time?"

Dr. Taylor laughed. "Leslie, you are fitter than most men your age and you have the resources to treat the issues you do have. I think you'll be alive and kicking long after I retire."

Leslie laughed and turned to his mom. She hugged him tight and sniffled. She wiped tears from her eyes and accepted a tissue from the doctor.

"So you heard that, right?" Randy said. "He said you're fine. So does that mean I can get back to beating him about the head and shoulders?"

The doctor laughed. "If you mean that figuratively then yes. You have no restrictions except that you need to avoid any sports or physical activities that have the potential for blows to the head. That includes diving into a swimming pool, martial arts sparring, boxing, etc. And no football, of course. Coach it all you want, but don't play it."

Leslie smiled and felt some of his fear dissipating.

"And one more thing. I think you should consider therapy. Working with a cognitive behavioral specialist can help you with the areas you may be struggling with and help to minimize them getting worse. It would also be good to get a baseline. And most importantly, to get support around managing your moods and recognizing any changes. It's better than waiting for it to just happen on its own. If you know what to look for and how to manage it, it will be better for you and your family."

Leslie nodded. *Damn.* What the doctor was suggesting was so reasonable. Why hadn't he done this already? Maybe he could have avoided some of this heartache with Joe.

Man, he had really fucked up. He'd let his fear get in the way of things with Joe, and he'd really hurt him. Leslie had a lot of work to do to make amends.

He went past the handshake and scooped Dr. Taylor up in a bear hug, which made the much smaller man laugh.

"You've got a lot of good years left, Leslie. Use them well. Take care of yourself, and I'll see you in a year."

The Paytons left the office a little lighter than they'd gone in. Except for one. They decided on Black Bear Diner for lunch and as they sat waiting for their food, Leslie finally addressed the elephant in the room.

"So it seems like I won't be needing the nursing home just yet, aren't you glad?" he asked Sandy.

Sandy stirred his straw around in his water and stared at the table. He shrugged and Leslie was taken back to the middle-school days with the twins, the period about a year after Rick died and it had finally settled in that their dad wasn't coming back this time. They'd been holy terrors before, but it had been hyperactivity and good trouble. But then it turned more destructive. Stink bombs in the cafeteria at school, vandalism, mean-spirited practical jokes at Leslie and Barry's expense.

"Guess so."

"So what's your damage, Brother Sandy?" Randy said. "I thought you'd be just as relieved, if not more, that you've been saved from wiping his ass for another year."

Sandy launched his straw at Randy's face, hitting him in the eye.

"Ow, what the fuck?"

"I *am* glad," Sandy said, sneaking a glance at Leslie. "I'm just...whatever."

"Sandy," Agnes said, placing her hand over his on the table. He pulled it back and dropped it in his lap.

"What the hell?" Randy asked, but Leslie put a hand out to shush him.

"Speak freely, Brother Sandy. You've earned the right. What's got you spitting fire?"

"I told Joe. Everything."

Leslie sat up, his body tensed and ready to spring into action.

"When?"

"Last night. I was in the kitchen when he was leaving."

"What did he say?" Agnes asked, placing her hand on Leslie's arm as if she could keep him in his seat.

"He asked me, 'what else?' What wasn't Leslie telling him. So I told him."

"That wasn't your place, asshole," Randy said, but Leslie kept his mouth shut.

"I couldn't stand it, you know? Joe thinking this was all his fault. You let him believe this was all him, and that wasn't fair. So I told him. Be pissed at me if you want, but it's out there. Don't ask me to keep shit from him ever again. Not after he's taken such good care of you."

Sandy pushed back from the table as the server brought their food. She set it down in front of them trying to keep a smile on her face while they watched Sandy walk out the door.

"I'll go," Agnes said.

"No. This is my doing. I'll handle it."

Leslie stood and walked out the door of the restaurant, noticing a few folks looking at him. Well, so be it.

"Hey," he said as he reached the Jeep. He leaned his elbows on Sandy's window and sighed.

Sandy sat back against the seat and stared out the windshield.

"You can be mad all you want, but he cares about you. He took care of you. It's not right keeping him in the dark, Leslie. You wanted to be with him for so long, and I've stood by you even when I didn't agree, but this—"

"You're right. I'm sorry."

Sandy wiped at his eye and looked at his hands resting in his lap.

"You're right, and you were right to tell him. I'm not mad."

Sandy nodded. "You need to tell him everything. Let him make up his mind."

"You're right."

Sandy turned to him and frowned. "Why aren't you mad?"

"Because. I'm mad at myself. I've taken you for granted, Sandy, and I apologize for that."

"No. You haven't, but this thing with Joe...you were so happy, and I didn't want to see you fuck it up."

"You're right. I fucked up. I should have told him."

"Man, stop agreeing with me. You're freaking me out."

Leslie laughed and it finally got Sandy to smile.

"It's not like I've ever been in love, you know, but I remember what it looked like with Mom and Dad."

Leslie squeezed his shoulder. "Yeah. They were in love. I wish you could have seen them before, you know?"

Sandy finally looked at him. "You're nothing like he was. You're not going to *be* him. I don't need medical tests to tell me that."

Leslie blew out a shaky breath. "How? How can you have so much faith in me when I don't have it in myself?"

Sandy turned to face him. "Because you raised us. You never raised your voice unless we deserved it. You were fair and tough, and you let us know you hated our actions but you loved us. We could never tell with Dad."

"He loved you the best he was capable of. Anything I did for you and Randy I learned from his example."

"What did you learn?" Randy asked as he and Agnes approached the car with to-go containers in hand.

"That my brothers are pretty damned smart. Now, let's get back to Ayre Valley. I have work to do."

They got back to Greenvale in time for football practice and Leslie let his brothers take the lead. When it was over, he walked over to Higdon and worked up the courage to go inside and face the music, like the moody stuff he heard coming from inside the common room. It seemed empty until he stuck his head in the doors.

Joe was alone, in front of the mirrors, dressed in snug black pants and no shirt. He moved in long lines, reaching at a diagonal and lifting the opposite leg and then he'd switch directions, making his way across the floor in a fluid movement. Joe's long limbs seemed to grow impossibly longer as he stretched them out as far as they could go and still be attached to his body. His feet were bare and his hair was loose and wavy, falling in his face.

Leslie stepped into the room and watched Joe move as if he were liquid, or a flower bending on its stem with the breeze or the weight of a bumble bee. He did a series of turns and then a leap that sent him rolling on the floor. He rose slowly, a little unsteady on his feet, and his facial expression was so full of passion, of longing and...sadness. He reached out with his hands, the muscles on his arms standing out, his fingers spread wide, articulating each bone with each grasp. He swung his leg in an arc and his toe hit the floor, leading into a lunge. His arms wheeled over and over until he brushed the floor with his fingertips and then he arched back, bending in half. He held that pose until the music ended and then he stood upright, his chest heaving as he stood in front of the mirror, glaring at Leslie.

"That was beautiful," Leslie said, moving forward tentatively. "What's it for?"

"New choreography for *Dance Machine* but also to show my beginning dance class." He tilted his head to the side. "How did the doctor's go?"

Leslie shoved his hands in his pockets, moving forward two more steps.

"Good, um, the doctor doesn't see anything on my scans to be concerned about. He wants me to see some specialists about my migraines and for cognitive therapy." He shrugged. "I'll do whatever he says," he added. *If it means I have more time.*

Joe nodded and chewed at a thumbnail. "That's good," he said. He turned back toward the mirror and looked around, finally grabbing his shirt. He slid it on and turned back around, but his body language seemed tense, as if he were looking for an escape route.

"Joe," Leslie said, holding his hands out. Then he let them fall. "I...I don't know what to say. I thought about it all day but I—"

"We said we would be honest. We wouldn't keep things from each other."

Boom. Joe's words hit Leslie hard. That was the truth of it. They had made that promise and Joe had done his part. He'd told Leslie about his job situation even though he knew Leslie wanted him to stay in Ayre Valley. He'd been honest. "I know."

"I kept wondering why you were in such a hurry, besides the fact that we'd waited so long. I didn't understand why the rush?"

"Because what if I don't have the time? What if my TBI becomes CTE? What if I lose myself?" Leslie blurted the words out. He laid himself bare before Joe, like the wooden expanse of floor between them. "My father was about my age the first time he threw a chair through a window in the house because he was pissed at my mom. That was how it started. He'd throw shit. It quickly descended into a time of terror for my family." He really didn't want to tell Joe the horror stories, hoped he wouldn't have to, not now. "I'll tell you more, I'll tell you anything, but it was bad, Joe."

"Leslie, I *know* you. I know your heart. Never for a minute—"

"And people said the same about my dad. Well, people who didn't live with him. He always had a bit of a temper, but he never hurt us, not before..."

Leslie blew out a breath. Their family had tried so hard to keep the details under wraps, but had that been the best plan? Had it allowed for more people to experience what Leslie's family had?

"I'm sorry for what your family went through, Leslie. I know it forced you into more of a parenting role with your brothers and it was tough on them and your mom. But *Leslie* Payton is not *Rick* Payton. I know who you are. And I thought," he said, messing with his hair, "I thought you knew me."

Leslie wanted to close the physical distance between them, but it was as if there was an invisible barrier holding him back, or his feet wouldn't work, so despite everything in him wanting to fix this, he couldn't move.

"I *do* know you, Joe. All I can say is I was afraid."

"Afraid I'd leave. I guess that means the Joe *you* know is not to be trusted. You can't trust me to know the truth about your health, you can't trust me to take care of you when you're sick, and you can't trust me to still work on my career and also be with you, even when you said you would support me always." He set his hands on his hips and his chest deflated. "You know me, but you don't trust me."

"I trust you in more ways than I've ever trusted a living soul," Leslie said. "I've told you things, let you see me at my weakest...I gave my heart to you!"

"But when you needed me most, when it mattered the most, you shut me out. You made me think I was wrong for wanting to keep working when really you didn't trust me to come back. Well that just fucking hurts, Leslie. After everything we've been through—"

"I don't want you to end up like me."

"What is that supposed to mean?" Joe asked, his voice going up in pitch.

"I hate to see you hurt. I know how much pain you're in and I don't want that for you. I know you love dancing, but is it worth it?"

"It's all I know! It's all I'm good for."

"That's not true—"

"Let me finish. I'd be nothing without this body," Joe said, gesturing to himself. "And my fucking talent. And it's going away. I have a very small window left before I can't do it anymore, and you showed me that I had something else to give by bringing me here. I love coaching, I love teaching, and I love that I can do that here and be close to you, but I'm not a wealthy man. I have to work, and I have to keep my options open, limited though they may be, in case the college doesn't hire me back. I can't just settle down without a plan. I have to think of the future."

Leslie felt this conversation slipping away from him like being down twenty-one points in the fourth quarter with the chances of scoring minimal.

"Is it more than that, though? I know you feel like coming here is settling." Fear was a monster that did ugly things to Leslie. "I guess that means I'm not good enough to settle down with if you think this is settling."

Joe flinched as if he'd been slapped.

"If that's what you think, if that's how little you think of me, then we have nothing else to say." Joe cranked up the music, turning his back on Leslie and the conversation.

A single tear fell from Leslie's cheek as he left the room, walking away from love for the second time.

TWENTY-SEVEN

Joe went through the motions for the next few weeks. The Jackets football team went on to win the conference championship, just as Leslie had hoped, and the cheerleaders were there to support the team, but Joe avoided all persons Payton. Basketball season was just around the corner and the cheer team shuffled personnel for the upcoming games. Some of the kids opted not to cheer for the games but wanted to continue working out for the upcoming national competition. His three-man hype squad expanded to seven and they were excited to perform. They already had their routines laid out and had been posting teasers on Instagram.

Joe spent every night and some time on weekends working out with the team, and the rest of his time was taken up working on his courses, making them challenging and fun, brainstorming with Marti ways that he could improve for the second semester. He already had kids, including football players, who wanted into his ballet and barre fitness class. He researched some local universities and spoke with their dance departments to learn everything he could. Why not? He had nothing else to do, and being productive made him feel better. Ish. He could almost say that this work was more fulfilling than anything he'd done in his life up to this point, including his Tony award-winning run in *West Side Story*. It just would have been better if he could have shared it with Leslie.

Several times he picked up his phone to reach out, but then he'd feel that gut punch once more.

Yeah, Leslie loved him, but he didn't trust him, didn't think enough of him to truly accept him as a partner. And what the hell was he supposed to do about that?

He spent the Thanksgiving break in LA rehearsing for *Dance Machine*, pouring his heart into new choreography, which the show's producers guaranteed him would win an Emmy. He got sick of hearing cracks like "that Iowa weather must have inspired you," or "there must be something in that Midwest water," as if Joe's pain was some kind of magic. Well, whatever, he used his pain and they used him to increase their ratings. Everybody used everybody. That was show business, right?

In early December, he met with Barry to discuss the degree program proposal.

"This looks really, really good, Joe. You put a lot of work into this and I appreciate it. Dance is a major I've always thought we needed to offer. My wife went to school here and always regretted that she didn't continue with dance. She was on the cheer squad a few years before you were here, you know. She loves what you've done this year."

Joe smiled. "Happy to have a Payton as a fan."

Barry's nice-guy smile fell. "Joe, I'm sorry, I know—"

"It's fine." The last thing Joe wanted to do was talk about his imploded romance with his boss's brother. The pain was enough. He didn't need to add humiliation to his résumé. "So, what happens next?"

"Well, we bring this before the board. You'll present your recommendations, and then it would require building each course, implementing them year by year so that by year four a degree would be possible. If the board approves, you'd be looking at a five-year contract, and in addition you'd need to determine faculty needs, and you'd be a part of the hiring process."

Joe's hand shook as he reached for his bottle of water and he nearly spilled it.

"Is that...you would want me for all of that?"

Barry smiled. "Of course. We hired you because we knew you had something very special to offer our community. It's true, you don't have an advanced degree in dance, but your experience more than makes up for it. I did my research, Joe. You've studied with some of the greatest experts and choreographers in the business. We may want to look at bringing someone on with a degree in dance who has collegiate-level teaching experience to support you, but your vision for the degree program is incredible."

Joe's chin quivered and he hid it by taking another drink of his water. "I guess I thought...well, I figured your brother bullied you into hiring me." He pushed his hair back out of his eyes and smiled.

"Leslie?" Barry laughed. "No, not at all. I was the one who asked for your contact information. We'd already been looking into alumni who might be a good fit and your name was on a shortlist pulled by the search committee."

"I didn't...I hadn't realized."

Barry laughed. "My brother may be a persuasive guy, but you were our top choice, Joe. It just worked out well for him. Well, I mean—"

Joe sighed and gave Barry a small smile.

"Thank you, for whatever the reason. I wanted to ask you, though, if I were to stay, if you were to offer me the position, I'd need to travel. Not only am I under contract with *Dance Machine* for another two years, but I'd want to visit some other schools, maybe take some workshops—"

"I'm sure we can work with that, and if we bring on an assistant that can cover your classes from time to time, that would free you up. It benefits the school for us to be flexible. We do the same for our other faculty members when the need arises."

Barry and Joe worked out a timeline for board approval of Joe's recommendations and deadlines for course descriptions for the new courses that would begin the following year. After spending his summer creating the ones for this year, he felt comfortable with the process and knew that with a little more legwork he could have all of it done by March like Barry was asking for.

Joe's chest relaxed a bit and he sat up straighter in his chair. They'd wanted him, not because of Leslie, but because of what he'd accomplished. He was elated when he shook Barry's hand and left his office. On the walk back to Higdon, he thought about the path he'd taken. To Greenvale, he wasn't just a handsome face with a great ass who could dance circles around the competition. He was an accomplished professional with a variety of experiences and skills that could benefit a small college program. Sure, his name and reputation helped, but that was earned.

He'd earned the college's respect. Maybe he could still earn Leslie's.

Because bottom line? Joe was a mess without him. His worst fears had come to be realized. He'd worried that if he and Leslie had tried to consummate their relationship when he came to Iowa, he'd lose his lifeline, he'd lose his best friend. And that might sound silly to someone who had close friends who'd been in their everyday life, but Joe had loved that Leslie could be his sounding board without being invested in whatever choices Joe made. Joe could tell him anything, which he basically had, and Leslie took it all in, never judging him.

Or so he thought.

It had been a big awakening for Joe to realize that the man he was, the man he had been, wasn't considered trustworthy by the one person he respected the most in the world.

Ouch.

He should be running to Leslie with this good news, but now he wondered if he'd ever be able to confide in him again.

Joe was great at licking his wounds, getting back up and trying again. He'd done it his whole career. So he gave his all to the Greenvale community through cheer, through his dance classes, and through his work behind the scenes preparing for his presentation before the board.

By Christmas break, he was dragging.

He had scheduled some rehearsal time for *Dance Machine*'s upcoming season, so it was off to LA once more. Marti made him promise they'd get together for a drink before he left, so the night before his flight, they met at the Goalpost.

Joe had been avoiding the bar, but Marti needed to stay in town because she was getting ready for her family to invade from Kansas City for the holidays, so the Goalpost it was. He just hoped the Paytons wouldn't be there that night. He wasn't sure he could handle a face-to-face.

Joe had managed to avoid Leslie since football season ended. Leslie came to the football offices to work sometimes, but the twins were running workouts for the team. Randy was in charge of the new fitness center that had finally been completed. It was gorgeous. Joe met with him for a tour and to schedule time for the cheer squad to work out and Randy had preened under Joe's compliments. It had to be hard to live in Leslie's shadow for both of the twins, but they were coming into their own. Randy would even be gearing up to take over the baseball program after the winter break. Joe knew how hard that transition could be.

Sandy texted Joe frequently just to say hi, send a funny GIF, or give him an update on Leslie's condition, but he didn't push. Joe knew Sandy had taken a big chance talking to him about Leslie's medical concerns. Talk about trust.

But Joe couldn't run from the face-to-face forever. Soon after he and Marti grabbed a booth at the back of the bar and got their drinks, the twins came in with some of the other coaches Joe had met but hadn't hung out with, and they headed back to the pool tables with pitchers of beer. Sandy waved to them and gestured for them to join in the fun but Joe held up a hand.

"I do play pool, you know. We could join them." Marti raised her eyebrows.

Joe pressed a hand to his chest. "Hurts still," he said. "They've been great, but...I miss him. He's everywhere even though I haven't seen him."

Marti took a sip of her beer. "You haven't seen him because he's gone."

"What do you mean he's gone?"

She shrugged and tore at the label on her bottle of Shiner Bock.

"Terrence said he left. He's got something going on, he wouldn't say what, but he's going to be gone for a while, I guess."

Joe was out of the booth and across the bar before Marti finished talking. He marched straight up to Sandy, who was in the middle of a beer-guzzling contest, and he grabbed him by the shoulder.

"What? Twi—Coach Judd, what's—"

"What's wrong? What happened?"

Sandy stared at him blankly. "What do you mean, what happened? What's wrong?"

Joe exhaled and rolled his eyes. "Where's your brother?"

Sandy showed all the signs of being well on his way to drunk off his ass. He'd probably had a few beers before they'd arrived at the bar.

"Brother Randy? He's—" He stumbled as he pointed across the pool table to where Randy was dancing with a group of women near the jukebox.

"Sandy," Joe said, snapping his fingers. "Focus."

"Brother Barry brought us here... Oh, you mean Leslie?" His smile fell. "He's gone and I'm not supposed to say where. It's top secret or something."

Joe never had patience for drunk people and he was ready to shake him when Randy danced over to the two of them, obviously less plastered than his twin.

"You'll have to ask Brother Leslie himself. Brother Sandy's not gonna spill the beans again, is he?"

Sandy shook his head and burped. "Nope. I have my orders and they don't involve trying to help my brother with his love life. Not anymore." Then he hiccupped.

Joe sighed. "Fine. I'll text him."

"Good luck. He didn't take his phone. He doesn't want to be disturbed."

Joe put his hands on his hips. "But you know how to reach him."

Randy sighed. "I know how to reach him."

Joe held out his hand. "Then do it."

Randy pulled his cell phone out, held it up, made a goofy face into it, and pressed the Facetime button. "He's under Ginormous Giraffe Turd."

"I'm not even going to ask." Joe took the phone and was about to hit the call button when he realized he should—

He turned and Marti was standing there with her beer. "Give me a kiss. I'll see you next year."

Joe kissed her and took Randy's phone outside where he might actually be able to hear.

Then remembered it was fucking December in Iowa and he'd left his coat inside.

He hit the call button and waited.

"I'm busy dipshit—Oh...Joe."

TWENTY-EIGHT

L eslie

"Hi."

God he'd missed that face, that voice. His eyes burned so bad he pinched the bridge of his nose for a minute to make it stop. He was done with crying for-freaking-ever.

"Oh God, a migraine? Are you okay? Where are you?"

Leslie laughed and it came out a sob. "No, I'm fine. I'm okay. How are you?"

Joe's face was lit up on one side, but the phone was shaking so Leslie couldn't get a bead on the background.

"I'm cold. Where are you, Leslie? What's wrong?"

"What do you mean, what's wrong? I'm fine."

"They said you left," Joe stammered out. His teeth were chattering. "Why?"

"I'm out of town, yes," Leslie said, confused. "Why?"

"Oh. But you're okay?"

"Yeah," Leslie said. "I'm fine. I'm working on something, that's all."

Working on the hardest thing he'd ever done in his life.

After everything blew up with Joe, Leslie had his last scheduled interview with Malcolm Darling and Malcolm had brought up the biography again.

"We can do it a number of ways. Either you can write down what you think is important, I can research on my own and you can fill in the details, or we can have a series of conversations...whatever you are comfortable with. Most people find the process a bit cathartic."

And boy, had Leslie needed some catharsis. He'd been shattered by his breakup with Joe. Destroyed, and it had been his own damned fault. He'd held onto this lofty ideal of what their relationship would be, ignoring the possibility of a grim future, and he'd held on so tight he'd let his fear choke the life out of what was the most important relationship in his life outside his family. Many times he'd found himself walking toward Higdon to find Joe and talk it out, but he realized he had a lot of work to do on himself. He couldn't just pretend like he didn't have cause for concern for his future, but he also couldn't hide from the real possibility of living with the effects of CTE. He'd let fear drive him so hard, drive him so far, he'd left Joe on the side of the road wondering what the hell had happened.

It wasn't fair, but Leslie knew he needed to take a time-out and regroup. If that meant Joe moved on, he'd have to deal with that.

He'd had a glimmer of hope, but that was it. He couldn't hope for a life with Joe. He needed to plan for a future that involved working on himself and taking care of his family.

He and Malcolm had been holed up at the Hawaii compound for the past two weeks talking for hours every day. Leslie had also found a fancy-pants cognitive behavioral therapist who was willing to do some intensive work with him, which had brought up a ton of stuff from his past that he'd shoved so far down into his mental locker he'd been shocked when it resurfaced. To round out his new dream team, he was doing a series of televisits with a migraine specialist in Seattle who had recommended a local nutritionist in Maui who was teaching him how to eat in a way that might minimize his headaches.

His previous dream team, his family, were told to stay away and leave him be. He depended too much on them and he needed to do this alone. He'd agreed they could come for Christmas, but that was it. He needed...time. Time to figure his shit out, time to learn how to be better, time to tell his story.

He had no idea where Joe fit in all that, whether he fit at all. Whether he *wanted* to fit.

"I'm sorry I worried you," Leslie said, his stupid, hopeful heart warming at the thought Joe was worried about him.

"Can I...C-c-can we...I miss you, Leslie. I'm—"

"I miss you too, Twinkle Toes."

Joe smiled when Leslie used his pet name.

"Well, I'll let-t-tch-ch-oo g-g-et back—"

"You need to get out of the cold, Joe. I'm fine, or I'm getting there. And I want to...talk, if you want. I need a little more time."

"Oh." Joe wiped at his eyes and his nose. "Okay, it's o-k-kay. I don't want to b-b-other—"

"No. No, Joe, you're not... Where are you going to be for break? Are you staying?"

"LA. Rehearsals," he said, the phone shaking more violently now.

"Can I call you there? Can we talk?" Because seeing his face, hearing his voice, it was all Leslie wanted, and it was killing him to wait.

"Yeah, if you have t-t-time. Merry Christmas, Leslie. I—" He smiled, but it didn't reach his eyes. "Merry Christmas. I b-b-better g-g-ive this back to Randy. I'd leave him with an inappropriat-t-te p-p-picture but he'd probably enjoy that."

Leslie barked out a laugh and he wiped at his own eyes. Stupid tears. "He'd probably sell copies. I wouldn't if I were you."

"You're right."

"Hey, Joe? I...I love you. I'm so sorry."

"S-s-st-t-top it," Joe whispered. He smiled wider.

"That's my line," Leslie said. He'd practically curled his whole body around the phone, wishing it was Joe in his hands instead.

"I love you, t-t-too. I'm turning into a J-j-joesicle, though. C-c-call me later."

"I promise."

They hung up and Leslie took in a deep, shuddering breath.

"Everything okay?" Malcolm asked. He'd gone to the kitchen for snacks and returned with arms full of food. Leslie's cook had been trying out all the recipes from the nutritionist and Leslie had gained ten pounds already sampling the goods. Okay, maybe five pounds, but it felt like his pants were a little tighter anyway.

"Yes and no," Leslie admitted. "It's probably time I tell you about Joe."

Malcolm hopped over the back of the couch and crossed his legs. He turned on the recorder and grabbed the big bowl of popcorn. "I've been *dying* for this part of the story."

Leslie shook his head. "It is a good story. One of the best parts of my story." Now if only he could make things right.

"So where does it start?"

"It started fifteen—almost sixteen years ago at the Goalpost on Spring Fling weekend. I was the returning hero, he was the current big man on campus, and we spent an entire night talking. And that's what we did. For fifteen years, we talked. And then when I finally had him where I wanted him, I screwed it up."

Malcolm frowned. "The end to that call didn't sound like you screwed it up, or at least not in an unfixable way."

Leslie had given Malcolm unlimited access to his life, well, after he signed a tightly worded nondisclosure agreement that gave Leslie all the master recordings when they were finished and final approval of the manuscript.

"Let me explain all the ways I screwed up and then you can be the judge...and maybe help me fix it."

Malcolm popped a handful of popcorn into his mouth. "I'm all ears."

TWENTY-NINE

J^{oe}

Leslie texted Joe once a day for the next few days just to make a connection, but they didn't connect for a conversation. Joe hadn't known what to make of their bizarre conversation and knew he needed to be patient with Leslie. Then came the most bizarre text Leslie had ever sent him in over fifteen years.

Do you have a couple of days off for the holidays?

Yes, dear. Even dancers get holidays off. I have Christmas Day through New Year's Eve. Why?

Prepare to be liberated.

. . .

Joe should have known that Leslie's cryptic text would turn into a fiasco.

Randy and Sandy showed up at the rehearsal space—Joe had no idea how they found out where he was—dressed in black suits and sunglasses, with earpieces in.

"I missed the memo where *Men In Black 5000* was filming here," Joe said to them, shooing them into the hall to not disturb the group that was performing at the time,

"We're under orders to collect the package and transport on a private charter flight in T-minus thirty minutes."

Joe's eyes flared. "You're kidding, right? I'm not done for another hour."

They looked at each other, their freaky twin synchronized moves making them seem more like the creepy guys in *The Matrix*. Nah, he thought. *Men in Black* was probably more their speed.

"Well make yourself done."

"Yeah," Sandy chimed in. "We're under orders."

Joe rolled his eyes. It really was no big deal. His routines had already been rehearsed. He was just hanging around to provide moral support, and there was the issue that he had nothing to do. Literally nothing. He'd already shipped out the few Christmas gifts he had for friends and co-workers before leaving Ayre Valley. He was going to be eating Chinese food with Arthur on Christmas Day since Arthur's main squeeze was away working, and neither felt like cooking. Then he planned on going to a friend's studio the rest of the week off to work on choreography for his second-semester classes.

"I need to grab my things—"

"You don't need to bring anything with you."

"My suitcase is at the hotel, though—"

"We've already retrieved it."

"What the... Okay, you guys are starting to freak me out. What the hell is going on?"

Sandy lowered his glasses and smiled. "Sorry," he stage-whispered. "We're just having some fun. We talked to your manager and he helped us out. We already packed up your stuff."

Randy cleared his throat and frowned. "No more stalling. We're taking you to our boss. You have a lot to answer for, Twinkle Toes."

"Not really," Sandy whispered as he led Joe out the door. "Just play along, he doesn't get to have fun like this much in Iowa. Just go with it."

Joe shook his head and pulled his zip-up hoodie a little tighter around him in the chilly air.

Out front of the soundstage where they'd been rehearsing was a long black limousine. Randy opened the door and held his hand to his ear. "The package has been acquired," he said, presumably to someone.

Joe climbed in the backseat, suddenly aware that he was a sweaty mess and wasn't wearing proper shoes. "Guys, really, can we go back to the hotel first?"

"Sorry, Joe," Agnes said with a little wave. "I gave birth to them, but please don't hold me responsible for their behavior."

She held out her arms for a hug and Joe winced. "I'm really, *really* sweaty."

She gestured for him to come on. "You know all four of my sons played football? And my husband?"

Randy and Sandy slid in and sat across from Joe and Agnes. Randy knocked on the window and the limousine pulled away from the curb with a lurch, nearly sending Joe sprawling.

Joe accepted a glass of champagne. "It's not drugged, is it? Do I get to know where we're going?"

"Oh," Sandy said. "Here. This will give you a clue."

He pulled two elaborate leis out of a brown paper bag and placed one over Agnes's head and one over Joe's.

"He *did* go to Hawaii," Agnes said with a laugh. "Oh good, I'm so ready to be in a warm place. I always forget how cold it actually gets back home." She turned to Joe, who was so glad for the fragrant lei that was hopefully covering up any unpleasant smells.

Joe's heart fluttered at the mention of Hawaii.

Things would likely have been very different in his life if he'd not chickened out on meeting Leslie there ten years earlier, and Joe had often wondered what would have happened. Would it have been too soon and they would've merely hung out, talked about what they wanted, and still went their separate ways? Or, maybe Joe would have been as swept away as he was in Iowa and he would have jumped at the chance to have Leslie in his life.

But Joe was a different man now. Ten years ago, he was chasing the next big thing. He hadn't been seriously injured yet. He hadn't thought about his career's expiration date. And he still thought dancing was the only thing he was good at.

Now he knew the truth.

And now, dammit, he was ready to face Leslie with all that he was, with all that he had, and he prayed it was enough.

"Joe? Are you okay?"

"Huh? Yeah, sorry. I was just thinking of the last time I was in Hawaii."

Agnes smiled and patted his knee. "He's going to be so glad to see you."

"I hope so."

They flew a private jet out of LAX to Maui and there were more surprises on the plane. More champagne, Joe's things, a bathroom with enough room for him to get cleaned up, thankfully, and a new suit, compliments of Leslie.

"How the hell did he know my size?"

"Apparently your manager is very knowledgeable about such things," Sandy said. "And he can be bought."

Joe scoffed. "Good to know."

A black Escalade met them at the airport. Joe had his third glass of champagne, or was it his fourth, at the urging of the brothers. Thankfully, there had been a boatload of snacks on the flight because Joe hadn't eaten anything since he'd had his morning smoothie.

"You're such a lightweight," Sandy joked as they climbed into the limo and Joe hit his head.

"Always have been." But he was also nervous. Could he and Leslie get past what had happened? The radio silence had been so painful, so awful. For the first time in the fifteen years since they'd met, he'd felt completely abandoned. He'd been hurt, maybe a little angry, but mostly he'd been able to channel it into solidifying his plans so that if Leslie came around, they could move forward together. The alternative to that was unbearable.

It was dark outside as they drove up a winding road and Joe was glad the driver was a local because there had been some hairy turns. Randy had led them in singing "Somewhere Over the Rainbow," and Joe wondered whether he'd ever actually learned the words, but he kept up with them. Somehow. Agnes held his hand, Randy and Sandy entertained them, and Joe was almost calm by the time they pulled up to a, well, a mansion lit up by floodlights.

"Leslie's working on getting this place all solared out because he wants to give back to the power grid. One of our companies deals with solar," Sandy was saying, but Joe was captivated by the figure standing at the edge of the driveway.

Joe pushed Sandy out of the way and staggered over to Leslie, who stood next to one of the solar lights, also dressed in a suit. Joe hesitated only a brief moment before he threw his arms around a surprised Leslie and squeezed him for all he was worth. It was probably much less force than Leslie had experienced in his NFL days, but it nearly knocked him over.

"Twinkle Toes ain't too twinkly once you get booze in him," Randy said. He shook his head at Joe, who wouldn't let go of Leslie, and accepted a handshake from his brother. Sandy also got a handshake, and Agnes a kiss on the cheek, and then they were left alone.

"I'm not letting go of you," Joe said, his face smushed against Leslie's chest. He smelled so good, like the Awapuhi body stuff he had all over his room back in Iowa. Joe was totally going to buy some when he was here so that if Leslie sent him away, at least he'd always have his scent.

"I'm not going to send you away," Leslie said, trying to lift Joe's chin to look up at him. "Joe—"

"No, not yet. I'm drunk. Don't say anything, just hold me. You can scold me, yell at me, argue with me, whatever, in the morning when I'm in charge of myself again. Just...hold me, dammit, so the world will stop spinning."

Leslie chuckled and squeezed Joe back. "Can we walk? I want to show you something."

"We can try. Yes, we can."

They managed to walk down a sandy path together, Joe's arms still clutching Leslie tightly.

"I can't believe you sent your brothers to kidnap me," Joe said. "The *Dance Machine* producers were going to call security when they grabbed me."

"Did they pull that *Matrix* shit?" Leslie let his head fall back and he laughed.

"I was thinking more like *Men in Black*. I was waiting for the flashy thingie."

Leslie rubbed his back and Joe felt those stomach flutterings like he had back in August. *Whoa.* So much had happened since then. It had been exciting and fun...and then scary and wonderful...and then awful. And now he was holding onto Leslie for dear life in Hawaii and he wasn't sure if these flutterings were nerves, the alcohol, or...

"What do you think?"

Leslie gently removed Joe's arms and turned him around.

"Oh, Leslie!"

A breathtakingly beautiful private beach illuminated by a full moon over calm waters. It was a picture out of a magazine, like *National Geographic*. It was pure magic. He wanted to weep, he—

"Babe, why are you crying?"

Joe's lower lip fluttered as he sucked in a breath.

"Why are you so fucking perfect, Leslie? Why? Why do you show me such beauty and then you show me this beach and you're so beautiful."

"And why did I allow my brothers to ply you with champagne? Come here."

Joe felt himself levitating and he thought maybe he'd died and gone to heaven. That would explain everything.

"Here, rest your head."

Leslie had somehow maneuvered them onto a wide lounge chair contraption and Joe was now curled against him, weeping.

"I am a weepy drunk, I admit it. I'm sorry. But it's your fault for being so perfect, too."

"Stop it," Leslie said, pressing a kiss against Joe's forehead. "I'm far from perfect. Let me hold you, Joe. I'm so sorry. For everything. I've missed you so much."

Joe wanted to beat on his chest and rage about their separation, but he knew it was the champagne. Damn, that had been a bad idea.

"You're awfully sweet when you're tipsy, Twinkle Toes."

"You better always call me Twinkle Toes," Joe said.

And shortly after that, while Leslie was in the middle of telling him something important, Joe fell asleep.

Joe didn't remember setting his alarm before falling asleep the night before. He didn't remember falling asleep. And his face was hot. And it was bright.

He covered his face with a hand and opened one eye to find Leslie's sleeping face next to his. Then it all came back in a rush. The twins acting weird, the abduction, the limo, laughing Agnes and her delicious champagne—

"No, no, no, no, not champagne," Joe moaned. He rolled over onto his back and threw his arm over his face. The sun felt so good.

"Good morning, Twinkle Toes. Or should I change it to Tipsy Toes?"

"God, no. Champagne is like truth serum or something, it makes me a wreck. But it's so good." He looked around, squinting in the sunlight and then looked down at himself. "Where'd this suit come from? And damn, did you pick it out? If so, you're shopping for me forever."

Leslie pushed himself up to sitting and smiled at Joe. "I liked shopping for you. I'll shop for you anytime. And here," he said, reaching over to a table next to their ridiculously large lounge chair and handing Joe a green smoothie in a pineapple-shaped glass with a little umbrella.

Joe gasped. "How did you find out?"

Leslie frowned. "Find out what?"

Joe took the drink from him and sucked down a few gulps. His eyes rolled back in his head. "How did you find out about my morning smoothies?"

Leslie's eyes went wide. "You mean, I now know your secret?"

Joe just blinked at him and hoped the goodness in the glass would clear up the rest of his foggy brain.

"This is what my nutritionist said I should be drinking first thing in the morning. I'm on a new eating regimen to help with my migraines."

Joe lowered the glass and put a hand over Leslie's. "I'm so glad. I wanted to bring it up, that food changes could really help, but I didn't want to be that douche."

Leslie laughed and Joe's eyes caught on the freckled skin of his chest peeking out from between the two sides of his unbuttoned dress shirt. He took a good long look at Leslie Payton lounging on the beach in a gorgeous black suit made from material as soft as butter, the same material as his.

"Did we get married last night?"

Leslie burst out laughing again. "Not that I recall." He took Joe's drink from him and pulled him into his arms for a long, lingering kiss.

Joe tangled their legs together and moaned. He yanked at Leslie's shirt until it was untucked and he could get access to Leslie's skin. He needed to be sure this was real. Joe scratched his nails down Leslie's torso and Les arched into him and groaned.

"Joe," Leslie sighed as Joe kissed his neck. Joe had learned early on that Leslie was like putty in his hands when he went to work on his neck. "Joe, can we...I want to tell you, I want a chance to explain."

Joe pulled back and reluctantly let go. He sat up straight with his legs crisscrossed. It was time to be grown up.

"I have things to say too."

Leslie pushed himself up to sitting and he raised the back of the chair. He stretched his legs out and stared at the ocean.

"When my father died, the autopsy showed that the multitude of concussions he'd received throughout his career had done irreparable damage. Chronic Traumatic Encephalopathy they call it, do you know what that is?"

Joe nodded. "I read the *Rolling Stone* article when it came out. I'm so sorry."

"The death certificate said complications from CTE. It made him a violent, confused, and terrified man at the end of his life. When I retired from the NFL, it was because I'd had a concussion, probably I've had five or six significant ones in my life, and I started having the migraines. My personal physician strongly encouraged me to retire, especially after what happened to my father, so I did. I probably could have had a few more years to play, but it wasn't worth it. My family was grateful. They'd been watching me and they let me know they had concerns. I'd been forgetting things a little, I couldn't seem to keep track of appointments, I forgot my mom's birthday. How much was stress, how much was my brain injuries, I don't know. So I retired."

Joe reached out and took Leslie's hand. He'd always wondered why Leslie had stepped away from the sport he loved. They had only just started to share personal information at that point in their unconventional friendship.

"And then the migraines got worse. I had a bunch of tests run, tried some different medications, but it made things very difficult while I was coaching at UKC. Sandy helped me as much as he could, came up with the voice memo reminders system on my phone, which became the twins' second business. It was the first app they created and it made them a million bucks when they sold it. Sandy nominated himself as my personal assistant and thank God he did. You can thank him for a lot of the little things I did for you over the years. They were my ideas, but he helped make them a reality when I couldn't."

Joe laughed. "Does that mean I am really dating your brother?"

Leslie rolled his eyes. "Stop it. You know better."

Joe smiled, but it faded.

"Why didn't you tell me, Leslie? Me, of all people. I thought...How could you think I wouldn't understand?"

"Because I was afraid—am afraid—I'll be like my father. The doctors are confident there are things we can do to help, but I wanted time with you before I lost my fucking mind."

Joe raised his eyebrows. "How was that going to work, exactly? One day you'd wake up and forget something and I'd be like 'I'm out of here'? Leslie—"

"I don't know," he laughed but it was hollow. "I don't ever want you to have to take care of me, but I guess I wasn't thinking you might actually want to stay."

Joe looked at their joined hands. "You wanted me with you, wanted a future together, but you weren't thinking 'til death do us part,' huh?" Leslie started to protest, but Joe held up his hand. "I get it, I do. And I never gave you a reason to think I was in it for the long haul. But I am, Leslie. I don't know how to make you see that. I have to travel for work sometimes, but I'm always going to be yours. I have to know that you'll trust me to come back." He swallowed hard. "Otherwise, I don't know why you brought me here. If you don't trust me, Leslie, then we need to walk away."

THIRTY

L eslie

The only thing keeping Leslie grounded was that Joe hadn't let go of his hand.

"And all this stuff about your father, and your potential future? You didn't even give me a chance to decide. Did I ever tell you about when my mom went on hospice?"

Leslie shook his head. "I know you went to her and it didn't go well."

"She sent me away, said she didn't want me to take care of her, wanted her boyfriend du jour to take care of her. Said it was more than a young man like me could handle and that she wanted me to remember her young and beautiful. I fought, hell, I even talked to a lawyer. But there was nothing I could do. When I'd go, her boyfriend would let me in for like thirty-minute visits and then he'd tell me to leave. Clint. I told you about him?" Leslie shook his head. "Oh, yeah, he was a football player too. Bragged about how he played for the

Patriots, but I looked him up. He was called up but didn't make the cut. Never played in a regular season game. He was a bouncer at my mom's favorite bar. He liked to 'wrestle' with me, you know? Thought he was funny. He'd pin me down and laugh when I fought to get free."

Leslie growled.

"Yeah," Joe continued. "That's who she chose to care for her in her last days. She left our house to him and I got a letter from her attorney with a check for ten grand, all that was left of her estate. She didn't think I was worthy of caring for her." He wiped at his eyes. "For you to think I'm not worthy of caring for you is even worse than that."

Leslie sat up and took Joe in his arms.

"God, no. It was never ever a lack of faith in you. Never. But Joe," he said, pulling back to make sure Joe was looking at him when he said this. "If I ever hurt you, if I got like my father was...He hurt my mom, Joe. The woman he loved more than anything in the world, more than his kids, more than football. He hurt her. I couldn't live with myself if I even...I am terrified to take that chance, Joe. Can you understand?"

"I would if I thought it was possible."

Leslie sighed. He wished Joe wasn't so stubborn. He was going to have to hear more. He took Joe's hands in his. "If we're going to do this, you're going to hear everything, okay? And I fully accept your decision to walk away after you know what happened. Did my brothers tell you what I'm doing here?"

Joe barked out a laugh. "You mean, you're not 007?"

"You are too much. God, I love you, Joe. I've missed you so." He cleared his throat. "I am here with Malcolm Darling, the reporter from *Time?*"

"Oh shit, really? I love him! He did that great article on Pete Buttigieg's campaign."

"Yeah, that's the one. We've been working on an article about my move to Greenvale, but he wants more." Leslie still couldn't believe this was all happening. Malcolm's agent was preparing to take their project to auction and was confident there would be a bidding war. "He's writing my biography, Joe. Well, we're doing it together. I brought you here so you could hear the tough parts, and to help me tell him our story, if you agree. I know it's personal, and you'd have full say in how much is included. What do you think?"

This was it, Joe would squeeze his hands, say thanks for the memories, and he'd be gone.

Joe tackle-hugged him and Leslie nearly fell off the chair. "Careful," he laughed, but he wrapped Joe up tight in his arms. "Doc says no contact sports."

"I'm sorry, but I intend to have all the contact with you. Let's do it. I love that you're telling your story. That you're sharing your beautiful self with the world."

"Stop it," Leslie said, his cheeks heating.

Joe sat up and grabbed Leslie's chin, holding it tight. "No, *you* stop it. You are beautiful, Leslie, inside and out, and I want the world to see you as I do. Just think of all the people who need your story. Think of kids like Terrell. Kids like I was."

"No matter what happens between us, Joe, I will always be grateful to you for our time together, for everything. If it's too much, though, I will understand—"

"Oh, fuck that, Leslie. I know you're afraid, but you need to get with the program. What's going to happen between us is that we are going to figure this shit out. We're going to go in there, give Malcolm a helluva story, then we're going to swim naked in that goddamned ocean and then go home to Iowa and freeze our balls off. You got it? And live happily ever after. That's the only thing that's going to happen between us."

Leslie ran his fingers through Joe's beard, letting his nails scratch through the coarse hairs. It was thick, as if he hadn't shaved for several days, maybe a week, which was unusual for him. It looked so dramatic against his golden skin, his dark red lips and his white teeth. Felt so good, too. Leslie's fair complexion and pale hair had always meant he couldn't grow a full beard, but God, he loved it on Joe.

"Does it have to be that order?"

Joe frowned. "Excuse me?"

Leslie's emotions were so close to the surface, had been the whole time he and Malcolm had been talking, that he just needed a release, and the kind he wanted was with Joe. He wanted to fly toward the sun and feel warm, feel loved as he let it all go, and when he came down, he would be cradled in loving arms and cared for. He wanted Joe.

"I mean can we get to the skinny-dipping part first? Or just sneak inside right now and crawl in bed together and make each other feel good until we can't walk, but in the best way possible?"

Joe licked his lips and went to work unfastening the rest of the buttons on Les's shirt.

"Can't we do both?"

Joe stood and slid out of his jacket, unbuttoned his shirt, yanked his pants and underwear off at once... "Hurry up," he said with an inviting smile and then he turned and ran naked into the ocean.

"Man, he wasn't kidding about no tan lines." Leslie admired Joe's athleticism as he ran down the path, over the sand, and dove into the ocean. He made quick work of the rest of his clothes, eager to touch all of Joe's golden skin...everywhere. Joe had waxed, apparently, which he'd explained he did when he was going to be performing for most shows. Said it helped with costuming, whatever that meant. Leslie didn't care, he'd eat Joe alive under any circumstances.

He hoped his family was otherwise occupied this morning and not thinking of coming down to the beach for a while. They were all supposed to take turns talking to Malcolm today. They'd scheduled it that way to give Leslie time to talk to Joe. And thank God for that.

Leslie didn't run for the water. He walked slowly, his chest feeling lighter as he drew closer and closer to Joe's smile. Joe reached for him like he did from a reclined position in bed.

"Come on in. It feels so fucking good."

Yeah, this really does feel so fucking good.

THIRTY-ONE

J oe

Their frolicking in the ocean was heavenly but they had to cut it short when Joe realized Leslie was getting fried. All that pale freckled pink skin couldn't handle the intense sunshine and rather than slide the lounge chair into the shade and make out, Leslie let Joe know he had a king-sized bed with soft sheets and a beautiful view in his private cabin separate from the main house. It seemed the best option.

"As long as I'm not keeping you from—"

Leslie shoved his tongue in Joe's mouth, reminding him that they had the entire day set aside for make-up activities, which very well could include sex, if they just moved inside...where there was a big shower. And supplies.

They yanked on their pants and Leslie led Joe up another path and then to the left of the main house. He let them inside and Joe gasped.

"This is incredible. I can't believe this view."

"I know. This was actually the original caretaker's house, but I had a bigger one built for the caretaker and his family. I wanted it in case, well..."

"Did you do this—"

"I hoped someday you'd come."

Joe's eyes filled and he dropped his clothes and shoes on the floor, pulling Leslie into his arms.

"If you want, I'll never leave."

Leslie buried his face in Joe's wild hair and Joe felt his whole body shudder.

"Let's shower."

This time, they were both relatively pain-free.

This time, they were both naked.

This time, Joe returned the favor and bathed Leslie.

"Except you're so freaking tall," Joe said, nearly slipping when he went up on his toes to wash Leslie's hair. "Even with my above-average height, I can barely reach you."

"Stop it," Leslie said with a smile.

"I love this shampoo," Joe said, inhaling as he covered his hands with the stuff and wove his fingers into Leslie's hair. "I've always loved this scent on you. You literally always smell like Hawaii."

Leslie grinned and tilted his head back, the soap running down his massive chest, over his slightly rounded stomach, and pooled around his semi-erect cock. Like the rest of Leslie's body, it was long, pink, and had all the right curves. His thighs were so powerful, his ass high and strong. Joe touched him everywhere and loved every second.

"I could do this every day and die a happy man."

"Then do it." Leslie grew serious, holding Joe's hands. "Move in with me."

They stared at each other and Joe's heart pounded out of control.

"Yeah?" he breathed.

"Yeah, I—ow." Shampoo had run into Leslie's eyes and they hurried to rinse them, laughing the whole time.

"But what about the rest of the Paytons? Are they ready for a fifth wheel?"

"They'd probably prefer you to me anyhow at this point. They love you, Joe. I know you've been on your own for a long time and there's a certain amount of tolerance necessary to live with my brothers—"

"Yes. Yes, I'd love to move in with you. But Leslie, you know we're going to be the talk of the town, there will be buzz..."

"Do you honestly think I care?"

Joe grinned. The idea of being a part of Leslie's family had been scary when they'd first agreed to give their relationship a shot, but now? He'd missed them almost as much as Leslie when they'd been apart.

"And I've got to work." Joe placed his hand on Leslie's cheek. "Whether it's at Greenvale for as long as they'll have me, in LA for *Dance Machine*, or New York...I have to work. As long as this body will cooperate. Will you accept that part of me as well?"

Leslie wrapped his arms around Joe and pulled him tight against him.

"As long as you come home to me, as long as we talk while you're away, as long as we continue to be honest... Yeah, Joe. I want to be your home. I want to take care of you when you need me, and I want to continue watching you soar."

This was a lot for Leslie, Joe knew. Something drastic had shifted between them and Joe was elated. Gone was any fear about committing, as long as Leslie was behind him unconditionally, they could have the kind of life people wrote romance novels about. That elusive happily ever after was in their grasp.

"And can we spend Christmas in Hawaii every year? Because this is awesome."

Leslie touched their foreheads together. "Whatever you want, Twinkle Toes."

They began to kiss and within moments they were ready for a horizontal surface. Joe's legs were shaking so bad and Leslie's height made things difficult for shower sex.

"Let me shave first," Joe said and Leslie shook his head.

"Leave it. I like it."

Joe raised his eyebrows. "Well, all right then."

They climbed into Leslie's massive four-poster canopied king and Joe sighed. "I might never leave this bed," he said and then Leslie reached over to the side table and used a remote to open the glass doors. A warm breeze drifted in and Joe moaned. "This is heaven."

"It's always tempting to stay in bed here," he said. "And with you beside me, it *is* heaven."

Joe dragged his fingers over Leslie's abs and then stroked his erection. "I think you should bring this heavenly body up here and make love to me."

"Actually..." Leslie ran his hand up Joe's arm to his shoulder and Joe recognized the uncertainty in his expression.

"You want me?"

Leslie nodded and lay on his back. "I've...I haven't—"

"I've got you," Joe said. "Not everyone likes it, though, and we can stop at any time." His heart was spilling over with love for this man who was so giving and brave enough to ask for what he wanted.

Joe talked Leslie through the prep, was so gentle with him, giving him time to adjust. When Leslie was trembling with need and begging for more, Joe slid on a condom and ran his hands over the backs of Leslie's thighs.

"I'm sorry I'm not as flexible as you." Leslie laughed nervously.

"You're gorgeous, babe." Joe was nervous, too. He hadn't ever been someone's first, and he didn't want to hurt him. He pressed in slowly and Leslie's eyes went wide before he smiled and relaxed a bit, his head falling back on the pillow.

"More."

A thrill shot down Joe's spine and he gave Leslie what he asked for, and when Leslie's cries of "more" turned into "yeah, baby," Joe let go of his hesitation, loving their closeness, loving that he could make Leslie scream, Leslie who was so prim and proper in every aspect of his life, who was so damn *nice*, and yet who turned into an unrestrained sex god under Joe's touch.

"God, yes, Joe, I'm coming." And Leslie came on his chest without Joe even touching his cock, his muscles rippling, his pink skin now red and splotchy and covered in a sheen of sweat and spend. Joe loved the view, so he pulled out, removed the condom and added to the mess on Leslie's abs.

"Fuck, that is the hottest thing I've ever seen," Leslie moaned. "You are so fucking good, Joe."

Joe dragged his cock against Leslie's and Leslie gasped. "I am here for your viewing pleasure." And then he collapsed next to Leslie and panted. "Although, my hip is warning me that an encore might not be the best plan."

Leslie cleaned them both up and then ran a hand over Joe's right hip flexor, bending over to kiss him there. "I'm sorry. And thank you, Twinkle Toes. That was awesome. I wasn't sure I'd ever want to, but I wanted to with you."

"I'm honored you trusted me," Joe said, pushing a wisp of Leslie's hair off his forehead. "Everything is better with you," Joe said. "Especially intercourse. I never really wanted anyone like that...never liked giving or receiving it much until you. Guess I'm demisexual after all."

"Everything is better with you, Joe. I love you."

"I love you, baby."

They reluctantly emerged from Leslie's casita to join the rest of the fam for dinner...and the inevitable razzing.

"I swear, I saw bigfoot in the bushes," Randy said. "I even got a picture."

"Stop it," Leslie said as he polished off his crab dinner. It was not the breathy, affectionate "stop it" that Joe was used to. This one had a warning behind it.

"I'm serious. Look," Randy showed Joe his phone and he nearly spit out his salad.

"Oh my god, Randy."

Leslie reached a long arm out and snatched his phone. His eyebrows went up at the sight of his pale ass in the bright sun moments before he leaped in the water. Joe wished he would have been able to get a copy of that picture before Leslie—

"Delete. Oh, and I'll delete that one. Oh, and that one. What the hell, Brother Randy? Are you looking at joining the paparazzi?"

"Thank goodness for the cloud," Randy said as he reached for his phone. Leslie gave him a hard look and punched a bunch of buttons on Randy's phone before handing it back to him.

"No, damn you! It's locked! Now I'll have to wait forever to get into it."

"You're lucky I didn't mess it up so bad you'll need to call. I know how much you looooove waiting on the phone 'for the next available agent.'" Leslie winked at Joe and Joe squeezed his knee under the table.

Malcolm watched the happenings with an amused expression. Joe had been a little starstruck meeting him and had to hold back all of the "what was it like interviewing Rita Moreno? What was Patrick Swayze really like?" type of questions. At least until after dinner.

"If you're finished, Brother Randy, I have news."

The three Paytons and Malcolm all waited eagerly for Leslie to speak.

"Joe's moving in."

Agnes threw her arms around Joe.

Sandy pumped his fist.

Randy groaned and rolled his eyes. "Man, now we're going to have to see the lovey-dovey shit all over the house, aren't we?"

"Oh relax, and Merry Christmas. I bought you snowmobiles. They're being delivered when you get back."

"Yes!" Randy said. He stood and hugged Leslie, kissing the thinning spot on the top of his head. "Thank you, Brother Leslie."

"And Sandy, your gift is first year's tuition for grad school."

Sandy dropped his fork on his plate, making a loud clang. "You're kidding."

"Nope. I saw your acceptance letter before I left the house. Congratulations."

Sandy stood and Leslie rose to hug him. "I'm proud of you, Brother," Leslie said. "You've done so much for me. Now it's your turn."

Sandy blushed and took his seat, tucking into his food. "I'm still going to be around. It's an online program. Someone's gotta help you with football when Randy starts up with baseball."

Leslie pulled out a box and handed it to Agnes. "And Mom—"

Agnes put her arm around Joe. "My present is that Joe's moving in. I finally have someone on my side."

Joe kissed her on the cheek. "And I want you to come to LA with me for the next taping of *Dance Machine*. Then we'll go shopping."

"I haven't been to LA in so long."

Joe was grateful Agnes had accepted him so easily and was looking forward to spending more time with her.

Joe smiled up at Leslie, who was still standing.

"What does Joe get for Christmas?" Randy asked.

Joe already got his Christmas present. Leslie must have been thinking similarly because he blushed.

"Joe gets a week of pampering," Leslie said and his look said all Joe needed to know. They were getting time together, time to be alone, time to spend with Joe's new family, and time to let their relationship settle into a comfortable groove. Joe was ready for it all.

"And Malcolm gets a bestseller," Sandy said and Malcolm chuckled.

"Speaking of, Mrs. Payton? Are you up for a conversation tomorrow?"

She smiled hesitantly. "Whenever you're ready." She turned to look at Joe and took his hand on top of the table. "I'd really like it if you'd sit with me while I talk to Malcolm about Rick."

Joe placed his other hand on top of hers. "Anything for you, Agnes. Whatever you're comfortable with."

Leslie squeezed her shoulder. "We're here for you, Mom."

She nodded at him and took in a shaky breath. "I would rather you boys not be there. It's too hard to be strong in front of you."

The boys all spoke at once and she held up her hand. "I'm going to be fine. This is long overdue. I just hope it will help some of the other football families."

"Very well. We'll talk tomorrow. Now, I believe I was promised a game night?"

Joe sat with Agnes the next morning and held her hand as she laid out the tale of her tumultuous marriage to Rick Payton. Malcolm was definitely a great pick for this project as he asked very gentle questions and gave her time to collect her thoughts in between crying jags.

She was the strongest woman Joe had ever met, and he was grateful she'd asked him to be there. Putting any of them through this hell was awful, but spurred on by her determination that she could help others, she was so brave. She'd wanted Joe to hear it all, wanted to spare Leslie from having to relive it, and Joe wanted to honor her request. He fully understood where she was coming from.

Leslie could very well experience devastating effects from his years playing football. His sense of urgency when it came to their relationship made so much more sense. It also explained why he'd been so hesitant to tell Joe everything. If he hadn't already been in love with Leslie, he might have had to pause when it came to jumping into a lifelong commitment after hearing the terrible things the Paytons went through.

It was obvious Leslie was still terrified Joe would change his mind. When he and Agnes emerged from the sitting room where Malcolm was doing the interviews, Leslie and the twins were waiting for them, terror in their expressions. Joe imagined the awful fear they must have all experienced near the end of Rick's life; two little boys who didn't understand and two grown men having to watch their beloved father unravel before their eyes and having to protect their mother from physical harm.

Leslie hugged a sobbing Agnes first and then handed her over to Randy and Sandy.

"Can we walk?" she asked them, and they fell all over themselves to honor her wishes.

"Are you...I'm sorry, Joe."

Joe pressed his fist against Leslie's chest. "Don't you dare apologize to me," he said, and then he pulled Leslie into a tight hug. "I'm so sorry, baby. You've been carrying all that around...I'm so sorry I wasn't there for you."

"We hadn't even met yet," Leslie said, his laughter thick with unshed tears. "I know if you had been in my life when this all went down that you would have done everything in your power to be there for me, just like you always have."

Joe brushed Leslie's fine hair back from his forehead. "You are the bravest man. And your mom...she's a goddamned warrior."

Leslie smiled and kissed the top of Joe's head. "She really is. And she's so happy for us, Joe. She pushed me to talk to you about this and I wasn't...brave enough. I'm sorry. I should have done better by both of you."

Joe pulled him down for a kiss and then held his face in his hands. "Stop it. That's all done with. All right?"

Leslie nodded and then the two of them returned to the room and found Malcolm staring out the window over the lush greenery.

"Leslie, your mother is a goddamned warrior."

Joe laughed. "That's what I just said."

Malcolm turned around and shook his head, his eyes red. "I'm going to put a lot of this in the draft, but I honestly don't know how much to share. I don't want your mother to be revictimized. I had no idea. The papers—"

"We kept it quiet. There was...pressure, but also, he was so loved by everyone. We wanted that memory people had kept intact. Now? I'm not sure that was the best move."

"We don't have to decide now," Malcolm said. "And we still have to talk to Barry. When is he arriving?"

"Barry and Evelyn will be here tomorrow."

Malcolm nodded and looked back out the window. "I need to... Yeah, I need to get out of here for a bit."

"No, of course," Leslie said. "Take one of the cars. Hell, my brothers will take you if you want to go tie one on. They know all the good spots."

Malcolm laughed. "I don't know. Is it safe?"

Joe and Leslie looked at each other and burst out laughing.

"Just make sure you have a passcode on your phone," Joe said. "And call us if you need a designated driver."

"Absolutely."

Hours later, Leslie and Joe sat on the beach, arms around each other, kissing lazily under the moonlight.

"This is the best Christmas I've ever had. Hands down."

Leslie smiled against Joe's lips. "Definitely the best since I met you."

Joe pulled back. "I bet the Paytons have had some great ones."

Leslie nodded. "Dad used to dress up like Mrs. Claus to bring out the gifts on Christmas morning when Barry and I were young."

Joe barked out a laugh. "Mrs. Claus, huh?"

"Yeah, he claimed his legs were too nice to hide under the big red pants." Leslie frowned. "His boobs were always crooked. That's what I remember the most. The crooked boobs, the presents, and then sitting on his lap watching football."

"Did you know even back then that you wanted to play?"

Leslie nodded. "I never *didn't* want to play. It was always a given. Play as long as I could, go as far as I could. But when I retired, it wasn't awful. I was totally at peace with my decision. I knew I'd always be involved with football somehow."

Joe sighed and snuggled closer to him. They were still naked from their afternoon swim but this time they'd moved their lounge chair into the shade to avoid sunburns. Joe hated the idea of having to wear clothes around Leslie ever again, but he doubted that Christmas miracle would come true.

"I hope when it's time for me to retire I can feel the same. It helps, you know, the coaching? The teaching? I don't even miss performing when I'm doing those things."

"You're so good with the kids, Joe. Really. A natural."

Joe smiled. "I never would have known if it hadn't been for you planting the seed. So, thank you. For so much, thank you." He ran his tongue over Leslie's lips, withdrawing when Leslie would try to catch him, teasing him over and over until Leslie caught his tongue and sucked it into his mouth. They both groaned and pressed their bodies closer together.

"Everything really is better with you," Joe said. "But I'd like to wash this sand off and—"

"Yes, God. Yes. Let's do it."

They hurried up the path, hoping the twins weren't out in the brush with their cameras this time. They made it into Leslie's room and into the shower without incident and after a quick rinse they fell into bed together, barely dried off, in a hurry to get closer.

Leslie's phone buzzed on the bedside table and they looked at each other. "Oh no. What did they do to poor Malcolm?"

Leslie grabbed it with a sigh and unlocked it. A flurry of pictures showed up of Randy apparently passed out shirtless on the ground with an apple in his mouth, Sandy in only a grass skirt with apparently nothing on underneath laying ass up on a lounge chair, and a selfie of Malcolm toasting the camera. All sent from Randy's phone.

"We better watch this guy."

Joe barked out a laugh. "He bested both of them?"

The last one was a selfie of Malcolm with Agnes toasting the camera, both wearing big smiles.

"Uh, is he looking a little smitten with your mom?"

Leslie frowned and shrugged. "I mean, he's a nice guy. Younger than her, but hell. She deserves all the fun."

"We deserve all the fun," Joe said as he slid down the bed and pulled the sheet over his head. "And I'm about to have my fill."

Leslie lifted the sheet and grinned, spreading his legs. "I want to watch."

Thirty-Two

Leslie wasn't a big pouter, but he definitely was a sore loser.

The fundraising numbers were in and he was kicking himself for losing focus. Not too hard, though, because when it came to life, he had won the best prize of them all. Joe Judd. Twinkle Toes. His true love.

The week in Hawaii had been emotional and emotionally satisfying. He and Barry had shared some harsh words when Barry learned the full extent of Leslie's secret project. Brother Barry wasn't sure he was ready to relive all of their family trauma and he declined his time with Malcolm. He didn't say never, he just wanted to think about it. Malcolm was more than willing to wait if it meant Barry was more comfortable. The family did have a nice dinner together where Evelyn announced she was pregnant. With twins. She surprised even Barry, who fainted. Flat on his face. Agnes was overjoyed and Evelyn really opened up to her, which Leslie had counted as a win.

Joe had to return to LA after New Year's for rehearsal and Leslie spent another week with Malcolm wrapping up the interviews. Agnes stayed on, too, and spent a lot of time with Malcolm, which was...interesting.

January was winter term at Greenvale so the students didn't return to class until the end of the month. That gave Leslie plenty of time to orchestrate Joe's move to Payton Manor as Joe liked to call it. For two guys who'd spent fifteen years dancing around each other, they quickly learned how to move together without stepping on each other's feet. Leslie was happier than he'd ever been.

He reminded himself of that as he sat in shorts and a T-shirt on a frigid March afternoon for Spring Fling...in a dunking booth. Losing the wager had gotten the football team assigned to the dunking booth and Leslie was the highlight of the day, apparently. He'd already paid a ridiculous amount to have his brothers dunked repeatedly during their time slots, so he was fully prepared for his dunking. At least he tried to be, but he was, again, a sore loser.

Until he saw Joe.

Then he grinned.

"Hi."

"Hi."

Joe had one of the balls in his hands, tossing it back and forth between his hands as a crowd grew around the dunking booth.

"You gonna do something with that ball?" Leslie asked him, raising an eyebrow. "I'm freezing over here."

Joe pressed his lips together. "Maybe. I wouldn't want you to suffer. But I have a question for you first, Coach Payton."

Leslie leaned forward, linking his fingers on the cage. "Anything, Twinkle Toes."

Yeah, his nickname for Joe had gotten out during basketball season and the cheerleaders had T-shirts made—Team Twinkle Toes—which raised them enough money to surpass the football team's fundraising total.

Joe linked his fingers around Leslie's on the cage and leaned in. "How much do you love me?" he asked in a voice only loud enough for Leslie to hear despite the fact that the crowd around them was growing by the minute. His smile was cocky, but his eyes were wet and wide.

"Desperately," Leslie growled. "You know that. What's this about?"

Joe sighed. "Just checking." He stepped back and hauled back his arm to throw the ball super hard at the target, but at the last minute, he tossed it over the cage and Leslie juggled it before catching it.

"What's this?" he said, realizing the ball was actually a plastic sphere.

"Open it," Joe said, linking his fingers and pressing them to his lip. "Carefully."

Leslie struggled to get the two halves of the sphere separated and when he did, there was a small black box in the middle.

He looked up so fast he lost his balance and slid off the plank and into the frigid water.

"Oh no. Leslie?"

"Shit," Leslie had dropped the box and he spun around trying to find it. Thankfully, it floated. He grabbed it and held it up.

Joe bit down on his lip as he leaned close to the cage. "Leslie? Will you marry me?"

The crowd gasped and Leslie froze.

"What?" He shook his head, opening the box. Inside was a gorgeous platinum band inset with three diamonds. "*No!*"

Joe stepped back and the crowd protested.

"No?" Joe asked, horrified. "You're saying no?"

Leslie sloshed water out of the cage, he moved so fast to the front.

"I was going to propose! Tonight! I had it all planned, dammit! You beat me!"

Joe's mouth fell open and he laughed as he approached the cage. "Well, yeah, that's why you're in the cage and I'm not. But Leslie! Will you freaking marry me?"

"Only if you'll marry *me!*"

"Jesus, you two, get on with it!"

Leslie looked over to see Randy filming them. Agnes, Barry, Evelyn and Sandy stood next to him waiting anxiously.

"Yes on three?" Leslie said to Joe.

Joe rolled his eyes. "One...two...three—"

"Yes!"

"Yes!"

The crowd burst out in cheers and Leslie kissed Joe through the cage, being sure to splash him and soon the two of them were laughing hysterically, tears streaming down Joe's cheeks.

"Does this mean we still have to do the stunt?" Terrell asked.

Joe spun around to see his cheerleaders there and he laughed. "You were in on his plan too?"

"I may not have convinced him to play for me, but he had my back when it counted," Leslie said, nodding to Terrell.

"Well get out of there, already," Joe said. "Hurry before I climb this damn cage."

Leslie climbed back onto the platform and Sandy helped him out of the dunk tank. He ran for Joe and nearly tackled him with the force of his hug, neither caring that it was freezing and now they were both soaking wet.

"I love you, baby," Joe said. "Put your ring on."

"No fair, yours is—"

"I got it, I got it," Sandy said, running over with the box.

Leslie opened it for Joe and Joe gasped at the gold band nestled in black velvet.

"I had matching ones made," Joe said and Leslie laughed.

"I did too!"

They hugged and kissed and everyone cheered. The Greenvale community had brought them both to the school a year earlier to help bring the community together. The plan had been for them to initiate a revamp of the athletic programs with alumni who were experts in their fields and to give the school athletics worth rooting for. Then a tornado ripped through campus and nearly derailed their plans.

Joe and Leslie had nearly been derailed as well. Their fifteen-year courtship was put to the test numerous times before they finally were able to set some ground rules and common language. Their future, however, looked bright, as did the rest of the Jackets' sports programs.

Joe's proposal for the dance degree program was approved. The dance major was created, and Joe was able to hire an assistant, one Marti Simmons, and Joe was able to talk one of his mentors, Mayra Delgado, into leaving Broadway and returning to her Midwest roots to head up the department, which gave Greenvale the academic experience the board felt was necessary. Joe did, indeed, receive a five-year contract, and he let *Dance Machine* know he would be available for the summer road show, but after his contract was up, he would no longer be available as a series regular, only a guest. As for Broadway, Joe opted not to audition for *Kinky Boots*, but Guillermo Diaz wouldn't take no for an answer to a future collaboration, so Joe got his dream of choreographing a major show, a revival of *Hair* that would start casting the following year. Joe would headline the first week and then step down. Leslie had been ecstatic for him.

Leslie's book did indeed sell at auction for well over six figures, and he donated all of his earnings to CTE research. Malcolm convinced him that they would write it together, that both of their names would receive equal billing, and Leslie was pleased to be so involved in the project that meant so much to his family.

"So how do you want to do it?" Joe asked him at the end of the night when they were tucked into bed together.

Leslie cupped Joe's generous ass and sighed. "I was thinking you could turn around and lay with your head that way and we could—"

"I meant our wedding, but I love where your mind is at."

Leslie covered his face and laughed. "I'm of two minds, really. Part of me wants to steal you away and elope, just the two of us, no stress, just fun."

"But?"

Leslie gazed at Joe lovingly. Joe had accepted all of Leslie, including his limitations and potential for a difficult future. He'd also accepted Leslie's more sappy side, therefore Leslie wasn't sure why he was so afraid to ask.

"But I think there are a lot of folks who are pulling for us and who have a vested interest in our future."

Joe cupped his cheek. "You want to get married at Greenvale, don't you?"

Leslie's eyes flared. "How did you know?"

Joe snorted. "It's where we met, it's what ties us together, yada yada."

"If you're going with that argument, we actually met at the Goalpost. We could get married there—"

"No way—"

"I'm kidding. Yes, I was hoping you would agree to a Greenvale wedding. The chapel for the service, the social hall for our reception..."

Joe sighed. "I draw the line at spending our honeymoon in Higdon, or—"

"Our honeymoon should be in Hawaii, don't you think?"

Joe gasped. "You mean...staying in bed for a whole week with the doors open and the ocean breeze on us? You got it. As long as we can do that, we can get married at The Buzz as far as I'm concerned."

Leslie wrapped him in his arms. "You've made all of my dreams come true, Joe. I'm so glad I waited for you."

"I'm glad you waited for me too, babe. Thank you for bringing me home."

Joe kissed Leslie and moaned as Leslie pulled him on top of him, skin to skin, just as he loved to be.

"Now how about we try that position where—"

Joe smiled down at him and went exactly where Leslie needed him. With their hearts, minds and bodies intertwined, all was right in Leslie's world.

"So good," Leslie moaned. "God, a tornado could rip through the house right now and I wouldn't—

"Stop it," Joe said, pushing up to scold Leslie. "Better not think about disasters. Your brothers are home."

"Good call."

So when the smoke detector started beeping a short time later and Randy shouted, "False alarm, false alarm," neither Joe nor Leslie missed a beat. They took their time bringing each other to mutual satisfaction, taking their time, of course, because they had all the time in the world.

THE END...

Acknowledgments

Huge thanks to my family for supporting me in this bookish endeavor. I swear, we'll get the carport decluttered one of these weekends.

To Rachael Herron and my 90 Day Cohort: Thanks to all of you for helping me find joy in the darkness. I can't wait to be back in September!

To Jen Graybeal: You are hands-down the best cheerleader in Romancelandia. Period.

To SBC: I know I'm not always around, but you're always in my hearts. Thanks for not giving up on me.

To Josanne, Janet, Debbie, and Suzanne. I learned from all of you. I grew from those experiences. Thank you.

About the Author

Whether she's writing swoon-worthy contemporary romance featuring quirky, queer, and relatable characters or diving deep into the supernatural to give readers a shiver, R.L. Merrill loves creating compelling stories that will stay with readers long after closing the book. Ro writes inclusive romance for the Happily Ever After collective, contributes paranormal hilarity to Robyn Peterman's Magic and Mayhem Universe, and pens horror-inspired tales and music reviews for HorrorAddicts.net. A mom, wife, daughter, and former educator, you can find her rocking out in her Bronco with Great Dane pup Velma, being terrorized by feline twins Dracula and Frankenstein, or headbanging at a rock show near her home in the San Francisco Bay Area! Stay Tuned for more...

Also by R.L. Merrill

Other Books By R.L. Merrill

Haunted Series: (Contemporary Romance)

Haunted

Fated

Bated

Jaded – (Coming Soon)

Minded Series: (Paranormal Spinoff of Haunted Series)

Minded

Blossomed

Father F'in' Christmas

A Peculiar Prom Night

Magic and Mayhem Universe: (Funny Paranormal Romance in the universe created by Robyn Peterman)

Shifted

Ghoul Me Once

Gator Me Twice

Magic and Mayhem/Shifted Collection

Fang Me Three Times

Fangtastic Four

Five Fanger Witch Punch

Hollywood Rock 'n' Romance Trilogy: (Contemporary Romance)

Teacher

Teacher: Act Two

<u>Teacher: The Final Act</u>

Contemporary Romance Series:

<u>The Rock Season</u>

<u>Road Trip</u>

<u>You Fell First</u>

The Heart Knows (Re-Releasing Soon)

<u>A Match Made in Spain</u>

LGBTQ Romance

<u>Pinups and Puppies</u> (Originally in Love Is All Vol. 2)

<u>I Want, More</u> – Bolder Breed Studios #1 (Love Is All Vol. 3)

<u>Love and Pride</u> – Bolder Breed Studios #2 (Love Is All Vol. 4, out solo November 2021)

Everything's Better With You: An MM Sports Romance

All I Wanna Do — Bolder Breed Studios #3 (Coming 2023)

The Banes of Lake's Crossing (Historical Horror Romance)

<u>The Fourth Man</u> (The Banes of Lake's Crossing) (Historical Horror Romance)

The Redemption of Nathaniel Bane

The Absolution of Jonah Bane

The Gifted Series: (Supernatural Suspense/Paranormal Romance)

<u>Healer</u>

<u>Connection</u>

Protector (Coming November 13, 2023)

Sundowners (M/M Paranormal Romance

Sundowners Book One

Sundowners Book Two (Coming 2024)

Forces of Nature Series: (Gay Contemporary Romance)

Hurricane Reese

Typhoon Toby

Earthquake Ethan (Coming Soon)

Summer of Hush Series: (Gay Contemporary Romance)

Summer of Hush

Brains and Brawn

You Can Do Magic: Carnival Of Mysteries (A Summer of Hush Tie-In) (Coming September 2023)

HEA Collective – A Patreon-Exclusive Series featuring Award-Winning and Bestselling Authors writing trope-based diverse and inclusive romance stories. Visit www.happilyeveraftercollective.com for more details!

Anthologies:

Thanksgiving Day Parade From Hell (Worst Holiday Ever) (Gay Contemporary Romance

Valentine's Day From Hell (Worst Valentine's Day Ever) (Gay Contemporary Romance)

Salty and Sweet (Summer Fair) (Lesbian Contemporary Romance)

The Fourth Man (The Banes of Lake's Crossing) (Historical Horror Romance)

A Piece of Him (Gone With The Dead) (Horror)

Breaking Bread—Dark Divinations from HorrorAddicts.net Press (Horror)

Exchange (Renewal) (Science Fiction)

Tap-Tap-Tap (Impact) (Horror)

Human Sacrifice (Innovation) (Horror)

The Sitter (Clarity) (Horror)

Joy Is A Phone Call Away – A More Perfect Union (Lesbian Contemporary Romance)

The House Must Fall – Haunts and Hellions from HorrorAddicts.net Press –

May 2021 (Horror)

<u>A Kept Woman – BAQWA Presents: Horror Show</u> 2021(Lesbian Horror Romance)

Gods of Rock 'n' Roll (email Ro for a copy at rlmerrillauthor@gmail.com)

<u>How Bittersweet is Karma?</u> Free on Wattled

Let Me Stand Next To Your Fire (Queer Cheer)

Midnight in the Renaissance Elevator

Holiday Romance

<u>A Peace Offering (Re-release)</u>

Love and Pride – Bolder Breed Studios #2

Audiobooks

The Rock Season (Kiss App)

Brains and Brawn (Kiss App)

Teacher (Kiss App)

Hurricane Reese (Kiss App)

A Match Made in Spain

Healer: Gifted Book One

Non-Fiction

Horror Addicts Guide To Life Volume 2 - Edited by Emerian Rich

Death's Garden Revisited - Edited by Loren Rhoads (Out Fall 2022)